ACTUAL STOP

Visit us at www.boldstrokesbooks.com

ACTUAL STOP

by

Kara A. McLeod

2016

ACTUAL STOP
© 2016 By Kara A. McLeod. All Rights Reserved.

ISBN 13: 978-1-62639-675-3

This Trade Paperback Original Is Published By
Bold Strokes Books, Inc.
P.O. Box 249
Valley Falls, NY 12185

First Edition: June 2016

THIS IS A WORK OF FICTION. NAMES, CHARACTERS, PLACES, AND INCIDENTS ARE THE PRODUCT OF THE AUTHOR'S IMAGINATION OR ARE USED FICTITIOUSLY. ANY RESEMBLANCE TO ACTUAL PERSONS, LIVING OR DEAD, BUSINESS ESTABLISHMENTS, EVENTS, OR LOCALES IS ENTIRELY COINCIDENTAL.

THIS BOOK, OR PARTS THEREOF, MAY NOT BE REPRODUCED IN ANY FORM WITHOUT PERMISSION.

Credits
Editor: Shelley Thrasher
Production Design: Susan Ramundo
Cover Design By Melody Pond

Acknowledgments

This book represents the culmination of about six years' worth of off-and-on writing (clearly, I'm the absolute queen of procrastination; you don't have to genuflect in deference to my reign, but feel free to bow your head respectfully), and then maybe a year of off-and-on editing after that. A great many people showed an inordinate amount of support during both processes, and I'd be absolutely remiss if I didn't express my sincerest gratitude for their contribution to this work:

Rad, who was an amazing friend and influence long before I started this journey and who has been nothing but encouraging since. Funnily enough, words are failing me at the moment, so I'll just say thank you.

My editor, Shelley, who I'm sure wanted to reach through the computer and strangle me at several points during the off-editing process but who somehow managed to refrain. You gave me a lot of great advice, some of which I actually remember, and I look forward to working with you on the sequels…assuming you haven't already told BSB you're busy that day. (Not sure I'd blame you if you did.)

Chief, who's tirelessly diplomatic even when telling me I'm a hot mess. You're so good at it, I didn't even realize that's what you were saying until now. I'm currently rethinking all our conversations. Don't worry. I'll catch up. Eventually.

My hetero soul mate, who patiently listens (and re-listens) to the plots of every book I have in the works whenever we're together and still manages to express the same level of enthusiasm each time. You're a trooper, lady. I managed to work in variations of your favorite words several times, that's how much I love you. Happy hunting!

Thing One, who's always down to read any draft of anything I write, who tirelessly boosts my ego by repeatedly asking when she can have the next installment, and who's unendingly positive in her comments and critiques. I miss you like crazy. Keep calm and UNGA on, my friend.

My dad, who's actually given me all the advice credited to Ben throughout the book. Just because Ryan sometimes acts bratty and rolls her eyes doesn't mean I don't appreciate the pearls of wisdom. Especially the one about the wagon. That one's my favorite.

And finally, to Glocamorra, whose generosity in allowing his name and likeness to be used can never be fully appreciated. I sincerely apologize for calling you a crocodile. I know you're an alligator. No disrespect was intended, I swear. Please don't eat me.

Dedication

For Pumpkin, who handled my "f-you attitude" toward the apostrophe with all the grace and poise anyone could ever hope to muster. You can't see it, obviously, but I'm clapping for you. I know how much you like that.

CHAPTER ONE

Thanks for coming with me," I said to Special Agent Meaghan Bates as we pulled out of the parking garage and onto Adams Street. "I really appreciate it."

"You owe me," Meaghan replied without hesitation. "I definitely didn't want to be out here this late. What are we doing exactly?"

"Going on an interview."

I didn't even have to look at her to know she'd rolled her eyes. "Gee, thanks. Do you think you could be any more vague?"

I grinned at her sarcasm. "A buddy of mine from WFO asked me to take a run at a guy who passed a counterfeit hundred down in Maryland."

"Since when do you do favors for the guys from Washington?"

"Since she did a favor for me. Quid pro quo and all that."

"Why didn't you just pass it along to the counterfeit squad?"

"Because she asked *me*."

Meaghan sighed and slumped down in the passenger seat. "You know Mark's going to crucify you for this if he finds out, right? That man has made it his mission in life to destroy you."

"Trust me, I know."

"So why are you taking this chance? Can't you find less consequence-laden ways of annoying your boss like a normal person?"

"I told you, because she asked me. Besides, how's he going to find out?"

"That man's the devil. If there's a way, he'll find out."

"I'll keep you out of it, if that's what you're worried about."

"It's only partly what I'm worried about."

"Where's your sense of adventure?"

"This has disaster written all over it," Meaghan muttered.

I grinned again.

In case you're wondering, I'm a special agent for the United States Secret Service. I won't be offended if you don't believe me. When most people think about Secret Service agents, they think of tall, broad-shouldered, dark-haired males wearing mirrored sunglasses, an earpiece, and no facial expression. Medium height, blond-haired, blue-eyed, smirking females never enter anyone's mind.

Because of that, I'm a natural choice for undercover assignments. And my air of innocence helps me get anyone to tell me anything during an interview, given enough time. Usually my friends laugh when I say as much. Okay, they always laugh.

Most people think we work only out of Washington, D.C. and only protect the U.S. president and his family. Not true. President Lincoln actually founded the Secret Service in 1865 to combat the growing counterfeit-currency problem plaguing America. We didn't even get in on the protection gig until 1901.

While every agent dreams of going to a permanent protection detail like the Presidential Protective Division or Vice Presidential Protective Division—commonly referred to as PPD and VPD, respectively—those have only so much room. The rest of us in the field—and we have offices covering every state, as well as several overseas—wait to be called to The Show by guarding visiting dignitaries and investigating various crimes. We deal with counterfeiting, financial-institution fraud, credit-card fraud, and identity theft. We also investigate threats against the president, vice-president, their families, former presidents, and foreign heads of state.

Meaghan and I are assigned to the Protective Intelligence Squad, which handles the threat cases. Any time anyone threatens a Secret Service protectee either verbally or in writing, an agent gets sent out to look into it. The majority of the threats we receive are made toward the president or the vice-president, but people also make them against former presidents and their spouses or other dignitaries sometimes, too.

Many times, the people making the threats are just venting. Or drunk. Sometimes they're just plain nuts. Occasionally, it's an interesting combination of the three. And every now and again, someone's just acting like an idiot. But we take each and every threat seriously and investigate it thoroughly because the person making the threat might like to do someone else harm, if given the chance. That's normally where I come in.

Today, however, I was getting into the spirit of Throwback Thursday. I'd transferred to the PI Squad from the Counterfeit Squad early last year, so I'd become accustomed to a certain type of investigation. This would be a good chance for me to reuse some techniques I hadn't needed to employ in my PI cases.

My phone rang before Meaghan could find another way to tell me to punt this to the counterfeit guys, and I smiled when I saw the caller ID.

"Hey," I said as I lifted the phone to my ear.

"Hey," Lucia Mendez, the NYPD Intel detective I'd been seeing, replied. "Where are you?"

"On my way to an interview with Meaghan. Where are you?"

A long pause. "So, I guess it's safe to say you forgot we had dinner plans."

My heart sank. I was such an asshole. "Oh, shit. Luce, I'm so sorry."

"Are you?"

I sighed and clenched the steering wheel. "Of course I am. I feel terrible."

"Yeah. I've heard that before."

"I didn't do it on purpose."

"You never do it on purpose."

"What's that supposed to mean?"

"It means that lately I feel like your job is more important to you than I am."

What the hell was she talking about? "Come on. You know that's not true."

"Do I?"

"Don't you?"

Another pause. "I'm starting to have my doubts."

Irritation swelled inside me, and I struggled to remain calm. She'd known about my lifestyle when she'd started pursuing me. Hell, we'd met on a detail, so none of this should've been a surprise. While I'd been wrong not to cancel tonight, I didn't appreciate her implication that I didn't care about her or my job was more important. She was a cop herself. She understood that things cropped up without warning. Or so I'd thought.

"Look, I'm sorry. I should've called. I'm still playing catch-up from UNGA, and I'm distracted. That's all. Once I get out from under my casework, it'll be better. I promise." No need to mention that what I was about to do wasn't strictly within my purview. Nope. None at all.

"Are you sure that's all it is?"

"Of course. What else would it be?"

"Nothing. Never mind."

Hmm. Clearly she had something big on her mind. Unfortunately, now wasn't the time to press her on it. For one thing, I wasn't alone. For another, we were almost at our destination. Time for damage control. "I'll be over as soon as I can."

"Forget it," Lucia said, sounding resigned. "We'll do it another time."

"I'd really like to see you."

"And I'd like to see you, too. I—I miss you."

"Well, then let me come over after I'm done. I promise I'll make it worth your while."

Lucia chuckled lightly, and my tension eased. "As great as that sounds, we both know there's no way for you to tell how long this'll take. And I have to get up early tomorrow."

Damn. She wasn't wrong. I didn't want her to be waiting on me. "How about tomorrow night? Are you free?"

She hesitated. "Yeah. Sure. Tomorrow night would be great. Be safe, okay?"

"You, too. See you tomorrow."

I took a deep breath as I re-holstered my phone. What would be the best way to make this up to her? Flowers wouldn't be enough. Jewelry would be too much. I could offer to cook for her, but I wasn't great in the kitchen. Maybe I could pick up dessert from her favorite bakery and—

"How's that going?"

"Hmm? How's what going?"

Meaghan let out an exasperated huff. "That was your girlfriend on the phone, wasn't it?"

"No."

"Then who was it?"

"Just someone I've been seeing."

Meaghan looked skeptical. "But not your girlfriend."

I shrugged. "Not officially."

"Ah. You haven't had the exclusivity talk."

"No."

"Why not? Is she seeing other people?"

"I don't know."

"Well, I know you're not."

I scowled at her. "What's that supposed to mean?"

"Don't you think I've realized you don't date?"

"I didn't realize my love life fascinated you. Something you want to tell me?"

Meaghan scoffed. "Please. Even if I were into girls, you wouldn't be my type."

"I am everybody's type."

"Stop quoting that stupid TV show."

"Hey, if you're going to open the door…"

"And stop trying to change the subject. Unless you want to tell me who made you swear off love. I'd be willing to let you distract me with that."

Every nerve ending in my entire body started humming in warning. I loved Meaghan like a sister, but no way were we going to talk about that. Now or ever. "I don't know what you're talking about."

"Sure you don't. Fine. Then let's stay focused on how this girl has managed to do what many others have tried and failed to achieve."

"There haven't been that many others," I muttered.

"There've been a few. Yet none of them have made it past what? Two dates? Three? I was starting to think you had commitment issues."

"I don't have commitment issues. I'm not opposed to the idea of dating someone exclusively. It just has to be the right girl. I refuse to settle just so I'm not alone."

"Well, this girl must be pretty special. I mean, she's made it a lot longer than any of the others."

"Good God. You make it sound like I've been participating in my own version of a reality dating show. There've been like three."

"Three who've never made it past a couple dates," Meaghan pointed out smugly as she moved the radio mike a little, shifted so she was facing me more, and crossed her legs. "And how long have you been seeing this one?"

I tugged on the cartilage of my ear as I did the math. "About six months."

"Wow. Isn't it past time for you guys to have moved in together and adopted a cat?"

I made a face and shook my head in exasperation, trying not to laugh. "If you try to tell me stereotypes exist for a reason, I'll be forced to punch you."

"Fair point. But still, that has to be some kind of record for you."

"You're an asshole."

She ignored my name calling. "So what is it about her?"

"She's persistent as hell," I quipped dryly, glancing at her out of the corner of my eye.

Meaghan's expression was disbelieving. "That's it?"

"That's it."

"That can't be it."

"What do you want me to say?"

"How about something real, for starters?"

"That is real. She wouldn't take no for an answer. Wore me down. And here we are."

"Maybe that's how it started. But that doesn't explain why she stuck around."

"She's a glutton for punishment."

Meaghan smiled. "Cute. But we both know I meant why you let her."

I tapped my fingernails against the steering wheel as I considered the best way to explain it. "It's easy."

"Did you just call your girlfriend a whore?"

I rolled my eyes and made a face. "Not my girlfriend. And I said *it's* easy, not she's easy. Jesus."

"Ah." A pause. "So what exactly does that mean?"

"It means we have fun together. She's funny and smart, and it's not any more complicated than that."

"Complicated by messy feelings, you mean."

"There are feelings. I'm not a sociopath. I really like her."

"If she's so amazing and she's managed to tie you down for this long, why the hell isn't she your girlfriend?"

"I don't know. We've never talked about it."

"Well, do you want to talk about it?"

"Meaghan, I don't like having women I'm actually seeing push me into talking about my feelings. What are the chances I'll tolerate it from you?"

Meaghan was unfazed and unrelenting. "So if she said she wanted to make it official?"

"I don't know. I think she likes things the way they are, too."

"Are you sure about that?"

"She's never said anything to lead me to think otherwise." Sure, I'd occasionally wondered whether she wanted something more official or permanent, but she was a big girl. I trusted her to use her words. I'd also suspected she had her own reasons for wanting something easy and casual, and the last thing I wanted was to be backed into a position where I'd be forced to reveal my own rationale for craving simple.

"Because women are so direct when it comes to feelings."

"I am."

"Yeah, well, you're the exception to just about every rule."

I grinned. "Thanks."

"Not a compliment."

"Oh, sure it was."

"Seriously, though. You know the talk's coming sooner or later."

"Yeah, maybe."

"And when it does?"

I pursed my lips and bounced my left knee. "Then I'll think about it."

"Okay, this is clearly going nowhere. New topic. How tired is your not-girlfriend of you always having to cancel plans because of the job?"

"Not nearly as tired as she is of me actually forgetting to cancel plans because of the job."

"How many times has that happened?"

"A couple."

"Ouch."

"I don't do it on purpose!"

She held up both hands. "Hey, I get it. I've been there. We all get caught up. She's a cop, right?"

I nodded. "Yeah. Intel."

"I'm surprised she's giving you a hard time. You'd think another LEO would understand." She gave me a pointed look I chose to ignore.

"Yeah, well, I should remember to call."

"You should date another agent."

The skin on my face was suddenly warm and a little too tight. "What?"

"It's easier. I can't tell you how much less stressful dating has been since I started seeing Carter."

Oh, thank God! She was just talking about generally dating someone else we worked with, not referring to the last agent I'd been involved with and telling me I needed to go that route again. What a relief. I'd taken great pains to hide that relationship for various reasons. And I didn't want to think about that right now. Or ever, if I could help it. Which I usually couldn't.

"I don't have to explain anything to him," Meaghan said. "He gets all the subtle nuances of our job, so we never have these problems."

"Great." When had the air become so stuffy and hard to inhale? I cracked my window.

"I just…I just want you to be happy."

"Mmm." I stared out the windshield as I circled the block, looking for a place to park, Meaghan's words ringing in my ears.

I didn't need a relationship to be happy, but since she'd brought it up, that particular brand of bliss had eluded me for some time: that ass-over-teakettle, rocket-ship-to-the-moon, heart-stopping, nerve-wracking kind of love that simultaneously hijacked and destroyed your entire existence. I'd tasted it once, several years ago, and it'd been achingly glorious.

Comparisons between holding my hand over a candle and jumping bodily into a five-alarm blaze didn't begin to describe the difference. Lucia was great, and I enjoyed her company. But what I felt for her was nothing compared to the pull—to be near, to touch, to hold, to protect—the draw, the all-consuming fire of the love I'd once felt for someone else.

"That right there tells me all I need to know," Meaghan said.

"What?"

"If you were happy, you would've argued with me." She pinned me with a mysterious look and opened her door.

I swung my own open and hopped out, taking a second to adjust the gear around my waist. I shut the door and rested my hands on the roof of the car. I tried to think of a rebuttal, but all I could come up with was, "I'm not *un*happy."

Meaghan's smile was laced with sadness. Or maybe it was pity. Whatever it was, I didn't like it. "I don't have to tell you there's a big difference, though, do I?"

She turned and headed toward the building, leaving me to stare after her. "No," I said softly, even though she couldn't possibly hear me. "No, you don't."

I snagged the file folder I'd need out of the backseat and hurried to catch up to her, determined to stay on task and keep all thoughts of love and happiness out of my mind for at least the next couple of hours.

CHAPTER TWO

*B*ang, bang, bang!
My very best police knock broadcast throughout the dreary hallway that something was about to go down. I winced. But people in New York tend to mind their own business. I wasn't knocking on their door, so they wouldn't get involved. Still, I looked up and down the hall. No one and nothing moved.

My back to the wall, my weapon side canted away from the door, I glanced across the doorway at Meaghan, who appeared to be listening for some indication of life inside the apartment. She lifted her eyes, head cocked to one side.

"Anything?" I mouthed silently. I hadn't heard a damn thing, but I'm not infallible. Maybe she'd picked up something.

Meaghan frowned and shook her head. The furrow in her brow deepened, and she broke eye contact. She leaned closer to the door, keeping to one side so she wouldn't be caught in the so-called fatal funnel.

Bang, bang, bang!

I pounded with the side of my fist, harder than before, then hesitated as I considered whether to verbally announce our presence. I glanced at Meaghan again. She shrugged.

"Police. Open up." Surely the occupant would hear my demand. Again, I checked the other apartment doors. Everything seemed still.

A soft scuffle sounded from just inside the doorway, and I met Meaghan's gaze. She nodded, and her right hand strayed toward the butt of her gun. We just wanted to interview this guy, not arrest him, and didn't suspect that he was either armed or dangerous, but Meaghan's weapon side was close to the doorway. It never hurt to be proactive.

I retrieved my baton from my belt and opened it, the clack ominously loud as the metal pieces fell into place. Using the weapon's tip, I pounded on the door again, a small part of me childishly hoping whoever was skulking there had their ear near the door.

"Police. Open the door." I struck the door a few more times.

Turning locks clicked, and I slammed the tip of the baton hard against the faded-yellow cinder-block wall. It collapsed back in on itself, and I jammed it back into its holster. The door opened as far as its chain allowed.

"Yes?" The slightly accented voice from within sounded mildly annoyed.

I held up my badge to the crack in the door. "Amin Akbari."

"Yes?"

"We'd like to talk to you."

A long pause followed. I held my breath. My patience with this situation was already becoming threadbare, and I was tempted to free the side of myself that had reduced grown men to tears and force this man to open the damn door. But I'd learned patience as well as situational awareness. It might be best to wait until I was actually inside to unleash the thunder and lightning. So, as the lone eye peered at me somewhat warily through the crack in the door, I flashed my brightest smile and tried to appear nonthreatening.

"Mr. Akbari, I'm Special Agent O'Connor. This is Special Agent Bates. We're with the United States Secret Service. We just have a couple of questions."

The eye blinked once, but at least the door wasn't slammed in my face. That was a good sign.

"I know it's late, and I apologize for interrupting your evening. We won't take up much of your time. Definitely less than an hour. We don't want to keep you from your evening prayer."

The eyebrow above the petulant-looking eye went up, and I spotted a hint of surprise in that dark gaze. The door shut softly but firmly, and my shoulders sagged. As I debated whether to resume my assault on the door, I heard the scrape of a chain being released from its fastenings. A moment later the door opened.

Mr. Amin Akbari wore a dark-blue galabia and a matching pair of linen pants. Comfortable-looking slippers covered his feet. He rubbed his close-cropped beard with one hand as he looked at me somewhat resentfully.

"May we come in?" I slid my commission book back into my jacket pocket and gave Meaghan a reassuring glance.

He stepped back, and we entered. The man's name and garb and the fact that he didn't refute my allusion to his evening prayer confirmed what I'd suspected. Akbari was Muslim. Crap.

Some Muslim men simply don't want to deal with women. Several I've encountered have flatly refused to acknowledge my presence, and Akbari's guarded expression indicated that might be the case here. I wished I had a male with me. This would probably go a lot better if I had.

The smell of spiced lamb hung heavy in the air. I cringed. Had we interrupted the man's dinner? The darkened kitchen behind him and the equally dim dining room to the left of it led me to think not. At least I hadn't earned any strikes there.

"Thank you." I walked into the apartment, giving Meaghan plenty of room to shut the door behind me, and gestured toward the empty dining-room table. "Would you like to sit here?"

Akbari merely turned away without a word.

Meaghan's long look said she was seriously contemplating kicking my ass later for dragging her out on this call. I shrugged one shoulder in apology and followed Akbari to the table.

"Before we start, Mr. Akbari, is anyone else in the house with you tonight?" The living room, visible from our vantage point in the foyer, was obviously empty, and I could see most of the bathroom through the open door at the end of the hall. That left the bedroom unaccounted for. I didn't detect any other signs of life.

"No." He flipped a switch to turn on a chandelier over the table and took a seat.

"So, you're here alone?" I wanted to be absolutely clear. You wouldn't believe the number of times I'd had someone wander out of a back room in the middle of an interview and then listened to the interviewee claim they hadn't understood exactly what I'd meant.

"Yes. It is just me." A pause. "And now you."

Akbari's intense stare was giving me the creeps, as if I needed yet another reason to hurry the hell up and complete this interview. I laid the packet full of papers I'd brought on the dining-room table and helped myself to a chair. The one I chose allowed me to face the bedroom, and I turned it slightly so I had a partial view of the front door out of the corner of my eye, if anyone decided to join us.

Meaghan hesitated for a fraction of a second before taking the seat next to me and arranging her chair in a similar fashion. She opened her notebook to a blank page and retrieved a pen from her pocket, ready to record the pertinent facts. She was taking notes so I could focus all my attention on the subject of my interview.

"Mr. Akbari, do you know why we're here?"

Akbari shook his head, but recognition flickered behind his eyes.

I nodded once, as if I accepted his answer, and put my hands on top of the papers I'd brought. His gaze was drawn to them, and now his expression was equal parts curiosity and caution. Perfect.

"I have some questions. As I said, we'll try not to take too much of your time."

Akbari remained mute.

Okay. He was going to make me work for it. I could do that. If he thought the silent treatment would intimidate me, he was clearly misinformed about the tenacity of American women. And he'd really misjudged me. I saw his reticence as a challenge and became that much more determined to break him.

I managed to restrain a smile. Barely. "Let's get the easy stuff out of the way," I suggested casually. "Do you have any identification?"

"Why?"

Interesting. He was reluctant to provide me with ID. Why?

Now I did smile. "I just want to make sure I'm talking to the right guy. Plus, it'll allow my partner here to get the necessary information, so you and I can keep talking. It makes this whole process go faster."

Akbari swallowed once and took a deep breath. He'd tensed, and I ensured that my own body language conveyed complete ease.

Akbari stood and retrieved a worn leather wallet from a nearby credenza. Slowly he fished out a driver's license, his hands shaking almost imperceptibly. If I hadn't specifically been looking, I'd have missed it.

I took the license and passed it to Meaghan without even turning my head. Akbari resumed his seat and fiddled absently with the wallet, which he'd placed on the table in front of him.

"How long have you lived here, Mr. Akbari?"

"Two years."

"And where did you live before this?"

"Anaheim, California."

"Did you like California?"

"Yes. It was very nice."

I inhaled deeply and adjusted myself in my chair, leaning forward and resting my weight on my forearms. I held his gaze until he dropped his eyes.

"Mr. Akbari, before we go any further I should probably explain something to you. Just because I ask you a question doesn't necessarily mean I'm looking for an answer."

Akbari appeared confused. His brow pulled down as he looked at me. "I don't understand."

"People don't tell the truth, Mr. Akbari. Unfortunate, I know, but those are the times we live in. Me? I like to know where I stand with people, whether I can trust anything they tell me. Many of the questions I'm going to ask you, I already know the answers to. I ask them anyway to see whether you're going to be straight with me."

I paused deliberately. Akbari's jaw tightened, and a light sheen of sweat broke out across his forehead.

"We're already off to a bad start, Mr. Akbari. You've just lied to me twice, which doesn't bode well for the rest of the interview." I paused again. "Are you familiar with criminal law?"

Akbari shook his head and licked his lips.

"Title 18, United States Code 1001 is a particular favorite of mine. I won't bore you with all the legalese. You can look it up yourself sometime if you're so inclined, but basically it says that it's a crime to lie to federal agents. Did you know you can go to jail for up to five years for violating that statute? Eight, if the matter under discussion relates to terrorism. And that's in addition to a hefty fine. You'd be amazed how often I need to bring that up. I'll admit, it makes me long for a simpler time when people were honest and respected the law and those who work tirelessly to uphold it. It breaks my heart when I have to remind people of their duty as human beings to do unto others."

Meaghan bumped my leg under the table, and I used my hand to hide my grin. Okay, she was right. I was laying it on a tad thick. But the bastard had lied to my first two questions. And they were the easy ones. What was I going to get out of him when I started asking questions I didn't know the answers to?

"Let's try this again, Mr. Akbari. How long have you lived here?"

"Three weeks." His shoulders slumped, and his voice came out a bit shaky.

I nodded. That was the answer I'd been looking for. "And where did you live before this?"

"Rockville, Maryland."

"Who did you live with down there?"

"My mother."

Three for three. Perfect. Now came the hard ones. I opened the folder on the table in front of me and retrieved a clear plastic envelope containing a counterfeit one-hundred-dollar bill. I laid it flat on the table between us and studied him to gauge his reaction.

Akbari's eyes went flat as he stared at it, and he clenched his hands together.

"Do you recognize this?"

Akbari hesitated. "It's a hundred-dollar bill."

"Very good. Do you have any idea why I might have driven over here so late in the evening to ask you whether you'd seen it before?"

Akbari shook his head, but he couldn't seem to take his eyes off the bill. I didn't expect him to recognize it. Not that exact bill anyway, which was a prop I'd borrowed from the Counterfeit Squad for dramatic effect. We'd gotten it from a bank in Manhattan, which had received it from some store's night drop bag. It was scheduled to be entered into evidence later in the week. We had no idea where it'd come from or who'd passed it off to the store. The only things that bill had in common with the one I was asking him about were that it was fake and it was a hundred. Everything else—identifying numbers, the paper it was printed on, the method in which it'd been counterfeited—was completely different.

Showing him the bill did serve a purpose, however. I mean, besides making him think I was a superagent and had gotten my hands on the fake hundred he'd passed at a grocery store down in Maryland. I peered at him as he looked at the note, watching carefully for the recognition I was positive wouldn't come. I was right. It didn't. And that alone said more than anything he could utter for the rest of the interview.

When my friend Sarah had called me from D.C. earlier that day to ask me to run down this lead, she'd suspected this guy was just a low man on the proverbial totem pole, and if he did have any involvement in the actual printing of the counterfeit currency—an unlikely scenario, as far as she was concerned—it was superficial at best. If his reaction, or complete lack thereof, was anything to go on, he wasn't involved in the printing at all. If he had been, he'd have recognized that the bill I was showing him wasn't his work and would've known I was bluffing. Clearly, this guy wasn't a major player in the operation. But I suspected he knew who was, and that was the information I was really after.

I gave him another moment to formulate a reply. He didn't. He just sat there looking at the bill with a dazed expression. Time to turn up the heat.

"A few weeks ago you visited a grocery store in Maryland and attempted to use a counterfeit hundred-dollar bill to pay for a carton of milk and some eggs." I was very careful to word my statement so as not to claim that the bill in front of me was the bill he'd used. "The clerk recognized that the bill was fake, and you left abruptly when she mentioned it to you. They pulled video surveillance of the cash-register and parking-lot areas and tracked you to your car. You were identified by your vehicle's license plate. The store footage of you that our agents in Maryland viewed matched your Maryland driver's license photo. There's no doubt it was you on the tape, but, just to be sure, the cashier was shown a photo lineup. She identified your picture immediately."

Akbari said nothing for a very long time. His unflinching eyes merely continued to look blankly at the bill in its plastic envelope. Every now and again his hands balled up into fists, but that was his only reaction. I let him wallow in his own thoughts for a bit. As he did, I leisurely read through the papers in the folder I'd brought with me, and every once in a while, I jotted down a note.

Eventually, I'd had enough. I glanced at my watch and noticed that we were quickly encroaching on prayer time. I cleared my throat to get Akbari's attention. He jumped and looked up at me for the first time in several minutes.

"Mr. Akbari, I just want to know where you got the bill." I retrieved my prop from the table and slid it back into my folder.

Akbari's expression was almost pained, and indecision warred in his dark eyes. "I don't know."

I raised one eyebrow and restrained the impulse to fold my arms over my chest, as most people saw that move as antagonistic. I wasn't quite ready to take that tack with him. Yet.

"You don't know." My tone was borderline questioning, though it'd taken a considerable amount of willpower to refrain from sounding sarcastic.

He shook his head. "No. I don't know."

"Do you often walk around with hundred-dollar bills in your wallet, Mr. Akbari?"

He didn't reply.

"What do you do for a living?" I asked, my voice light. I regarded him steadily as I awaited his reply.

"I am sorry?"

I held out my hand to Meaghan, who wordlessly deposited Akbari's driver's license into it. I glanced at it for confirmation of his age before I handed it back to him. I'd been told he was in his mid-twenties. The date on the license verified that fact.

"For a job," I said. "Where do you work?"

Akbari hesitated. "I'm a graduate student."

"So you have no means of income?"

He shook his head.

"Yet somehow you have enough hundred-dollar bills at your disposal that you can't remember where you got the one you tried to use three weeks ago to buy milk and eggs?" Now I allowed my skepticism and disbelief to bleed into my words. I didn't ask where he went to school. Since I was fairly confident he was lying to me, I didn't really care. There was no need to poke more holes in his story. We both knew he was full of shit. And we both knew that I knew.

The uncertainty was back in Akbari's eyes. He picked at the edges of the driver's license in his grip but didn't seem aware he was doing it. The sweat on his brow was more pronounced, and beads of it dotted the visible skin of his neck.

"Tell you what. I know you have to pray. I'd never stand between a man and his God, so I'll leave you to it. Why don't you think about it after you've communed with Allah. Try to remember where you might've gotten the bill, and give me a call. How does that sound?"

"All right."

I stood up to go but stopped just short of actually making a move toward the door. "Is there a number where I can reach you?"

"I don't have a phone," Akbari said quickly.

I glanced pointedly toward the credenza where a cell phone lay. Akbari said nothing to refute his previous denial. I sighed theatrically and walked over to pick it up. Akbari didn't move as I placed it on the table in front of him. While I was doing that, Meaghan had risen and plucked the landline phone off the wall in the kitchen. She nodded when I looked to her, letting me know there was indeed a dial tone.

"Do you want to try that again, Mr. Akbari? I can get these numbers another way if I have to, but doing that extra work won't make me feel very kindly toward you. You do want me to feel kindly, don't you?"

Looking almost angry, Akbari rattled off two telephone numbers in rapid succession. Meaghan jotted them on her notepad and gave me a thumbs-up to indicate she'd gotten them. I extracted one of my business cards from my commission book and laid it on the table next to his cell phone.

"Thank you for your time this evening, Mr. Akbari. If I don't hear from you in a few days, I'll be in touch." I moved to the door and opened it to allow Meaghan to exit ahead of me. I hesitated in the doorway and looked at Akbari until he met my eyes. "Amin. It means 'honest,' doesn't it?"

Akbari's own eyes grew wide, and his mouth dropped open.

I smiled. "Your parents named you well." I stepped out of the apartment and shut the door softly behind me.

Meaghan gave me a look of exasperation as I joined her in the hallway. She smiled slightly and shook her head as we walked. She managed to maintain her silence until we'd gotten into the elevator, but I could tell the effort was killing her. When we began our descent she turned to me.

"That was much, even for you."

"I don't know what you're talking about."

"Sure you don't." Her tone was teasing, and she playfully bumped my shoulder with her own before she mimicked me. "'It makes me long for a simpler time.'"

"Hey, I thought that one was pretty good."

"You have to stop shoveling that bull in interviews, Ryan."

"Works, doesn't it?"

"Yeah, but do you have any idea how hard it is for me not to burst out laughing?"

"And there's the other upside." I grinned at her.

Meaghan shook her head again and exited the elevator ahead of me. She was trying hard to affect a demeanor of annoyance, and I think she was becoming irritated that it wasn't working.

"What was in the folder, anyway?"

I opened it and held it up so she could see. "Crossword puzzles."

Meaghan threw back her head and laughed.

CHAPTER THREE

I'd barely walked through the door to my office early the next morning when I heard my immediate supervisor, Mark Jennings, bellowing my name from the other end of the hall. Clearly, he required my presence in his office, though I wondered what I could've managed to pull off in the two minutes I'd been in the building that made him feel the need to yell with such contempt. Maybe if I'd had a chance to stop for coffee on my way in, I'd have had enough brain power to figure it out.

Rolling my eyes at yet another blatant display of unprofessional behavior on his part, I made my way to his office. The sooner I got this over with, the quicker I could search for caffeine, and the happier everyone would be.

I entered Mark's office mildly aggravated and ready to make that fact abundantly clear, but then I noticed the prominent theme of his office décor and stopped.

Pirates, I thought dumbly. Mark must've had some sort of weird pirate fetish I was just finding out about. I never ventured anywhere near his office, so I hadn't known about this quirk. Someone really should've warned me. It's tough to school my face into a completely impassive expression when I'm surprised.

And, boy, was I surprised. Signs of pirates abounded: Jolly Roger screen saver and mouse pad, pirate calendar, skull-and-crossbones coffee cup, little skull heads wearing bandannas as erasers on his pencils, a sticky-note pad, a row of tiny pirate figurines accompanied by miniature ships and cannons and treasure chests lined up like sentinels on the bookshelf. (Admittedly, I wanted to play with those.) A print with a skull and crossbones and the motto "The beatings will continue until morale improves" adorned one wall. A skull-and-crossbones tie even hung lazily from the doorknob.

I frowned as I took it all in. I mean, hell, I like pirates as well as the next girl, but this was bordering on an obsession. One that made me wonder—completely and utterly against my will, I assure you— whether he was wearing pirate boxer shorts. Which then led to musings of whether he was a boxers or briefs type of man. I shuddered, vaguely sickened, and banished the thought.

I'd been so busy examining my surroundings and trying to combat my nausea at the detour my mind had taken, I'd failed to notice Mark was looking at me intently. He didn't seem particularly happy. I allowed my eyes to hold his for a long moment but didn't speak. He'd called me in here. He could be the first to break the silence. I'm terribly stubborn about some things, and this happened to be one of them.

"I have just one question for you, Ryan," Mark said finally, his voice a low rumble in his chest. His eyes were narrowed, and I'd bet that if I could see his mouth through his large, bushy, seventies-porn-star mustache, I'd see that his lips were pursed as well.

I waited impatiently, trying not to roll my eyes or let my annoyance show. I had things to do. I didn't have time for these ridiculous power games.

Mark let out an irritated huff—presumably at my refusal to speak, though who could really tell—and finally got to the point. "What were you doing on Utica Avenue last night?"

Just beneath the surface of my skin, a flash of blistering cold turned immediately boiling. Of all the accusations I'd been expecting, that hadn't been an option. I stalled for time and fought to keep my expression neutral. I inhaled slowly, willing myself not to flush. No small task when you have Irish skin as fair as mine. "Excuse me?"

A dimple stood out on Mark's cheek, indicating he was smirking behind his mustache. I was caught, and we both knew it. "Utica Avenue," he repeated, a note of triumph in his voice. "What were you doing down there?" His eyes were positively gleeful as he waited for my reply.

Let it be known that, unfortunately, loving my job does not translate to loving my boss. Mark and I'd had a rocky relationship ever since I'd started working for him about eighteen months ago, and judging by the encounter we were currently engaged in, our relationship wasn't going to smooth out any time soon.

Mark's title is Assistant to the Special Agent in Charge—AT for short—of the Protective Intelligence Squad, and Meaghan had been right; he did appear to hate me. Ever since I'd transferred, my life had been a living hell, through absolutely no fault of my own. Now, I know that when most people say things like that, they're usually sugarcoating a situation to avoid taking responsibility for some bad choices. I'm also aware that ninety-nine times out of one hundred, I'm the author of my own misery, which anyone close to me will be more than happy to confirm. In this instance, however, I did nothing more to earn Mark's disdain than be in the wrong place at the wrong time. I swear.

One of the very first threat cases I'd investigated after joining the squad had been a veiled threat to the President of the United States, or POTUS, that'd been included in a high-school senior's current-events term paper. Normally, I wouldn't have been allowed over into New Jersey to look into the matter, as the Secret Service is an extremely territorial agency and that particular case was something the Newark Field Office really should've investigated. However, I'd grown up in Jersey. I'd actually attended the high school in question, so I already had a rapport with the majority of the kid's teachers, who'd all need to be interviewed as part of my investigation. Also, my mother had reported the threat, since it'd come from one of her students. In light of all that, the bosses of both offices thought perhaps the investigation would go more quickly if I handled it.

On the afternoon when my life began its downward spiral, I'd arrived at the high school to start the corroborating-interview phase of my investigation. Armed with a copy of an extremely hostile and disturbing rant of a term paper straight from the mind of an angry teenager and mountains of forms to be filled out, I'd been ready to work.

School had just let out as I'd arrived, and I'd been busily dodging hordes of screeching adolescents, cursing the parents who'd had the nerve to raise such inconsiderate, insolent little brats and vowing never to procreate as long as I lived, when I'd caught sight of someone across the parking lot I thought I knew.

Mark Jennings, my new boss, had been there picking up his daughter and some of her friends from class, loading the riotous crew into the backseat of his government vehicle, which is a huge no-no as far as Uncle Sam's concerned. His gaze had snagged on mine, and we'd looked at one another for a long moment before I'd sketched a tiny wave, shaken my head, and turned to head inside the school.

In my opinion, what he did on his own time was his business. Unless one of the higher-ups asked me specifically whether I'd ever seen him putting nongovernment employees into his government vehicle on a day he was supposed to have been on sick leave, I was keeping my mouth shut. These things had a way of working themselves out that didn't involve me. I'd also figured the incident was a nonissue. Naïveté at its best.

The repercussions of that inadvertent sighting had been swift, severe, and ongoing. Mark had done his best to make my life as miserable as possible, giving me the crappiest cases and shittiest assignments to send me a very clear message: it would only get worse if I fucked with him. Somehow I'd been unable to convince him I wasn't a danger.

Which brings us back to Mark still trying his damnedest to make his power obvious as he glowered at me from amid all his pirate memorabilia. He was sure he had something on me. And, for once, he was right.

If another office is investigating a case whose leads redirect the case to another district, that office has to send the other district a formal request for assistance, describing the leads to be run out in as much complicated governmental jargon as one can cram into the report without being overly obvious. It could be a real inconvenience, but it was policy. Until last night, when I'd broken it.

My interview the previous evening with Amin Akbari had been a favor to an old friend, off the record and completely against the rules. Obviously, I'd known exactly what I'd been doing when I was doing it; I just hadn't thought I'd get caught. How had Mark even found out I'd been in that section of Brooklyn at that time of night? I guess it didn't matter. Either way, I was busted. The transgression wasn't worthy of formal disciplinary action, but I was going to pay. Somehow.

Fantastic.

"I asked you a question, O'Connor," Mark barked.

"Agent O'Connor." My voice was low and icy.

"Excuse me?" Mark demanded after a startled pause, sounding thoroughly outraged.

"It's either Ryan or it's Agent O'Connor. I respect you enough to address you as AT Jennings. I expect the same courtesy from you. I worked hard to earn my title. Use it."

Okay, that line about respect was a lie. But he was my boss—someone somewhere probably respected him, at least a little—and I wanted to keep my job.

Maybe I should've just let that go and not stood on principle, just this once. Nah. I folded my arms across my chest as I waited. I scowled and briefly entertained the idea of trying to don a neutral expression. But I blew past that thought as swiftly as the last. Fuck him. He'd disrespected me one too many times. I didn't care if he knew I was angry.

"Fine." Mark's voice was clipped and strained. "Agent O'Connor." The address sounded more than a little sarcastic to me, but I let it go. For now. "I asked you a question. I'd like an answer."

"Very well. I was looking into something." I played the semantics game extremely well. If he wanted answers from me, he'd have to work for them.

"I was unaware of any threat calls connected to Utica Avenue. You weren't even the duty agent last night. You don't have any active cases right now. Your annual report on Webster isn't due for another three months, and he's confined to a mental hospital in Queens, not Brooklyn. So whatever you were doing, it wasn't threat-related. What was it?" That last was definitely more of a statement than a question.

"Counterfeit." I answered him only because it seemed pointless to lie. I was screwed regardless. He was going to hammer me for this. No sense making it worse.

"You don't work counterfeit anymore."

"I know."

"Did the Counterfeit Squad need extra bodies for something last night?" He frowned, and I was willing to bet he thought he'd been left out of the loop.

"No."

He eyed me, his expression speculative. "Who were you doing counterfeit for?"

"A friend."

"What friend?"

I shrugged. "Doesn't matter."

And it honestly didn't. At least not as far as I could see. Nothing would be gained by giving him Sarah's name. She'd most likely get into trouble for even asking me to talk to Akbari. That she'd broken protocol with the unofficial request was problematic enough, but I wasn't supposed to be working anything except threat cases. Counterfeit was off limits to me because I wasn't in that squad anymore. Sarah hadn't known that.

She also hadn't known what a complete prick my boss could be, or she wouldn't have bothered asking. But I'd known. And I'd chosen to help her anyway. I refused to drag her under the bus with me. Mark would call her boss just to spite me.

"It matters to me."

"Well, I'm not telling you."

"You're not telling me," he repeated flatly.

"Like I said, it doesn't matter. I was looking into something for a friend. You don't need any more explanation than that."

Mark glared at me for a long time. "I can slaughter you for this, you know."

"I know."

"You still won't tell me?"

"I don't rat out my friends."

"I ran," he murmured.

I blinked at the abrupt change in subject matter. "I hate running." Where was he going with that remark, and why had he suddenly decided to exchange workout tips?

Mark appeared confused. "What?"

"What?"

"Why did you say you hate running?"

"Why did you tell me you ran?"

Mark looked a touch smug. "No. The country. Iran."

"Oh." I paused and waited for him to elaborate. He didn't. "What about it?"

"Iran comes in next Thursday. He's scheduled to stay eleven days. The visit may get extended."

"I heard." I definitely didn't like the direction this conversation was headed.

"I want you to do the intelligence advance."

"Jay's doing the intelligence advance for Iran."

"I'm pulling him. His son's sick."

"His son has a cold," I shot back. "I'm sure he'll be better by Thursday."

"Still, I want him to be able to spend some time with his family. You take the lead."

"Fine." It could've been worse. I could use the overtime anyway.

Mark's eyes positively glinted. Clearly he hadn't quite finished doling out my punishment. "I'm also reassigning the Dougherty case to you."

What sort of game was he playing, and how was he planning to get away with playing it? A few months ago, I'd been assigned as the Secret Service rep to the Joint Terrorism Task Force. The JTTF was an FBI-run collection of law-enforcement officers from different agencies who worked together to combat the country's ever-expanding war on terror. When I wasn't on a protection assignment or doing my required timekeeping paperwork for my own agency, I reported to an FBI-controlled office in Manhattan and assisted with investigations into targets suspected of funding terrorism in one way or another.

I still wasn't sure how I'd managed to score such a coveted assignment. Mark would never nominate me for the position. I had my suspicions, of course, but no concrete proof. And the how behind my good luck wasn't important enough for me to make a proverbial federal case out of it. I loved the task force, and I got to spend less time under Mark's thumb. No way was I going to argue with that.

Being assigned to the JTTF also relieved me of the burden of conducting regular threat investigations. Since our threat cases were extremely time sensitive, and my duties at the JTTF would keep me from getting them done, all my ongoing cases had been reassigned when I'd transferred. I had only one annual update to status for a subject confined in a local mental institution.

"Okay," I said, drawing out the word. I wasn't yet positive whether I should point out that I wasn't supposed to be carrying a regular case load, so I refrained.

"You don't have a problem with that, do you?"

"I suppose not." I mentally reviewed my JTTF caseload. I could probably manage to squeeze in the Dougherty case without too much hassle. But why had Mark suddenly departed from his beloved protocol? As I turned to go, he revealed his reason.

"The report—which should be a final, closing report, by the way—is due in five days." Mark sat back in his chair and laced his fingers behind his head, looking relaxed and smug.

"What?"

"Five days. Timing fits perfectly with the visit, doesn't it?"

That did it. My stoic veneer, which'd been shaky at best, finally shattered. "How the hell am I supposed to start the lead for Iran and conduct interviews for a thirty-page report due in five days?"

"Hmmm, it'll be tough, but I'm sure you can handle it. You're a superstar, right? Isn't that why you're in this squad?"

A knock on the door saved me from torpedoing my career.

"Come in," Mark said.

Still seated, I cast a glance over my shoulder so I'd know who to thank later, and my gratitude quickly vaporized as the ground seemed to disintegrate beneath me the instant my eyes fell on the new arrival.

Allison Reynolds stood in the doorway, her near-black eyes sparkling with amusement. My heart promptly stopped, skipped a beat or two, and resumed pumping double-time. An unwelcome heat rose to my face, which contrasted to the icy feeling that slithered down my spine, freezing all my internal organs on the way down. The bitter notion that this day kept getting better and better flitted through my jumbled thoughts.

"Agent O'Connor," Mark said, his voice sounding far away and tinny. "You remember Agent Reynolds. Agent Reynolds, please come in. I was just about to tell Agent O'Connor the good news."

Allison stepped into the office and moved to take the seat beside me. My body was humming unpleasantly, and my mind had gone completely blank. Allison's sudden reappearance had been so out of left field I couldn't have prepared myself for it if I'd wanted to. I also couldn't adjust to it, apparently.

Mark's phone rang, giving me something else to focus on besides the vision now seated next to me. "Excuse me." He picked up the receiver and spoke into it. "Secret Service, Jennings."

Allison turned to me then, and my muscles seized. "It's great to see you, Ryan."

Her low, throaty voice sent the chills back up my spine and sparked warmer feelings in other, more intimate places. The air molecules in the room were suddenly too large to fit comfortably inside my lungs and seemed to have a weight and texture to them. Damn, even smug, the woman looked incredible. Stop thinking about her like that, I scolded myself. My tongue felt like it had swelled three sizes, and a horrendous taste dribbled down the back of my throat.

"Allison," I finally managed, ignoring how choked the word sounded. My body felt both feverish and clammy. I tried to swallow, but my mouth was completely devoid of moisture. It didn't take a genius to figure out where that dampness had gone, and I couldn't seem to stop the tumult in my heart. I also couldn't think of anything else to say. Not something I wouldn't later regret, anyway.

Allison tossed her jet-black hair back off her forehead and out of her eyes in a familiar careless gesture that made me clench my teeth and catch my breath. Her olive skin was, of course, absolutely flawless, and as much as I hated to admit it, she was a vision of strength and beauty in her exquisitely tailored pin-striped suit. A bittersweet ache spooled inside me and continued growing larger and larger until I was sure my body would no longer be able to withstand the pressure. I wouldn't have been surprised if I'd burst open, gushing an embarrassing array of emotions messily onto Allison's shoes.

"I'm sorry, Agent Reynolds," Mark said, his voice breaking against my dark thoughts. "I have to take this. Would you mind getting Agent O'Connor up to speed?"

"My pleasure," Allison said. Her gaze slid back over and locked onto me with such force that I was pinned to my chair. "Agent O'Connor, is there somewhere we can speak privately?"

I nodded, but my mind had fixated on the "privately" part of that statement, and I had to force myself not to hyperventilate at the notion that I was going to be alone with her for the first time in years. Heads couldn't explode like they did in the movies, could they? I hoped not.

"Sure. Follow me."

I left Mark's office in a daze, acutely aware of Allison Reynolds trailing me.

CHAPTER FOUR

The walk to my office wasn't far, but it gave me more than enough time to tie myself up in knots. I tried forcing my muscles to relax, but my efforts didn't make so much as a dent. My thoughts were rapidly traversing some seriously rough terrain, and all the twists and turns rattled me.

I opened the door to my office with a trembling hand and blinked at Meaghan, seated behind her desk. She grinned at me, but her face fell almost immediately, and she appeared concerned.

"Ryan? Are you okay?"

I didn't answer. I didn't know how. I shook my head a little and took a step inside. Allison was hot on my heels, literally, so close I could actually feel the heat radiating off her body. I so didn't want to go there. Trying to ignore her, I moved toward my own desk in the hopes of gaining some distance and much-needed perspective.

"Meaghan." Allison's voice was warm as she greeted my officemate, who'd stood and approached the door. She opened her arms and hugged Meaghan briefly. I was irritated that the move ignited a small fire of jealousy in me, though I pushed it aside. I didn't need even one more negative emotion churning inside me. "It's nice to see you. How've you been?"

Meaghan returned the hug, although her expression seemed odd. Guarded. "It's nice to see you, too. How's D.C.?"

Allison gestured with one slender hand, and the sight of her unadorned fingers sparked memories I really didn't want to get lost in at the moment. "I hate it. I absolutely do not want to be there, and I'm practically counting the minutes until I can come back. But I'm making the best of it. How about you? Are you ready to move on yet?"

"No. I'm content to stay here for the rest of my career." Meaghan glanced at me again as she said that, her face still unreadable. "What brings you up this way?"

"You haven't heard? Harbinger planned a last-minute trip to the Stock Exchange for Monday. I'm doing the lead advance."

That explained a lot. The President of the United States, codename Harbinger, was coming here. Allison was on PPD. In fact, now that I thought about it, the only thing that surprised me was that she hadn't returned to New York sooner. She'd been on the detail for years now. POTUS was up here all the time. She should've been up at least a handful of times, even just to work the shift, but as far as I knew, she hadn't set foot in New York since she'd left several years ago. Maybe she'd engineered that deliberately. The only way for me to know would be if I asked, and that wasn't about to happen.

"Congratulations." Meaghan's expression and her tone contrasted with the word.

I'd quickly begun to tear through the disaster that was my desk, trying to locate the office phone list. That intelligence advance for Iran wouldn't conduct itself. Plus, I wanted to seem hard at work. I was staying out of the conversation and focusing all my efforts on extinguishing the fire in my cheeks. And I was becoming annoyed because my blush might actually be getting worse. I inhaled slow and deep as I counted four beats and then exhaled to the same tempo. It helped. Somewhat.

"Hey, Meaghan," a voice called from the hall. "Can you come read this over for me?"

Meaghan's smile was flat. "Excuse me. Duty calls. It was nice to see you again, Allison. Good luck." She breezed out the door and disappeared before I could think of an excuse for her to stay.

Allison refocused her attention, and the force of her gaze settled heavily on me as if it had actual weight. Her smile widened even more, and she sauntered farther into my office, her movements and posture radiating confidence and purpose. Her eyes seemed to bore into mine, and she exuded sexuality.

I was having a hard time remembering how to breathe, and the dull roar I was hearing had to be my own blood rocketing through my veins. My head was too full of thoughts all of a sudden, and it was hard to get a firm handle on any one in particular. Not that it would've mattered. None of them would be remotely helpful in getting me through this conversation with dignity. I attempted to ignore the useless litany and appear unaffected. I didn't think it really worked, but I tried.

Allison shut the door behind her without averting her gaze, and I gulped, marveling at the effect she still had on me. It'd been more than four years since Allison had ended our affair—not that I was keeping track—yet an excruciating ache still pierced my chest every time I thought about her, every time anyone even said the name Allison, whether they were talking about her or not. The hope that my agony would eventually subside flickered through my head, there and gone in an instant.

"Don't I get a hug?" she asked finally. Her soft voice with its slightly teasing edge made me bristle.

Refusing to comply would only make me look petulant and immature, so I rose from behind my desk and wrapped my arms around her. For a moment, I closed my eyes and allowed myself to take in her familiar scent, a combination of shampoo, perfume, and her naked skin that still made me want to bury my face in her hair and never let go. I pulled away and resumed the much safer position of having a desk between us. Straining to find normalcy in a situation that presented none, I gestured to the chair opposite my desk. "Have a seat."

"Thanks." Allison settled herself across from me, her face still alight with some secret I had yet to figure out. "How've you been?" Her low intonation was intimate. It spoke of our history together, the history she'd thrown away as if it'd meant nothing to her. That tone sparked a painful fury inside me.

"I've been fine. How about you?" I struggled to keep my words from sounding sharp, but even I thought I sounded a touch huffy.

Her smile never faltered. Was this all some sort of game to her? "I've been great, thanks. How's your family?"

"They're doing well, thank you. And yours?"

"The same as always. Mom's busy with some committee or another, and Dad's just now realizing that his rush into retirement means he has to spend more time with Mom."

"Mmm," I murmured, noncommittally. "Glad everyone's well."

The silence stretched out for a time, heavy and viscous. Allison continued to smile at me, and I continued to let it annoy me. Again, my stubbornness kicked in, and I refused to be the first one to speak. After years of no contact whatsoever, she'd sought me out. It was up to her to drive this conversation. It was her show. Besides, I'd said plenty to her the last time we'd spoken, during which I'd made a complete fool of myself, crying so hard I was barely coherent and insisting I'd love her forever. She had the majority of my dignity. No way in hell was I just going to hand her the rest.

"So, I just had a chat with your boss." Allison's demeanor became distinctly more businesslike.

"Better you than me."

Allison's brow furrowed, and her expression became confused. "I thought you liked the SAIC. He certainly seems fond enough of you."

I sucked in a startled breath and willed my own countenance to remain completely neutral. I hadn't realized she'd been talking about the Special Agent in Charge, although that did make more sense. "Oh, I thought you meant Mark. What'd you talk to him about?"

"I've requested that you be my field-office counterpart for the visit."

I blinked and stared at her for a long moment waiting for the punch line to what was obviously an extremely unfunny joke. There wasn't one. "What?"

"You heard me."

Sure, I'd heard her, but her statement had made no sense. How could I be the field-office counterpart for a POTUS lead? I was in PI. In this squad we only did intelligence advances. Ever. I couldn't think of one good reason to alter that policy. Not only that, but the bosses didn't generally allow the PPD leads to handpick their counterparts. Something about this entire situation felt off to me, and I didn't even try to hide my suspicion.

"Why?"

Allison waved in an offhanded way. "They thought that since we have so little time to complete this lead, it'd be in everyone's best interest for me to work with someone I'm comfortable with. The SAIC agreed. And here we are."

The last thing this disaster was sure to be for either of us was comfortable, but I didn't think pointing that out would help. "And whose brilliant idea was this?"

"Mine. But I ran it by my SAIC, who called ahead and floated it to Flannigan."

"Ah. Of course."

I gritted my teeth, grounding myself by concentrating on the throbbing ache in my jaw, and took extreme care to make my expression go blank, although I didn't know whether I succeeded. Allison was the golden child. The superstar. She always had been. That had been true when she'd been here in New York, and I had no doubt the trend continued down in D.C. She got everything she asked for. It's just the way it was. And, secretly, even still, the thought filled me with a kind of pride.

Well, normally. Now, not so much. I shoved my hands into my lap so they'd be hidden behind my desk and she wouldn't see me clenching them into iron-tight fists. My fingernails dug deeply into the flesh of my palms, and hot little bursts at my temples felt like someone was setting off tiny dynamite charges. What about what I was comfortable with? Did she even care? Probably not. I suspected that my comfort level, or lack thereof, was most likely last on her very long list of considerations, which is why I didn't bother to argue. So what if I was in a squad that didn't do that kind of protection work? Who the hell cared that this would cause office gossip for months to come? Allison Reynolds had asked for something. Who was I to stand in her way?

Not that my opinion really mattered anyway. That Allison and I were even having this conversation indicated that the bosses had already given her their blessing. It'd been decided without requiring any input from me, apparently. Oh, I might be able get out of this if I really wanted to, but there was no guarantee. And my reticence would most likely cause more of a stir than just going along with what everyone else clearly wanted. Sometimes you had to pick your battles. Even I knew that.

Allison seemed to sense my acceptance of the situation even before I said anything, because when I looked back into her eyes, they were sparkling again, and she was grinning. "Come on. You know we've always made a great team." The low, intimate tone slipped back into her voice as she spoke, and something I couldn't quite place flickered briefly behind her eyes.

No comment.

"Can you give me an hour or so to tie up a few loose ends?" I asked finally, trying to convince myself that I didn't sound as beaten to her as I did to me. How was I supposed to finish everything else when I'd be spending the next few days wrapped up with this assignment? I fought the urge to massage my forehead.

"Take the rest of the day," Allison replied. "Pick me up at my hotel at oh-seven-hundred tomorrow morning. I'm staying at The W on Lex. We'll grab a quick breakfast and get started."

I nodded absently as she stood and exited my office. Only after she shut the door behind her and I knew I was completely alone did I put my head in my hands and squeeze my eyes shut.

Son of a bitch! I ran my fingers through my hair and let out a sigh. This was going to suck in so many ways, and I couldn't do a thing about it. Just my luck. I took a deep breath and stared at the mess on my desk, marveling at its resemblance to my life all of a sudden.

This wasn't helping. I needed a plan. No way was I just going to sit back and embrace the suck. That wasn't my style. But in order to come up with a realistic coping mechanism, I'd need to stop lying to myself and start getting real. Okay, so not a single day had gone by that I hadn't thought about Allison. Not one. I'd thought about her yesterday, as a matter of fact. But first love is like that, from what I'd heard, though that old adage never made me feel any better about it.

It'd been getting better though. Slowly. In the beginning, thoughts of her had been nearly constant and had made it impossible to concentrate more often than not. But they'd slowly tapered off as time had passed, and the agony that'd seemed permanent had eventually faded into a dull ache. Yet I'd be a fool to deny that I did still think about her. And not all my reflections were appropriate.

Almost immediately, my mind shifted gears, and I smiled wistfully as I drifted to memories of Allison back when we'd been happy and in love. The playful way she used to cock her head to the side when she'd been teasing me. The light in her beautiful eyes when she smiled. The naked desire on her face when she'd looked at me. The smell of her skin. The feel of her silken hair sliding between my fingers. The taste of her lips. The sound of her breathlessly moaning my name in my ear while I—

"Ryan?" A voice broke into my reverie.

"Huh?" My head shot up, and I balled my hands into fists in my lap, trying to banish the almost palpable memory of what it felt like to slide my hands over Allison's flesh. That was *not* a good coping mechanism.

Meaghan stood framed in our doorway looking at me with a curious expression. "You okay?" Her voice was soft, her expression tinged with concern, which caused a heavy pang of guilt to resound deep in my gut.

"Yeah." I rubbed at my eyes without thinking about what I was doing and then swore softly. I'd probably just smeared my makeup everywhere. Great. "Just tired."

"You sure?" Meaghan stepped closer to my desk to peer at me intently.

I nodded, but my thoughts kept drifting elsewhere. I was trying, I really was. But Allison's sudden and completely unexpected reappearance had stirred up a whole host of emotions I'd spent a considerable amount of effort burying. Unsuccessfully, it seemed. With barely a thought, she'd thrown my entire world into chaos. Again.

"Here." Meaghan handed me a manila envelope. She was obviously choosing to accept my explanation, though not looking as if she really believed it.

"What's this?"

Meaghan's eyes twinkled with something close to pride as she took the seat Allison had just vacated. "Photos. From last night."

"Really?"

Meaghan nodded, and her smile widened as I shook the pictures loose from the envelope. "What do you think?"

Impatiently, I shoved some of the clutter on my desk to one side, so I could splay the photos out in front of me.

Meaghan was something of an amateur photographer, a hobby she studied tirelessly in what little free time she had. She'd even converted her spare bedroom into a darkroom. I found her work absolutely breathtaking and actually had a few of the pictures she'd taken while we'd once gone hiking hanging up in my living room. But she always shrugged and gave an absent wave of her hand when I complimented her considerable skill, stating she was merely okay.

Meaghan's new obsession of late had been night photography. She'd been raving for weeks about this fancy, high-tech-sounding equipment she'd bought, and her entire body had practically vibrated every time the subject came up. It was all way over my head. She might not have wanted to go interview Akbari with me, but once she'd gotten over being mad at me for dragging her along in the first place, she'd decided it was the perfect opportunity to test her new toys.

"These are great, Meg." I marveled at the work spread out in front of me. She hadn't been after photos of anything in particular when she'd set out. But the details I could make out of people's faces, even in the almost nonexistent light, amazed me.

"They're okay."

"They're fantastic." I pushed one across the desk at her, so she could admire it, too. "Look at this. You can see this guy's face perfectly. And that right there." I ran my fingertip over the area in question. "You can see the license plate on that car. Hell, you can even almost make out that sticker in the back window. It was nearly black out when you took these. Great job."

Meaghan gathered up the pictures and slid them back into the envelope she held. "Thanks. I'm just glad I was able to test my new stuff. I'd been dying for an opportunity."

Something clicked in the back of my mind as she said that, and I was suddenly apprehensive. "Uh, Meaghan? Did you see Mark today?"

"Yeah, why?"

I hesitated. "He lit into me about going to Utica Avenue last night."

"I told you he'd find out. Wait, how did he do that?"

"I have no idea. Did he say anything to you?"

"No."

The relief that surged then made me dizzy. I hadn't dragged her down with me. "Good. He didn't mention your presence to me, either. I'm hoping he didn't see you."

Meaghan shook her head, a small smile touching her lips.

"What?"

"Where's all your bravado from yesterday? Not so much of an adventure now, is it?"

My thoughts wandered immediately to Allison. "My life's a nonstop adventure. That's the problem."

CHAPTER FIVE

So, are you going to tell me what's bothering you?" Lucia murmured into my ear, her voice a throaty whisper.

Splayed on the couch in her apartment, I nestled between her legs with my back propped up against her chest like she was the world's most comfortable chair. Her arms were wrapped around my waist, and her chin rested on my shoulder. Her petite hands lightly stroked my thighs.

"Mmm?" I murmured, my mind still whirling. My eyes were closed, and much to my disgust, I'd been lost in memories of sitting like this on the couch with Allison many moons ago, remembering what it'd felt like to have her hands in a similar position. And then what it'd felt like when they'd moved with more purpose.

Lucia grew still. "You're quiet. You were quiet all through dinner, and you've barely cracked a smile during the movie. It's not like you."

"I'm sorry."

"What's wrong?" Lucia's voice was low and soothing as she pulled me tighter against her and placed a gentle kiss on my shoulder. "You're not still upset about yesterday, are you? I thought we were past that."

Sighing, I turned in her lap so I could meet her eyes. She opened her legs a little wider to accommodate me, but one of my arms remained trapped between our bodies. I traced feather-light patterns on her arm with one finger of my free hand, enjoying the softness of her skin, which always amazed me.

Even now, despite seeing her as often as I did, her beauty left me speechless. Lucia's thick black hair was pushed back off her forehead and fell just past her shoulders in luxurious waves. Her skin was the color of lightly sweetened coffee, and her eyes were an amazing shade of golden brown flecked with hazel, yellow, and green. No single word could describe them save for, possibly, magnificent. And even that fell a little short.

I smiled at her and gave her a small kiss. I'd only meant for it to be a quick reassurance, but somehow, I became totally lost in the soft feel of her lips against mine. I deepened the kiss, exploring her slowly. Time lost all meaning, and when I finally pulled back, I was breathless.

"Wow," Lucia said after a long moment of gazing into my eyes. Her own were slightly hazy, and her lips quirked up in a dreamy smile. She kissed me again and ran her fingers up and down my sides. "Not that I'm complaining, but what was that for?"

"It was an apology. For yesterday. For tonight. You're right. I've been completely distracted lately. I'm sorry." I sighed again as thoughts of my hectic day threatened to intrude. I managed to push them back with a colossal effort, and I'd be lying if I said I didn't have a very brief memory of giving Allison a kiss just like it. God, I was being an ass! I closed my eyes and shook my head to break the spell.

Lucia waited silently, knowing me well enough to realize that if she was patient, I'd talk. She never pushed, which I appreciated. Her warm eyes were encouraging as she lovingly brushed an errant lock off my forehead. I captured her hand with my own and kissed her fingertips.

"Work was kind of rough. Mark hit me with a lot of assignments that have very specific and fast-approaching deadlines. I'm just a little stressed. I didn't mean to let it ruin our evening." I kissed her again—once, twice, a third time—each kiss lingering longer than the one before it.

"I'm so sorry," Lucia murmured, when I finally allowed her to use her lips for speaking. "I know Mark has been coming down hard on you lately. I shouldn't have given you a hard time yesterday."

I shrugged as much as I was able, trapped in her embrace. "It's my fault. And you're right. We're past it. As for Mark, I'll manage. I just need to try to put it out of my mind."

"Hmm. If only I could think of a way to distract you." Her eyes glinted, and she grinned mischievously. She cradled my face in one hand and slipped the other up the back of my shirt to rake her fingernails over my skin. I shivered and closed my eyes.

"If only," I whispered.

"What can I do?" Lucia tilted my head back and nuzzled my now-exposed neck with her lips.

"I don't know." My eyes were still closed, and I thoroughly enjoyed her grazing the sensitive spot just under my ear with her teeth. My nipples hardened instantly, and sparks of pleasure shot straight to my already aching sex. "I'm really concerned. It might take a lot."

"Yeah?" Her tone was light as she nibbled on my earlobe. "Guess I'll have to be resourceful."

I threaded the fingers of my free hand through her hair and tugged gently to pull her away from her exploration. The passion in Lucia's eyes made my breath catch in my throat.

As I looked at her, my conversation with Meaghan from the day before echoed in my head, and I deliberately reviewed the long list of things I liked about Lucia. She was smart. She was strong. She was an unbelievably hard worker, dedicated to her job. She had a wickedly sharp sense of humor. Her capacity for tenderness and caring was limitless as far as I'd been able to tell. She was compassionate and understanding. You couldn't ask for anything more in one human being. I considered myself lucky.

I traced my thumb lightly over Lucia's full lower lip. Perhaps I was overthinking the entire situation. In fact, maybe I was trying to talk myself into—or out of—something. Definitely not what I'd had in mind when I'd started my introspection.

I held Lucia's scorching gaze as I slowly pushed myself to a standing position. One day soon, I'd have to stop fighting and really analyze what was happening between Lucia and me and where—if anywhere—our relationship was going. But not tonight. I'd done more than my share of thinking for one day. Tonight I just wanted to feel. More importantly, I wanted to make her feel.

Lucia watched me with a knowing smile. Returning it, I held out a hand and pulled her to her feet. We stood there, face-to-face, our lips scant inches apart, just staring into one another's eyes. I allowed the fire between us to smolder for another moment or so before I turned and led her down the hall to her bedroom.

The light from the streetlamps filtered in through the window to paint the room in dimly lit shadows broken here and there by yellow swaths of illumination. My eyes raked hot trails down Lucia's body, and when they made it back up to recapture hers, the desire there made my knees wobbly.

"Ryan." Lucia's voice was a whispering plea.

"Soon." I cupped her face in my hands and pressed my lips to hers, reveling in their softness, their taste.

A moan escaped her throat, and she parted her lips to allow me entry. I teased her with the tip of my tongue, first running it over her upper lip and then her lower, but I refused her blatant invitation and had even gone so far as to pull back with an admonishing "tsk" when I felt her tongue attempt to explore the depths of my own mouth. Lucia let out a groan, and an adorable frown wrinkled her brow.

"Ryan." Her tone was complaining now, and she reached for me. I grabbed her by the wrists and stopped her before she could touch me.

"Not yet."

Lucia whimpered, and her eyes fluttered as I placed a kiss in the palm of each of her hands. Her breathing was a touch ragged, and I smiled, intoxicated that I could have this effect on her. I hoped, as I always did, that I'd manage not to disappoint her somehow.

"Are you trying to kill me?" I think she wanted to sound sharp and irritated, but her tone spoke only of lust and longing.

I chuckled but didn't justify her question with a verbal response. Instead, I took her hands and placed them around my neck, patting them decisively, my meaning clear. She was allowed to touch me, so long as she kept her hands there. Immediately she tangled her fingers through my hair, her grip rough and just this side of painful. I'll admit that flipped some switches for me, but I was determined to remain focused on Lucia for the time being.

Satisfied that she intended to comply with my unspoken command, I shifted my attention to other areas of her body. If the look in her half-lidded eyes was any indication, I didn't have much longer before her fragile control shattered. Idly I made a bet with myself about how much more she could stand and, after she finished enduring my torture, whether she just took what she wanted or begged. It was a fool's wager. Either outcome would more than suffice.

Using the lightest touch, I ran the tips of my fingers back down her arms to her shoulders, delighting in her shiver. Her nipples stood out clearly through the fabric of her shirt, making my mouth water. I held my impulse to taste them in check and continued my teasing exploration, working my way slowly over her collarbones and down her chest to trace the contours of her breasts, deliberately avoiding those hardened peaks.

Lucia's breathing came fast now, and she squirmed as if to force my touch where she wanted it. The desire on her face was one of the most captivating things I'd ever seen, and my heart swelled with the knowledge that I'd put it there. I wanted nothing more than to give her the pleasure she deserved.

For the briefest of instants, thoughts of Allison threatened to intrude and splinter the intimacy of the moment. I closed my eyes, took a deep, shaky breath, and willed them away. Lucia. This was all about Lucia. I opened my eyes again to see her looking at me. She smiled, and my heart fractured, leaving a pronounced ache in my chest.

"Are you going to do something with those?" Lucia's teasing tone was slightly breathless, and I couldn't help smiling back.

I cupped her breasts and ran my thumbs over the hardened tips of her nipples. Lucia moaned and arched her back, pressing herself into my hands. Her heart was pounding against the pads of my fingers, which kicked my own heart into overdrive.

"Tell me what you want," I whispered roughly, nuzzling the inner curve of her breasts with my cheek. Even after all this time, I still couldn't decide what turned me on more: her facial expressions, the little noises she made, or her spelling out for me how she wanted me to touch her.

"I want you inside me." Her sure, immediate answer robbed me of the ability to think momentarily.

I lifted my head so I could look into her eyes. "Already?"

That small smile was still gracing her full lips. "Unless you want me to go off without you."

I quickly took off her shirt and tossed it across the room. Her warm skin was smooth and inviting, and I wasted no more time on teasing. I bent to capture one pebbled nipple between my lips as I worked furiously on the button of her jeans. Impatient now, I moved to shove them down off her hips. I groaned in the back of my throat when I realized she wasn't wearing any panties and nothing stood between me and the silky wet heat of her sex.

Lucia stepped out of her denims and allowed me to maneuver her onto the bed. The sight of her stretched out naked there stopped me. The need in her gaze held me captive. I couldn't help myself. I stared.

"What?"

I blinked like someone waking from a dream and carefully lay down on the bed beside her. I reverently traced the contours of her cheek with my thumb and rested my other hand on the back of her neck.

"You're exquisite."

Lucia looked shy for a beat before regaining her composure. "And you really are trying to kill me."

I shook my head, allowing my hand to stray and sketch a light trail over her collarbone and down the center of her chest. "Never."

I drew tiny circles on her abdomen before inching my way over to her hip. Lucia's breath hitched as I caressed the crease at the top of her thigh, but I purposely avoided going any closer to her sex.

Lucia growled, her face a mask of tortured frustration. She grabbed my hand, and I relented, allowing her to force my touch to go where she needed it most. I smiled at her impatience and silently promised to pay up on the bet I'd just lost to myself.

I gasped at the silken heat that awaited me. My fingers easily slid through her folds, and I regained what little control I had over the situation by slowly exploring her length without entering her, which the insistent tilt of her hips told me she clearly wanted.

"You're soaked," I whispered. I closed my eyes, wanting to fully concentrate on the experience. I loved the feeling of her arousal coating my hand. Knowing she was this wet for me caused a new flood of moisture to collect between my own thighs.

When I looked up, Lucia had thrown her head back and closed her eyes. Her bottom lip was pinned between her teeth, and the tendons stood out on her neck. She nodded. "Been thinking about you all day."

"Really?" I drew my hand through her heat again, touching her more firmly. She was so ready.

"Uh-huh. Going crazy." Her eyelids fluttered, and she gasped before emitting a low moan as I slipped my fingers inside her.

"Why didn't you tell me?" I drew my fingers out of her at an agonizingly slow pace, enjoying the furrow of her brow.

"You seemed—oh, God—upset earlier."

I pushed back into her just as slowly and let my thumb lightly circle the place that would make her come undone, enjoying the feel of her as much as her reactions to my motions. "So?"

"Jesus, Ryan!" Lucia was quiet for a few seconds. She took a long, deep breath and lifted her hips again. One of her hands wandered up to fondle her own breast, rhythmically rolling the taut nipple between eager fingertips. My mouth went dry at the sight. I loved watching her touch herself.

I prompted her when I could finally think again. "And?" I could barely make out my own voice over the distant humming in my ears.

"And what?" Her gasps were faster and shallower. Her other hand tried to assist me with what I was doing, but I pushed it away and pinned it against the bed.

"Why didn't you tell me you were waiting for me?" My voice may have come out as a hushed whisper. I may not have actually spoken at all. I was now completely caught up in her pleasure. My one hand took up the rocking motion of her hips, and the other moved to attend to her neglected breast.

Lucia's free hand fisted in my hair, and she roughly pulled me to her. "Kiss me," she demanded, even as she brought her mouth up to meet mine. Her lips were hot, possessive, and a moan escaped my throat as she nipped at me.

She was panting now, her body tense and covered in a light sheen of sweat. Low grunts and groans escaped her throat as she rode my hand and kissed me breathless. Her muscles began to tighten around my fingers. She was close.

Lucia tore her lips away from mine abruptly, and her eyes locked onto mine, holding me spellbound. The emotion laid bare in front of me honored yet terrified me. I opened my mouth to say something, to acknowledge the precious gift of her passion, but nothing came out.

A small smile ghosted over Lucia's lips, and she caressed my cheek, her hips pumping furiously. Her other hand dug into my shoulder hard as I drove her to climax, and her grip became almost painful in the seconds before she tumbled over the edge. I knew I'd bruise, and I didn't care. In that perfect moment, I'd have given her anything she asked for, no matter the cost.

Lucia shuddered and closed her eyes as she rode the waves of her orgasm. Her inner walls clamped around my fingers like they were trying to draw me all the way inside her, and my heart beat a matching rhythm. One lone tear leaked out of the corner of her eye, and I kissed it away and settled down next to her. I sighed as I buried my face into her neck.

The throbbing of my own need was distant, barely a concern. As long as she was happy, so was I. Could I make her come again? I stroked her most sensitive spot once more with my thumb in an effort to find out. My lips and tongue fed at the hollow of her throat, savoring the taste of her.

Lucia let out a light laugh and grabbed at my wrist halfheartedly with one hand, silently urging me to stop. I did so reluctantly as I felt a soft kiss deposited on my temple.

"I knew you were trying to kill me," she whispered.

"Didn't work. Guess I better try again." I maneuvered my hand up to cup her breast, but Lucia intercepted me before I'd reached my desired destination.

"Just give me a minute."

"Take all the time you need."

We lay together for a while, me half on top of her, limbs tangled haphazardly. Only the sound of our mingled breathing and the occasional contented murmur or sigh cut through the silence.

"So, why didn't you tell me you were waiting for me?" I wanted to know.

"Hmm?" Lucia had been slowly relaxing by degrees, and she sounded pretty close to the edge of sleep.

"You said you'd been thinking about me all day."

"Oh. Yeah. I had." Her lips moved against my forehead.

A sharp tug of guilt bit at me. Apparently, I'd been so wrapped up in myself I'd completely missed the signs. I frowned and wallowed for a moment in self-loathing and disgust. "You should've told me. I'm sorry."

Lucia lifted the shoulder I wasn't occupying in a careless shrug. "'S okay. You were worried." She patted my hip, and her fingers came into contact with the bare skin just above the waistband of my pants where my shirt had ridden up, making me tremble. "I was supposed to be distracting you." Her tone suggested she wanted to be aggrieved by the recent turn of events, but she wasn't quite able to muster up the required energy.

"Oh, honey, you did. Trust me."

"Mmm. Not exactly what I had in mind."

"Are you complaining?"

"Not even a little bit."

I smiled. "Then shut up."

Lucia shivered and wrapped her arms around me tight. "Turnabout's fair play."

She yawned, and I could tell she was beat. I hated to admit it, but a tiny part of me was relieved. I hurriedly buried that emotion without examining the reasoning behind it. I stripped quickly and pulled the covers up over our naked bodies. Lucia turned on her side, and I snuggled in behind her, wrapping one arm around her waist. I kissed her shoulder.

"You're in trouble," she muttered sleepily.

"I know."

"You just wait 'til I catch my breath."

"I'll count the seconds."

"Paybacks are a bitch."

I smiled. "So I've heard."

Some of her muscles tensed as though she was trying to gather the strength to turn over, but they relaxed again almost immediately. She was simply too tired. I heard her sigh. "Gotta return the favor," she mumbled.

I placed another kiss on the back of her neck and closed my eyes. "Tomorrow."

CHAPTER SIX

A very long while later, I lay silently in the dark bedroom listening to Lucia's deep, even breathing, barely aware of the sounds of the occasional passing car on the streets below. It was official. I was the biggest asshole on the entire planet because, as I lay there attuned to the sounds of my lover sleeping soundly by my side, I couldn't purge thoughts of Allison from my mind.

I didn't want to think about her. I didn't want to get lost in memories of the good times we'd had because they only led to recollections of how easily Allison had been able to forget me, and that shattered me all over again. I didn't want to relive every word and touch and look we'd shared. Well, I did, but even I was smart enough to know that, in the end, I'd only be hurting myself. Nothing good could come of it. So why bother?

I drew a ragged, frustrated breath. I don't know if there ever would've been a good time for Allison to make a reappearance, but I was absolutely positive her timing couldn't have been worse. Between the stress of an impending PPD visit, the looming Iran advance, and the lengthy case report due in a few days, I had more than enough on my mind. That I now had to add working closely with her to my list of potential distractions filled me with dread.

A strange, hollow ache in my chest made it hard to breathe, and every thump of my battered heart compounded that emptiness. It was time to stop. I couldn't get sucked further into my current line of thinking; it was more dangerous than wading through quicksand. Sorrow, anger, and regret would undoubtedly drown me. I couldn't handle that today. Not when I had to spend the entire day with the woman who'd made me feel this way.

No. This was unacceptable. I needed to change my outlook on life, and I needed to do it quickly, or the next few days would be utter torment. When Allison and I had been together, I'd spent a lot of time reacting badly to situations. I'd shed a lot of tears after she'd broken my heart and allowed bitterness and rage to fill the cracks her absence had left. I hadn't been myself for a long time after that, and I was still ashamed that I'd fallen apart so completely and lost sight of who I was, who I wanted to be. Some of that had happened in front of her. The rest of it she never needed to know. And if I was going to keep whatever self-respect I had left, I needed to put on a good face and not let anything she said or did get to me. Probably easier said than done, but that didn't mean I wasn't going to try.

Quietly, I crawled out of bed. I'd perfected my technique of dressing noiselessly in the dark, and today was just another chance to exercise those skills. I pulled on a sports bra, T-shirt, and shorts.

I needed to burn off some of this frustration. Nothing a trip to the gym wouldn't fix. I jammed a hat onto my head and spent a few moments shoving my tangled hair underneath it. After a quick stop in the bathroom to wash my face and brush my teeth, I hurriedly gathered my keys, my phone, my iPod, the backpack I carried to work, and the gym bag I always had packed and ready to go. I slid the headphones on, chose a playlist I'd deliberately compiled to combat dour moods and bad days, and slipped out the front door, silently trying to convince myself this was the best day I'd ever had.

Nothing quite like the power of positive thinking.

At the ungodly hour I'd decided to start my day, there was almost no traffic, and I made it to the office a lot faster than usual. The gym was completely empty, so not only did I have my choice of machines, but I also got to pick the television stations. That improved my mood immensely. I could only take so much ESPN and CNN, and none of that limited tolerance extended to when I was trying to work out.

I started with some light calisthenics to warm up and then hopped on the treadmill. I hadn't been kidding when I'd told Mark I hated running. I did. More than most things, actually. But running was one of the requirements for our quarterly physical-fitness tests, so I forced myself to do it. However, I was never pleased about it.

I spent a minute or so adjusting the settings of the treadmill to my liking, and then I zoned, running at a clip fast enough to challenge me but not make me pass out. I watched the television as I pounded along to the music blaring in my ears. I mouthed the words to the songs, wanting to sing as I ran but being just a little too winded to do so. I also carefully monitored my thoughts, lest they stray to unpleasant topics and undo all the work I'd just done.

I finished my four miles and moved on to the mat room to muscle my way through a grueling pyramid of push-ups, pull-ups, and sit-ups. I pushed myself extra hard, determined to keep distracted. Then I spent another few minutes stretching my entire body before I went to get ready for my day.

I said a few hellos to the guys who'd commandeered the television and flipped it to ESPN Sports Center and made my way to the locker room. My body felt rubbery, which I took as a sign that I'd done a good job tiring it out, and I sighed happily.

Alone in the locker room, I lost myself in the familiar routine of gathering my shower supplies and ironing my wrinkled shirt, singing along with my iPod as I did so. A few other gym bags lay strewn around, indicating that other women from the office were milling about somewhere, and I picked my way through them on my way to the shower.

The hot water sluicing over my body felt wonderful, and I took my time standing under the spray, letting it wash away my aches and cares. I had a while before I had to leave to pick up Allison at her hotel. No reason to rush into that storm before absolutely necessary.

Eventually, I got out of the shower and leisurely dried off, humming under my breath. The run had burned off some of my stress, and the good music had lifted my spirits. I was actually smiling as I donned my bra and panties, convinced that it was going to be a great day.

As I unwrapped the towel from around my head to rub at my wet hair, I felt a slight tug and heard the distant clatter of metal against tile. I froze, my eyes wide. I knew exactly what'd happened, but that didn't stop me from putting a hand to my ear to confirm it.

"Damn it." I sighed and cast a helpless glance around the floor, trying to spot the earring that'd been pulled out. I wadded up the towel and threw it on the ground, so I had something to kneel on as I searched. It took another minute or so, but eventually I located the rogue piece of jewelry.

"Aha!" I murmured triumphantly as I closed my fingers around it.

"Lose something?" someone asked from behind me.

Startled, I flew to my feet. Having not bothered to look before I leapt, so to speak, I bashed my forehead on the corner of an open locker on the way up. White-hot pain slashed through me as I drew in a hissing breath. I raised my hand immediately to the source of the agony and closed my eyes.

"Ow." I squeezed my eyes shut even more tightly. Holy hell, that hurt! And I was now battling mortification as well. Terrific.

"Oh, my God, Ryan!" Allison rushed to my side. "Are you okay?"

As my eyes were still closed, I couldn't see her, but the touch of her hand closing over my wrist was unmistakable. My pulse started racing, and the ragged inhalation I drew now had nothing to do with pain.

"Let me see it," Allison said gently.

"It's nothing." My teeth were clenched against the sting, and I was absolutely humiliated.

"Oh, stop it. Let me see."

The hand on my wrist pulled lightly, and I allowed her to remove my own hand from my head. I opened my eyes to look at her, which only made my heart start pounding faster. Her skin was sweaty and flushed, as though she'd just completed a fairly strenuous workout, too. Her hair was pulled back into a messy, haphazard ponytail, some stray wisps of which had escaped and now floated around her head, creating a chaotic halo. She was quite possibly the most beautiful thing I'd ever seen. I silently scolded myself for even entertaining the notion.

"Oh, Ryan," she exclaimed. She took a step closer—which had the added benefit/disadvantage of putting her lips scant inches from mine—and frowned at my forehead. "You're bleeding."

"It's nothing," I said again. My humiliation hadn't lessened. Neither had any of the pain.

Allison snorted as she went to a gym bag on the floor and pulled out a small pouch. Deftly, she retrieved an antibacterial wipe and dabbed at my head. I winced at the sting but made no noise.

Allison glanced into my eyes. "Does it hurt?"

"Mmm." I fixed my eyes on the locker-room wall over her shoulder and concentrated on showing no emotion, belying the maelstrom swirling inside me.

After what seemed like an eternity, she stopped dabbing at my forehead and tossed the wipe onto the floor, where it landed on top of my previously discarded towel. She made no move to increase the distance between us and took a long moment to look me up and down. I was now acutely aware that I was still in my underwear and wished I could cover myself without revealing my feelings of vulnerability.

"Wow, Ryan! You look fantastic."

"Uh...Thanks."

Her smile widened into a full-fledged grin, and she ran one thumb lazily across my cheek. "Why are you all red?" Her teasing tone caused a new tumult in my already racing heart.

It was an old joke between us, and she knew damn well why. How could she not? I absolutely hated that she was enjoying this so much. My face only got hotter as she pointed out my rosy hue, and I tried not to revel in the tingles that the brush of her finger had sparked in me. I gritted my teeth, turned on beyond belief and completely annoyed with both of us.

In an effort to escape the awkwardness of the situation, I cleared my throat and sidled by her, snagging the bloody wipe and carelessly discarded packaging as I went. "What are you doing here?" I asked, completely ignoring her question. "I thought I was picking you up at your hotel."

She leaned casually against the row of lockers and folded her arms across her chest. She was openly studying me—all of me—which was very distracting. My face was on fire, and I'd started to sweat, to say nothing of the moisture collecting in other places. I set my shoulders and my jaw and looked her in the eye.

"I just came in to run the bridge with Eddie. We have a countdown meeting today at eighteen-hundred hours, and I wasn't sure I'd be able to fit it in after that." She shrugged as if the subject didn't interest her.

I wandered over to the row of sinks lining one wall and turned my back on her to study my new wound in the mirror. I frowned at my reflection and sighed. The cut was extremely noticeable. I pursed my lips and prodded the gash experimentally, wincing at the splinters of pain that exploded at the touch.

In the mirror, I saw Allison step up behind me. She leaned over and put her hands over top of mine to still them, and the majority of her body pressed up against my back. I froze and forced myself not to gasp. Once the initial haze of arousal subsided and I was thinking clearly, I spun around so we were face-to-face. I narrowed my eyes at her. What the hell was she playing at? She knew damn well what kind of turmoil her caress induced, yet she did it anyway.

"You shouldn't poke at it," Allison said softly, staring into my eyes. She brushed a lock of hair back off my forehead, and I fought the urge to shiver at the rush that ignited just about everywhere. We continued to look at one another for a long moment, the tension between us thick and heavy. "You might need stitches." Her hand moved to cup my cheek. The touch was brief, there and gone in an instant. But the sensation was seared into my soul.

I refused to drop my gaze, even though every cell in my body screamed at me to get the hell out of there. It was a test of wills now, and although we both knew she got to me, I refused to let her win all the points in this ridiculous competition.

"I'm sure it's fine." I couldn't keep the haughty tone out of my voice.

Allison's eyes darkened, and her expression said she knew exactly what was going through my mind. Even after all this time, she could still read me. I wished I was able to keep something from her.

"At least put a Band-Aid on it."

I ignored her and slipped past her to my locker. As I applied my deodorant and shrugged into my shirt, I glanced at her over my shoulder. I'd seen her expression a million times before, and as always, it made me uneasy. She was wearing her closed mask, a surefire indication she was about to treat me like someone she barely knew. I'd refused to play by her rules; she was taking her marbles and going home, figuratively speaking.

Pushing my edginess aside, I turned back to face her, buttoning my shirt. She was digging through her bag, obviously rummaging for the supplies she'd need to take a shower. I watched her in silence for a few long moments, but she refused to look at me.

"So," I said finally, unable to bear the silence any longer, "since we're both here, do you want to grab breakfast before we head over to Manhattan? Do we have time?"

"Sure." The chill in Allison's voice sent a ripple up my spine and made me faintly nauseous. She focused solely on her bag, almost as if I weren't even there.

I bit back the aggravated retort that swam to my lips, refusing to let her know that she'd thrown me. I hated it when she behaved like this, and I hated it even more that I still cared. But she didn't need to know that. "Any place in particular you'd like to go?"

"No." Her movements had become quick and jerky, her search obviously not going well.

I sat down on the bench and began drying my feet with a paper towel so I could put my socks on. I continued to watch her silently from beneath my eyebrows. The out-of-control thudding in my chest now had more to do with my discomfort caused by her mood than any lingering arousal.

"Damn it."

I jumped. "What's the matter?"

Allison sighed, her irritation plain. "I forgot my flip-flops in my hotel room."

I slipped on my shoes, retrieved my flip-flops from the floor in front of my locker, and put them down in front of her.

She glanced up at me and looked somewhat surprised.

I shrugged and grinned. "Easily remedied."

"Thanks." Her cool demeanor was beginning to thaw somewhat.

I shot her another quick smile, sloughing off a vague sense of relief. As I finished getting dressed and donned all my equipment in silence, I stole glances at Allison in the mirror whenever I thought I could get away with it.

She padded back and forth between the shower and her duffel bag, carefully setting out her shampoo, conditioner, and soap, singing along with the song playing on the radio. She ironed her shirt and organized her clothes while I put on my makeup.

I spent several long minutes arranging my hair so it fell down artfully over my forehead on one side in an effort to hide the gash. I turned my head back and forth a few times, examining my work. I bobbed my head once, pleased with the result, and twisted away from the mirror just in time to see Allison streak past me, naked.

The fire reignited in my cheeks, and I dropped my eyes. My breath caught in my throat, and my heart stopped beating. Damn, that woman was gorgeous!

"You okay?" Allison asked.

"Sure," I lied, my voice cracking. I winced and cleared my throat, turning my back on her to gather my belongings, grateful to have a task that gave me a reason not to look at her. I swung my bag up onto my shoulder. "I'm going to my desk for a few minutes to get some stuff done. Meet you down at the car. I'm parked out front. Black Impala across from the fire hydrant."

"Okay," Allison replied as she disappeared into the shower. "I'll be down ASAP."

I breezed out of there as fast as I could, never looking back.

CHAPTER SEVEN

As I made my way back upstairs to my desk, my mind was spinning like Brody's fishing reel as Jaws was pulling it. I couldn't remain focused on my upcoming assignment and all the tasks that lay ahead of me. Instead, I thought about Allison's complete lack of modesty in the locker room just now and what, if anything, it'd meant. Not that it should've mattered. I had a not-girlfriend, and Allison had broken my heart ages ago.

The sound of barely contained shouting interrupted me. I frowned and consulted my watch. Who could even be in at this hour, let alone engaged in such a heated argument? Only the gym rats should've been in the office. And I couldn't think of anyone who would've been yelling.

The shouting grew louder the farther I went down the hall.

"Goddamn it, Dharma! What the hell's the matter with you? Are you a complete fucking moron? What did I tell you? Huh? How many times have we had this conversation?" A pause. Then, "Stop! Just fucking stop. How hard is that? Jesus Christ! I don't know why you can't just get this through your thick skull."

I hesitated just outside the open doorway to my boss's office as he continued to berate his wife. I debated turning back and taking another way to my own desk. I didn't want him to know I'd heard any of that. I could only imagine how that would go over. I was already in enough hot water with him. Taking a deep breath, I rushed past the doorway, only chancing the swiftest of glances inside as I scurried. Thankfully, his back was to the hall.

I cringed as the slew of curses and insults continued to pick up steam and become increasingly more hateful until I was no longer in earshot. I'd always been amazed that a man as prickly as Mark had managed to get someone to agree to marry him. After what I'd just heard, I was flabbergasted he'd somehow gotten her to stay. I couldn't imagine what poor Dharma had done to garner that sort of scolding, but I seriously doubted it warranted such cursing and belittling.

The sound of my own phone ringing floated to my ears, and I hurried the rest of the way down the hall. I made it to my desk just in time to grab it before the call got kicked over to voice mail.

"Secret Service."

"Hey, Ryan. It's Sarah."

"Hey. What's going on?"

"You okay? You sound a little breathless."

"Yeah. Just got back from the gym. What's up? You're in early."

"I could say the same for you. I didn't expect to catch you. I was going to leave you a message."

"I've got the POTUS visit on Monday. You?"

"I have a protection assignment today. I needed to grab some equipment from the office."

"Ugh. Hopefully it's a short one."

"Yeah. Couple hours. I should be done around lunchtime."

"Good luck."

"You, too. I won't keep you. Just wanted to touch base. Did you get a chance to talk to Akbari?"

I pulled the file folder containing my notes from the interview as well as the envelope with the pictures Meaghan had taken out of my desk drawer. "I did, actually. Night before last. I'm sorry I didn't call you to fill you in. It's been crazy here."

"Don't worry about it. I was out all day yesterday on a protection assignment and couldn't really talk anyway. So what'd he say?"

"About what you'd expected. He claimed he doesn't know where he got the bill."

"Do you believe him?"

I snorted. "Of course not."

Sarah chuckled. "Didn't think so. Did you bring up the lying-to-a-federal-agent statute?"

I grinned. "Don't I always?"

"That's my girl." Sarah's tone was wry. "And it wasn't enough to crack him, huh?"

"No, but it made him sweat a little. Literally and figuratively. I don't think he's involved in the actual printing, though. I took one of our evidentiary notes with me to play a little game of show-and-tell, and he didn't even blink."

"What kind of bill? How was it counterfeited?"

"On an ink-jet printer."

"Oh, yeah. He'd have picked up on that difference right away if he was our guy."

"Yeah, I thought so, too. But just because he isn't printing them doesn't mean he doesn't know who is. In fact, I'll bet you a genuine hundred that he does."

Sarah made a clicking sound with her tongue. "A fool's wager, since I want to believe that he knows. Think you can get it out of him?"

"I'm planning to try. I left him to think it over with the promise that I'd be back. I have the visit Monday, and then I roll into Iran on Thursday, but I plan to try to squeeze in another chat with him somewhere between them."

"Jesus, you guys are almost as busy as we are."

"Sarah, we're busier than you are. We actually work cases." I liked to tease her.

"Whatever."

I laughed.

"Shut up. Oh, by the way, I've been meaning to thank you."

"For what?"

"For my fruit basket and for sending those NYFO shirts down for Lydia. I take it that means your girl enjoyed the tickets?" The mischievous edge to her voice made me smile.

Lydia, Sarah's boyfriend's sister (or cousin or aunt or someone), was a trainer for the Connecticut Sun. Through Sarah, she'd provided me with front-row seats for a home game against the New York Liberty, which I'd used as a birthday surprise for Lucia—whose obsession with the Liberty bordered on fanatical.

Sarah had mentioned that Lydia was what we affectionately called a "holster sniffer"—someone with an affinity for law-enforcement officers—so I'd sent her a couple of NYFO Secret Service shirts as a thank you. Lucia'd had a blast, both at the game and then upon meeting some of the players afterward, so sending the trainer a few shirts and Sarah some fruit for her part in arranging it to show my gratitude was definitely the least I could do.

"Yeah, she was thrilled. Please thank Lydia again for me."

"Can I tell her that her tickets got you laid?" Sarah sounded as though she was struggling not to laugh.

"No, you cannot tell her that!" My God, did the woman have no class?

"Oh, so you didn't get laid?"

"I'm hanging up now, Sarah."

Sarah wasn't even trying to contain her laughter anymore. "Oh, come on. Brian's overseas and won't be back for months. I've got to live vicariously through someone."

"I'll talk to you later."

I hung up, and the sound of hurried footsteps approaching my open office door made me tense and look up. It was still too early for most people to be here, and whatever would cause someone to move with that much purpose at this hour couldn't be good.

Mark burst into my office suddenly and stumbled to a halt. He looked nearly as surprised as I felt, and I hurriedly slammed the folder with the Akbari notes shut. I hoped I didn't look too guilty but somehow doubted it. Why the hell was he was running around the nearly empty office, and what'd prompted him to come charging into my work-space?

"O'Connor." Mark's eyes darted around the room skittishly before settling back on me. He appeared to be even more wound up than usual.

I was so flummoxed I completely forgot to argue with him for calling me that. "Sir."

We stared at one another for a long moment.

"Aren't you supposed to be conducting a PPD advance today?"

Ire, sharp and acrid, clawed at the back of my throat and grated painfully like sand behind my eyes. Was he checking up on me? It wouldn't surprise me. Tripping me up seemed to be his goal in life lately. But there was no way for him to know I'd be in this early, so that couldn't have been it.

"Yes, sir." I wanted to snap at him, but a small part of me thought it might be time to at least attempt to keep the smart-ass-ery to a minimum. Especially considering his current mood.

"Do you plan to do that from behind your desk?" I gripped my kneecaps tightly, using the dull ache the pressure produced to ground myself. "No. I'm waiting for the PPD lead. She's at the gym. I was just catching up on a couple phone calls."

Mark regarded me intently for a long moment, and I had to force myself not to fidget or squirm under the scrutiny. For lack of anything better to do, and in an attempt to retreat from this awkward situation as fast as I could, I swept the Akbari folder into a pile with some other advance paperwork I had lying around and shoved the whole lot into my bag. I stood and moved out from behind my desk toward the door.

Before I could walk past him, Mark abruptly spun around and stalked out without uttering another word. Frowning, I closed and locked the door behind me. It wasn't until I'd almost made it to my car that I realized he hadn't said a word to me about why he'd come to my office.

CHAPTER EIGHT

About an hour after I'd fled her naked presence in the locker room, Allison emerged from the building. She looked stunning in a charcoal suit and pale-ivory button-down shirt with a leather satchel over her shoulder. Her hair tumbled loosely to her shoulders, and she moved with the easy confidence I remembered. I clenched the steering wheel, determined to stop being turned on by every single thing she did.

Allison slid into the passenger seat next to me, focused completely on her BlackBerry.

"Any thoughts on breakfast?" I asked.

"Mmm? Oh. Uh, yeah. Why don't we go to that diner I like in Chelsea. Is that okay?"

"Sure." I carefully pulled out into traffic and pointed the car in the direction of the Brooklyn Bridge. Allison was reading an email, so I stayed quiet.

"We have a walkthrough at oh-nine-hundred," Allison said. "A police meeting at thirteen-hundred and a countdown meeting at eighteen-hundred. Oh, and we need to find time to meet with the second supe."

I wrinkled my nose at the mention of a meeting with her boss as I tried to mentally schedule the day. My work cell phone vibrated on my belt, interrupting me. I pulled it out of the holster and started to answer it.

Allison snatched the phone out of my hand. "Oh, no, you don't."

"What are you doing?"

"Keep your eyes on the road." I grabbed for the phone, and she jerked it out of reach. "Both hands on the wheel." She slapped at me with her free hand.

"I need to answer that!"

She shook her head and answered. "Hello?"

"Uh...Hello?" a voice said through the speaker.

"Hello?" Allison said again.

"Ryan?"

I made a face as Allison held the phone up closer to me. "Yeah?"

"Oh, hey, Ryan. It's Jim."

He was the backup of the squad. Kind of like the assistant manager. He was the same pay grade I was, only the poor guy had a hell of a lot more headaches and responsibility and none of the fun.

"Hey, Jim. You're in early. What's up?"

"I have a problem. Aaron's on vacation, and we've got guys who didn't take their PT tests last quarter. We need to administer them to the squad ASAP and backdate them so they're in compliance."

I sighed. I was in no mood to oversee anyone's physical-fitness tests, let alone falsify government documents. "I'm the field office counterpart for the POTUS visit Monday. Then I have to do some interviews before I roll into the Iran visit Thursday."

"I know. The timing sucks. I'm really sorry."

I searched for a way to make the situation work. "Okay, wheels up is scheduled for twelve-hundred hours Monday. I'll just come to the office after the visit. I can administer the test to half the guys and take care of the rest Tuesday morning."

"Just make sure you enter the results into the mainframe by the end of the week."

"No problem. Hey, can you make sure Meaghan's schedule stays clear Tuesday and Wednesday? I'm taking her on those interviews with me."

"Consider it done."

"Thanks. Also, I forgot to tell you, my recertification for rescue swimmer is coming up. I need you to block out the dates for me so I don't get picked up for another assignment."

"Okay." I could hear the scratching of a pen on his end of the line. "Do you know exactly when that is? You need to go back to Beltsville for that, right?"

"Yeah. It's the week of the twenty-first."

"Sounds good."

"Do you want me to email the guys to tell them the good news about their PT tests?"

"No. I'll take care of it. You concentrate on the visit."

"Thanks, Jim. Talk to you later."

"Sure thing. Stay safe."

I nodded at Allison to hang up and tried to ignore her strange expression. I held out a hand for the phone, which I returned to my belt, as she continued to stare at me.

"What?" The unwavering attention unnerved me.

"You're a PT coordinator?"

"Yeah."

"And a rescue swimmer?"

I nodded.

"Huh." She appeared amused.

"What?"

"Nothing."

The ringing of my personal cell phone stopped my sharp retort. I pulled it out to answer it, and Allison snatched it out of my hands. Again. I gave her a look meant to wither, but she only laughed.

"You are the worst driver ever." She gestured toward the windshield. "I need you to keep both hands on the wheel and as much of your focus on the road as you can, so we don't die."

"I'll kill you myself if you don't give me back my phone."

Allison chuckled, hit the "accept" button displayed on the touch screen, and held it up for me. Her eyes danced. Clearly, she thought she was very clever.

"Hello?" I said, rolling my eyes at her to let her know exactly what I thought of her cute little quips.

"Hey, baby." Lucia's voice floated to me over the airwaves.

Blood rushed into my cheeks with all the subtlety of a massive volcanic eruption, and while I deliberately avoided looking at Allison, I could feel her dark eyes boring into me. "Hey. I've got you on speaker," I said quickly. I wanted to make sure she didn't say anything too personal or revealing. I refused to attempt to decipher why having

Allison listening in on my interaction with the woman I was seeing would bother me.

"So that's why you sound so funny," Lucia said.

"Uh-huh." It probably had more to do with Allison than the speaker phone, but she didn't need to know that.

"Where are you right now?" Lucia asked

"On Chambers. Why? Do you need something?"

"Just my phone. You grabbed the wrong one when you left this morning. You got dressed in the dark again, didn't you?"

My face burned even hotter. But I guess that's what happens when your not-girlfriend teases you in front of your first love. I glanced at the clock on the dashboard.

"We're on our way to grab something to eat," I told Lucia, deliberately not answering her question. "We have a walkthrough at oh-nine-hundred. Do you have time to meet me someplace?"

"Of course. I can stop by the restaurant, if you want."

"That works." I gave her the name and the cross streets and said good-bye. Without turning my head, I took the phone from Allison, feeling as if the stupid thing had betrayed me somehow.

The silence in the car stretched out for an eternity. I kept my eyes on the road ahead, while Allison continued to watch me.

"That your girlfriend?"

"Uh…Yeah." I decided it was easier to say that than to explain the nuances of our relationship. Besides, it wasn't any of her business.

"I didn't realize you were seeing anyone."

I searched for a hidden meaning in her words but could divine nothing from her even tone.

"Yeah" was all I could come up with. I felt like a jerk because I'd spent the entire morning lusting after Allison, and Lucia hadn't cropped up in my thoughts even once except during the conversation I'd had with Sarah. What the hell was the matter with me?

I lucked out and found a parking place right in front of the diner, which I managed to get into on the first try. I threw my police-issued parking placard on the dash and jumped out, drawing in a contented lungful of crisp, cool air.

"So, what's she like?" Allison asked as she fell in step beside me.

I shrugged, distressed. It was childish, I'll admit, but I hated that she could talk about my love life with such ease. It didn't appear to bother her at all that I was seeing someone, and that stung. "She's great." I pushed open the door with my shoulder and walked into the restaurant.

The hostess, a matronly woman who didn't look a day under eighty years old, led us to a booth near the windows and left us with our menus. I deliberately kept my eyes down and read every item listed with extreme care, even though I already knew what I wanted. I could feel Allison's eyes on me.

"That's it?" Allison demanded. "She's great? That's all I get?"

"What more do you want?" I still didn't look up.

She dropped the menu on the table and abruptly stood. "I'm going to wash my hands," she announced coolly as the waitress came over to deposit silverware and glasses of water on the table. "Order for me?"

"What do you want?"

"Surprise me."

I nodded and turned my attention to the waitress. "I'll have egg whites with peppers, mushrooms, and spinach in a wrap; dry wheat toast; and the largest coffee you can get me. My friend will have a bowl of oatmeal with some brown sugar and raisins, the fruit plate, and a cup of tea with honey."

"Sure thing," the waitress said as she wrote. "I'll be back in a moment with the tea and coffee."

"What did you get me?" Allison asked when she returned a moment later. I told her, and she smiled almost tenderly. "You remembered." She sounded oddly pleased.

I shrugged and stood, feeling a tug around my heart. I struggled to keep both my face and my voice neutral. "Be right back."

I needed the few precious moments the trip to the bathroom provided in order to corral my wildly careening emotions. When I returned from washing my own hands, Allison was looking out the window at something with great interest.

"What's up?" I asked as I slid into my side of the booth.

She grinned at me wickedly. "You should've seen the woman who just walked by. She was stunning."

I tried not to let my annoyance and hurt show, but I must've failed because Allison gave me a look that said I was being silly. As if pangs of jealousy at the thought of the former love of my life openly ogling someone in front of me were a ridiculous idea.

She looked over my shoulder. "That's her," she whispered.

I whirled around to find Lucia standing just inside the door, talking with the hostess. Of course it was. Why wouldn't it be? And I agreed with Allison. She did look gorgeous. But Allison's appreciation of any woman's beauty still hurt me. That it was Lucia somehow made it worse. How much longer until I was over this?

I waved to catch Lucia's attention, and she said something to the elderly woman before heading our way. These next few minutes were going to be the most awkward of my life. My face got hot again, and I silently cursed my fair skin. Perhaps I should visit the tanning salon.

Lucia gave me a strange look. "You okay?"

"Yeah, why?" I said, probably a little too quickly.

"Your face is red." Lucia affectionately touched my hair as she smiled down at me.

"Is it?" Not knowing what else to say, I opted to play dumb.

"I'm Lucia." She offered her hand to Allison and gave me a look equal parts puzzlement and scorn.

Allison accepted the handshake gracefully and favored me with an almost-matching expression. "Allison. It's very nice to meet you."

"It's nice to meet you, too."

I scooted over a bit on the bench, feeling like a moron. I couldn't believe I'd forgotten the simple courtesies of introductions. What were the odds I'd be capable of coherent speech any time in the near future? Somehow, I suspected they were slim.

"Do you want to join us? Do you have time?" I asked Lucia. There. Those were sentences. I was proud of myself. I was also secretly praying she didn't have time because I was positive prolonging this experience would kill me. But it'd seemed polite to offer.

"I can't." Lucia sounded truly sorry, which made me feel like an even bigger asshole, especially since my immediate reaction was relief. "Jessie's in the car waiting for me. We have our firearms requalifications this morning and need to hustle."

The mention of Lucia's ex-girlfriend, who she still sometimes had to work with, gave me pause, and bile rose in the back of my throat, thick and cloying. Talk about irony. Apparently ex-girlfriends were running around all over the place today. Oh, goody.

With an extreme effort, I kept my expression neutral and successfully hid my distaste for the woman. I'd met her only once, but she'd made no secret of her instant dislike for me. Which had been fine with me because there was something about her I didn't quite trust either. I suspected she wanted Lucia back and saw me as an obstacle, but Lucia had laughed at me the one and only time I'd suggested it.

Lucia took my phone out of her pocket and handed it to me with a smile while staring directly into my eyes. Her expression of tenderness and affection was lit with an underlying spark of desire. My heart skipped a beat and my mouth went dry. I was aware of Allison watching us from the other side of the table but forced myself not to look away. Lucia was my...well, something. She deserved to have me return her attention. I favored her with what I hoped was a passing imitation of a similar look. I didn't want to hurt her.

"I'll see you later," Lucia told me, her voice soft, her tone intimate. I'd apparently done a pretty good job covering up my discomfort. She turned to Allison. "It was nice meeting you."

"Nice meeting you, too," Allison said.

Once Lucia was gone, she sat still and studied me, her countenance serious and thoughtful.

"What?"

"Nicely done, Ryan." Allison winked at me.

"Thanks," I muttered. I shifted my attention to the number of water spots on the spoon lying on the table in front of me.

"How long have you been seeing her?" Allison laced her fingers together and rested her chin on her hands and her elbows on the table, her expression intensely curious.

"About six months."

She cocked one dark eyebrow at me and gazed at me for a long time. "Do you love her?" Her voice was low and even as she spoke, but I wasn't sure whether she was just making conversation or if my answer mattered.

The inquiry itself wasn't nearly as complicated as the emotions the answer evoked. I enjoyed being with her. She made me laugh. I never wanted to do anything to hurt her, no matter how remotely. My day somehow wasn't complete until I'd heard her voice, and my daily goal was to make her smile. I'd miss her terribly if I ever lost her. I guessed some people would consider that love, right?

I thought about the conversation I'd had with Meaghan the other day and chewed on the inside of my lower lip. For the second time, I was reflecting on the difference between what I had with Lucia and what I'd once had with Allison. I didn't like what the comparison forced me to admit. And while these weren't exactly new thoughts, they somehow seemed more real, more urgent, with Allison sitting in front of me looking at me the way she was. Well, didn't this just suck? Things with Lucia had been fine until yesterday, until Allison had stirred up a whole host of emotions I'd spent a considerable amount of time and effort burying. Why should one have anything at all to do with the other, anyway? It shouldn't, as far as I could tell. Yet it did.

The thoughts now roiling inside me were scalding and poisonous, and I had to force myself to take a breath and look at this situation rationally. It'd do me no good to get mired in sentiment. Especially not now. Not when it looked as though I was going to analyze this thing I had with Lucia sooner rather than later.

Okay, so maybe my feelings for Lucia weren't as strong as the love I'd felt for Allison, but that didn't invalidate them completely, did it? Did I have to feel exactly the same for every woman I ever dated in order to call it love? That seemed unfair. I mean, I felt differently about mint chocolate-chip ice cream than swimming in the ocean, but my feelings for one shouldn't carry more weight than my feelings for the other. They were completely different experiences, and Lucia and Allison were completely different people.

A soft sigh slipped from me before I could stop it, and Allison's scrutiny stripped me completely. She was the only woman ever to have touched me that deeply, and the look in those dark eyes as she gazed at me now made me wonder whether she knew it. Whether it even mattered.

I decided not to answer her question. I still didn't have a handle on exactly what I was feeling for Lucia, let alone tell Lucia whatever those feelings might be. I refused to be manipulated into making a declaration that—if and when it became necessary—should be for Lucia's ears only.

Allison's expression melted into something almost tender, and it was clear she'd taken my silence as confirmation. I didn't want to argue, and I didn't want to offer explanations. Instead, I stared at her, daring her to contradict what she thought she knew, daring her to speak aloud the comparisons I could barely stand to have echo in my head. The silence as we looked at one another stretched on for an eternity. The connection was familiar, intimate, and altogether inappropriate.

"She's a very lucky woman, Ryan," Allison whispered softly. "I hope she knows that." For a fraction of a second, I'd have sworn her expression bordered on pain, but it fluctuated so swiftly I couldn't be positive I'd seen it at all. But that was stupid. What would she have to feel bad about?

"Thank you." *That's right. My feelings for her are tentative and underdeveloped compared to my love for you, but she's getting the best I have to give.*

Fortunately, the waitress chose that moment to bring our breakfasts, breaking the spell and giving us both the opportunity to pretend our conversation had never happened.

CHAPTER NINE

The rest of the day passed fairly well, considering our rocky start. We were unbelievably busy, which helped a lot. This trip was so last-minute, and we were swamped with a million tasks. That made it easy to ignore whatever had once been between us and allowed us to interact with one another with relative ease. Well, relative for me. Allison never had any problems interacting with anyone easily.

By the time we finally finished all our meetings, I was almost able to forget our earlier conversation in the diner. Almost. But things were comfortable between us for the time being, which was all that really mattered.

As we walked out of the field office, Allison bumped my shoulder lightly with her own. "Nice save." She cast a sidelong glance in my direction, a small smile on her lips.

"What?" I readjusted the shoulder strap of my bag so it didn't bang into my hip quite so much when I walked.

"That note you scribbled on my note pad about getting the loading dock cleared around the back of the building. I'd completely forgotten about that."

I shook my head. "No, we talked about it earlier."

"I know, but I'd forgotten to mention it in the meeting. What if we'd adjourned without bringing it up?"

I shrugged. "No big deal. We still have a few days. We'd have figured it out."

"Ryan, it's Saturday night. If we hadn't told the sanitation department today that we wanted them to remove all those giant dumpsters from the arrival area, they wouldn't have done it. If the motorcade rolled up on game day and couldn't park because dumpsters were in the way, I would've gotten my ass handed to me."

"Oh, come on. Stop exaggerating. We would've found somebody to take care of it. You can't tell me no one has emergency home numbers for those guys. I would've tied a rope to them and pulled them away myself if I'd had to. Can't have anyone touching your ass, now can we?"

Allison rolled her eyes and stopped, tugging gently on my arm to get me to break my stride as well. I opened my mouth to protest but was silenced by her fingers pressed lightly to my lips. "Just say 'You're welcome,' would you?" she said softly, looking into my eyes.

A shiver went up my spine. Her feather-light touch on my lips was warm, and I had to fight the urge to give her fingers a soft kiss. I wrapped my own fingers around her wrist and slowly removed her hand. "You're welcome."

"That's better." Her eyes held mine for a moment longer before she finally broke the contact and resumed her gait. "Give me a lift to my hotel?"

"Sure. Hungry?"

"When am I not?" Allison tossed her bag into the backseat of my car with an almost-euphoric sigh. She rolled her shoulders as if working out some residual tension and opened the front passenger door. "But I'd like to take a shower first, if that's okay."

"No problem. Just give me a second to make a phone call." I stowed my own gear and started the engine.

"No talking and driving." Allison put her hand over the gear shift, preventing me from shifting out of park without a struggle.

I threw up my hands in a huff. "Fine." I punched in the numbers with more force than was really necessary and waited for someone to answer on the other end.

"La Traviata. Can I help you?"

"Hey, Kendra, it's Ryan."

"Oh, hey, Ryan. How's it going? Are we still going to see you tonight?"

"No, that's why I'm calling." Allison's fiddling with the programming on my radio distracted me. I slapped at her hand. "We're not going to be able to make it. I figured you guys would be slammed, so I wanted you to know. I didn't want you to be waiting on me."

"Oh, well, we'll miss you, of course, but we can always use the table," Kendra said over the roar in the background.

"I'll stop in soon. Say hi to the guys for me."

"Will do. Take care, Ryan."

"Thanks. You, too." I hung up the phone and rounded on Allison. "I'll shoot you. Stop messing with my stations."

"What was that?" Allison stopped playing with the radio and looked at me.

"What?" I was now completely focused on pulling out into Saturday night bridge-and-tunnel traffic. I chanced a peek at her out of the corner of my eye and spied her smiling at me enigmatically.

"The phone call. What was it?"

"Nothing," I lied.

"You made dinner reservations." Her voice was soft, and her tone was oddly tender.

"Just for the Italian place down the street. I figured we'd be hungry, but they're always busy at this time on a Saturday night, so I thought a little insurance wouldn't hurt."

"That was very thoughtful, Ryan. We can eat there if you want."

I shook my head and narrowed my focus to the side-view mirror as I merged onto the Brooklyn Bridge. "Nah. You're tired, and you want to take a shower. It's fine."

"Are you sure?"

"Of course."

"I thought we could order room service, a couple of beers, and maybe start hammering out some of our paperwork. Is that okay?"

"You mean, you thought I could start hammering out some of our paperwork?"

"Well, yeah." She was unrepentant as she picked lint off her sleeve. "We're a team, aren't we?"

"Mmm-hmm," I muttered, amused. She was hopeless when it came to filling out the required forms for visits, and we both knew it. For some reason I had yet to figure out, it took her damn near forever. To say that it would just be faster if I did the whole thing was a gross understatement. If I let her do it, the visit would be over before she had anything that was remotely usable. It was sad, really. And somehow absolutely adorable. "How do you fudge your way through other visits? I mean, you can't possibly con everyone into doing your work for you?"

"Why not? Besides, I don't think of it as conning. I consider it the spirit of teamwork."

"The spirit of teamwork," I repeated skeptically.

"Of course. They have the pleasure of working with me, and in return, I offer them the chance to gain invaluable experience by doing the paperwork. It's win-win."

I laughed and shook my head, knowing when I was beaten. I also knew Allison was just joking. Though she deserved her status as the golden child, she was truly the most modest woman I'd ever met, which made it difficult for anyone—no matter how jealous they might be of her success—to dislike her.

Traffic on the bridge was packed with people looking to go out and have a good time and was crawling. I took advantage of the situation and got out my cell phone to send a quick text message while I had the chance. Once we were on the FDR, I wouldn't be able to.

"Hey!" Allison made a grab for the phone. "No texting and driving. It's bad enough you try to talk and drive."

I had to be quick to maintain possession of the phone. Keeping it out of her reach with one hand while fending her off with the other wasn't easy. "We're sitting in completely stopped traffic." Her flailing arms were now smacking me in the face in their attempt to pry the phone from my grasp, but I continued to text badly with my left hand while elbowing her across the chest with my right. "We haven't— ouch—moved. Stop it!" I slapped at her hands with my free one and was rewarded with a surprisingly forceful backhand across the nose. "Ow! The message is already sent."

"Put it away," she ordered me. "We're moving now."

"You're not the boss of me," I shot back maturely.

"Away."

I scowled and touched my nose gingerly before complying with her request. "Has it occurred to you that brawling with me while I'm operating a motor vehicle is slightly more dangerous and apt to get us all killed than my texting?"

"Just leave it in the holster while you're behind the wheel." Allison narrowed her eyes and pointed one finger in my direction.

"I love it when you get all domineering," I told her, allowing my voice to turn low and throaty at the end. I grinned at her and wiggled my eyebrows suggestively, marveling at how easy it was to slip back into playful banter with her. Like not a minute had passed.

Allison was not amused. "How about when I spank you like the spoiled brat you are? Do you love that?"

I made a show of closing my eyes, letting my head loll back, and moaning softly. "Don't tease me. It isn't nice." That earned me a hard punch on the arm and a glare, which made me laugh.

"Uh...Ryan?" Allison said in a small voice.

My insides flipped at her tenor, and I was immediately wary. She did know I was only kidding...right? "What?"

"You're bleeding."

"What?"

"Your nose." Her tone was just this side of apologetic. She pointed, as if I couldn't be trusted to find my nose on my own. "It's bleeding."

I touched my fingers to my upper lip and discovered she was right. "Wonder whose fault that is?"

"Whose?"

"You're kidding."

"What?"

"You really don't see how you might've had something to do with this?"

Allison shrugged lightly, but I could see she was struggling not to smile. "I plead the fifth."

"I'm sure you do." My tone was wry. I made a faint gesture with my now-bloody hand before returning it to its previous task of trying to catch the crimson flow. "You'll find some napkins in the glove box."

With an expression that was an odd mixture of amusement, wistfulness, and contrition, Allison grabbed a couple and handed them to me so I could clean myself up. "How long?" She sounded concerned.

"How long what?" I was busy trying to wipe my nose, assess the damage in the mirror, and drive at the same time.

"Since you were sick? How long?"

Bloody nose momentarily forgotten, I turned my head to gape at her. "Huh?"

"You always get a bloody nose easily right after you've had a sinus infection. So I was wondering how long ago you'd been sick."

I was shocked she even remembered but tried not to show it. "Are you trying to blame this mess on something other than you and your flailing limbs of fury?"

Allison snorted. "Call it shared culpability if you like. I refuse to accept all responsibility for this situation. But if you were recently sick, it wouldn't take much."

"Hmm. I only admit it because I want you to know I'm tougher than that, and it'd take more than that pop you gave me to really hurt me."

Allison smirked. "Of course. You're a total badass."

I laughed, and she looked at me expectantly. "What?"

"How. Long."

"Oh. About three days, I guess." I was concentrating much harder than necessary on weaving in and out of traffic on the FDR. "Maybe four." I was oddly touched she recalled something so trivial about me. Especially since I'd been under the impression she'd completely purged everything about me from her memory. A lump began to form in my throat, and I tried to swallow it.

Allison sniffed and glanced in my direction. "You'd better not get me sick," she said, her tone threatening. She pointed one finger at me as she gave me the command.

"How the hell do you think I'm going to get you sick?"

"You'd just better not."

"Well, don't kiss me, then," I shot back, regretting the words the instant they were out of my mouth.

"I wasn't planning on it." Allison fished her BlackBerry out of its holster in response to the vibration that even I could hear in the weighty silence filling the car.

My face immediately warmed, and the slash of regret that sliced through me was agonizing. I hadn't been expecting her to kiss me, of course, but would it have killed her to want to? Even a little? I inhaled deeply and let out a heavy sigh. I hastily resumed wiping my face with the napkin in an attempt to hide my expression. Fortunately, Allison didn't appear to notice. She was completely consumed with reading and then answering an email on her BlackBerry, leaving me to wallow in my own unpleasant thoughts.

"How many post-standers do we have for the LZ again?" Allison's eyes were glued to the device in her hands as her thumbs flew over the keys.

I wracked my brain, trying to remember how many bodies the scheduling guys told us we could have for the landing zone we used for Marine One. I was pretty sure she wouldn't like the answer. "How many did we ask for, or how many did we get?"

"Those numbers are different?"

I nodded, speeding up in order to pass a slow-moving car in the right lane and then returning to that lane quickly so we didn't miss our exit. "They always are, out there. But we can use NYPD detectives on the outer-perimeter, nondiscretionary posts. I'll show you. It isn't a big deal."

Allison was pursing her lips and annoyance flickered across her features, but I could tell it wasn't directed at me, which made me nearly dizzy with relief. I must have hidden my emotions better than I'd thought. Either that or she was more distracted than I'd realized.

Allison let out an irritated sigh and punched the keys on her BlackBerry with a little more force than she'd been using. "What'd they give us?" Her tone was borderline resigned but with a touch of exasperation.

"Fifteen."

"Are you kidding me?"

"Why are you worried about this, again? You have coworkers up here with you getting paid to work out those details. You don't have to do everything yourself. We have enough to concentrate on without getting involved in things that aren't our job. Trust your peers to do theirs."

"I do trust them. But I want to know everything about every single, solitary part of this visit. Right down to the smallest detail."

I tried hard not to smile because showing any mirth would only irritate her. But it was tough. She was too cute when she was all anal retentive. "Of course. When we get to the room, I'll go over the diagrams for each site with you one by one. Then you can work it out with the site agents how you want it structured. Don't worry. It'll all be fine."

"You have working copies of the diagrams already?"

I nodded, piloting through the traffic on the surface streets with care, keeping a particularly wary eye on the yellow cabs zipping around. "Yeah. I sketched them while we did the initial walkthroughs." That made me as much of a control freak as she was.

"Fantastic." Allison sounded relieved.

"You asked the boss if you could work with me and then expected a half-assed job?"

"Do you really think I'd stake my reputation on anything less than stellar?"

"Then why do you sound so surprised that I made diagrams?"

"I don't know. I just wasn't thinking that far ahead. This whole thing sort of took me by surprise. And then there was the shock of actually seeing you." Her words made me inhale sharply, but I didn't have time to follow up on them. She held up her BlackBerry and wiggled it at me as she rushed on. "The boss wants to do preliminary walkthroughs tomorrow afternoon. I want to have everything squared away by then."

"No problem."

I forced myself to focus on the parking situation and tear my mind away from her cryptic comments. I'd spotted a space just up the block that would put us less than thirty steps from the front door of Allison's hotel and had convinced myself if I didn't take my eyes off it, I'd be able to save the space through willpower alone.

I effortlessly slid the Impala into the spot, pleased with my luck. Throwing the car into park, I leaned back between the seats to retrieve my parking placard, unsure how it'd ended up there in the first place.

The resulting position put my face in very close proximity to Allison. When she turned to look at me, her lips mere inches from mine, and I again had the disconcerting notion she was staring directly into my soul. She leaned toward me, causing my head to swim; the scent of her was intoxicating.

Allison's near-black eyes flicked to my lips for an instant, and she shifted just a fraction of an inch closer, her lips quirked in a small smile. I was pretty sure my heart would give out at that point.

"I thought I told you not to get me sick," she whispered. Her breath ghosted gently across my cheek, and I had to fight not to close my eyes.

"I thought I told you not to kiss me," I whispered back. I flashed her a small smile of my own, amazed I had the presence of mind to form coherent words, let alone attempt wit.

"I wasn't planning to." She tried to make her protest sound haughty, but the heat in her voice fizzled and died. She didn't make any move to increase the distance between us.

"Uh-huh."

My heart lurched. I'd seen that expression before and wasn't liable to forget it. She might not have planned to actually do it, but she'd definitely thought about it. If only for the briefest of instants.

In the end, the loud honking of a car horn on the corner shattered the moment. I folded my fingers around the police placard but took my time returning to a completely upright position.

"Come on, supercop," I said. "Let's go."

Allison smiled back at me as she gathered her belongings and followed me out of the car.

CHAPTER TEN

The New York Field Office of the United States Secret Service leads the entire agency in arrest stats as well as protection visits, surpassing even the Washington Field Office. The guys in WFO like to argue that we're only on top due to a technicality because our stats are bolstered every year by the United Nations General Assembly, which usually attracts upward of two hundred protectees to the NYFO district. In response to those allegations, I normally choose to respond with a well-timed raspberry. I find that tends to end most arguments rather quickly.

In addition to the yearly meeting of the UNGA, New York has numerous visiting dignitaries in and out of the city throughout the year. Because of that, we tend to have a close working relationship with the many hotel chains scattered in and around here. Most hotels have housed either agents or visiting foreign delegations.

The W Hotel on Lexington Avenue is located near both the Waldorf Astoria and Intercontinental, two favorite hotels of our own president and of foreign heads of state. As such, it's the perfect location to house our agents when necessary. The agency has a very good working relationship with the hotel staff, and I'd personally made some friends there over the years.

That fact would explain the loud, "Well, well, well" that carried across the entire lobby upon my arrival.

I turned toward the greeting, both unwilling and unable to hold back my grin. "Well, yourself," I shot back. "Looking pretty good." I allowed my eyes to sweep up and down the curvaceous form of my personal welcoming committee, lingering very obviously on specific parts of her anatomy.

Allison's eyes shot from me to the woman heckling me, but the ringing of her cell phone spared me any commentary. She walked a few paces away to take the call in relative privacy while I rested my hands on my hips and waited.

The blond woman headed my way snorted as she approached and rolled her hazel eyes theatrically. She made a show of fluffing her hair and sweeping nonexistent lint off her impeccably pressed uniform. Her general manager's nametag gleamed brightly under the lobby lights.

"Pretty good? Please. I look fabulous, as usual. And stop trying to butter me up. I got your text." Her tone was dry, but her eyes were shining, so I knew she wasn't really as annoyed as she pretended. "That's always the way with you agents. We don't hear from you for months, and when we finally do, it's only because you want something."

"Oh, come on, Stace. That is so not true. I asked you out to dinner just last week." I paused as I rethought that statement. "Or maybe it was two weeks ago? I think last week I was on Trinidad. Anyway, whenever it was, I didn't want anything from you then aside from the pleasure of your company."

"Really?"

"Of course, really. What else would I want?"

Stacey shrugged, but I recognized the mischievous gleam in her eye all too well. It always meant trouble. "Oh, come on, Ryan. We both know you're hopelessly attracted to me. Why deny it any longer?"

I scoffed. "We do, huh?"

"We do. And I'm flattered. Really. But you know I'm happily married. Besides, I just don't think I could get on board with the whole woman scene."

"The hearts of lesbian and bi-curious women everywhere are breaking." She was such a trip.

She went on airily, almost as if I hadn't spoken. "Even if I were inclined to make all your wildest dreams come true and give the girl-on-girl thing a shot, Jeff would be devastated. You know he called first dibs on you. And I don't think he'd want to share you, even with me."

I bit back a laugh, unsure, as I always was, whether Stacey really was that cocky or whether she was just messing with me. I really hoped it was the latter. "That's a damn shame. And as attractive as I think your husband is—you know, for a guy—he just doesn't do it for me. But don't tell him that, okay?"

She laughed at my joke, and her gaze slid over to Allison, who had her back to us and was giving no sign of paying any attention to our banter. "Speaking of attractive."

My chest was suddenly tight, and my face burned as my eyes flicked to the woman in question. I clenched my teeth together for an instant before making a conscious effort to dispel the tension from my body. It helped. Well, a bit.

"What happened to Lucia?" Stacey wanted to know. "Did you finally break up with her? Because it's about damn time."

I blinked, startled, and returned my attention to Stacey, who was eying Allison speculatively. After a moment, her focus shifted back to me. "Not that Lucia isn't very sweet and completely gorgeous if you go for that Michelle Rodriguez type, but you know…" She sketched a wave in the air, as if she'd made her point.

"Lucia and I didn't break up." I had trouble getting the words out, and I didn't even want to think about why the air in the lobby had just become stifling.

Stacey's eyes widened, and she put one hand to her mouth. "Oh, my God, Ryan. I'm so sorry. I just assumed, well, I mean, I never really thought you and Lucia clicked all that well, and now here you are with this walking wet dream—"

"Stacey," I barked, a little louder than necessary, which caused Allison to turn her head in my direction and examine me briefly with her hawk-like gaze. Two things were bothering me about Stacey's statement, and I still wasn't sure which affected me more.

First was her opinion that Lucia and I had never really clicked. I'd thought we actually clicked pretty well. And what the hell would she know about it anyway? She'd seen us together on maybe three occasions and only long enough for us to grab dinner. That was hardly time enough to accurately assess an entire relationship.

Second, something about her categorization of Allison irritated me. A lot. Not that it wasn't accurate. Not by a long shot. Hell, I'd been teetering unsteadily on the razor edge of arousal all freaking day because Allison Reynolds and I were occupying the same space, but still, to hear someone else say it out loud...

Stacey's features softened, and her expression became a cross between sympathetic and incredulous. "Oh, wow. You've got it bad." Her voice was hushed, almost a whisper, her tone colored with quiet wonder.

"I do not!" I'd have done better to pretend not to know what she was talking about. My fervent denial pretty much confirmed her suspicions. For both of us.

Shit.

"Come on, Ryan." Stacey placed a tender hand on my shoulder, and the gesture touched yet aggravated me. "I see the way you look at her. It's obvious that—"

I held up my hand to stop her, positive I was better off not knowing what she intended to say. I believed in plausible deniability. Oh, and plain old denial. I was a definite fan of that, too. At least in this instance.

"Stace, we really gotta go." I turned abruptly and walked away from the conversation, trying to sweep the entire conversation—revelations and all—to the back of my mind. I brushed the palm of my hand along Allison's back briefly to get her attention on my way to the elevators but averted my eyes. Stacey's words had resonated within me on several levels, and I was sure Allison would immediately know something was up.

"Ryan." Stacey's voice carried after me and sounded a touch upset.

I got into the elevator with Allison following closely behind and turned back to face the now-closing doors. "I'll call you later."

I suffered a brief stab of remorse at Stacey's forlorn expression. Like I needed that on top of everything else. I sighed and roughly removed the hair tie keeping my tresses pulled back, twisting it around and around my index finger until it hurt.

Allison terminated her call and returned the phone to its place on her belt, turning to study me intently. Silence reigned, and my face grew hotter the longer she stared at me. I resolutely kept my eyes on the doors in front of me and wrenched the rubber band around my finger so hard I had to bite the inside of my lip to keep from crying out.

"You okay?"

"I'm good." I didn't meet her stare, preferring instead to step off the elevator the second the doors opened and stride with purpose down the hall to her room. I released my now-purple fingertip from the hair tie and shoved it in my pocket.

Allison kept pace with me. "Did that woman say something to you?"

"Nah." I kept my attention focused on the room numbers as we passed.

"You sure?" She sounded skeptical.

I glanced at her and decided to change the subject. "You know what I am sure about?" Allison shook her head, and I threw one arm companionably around her shoulders. "I'm sure someone promised me a whole lot of beer." I gave her a final squeeze and let her go as we stopped in front of her door.

Allison chuckled and slid her key card into the lock, shaking her head, and a few stray locks of her thick black hair tumbled across her forehead and into her eyes. The longing to brush them back was almost painful, and I thrust my hand into my pocket to finger its contents in an effort to have something else to occupy me.

"You Irish girls are so easy." She gave me a sly grin as she opened the door and led the way into her hotel room. "Give you a beer, and you're thrilled."

"Hey, that's not always true. Sometimes we require whiskey."

Allison laughed again and deposited her bag on the floor in the corner. She shrugged out of her suit jacket and hung it carelessly over the back of the chair at the desk. I started to set up my computer while she methodically removed her equipment and laid it out neatly across the dresser.

"You don't mind if I take a shower, do you?"

I glanced up at the question. She'd turned to face me, and her fingers were poised over the buttons of her dress shirt as though she were awaiting my permission to take it off. I ducked my head to continue scrutinizing the diagram I'd sketched for the LZ site while I waited for my laptop to boot up.

"Knock yourself out," I managed to say, pleased that I didn't sound too shaky. Peripherally, I could see her unbuttoning her blouse. She was clearly trying to kill me. I took a shuddering breath and deliberately concentrated elsewhere, although, admittedly, I wasn't really seeing anything at all.

Once Allison finally tired of trying to incite an aneurysm by prancing around the room in her underwear, she disappeared into the bathroom, and I could finally breathe somewhat normally and use my scrambled brain.

Sure, occasionally my thoughts strayed back to Allison and what I knew her lean, taut body looked like as she stood under the scalding hot spray, rivulets of water running down her silky smooth skin. And, okay, maybe I entertained a few images of joining her and licking all those stray droplets off, making her moan with pleasure. But mostly I just concentrated on work. More or less.

"Hungry?" Allison asked softly from behind me.

I jumped and hastily shot to my feet, then spun around. For the briefest second, we stood face to face. Our eyes were locked, and our lips were far too close to touching for my comfort. The clean scent of her shampoo intoxicated me, and I had to fight not to lean into her.

Fortunately, a knock sounded at the door before I could fall too far into her midnight gaze. I could only hope my jumbled emotions hadn't been too clearly on display for the length of time she'd held me prisoner. Fat chance. But at least I hadn't made an idiot of myself. That was something.

"Stay here." My voice was barely louder than a whisper. I was aware of how breathy and desire-laden I sounded but was unable to disguise my tone. I ran one hand over the soft skin of Allison's bare upper arm as I went to answer the door, marveling at the tingles along my own skin.

A quick peek confirmed it was the room service I'd ordered, so I paid for the meal and assured the puzzled waiter I could take the cart in by myself. That was probably best, considering Allison's state of undress.

My heart started to thud within the suddenly-too-small confines of my chest. I took a deep breath and quickly swiped my hand across the side of the ice bucket, then rubbed the moisture onto my hot cheeks. *Stop acting like a complete dolt.*

While I was at the door, Allison had donned her pajamas. She was now wearing a light-gray T-shirt we're all issued in the academy with the initials of our training center—JJRTC—stenciled across the left breast and a pair of faded red flannel pants with tiny, white lips printed all over them. The vision of how sexy she was in her casual nighttime attire, her dark hair carelessly finger combed back off her forehead and leaving wet spots on the shoulders of her shirt, struck me dumb.

Allison didn't lift her head from the sheaf of papers resting in her lap as she sat cross-legged in the middle of the king-sized bed, but she did shift her gaze toward me. When she noticed the cart, her expression became contemplative.

"What's this?"

"Dinner." I snagged a beer from the silver ice bucket and used the strike plate nestled in the jamb of the bathroom door to pop the cap off. I grinned, sauntered over to the bed, and held out the bottle. "And the beer someone promised. I got tired of waiting for you to provide for me."

Now Allison's head did come up, and she smiled at me as she accepted the beer. She took a long swallow and then offered it to me, so I could have a gulp of my own. I accepted the bottle and tried like hell not to dwell on the fact that my lips were touching the place where hers had just rested. If the painful clench of desire low in my gut was any indication, the attempt didn't go as planned.

Allison waved a familiar-looking manila folder at me. "I can see that it's dinner. I meant what's this."

My eyes flicked to exhibit A. The folder with the stuff for the Akbari interview. "Oh, that's a case folder. It's nothing. It must've gotten mixed up with the rest of my things when I packed up this morning."

Allison flipped through it casually. "It's a counterfeit case."

I held my hand out for the folder and its contents, and she handed them over without comment. "Yup. I was checking on something for a friend." I tossed the folder onto the chair I'd been occupying earlier.

"Since when do you work counterfeit?"

"I don't. Not anymore."

"You used to? When was that?"

"Not long after you went to D.C."

"Huh. I didn't know that. Did you like it?"

I shrugged. "You know me. I'm pretty content wherever I am."

Allison eyed me with skepticism. I was certain she'd push that issue, but then she picked up another piece of paper lying off to the side of the pile of diagrams she'd been perusing.

"And what's this?" She waved it at me, but I couldn't make out what it was.

"I dunno. What is it?"

"Looks like a bingo board to me."

Oops. Busted! I checked my BlackBerry for nonexistent emails.

"Really? Huh. That's weird."

"Mmm-hmm. Weird. Right." She raised her eyebrows and began to read aloud what was written in the little squares. "Tip of the spear. The beast. Terrain feature. Plenty of relief built in. Game day. Crickets. The jackal. Marry up. Clicks. Grip and grin. Nobody's gonna get hurt."

"Yup. That's what it says."

"What is this?"

"Uh…PPD Briefing Bingo?"

"What?"

"PPD Briefing Bingo," I repeated more firmly.

"You've made a game of our briefings?" I couldn't determine the exact nature of her tone.

"Just the ridiculous parts."

"Ridiculous?!"

"I'm sorry. Would you prefer another description?"

Her eyes flashed in anger. "How would you like us to impart important information, then?"

"Beats me. But it'd probably sound a lot less stupid if you all at least used the terminology correctly. A person is not a 'terrain feature.'"

"I've never once uttered the words 'terrain feature.'"

"I never said it was you."

Allison glared at me, and I took a deep breath, caught somewhere between shame and amusement.

"Look, it's a campaign year, which means POTUS is up here on average once every two to three weeks. We barely get a break from you people, and you're back. It's exhausting. And every single time he comes into district, we have to sit through one of those briefings. And we get it. We do. We all need to hear how the visit is laid out because you can't take the chance on what might go wrong if we skip it even once. We appreciate that. But every single briefing is always exactly the same as every other one before it. And having so many so close together, it gets kind of hard to focus." I made a helpless little gesture with my hands, almost begging for her understanding. "Making a game of listening for those particular phrases seemed like a good way to keep from falling asleep. It was never meant to be disrespectful."

"You do this every time we come up?"

"Um...Maybe?"

Allison's eyes narrowed at me, glinting with suspicion. "Was this your idea?"

"I can neither confirm nor deny."

"Right." She appeared to consider this, and I changed the subject. No good could come of this line of questioning. I certainly didn't need for the bosses to find out we played this game. I couldn't imagine they'd have a sense of humor about it.

"So, are you hungry? Because I'm ravenous."

Allison regarded me silently for a long moment, and I had a flash of fear that she wouldn't let me divert her attention. Thank goodness she opted to chug the remainder of her beer and hold out the empty bottle to me.

Sighing quietly, I took it and automatically prepared two more, one for her and one for me. "Burger?" I asked, lifting the lid off one dish and carefully setting it upside down on the edge of the dresser, out of the way.

When no answer came, I looked back over my shoulder to find Allison staring at me. I gestured toward the steaming plate with one hand as I took a small sip of the beer nestled in the other.

"What if I wanted pasta?"

Smugly, I lifted the metal cover off the other dish and set it inside of the first. I took a step to the side to reveal the plate of fettuccini Alfredo topped with grilled chicken. "Then I'll eat the burger. But I'm not sharing my fries."

I placed the plate of pasta with its garlic bread on the desk, then removed the cling wrap from one of the two glasses of water that'd come with the meals and set that down to the right of the plate, just above where I'd laid the still-wrapped silverware. The small vase with its single rosebud joined the place setting, and I pulled the chair out for Allison and waited for her to take a seat.

The odd expression on her face as I finally turned to look at her was difficult to interpret, so I didn't even try. I merely held out my hand to her.

Allison pushed the papers off her lap with no regard for order or destination and slid off the bed, the beer bottle dangling loosely from her fingers. Her eyes held mine as she took the offered chair, and I slid it in for her, helping her get comfortable. Once she was settled, I gathered the papers and my laptop off the ottoman and deposited them on the floor where they'd be out of the way while I ate.

The room was silent but not uncomfortably so, though I did wonder what she was thinking about a couple of times. Once I'd inhaled my burger, I went back to studying my scribbly diagrams and making more notes as I worked on my fries.

"The text message." Allison's voice was hushed and tinged with realization and something else I couldn't identify.

I was completely absorbed by my work, and perhaps that's why Allison's statement surprised me. It took a few seconds for her words to penetrate, and I frowned as I dragged my eyes from my papers to look up at her.

"Huh?" I was trying to shift gears and catch up with her, I really was. But nothing was sticking.

"The text message you sent in the car."

"What about it?"

"That's how dinner got here so fast, isn't it?" Her gaze was sharp as she studied me. "You texted ahead and asked them to have dinner waiting." Her dark eyes clouded. "That blond woman from the lobby," she murmured quietly, almost to herself. Her attention shifted from the cart to the plate in front of her to the flower back to my face.

"Stacey," I supplied with a nod, popping a ketchup-covered fry into my mouth.

Allison's eyes now cleared as the pieces fell into place, and something not unlike affection flooded her features as she looked at me. I tried hard not to blush. "Thank you," she said finally.

I smiled at her, secretly thrilled that she was pleased. "No problem." I quickly shifted my focus back to the papers in my lap, anxious to dispel the intimacy of the moment.

"That was very thoughtful."

"Well, I know how you get when you're hungry." I deliberately kept my voice light, falling back on one of my most relied-upon tools: using humor to gloss over a situation I wasn't entirely comfortable with. "Frankly, I don't have the energy to deal with you when you're like that."

"Ha, ha. Think of that all by yourself, smart-ass?"

"Yes, I did. I'm unbelievably clever."

"Oh, you're something all right," Allison mumbled.

I ducked my head to avoid further eye contact and made a show of working. While I may've actually been getting some things accomplished, my underlying thoughts were distracting me.

Coming up to Allison's hotel room had been a terrible idea. A small part of me had recognized that when she'd first suggested it, then worried when we'd been so close to kissing in the car. And now that she was sitting just a few feet away from me engaging me in witty banter like she used to and looking at me with that special smile as if not a day had passed, I was certain. Worst idea ever. What had I been thinking?

I wanted to resent her but was having a tough time justifying that emotion. This wasn't her fault. I was the one having a problem keeping this encounter strictly friendly. I was also apparently the only one who still felt the attraction that'd once flared between us. I mean, aside from the flash of desire on her face in the car, she hadn't indicated that she had any feelings for me not rooted in professional respect or nostalgia for what we'd once shared.

I dug my knuckles into the edge of my eyebrow hard and forced myself not to frown. I didn't want to still be attracted to Allison. She'd hurt me. Badly. And while a small part of me was still angry, she'd somehow managed not only to quietly overcome my ire but also to reawaken emotions I'd kept buried for a long time.

I glared at the diagrams in front of me, upset with myself and now inanely with her for making me this tied up in knots. I wanted to be over her. But I had to accept that I wasn't, that I'd barely made any strides toward that end, and the realization was killing me.

Of course, I was seeing someone, which was also contributing heavily to my dismay. I didn't want to hurt Lucia. She was such a wonderful person, and I really did like her. She deserved so much better than someone who clearly had trouble letting go of the past. She was worthy of someone who would offer her a fairy-tale future. My heart was breaking slowly and painfully as I questioned for the second time that day whether that someone was me.

I crumpled one of the diagrams roughly in my fist and then smoothed it out against my thigh. When it was as unwrinkled as it was going to get, I placed it back on the ottoman. Then I clenched my hands together in my lap, pushing my palms against one another hard as though I could compress the guilt that was threatening to tear me apart.

I chanced a quick glance at Allison, relieved to see that she was intently focused on her own work. I didn't want her to catch even a vague hint of my turmoil, didn't want her to question it. I don't think I could've articulated to her exactly why I was so vexed even if I'd wanted to. Not only did I not want to get into it with her, but I also wanted to save face. We weren't together anymore. Hell, we weren't even friends. Not really. I hadn't heard from her once since she'd left. I definitely didn't owe her any kind of explanation for my moods.

What I did owe her was complete and undivided attention to this job. We had a mission to accomplish and not a lot of time. I took a long drink of water and cleared my throat.

"What have you got?" If Allison noticed that something was bothering me, she was polite enough not to mention it. Either that or I'd done a bang-up job of hiding it.

I turned the copy of one of the uncrumpled diagrams around so she could see it and laid it flat on top of the ottoman. When she leaned over to study it, I began to explain what post-standers we usually used and what I'd changed and why, gesturing to key points on the schematic with my pen.

Allison nodded and asked the occasional question or interjected a comment, but mostly she was silent. When I'd finished, she remained quiet for a long moment, obviously thinking.

"Can you get these changes inserted and have a working copy sketched out by tomorrow afternoon for the walkthrough with the boss and the site guys?"

A fissure of relief skittered through me. Without realizing it, Allison was offering me a perfect excuse to flee the scene. I tried to keep my expression from suggesting I was thrilled at the prospect of running away from her and handed her the other diagrams to look over, praying she wouldn't ask about the one I'd mangled.

"Tell me if these are okay, and I'll go take care of it now."

"Ryan, it's almost nine o'clock. We can stop at the office tomorrow morning and do it."

"I know. But the more we get finished today, the less rushed we'll feel as the visit approaches. If I can make the majority of the changes now, the site guys will have less work to do after the supervisor walkthroughs."

Allison eyed me for a long moment before she shifted her attention to the diagrams in her hand. She appeared reluctant yet resigned, and I was glad she wasn't trying to argue with me or talk me out of this.

She made a few quick notes and handed the papers back to me. As I accepted them, she padded over to the dresser and started lifting off her shirt.

My heart collapsed in on itself and rocketed off to another part of my body. I turned my head, covering my eyes with my hand. "Whoa. What the hell are you doing?" I hadn't meant to sound so harsh, but the threat of spontaneous nudity had taken me by surprise.

I could see through the tiny gaps between my fingers that Allison was looking at me like I was crazy, but she'd stopped trying to remove her clothes. Thank God.

"I'm getting dressed."

"Why?"

"What do you mean 'Why?' I'm coming with you, and I refuse to show up at the office in my pajamas."

I shook my head. I'd planned to make the changes from the comfort of my own apartment. But I didn't want to tell her that. Heaven forbid she want to accompany me there.

Instead, I said, "Allison, you don't need to come."

"Well, I don't want you going by yourself."

"Don't trust me not to screw it up?" I flashed her a grin. I was purposely trying to lighten the mood. If she continued to press the issue, I was afraid I'd blurt out that I really just wanted to go home, and some small part of me really didn't want her knowing that. It was as if admitting that would be admitting to every other outrageous thought that had recently cut jagged trails through my tangled little mind.

Sure, I recognized that one had absolutely nothing to do with the other. And regardless, Allison couldn't read minds, so it shouldn't make a difference. Besides, did it matter what Allison thought? Unfortunately, the rational part of me was nearly silent at the moment. So I went with misdirection.

"Well, there is that. But we're a team. I don't want you to think I'm not doing my share." Allison's expression was serious, and she was staring at me with an intensity that made me vaguely nervous.

The idea that she cared what I thought touched me and warmed my soul in places it probably shouldn't have. That was a surefire clue that I needed to get going. Like now. Because having feelings like these was only heightening my confusion and, by a directly proportional degree, my guilt. So, yeah, the sooner I made my grand escape, the better.

Despite myself and my nearly compulsive desire to run from the room, I softened my smile and couldn't resist squeezing her forearm. "I promise you I won't think that." As she opened her mouth to protest, I went on. "Look, you're already showered and dressed for bed. It makes no sense for you to go back out now. Not for something this trivial. It'll take me fifteen minutes, tops."

Uncertainty flickered behind Allison's eyes. "Are you sure?"

"Positive. I'll see you tomorrow, okay?" I hastily gathered my belongings and shoved them haphazardly into my bag, grateful for a legitimate excuse to divert my attention. It was a relief to escape her gaze, if only momentarily. I slung my bag over my shoulder and took a deep breath before I looked at her once more.

"What time do you want me to pick you up tomorrow?"

"That depends. Do you want to grab breakfast first?" If I didn't know better, I'd have thought she was afraid I might decline. But that made no sense.

I pretended to consider her question. "That depends." My use of the phrase was deliberate. I was teasing her, but her expression made me wonder whether she knew it.

Allison folded her arms across her chest, her countenance cool now. "On?"

"On whether you agree to split an order of chocolate-chip pancakes with me." I grinned at her and waited to see whether she'd pick up on the reference to one of our old breakfast rituals.

I don't know what reply she'd been expecting, but the surprise on her face told me it wasn't that. She threw her head back and laughed. "Only if you promise to actually share them with me and not eat them all before I can grab a bite."

We meandered to the door still chuckling at the inside joke and said our good-byes, agreeing that I'd pick her up the next day at seven and let her have at least five bites of our pancakes before I even waved a fork in their direction.

It was only after the door was safely shut behind me that I quietly responded to the innuendo I imagined her statement about sharing had held.

"I wouldn't have it any other way."

CHAPTER ELEVEN

Human beings obviously aren't perfect, and I can easily admit I probably have more flaws than most. I'm stubborn. I can be overly emotional at certain times yet oddly cold and detached at others. I'm a pro at using humor as a tool for avoidance. And I'll procrastinate with my vacuuming until the end of time. Just to name a few.

At the moment, the fault giving me the most trouble was my ability to obsess over a situation until it was resolved. No matter how much I tried, it was tough for me to push specific things from the forefront of my mind.

My dad always told me never to waste time or energy worrying, especially about things completely out of my control. He'd always said situations had a way of working themselves out and my constant fretting wouldn't affect the outcome one way or the other. Best to just concentrate on the parts I could influence and deal with the consequences.

I envied him that particular ability and had wished more than once that I could adopt that outlook. Though I'd left the desire unspoken. I'd wanted to avoid being hit with his second favorite piece of advice, which had something to do with wishing in one hand and spitting in the other to see which filled up first. That one had always irritated me a little. It was human nature to wish for things, and I didn't appreciate being told otherwise. Also, once he trotted out that adage, he soon mentioned if his grandmother had wheels, she'd be a wagon, and I never knew what to say to that one. Best to completely elude that pitfall altogether by just keeping quiet.

Not that I needed him to have a full-blown conversation about worrying or wishing or even wagons, apparently, because I'd heard his voice inside my head doling out all sorts of less-than-helpful advice since I'd left Allison's hotel room. That I could still hear him was grating, and my sour mood and blatant annoyance with myself certainly weren't helping matters.

Huffing in frustration, I slapped the newly printed copies of the site diagrams down onto my coffee table and flounced back on the couch. My fingers tapped out a nervous, restless rhythm on the tops of my thighs as my eyes ricocheted around my living room. After a slightly schizophrenic car ride home, I'd forced myself to focus on work just long enough to accomplish the task I'd told Allison I'd perform before my brain rebelled and refused to be coerced any longer.

Now my mind was racing back and forth between Lucia and Allison, past and present, guilt and anger, sadness and pain. My thoughts crashed violently only to bounce off one another and zoom crazily in another direction like pin balls in a pin-ball machine at some sort of fucked-up carnival. I was about ready to tilt.

I reviewed the situation and ran through my reasoning for what must've been the fifteenth time since I'd walked out of The W. While I'd pretty much made up my mind, and it was difficult to dissuade me once I reached a firm decision, I couldn't shake the doubts that danced inelegantly at the dark edges of my thoughts. I poked at them the way I'd worry a loose tooth with the tip of my tongue, almost perversely enjoying each dull throb of discomfort.

Allison had shattered me once upon a time, and though I'd never denied that fact, it was about damn time I confronted it, got the hell over it, and moved on with my life. I couldn't hang on to the hurt and anger forever. If I couldn't learn to let it go, I'd never be able to build a life with anyone else. Not a whole one, at any rate, because I couldn't give myself completely to anyone as long as any part of me still belonged to her.

How, then, could I make a break? How did I reclaim that part of myself I'd allowed her to retain even after she'd made it clear she didn't want it? Maybe that was part of the problem. Maybe I didn't really want it back. Because if she had it, if I kept it "safe" with her, then theoretically I couldn't be hurt again. Perhaps I simply didn't want to risk living through that kind of agony another time by falling for someone else.

I blinked slowly and frowned as I considered. Was that what I'd been doing all these years? Making sure no one else could ever break my heart by refusing to wholly give it to another? Surely even I couldn't be that messed up. Could I?

So, how to fix this, then? That was the question. How could I completely eradicate any and all feelings I still had for Allison Reynolds? I wasn't sure, and my overtired brain wasn't helping a whole hell of a lot. It just kept spinning, like tires slipping on an icy road, unable to gain traction.

Lucia was the key. She had to be. I might not be ready to say I loved her quite yet, but that didn't mean I couldn't someday. She was the only woman since Allison I'd even considered having any type of relationship with past three or four dates. That had to count for something, right? I hoped so. Because if it didn't, I was screwed.

I crumpled, bent at the waist, and rested my elbows on my knees, lightly clasping the back of my neck. I studied the wiggling tips of my toes peeking out from beneath the cuffs of my slacks. It was as if the feet I was looking at were completely detached from my body. I wished I could disconnect my mind that easily. I simply didn't have the energy to try to solve this puzzle tonight.

A quick glance at the clock told me it was rapidly approaching eleven. I doubted I'd be able to get any sleep. My thoughts were too fractured, and I was still too wound up.

I wouldn't be able to keep this up much longer. I was terrible when I was tired. My emotions were more raw and closer to the surface than they'd otherwise be, and my normally tight grip on them was noticeably looser. It was a recipe for trouble and most likely would make me make an ass of myself. Probably more than once and possibly in front of a small crowd.

I pushed myself awkwardly to a standing position and turned toward my bedroom, flipping off the table lamp as I went. I intended to cuddle up in bed with a favorite book and read until I couldn't keep my eyes open any longer. I hoped that wouldn't take all night. The sound of a key in the lock on my front door stopped me, and I froze. Who even had a key to my place? I eased my right hand toward the butt of my pistol and prepared to unsnap the retention strap.

Lucia let herself in and quietly closed the door behind her, sagging against it after it'd shut. Her eyes were downcast, and she looked miserable. I tried to rein in my wildly galloping heart and scolded myself for having forgotten I'd given her a key a few weeks before so she could pick up some USSS swag she'd asked me to get for her.

I allowed my hand to drop to my side—telling myself not to freak out because I'd almost just drawn down on her—and gave her a careful once-over. As I took in her expression, my pulse resumed its previously racing tempo. Last I'd heard, via a recent text message, she'd planned to spend the night at her place. It'd been the only time she'd contacted me all day. What could've happened?

"Luce?"

Lucia dragged her eyes up to meet mine and simply stared at me as an ever-changing array of emotions paraded across her features: dejection, anguish, fury. Others I couldn't begin to put a name to. My fear ratcheted up a few more notches, and my hands trembled.

"What happened?"

I immediately thought someone was dead. Once that idea had solidified, my brain glommed onto it and ran. A million different scenarios burned hot trails through my consciousness, each more gruesome and heartrending than the one before it. I had to force myself to stop jumping to conclusions before I drove myself mad. My father's calm voice sounded in my head, a variation on a theme, reminding me not to invent things to worry about.

I took a tentative step forward and reached out, the gesture careful, hesitant. I didn't want to do anything to spook her. But I wouldn't have the first clue how to comfort her if she didn't tell me what was wrong.

Lucia zeroed in on my hand as it approached her and allowed me to touch her lightly on the shoulder, but she stiffened, and the muscles under my fingers tensed and held as if my touch hurt her. Or was unwelcome.

"Sweetheart, what's wrong?" I made sure to keep my voice low and calm. I'd had a lot of practice managing emotionally disturbed people in the past few years. I'd just never thought I'd need to rely on those skills when dealing with someone I cared about.

I scanned Lucia for any outward signs of injury, relieved when I found none. Whatever was bothering her, it didn't appear to be physical.

I was glad she wasn't in pain, but afflictions of the heart or soul weren't much better. I'd rather she wasn't distressed at all. My father's adage about wishing in one hand flitted absurdly through my thoughts, and I pushed it away.

I trailed my hand down her arm and threaded our fingers together. Tugging lightly, I led her toward the sofa. She followed silently, not putting up any resistance, for which I was grateful. I sat down on the couch, and Lucia sat beside me, depositing the cell phone in her hand on the coffee table next to mine. Then she sat back, stiff and still. I cradled the hand I was already holding in both of mine and waited for her to speak.

Lucia continued to look straight ahead, her eyes glassy, her expression dazed, broken only occasionally by brief flashes of other, darker emotions. She took deep, controlled breaths, inhaling for a four count and exhaling the same, and I deliberately timed my own breathing to match hers. This seemed to go on for an eternity, but the calming technique appeared to have the opposite effect on her. Every muscle in her small frame was taut, and her jaw was clenched so tightly, I was positive she might shatter her molars.

To say that I was uneasy with the situation would have been akin to remarking that the ocean was wet. But this wasn't about me or my state of mind. It was about her. I didn't know what to do. She was obviously extremely distraught about something, and instinct told me not to push her, yet obeying that impulse was killing me.

When I shifted a bit closer so I could put my arm around her, a strangled sound somewhere between a moan and a wail wrenched itself from her throat, and she shook me off. She whipped her head around and, for the first time since she'd arrived, looked me square in the eye. Her naked feeling made me recoil before I could stop myself. Lucia was upset with me.

My insides lurched, and I mentally ran through all the things I could've done to put that look in her eyes, completely ignoring any advice regarding inventing things to worry about. It wasn't her birthday. I hadn't broken any plans that I could recall. And I didn't think forgetting to pick up something from the store would garner what I was seeing in her eyes.

It took a while, but finally I reached my own breaking point. I couldn't stand Lucia's calculated silence any more than I could bear her accusing glare. Frankly, both were starting to piss me off. I'm all for owning up to my mistakes and taking my lumps if I deserve them. But you have to at least tell me what I did wrong.

"What?" My tone was snappish, my voice harder than I intended, and I immediately regretted it. I ran one hand through my hair, tugging viciously at the snarls I encountered, knowing my frustration would continue as long as Lucia wanted it to. She was keeping me trapped there on purpose.

Lucia stared at me a moment longer, evidently gathering her resolve; the courage collecting in her glassy eyes was practically visible. The muscles along her jaw tensed, and she inhaled slowly. She clenched her hands into fists on top of her knees and opened her mouth. I caught the faintest whiff of alcohol, and my anxiety spiked. Lucia wasn't much of a drinker.

"Is it her?"

I blinked once, my mind blank. I had no freaking idea what the hell she was talking about.

"Is what who?" But the instant the words were out of my mouth, I knew. Well, at least who the "her" was. The "it" was still fuzzy. My heart bounced back and forth between my lungs, and a cold dread corkscrewed down my spine.

"The woman I met at the diner this morning." Lucia's eyes flashed, but her lower lip quivered the way it always did just before she started to cry.

"Allison?" The unease balled up inside me was growing heavier and more oppressive by the second.

"Yes. Allison."

"What about her?" I felt as though I was creeping precariously across a frozen pond, the thin, brittle ice ready to splinter and crack if I misstepped. My heart thudded painfully. Could she hear it? She had to be able to.

"She's the one, isn't she?" Lucia's eyes were sad now, glistening with unshed tears.

"The one what?" I still wasn't positive where this conversation was going. I'd never talked about Allison to Lucia. Not once, not ever. And she'd only crash-landed back in my life a little more than twenty-four hours ago. How could Allison be the one anything?

"She's the woman you were with before me." Lucia's voice was a low, pained whisper. "She's the one who broke your heart."

I gasped, surprised she'd so easily reached the correct conclusion. How had she done that? Maybe I hadn't given her enough credit. Or maybe I wasn't as unreadable as I'd always tried to be. I wasn't quite ready to concede defeat, however.

"What makes you say that?" I intentionally made my voice soothing and light, trying the exact tone I used when talking to a threat subject who'd just said something bat-shit crazy. And the glint of fury in Lucia's eye now told me she knew it.

"Are you denying it?" Her voice was louder now, more sure. Its shrill edge made me grimace. It completely contradicted the way she normally spoke, even when upset. How much had she had to drink?

"I was merely wondering what made you deduce that."

She refused to be diverted. "So it was her?"

I nodded once. "Yes. She's the last serious relationship I had before you."

The pageant of varying emotions resumed its play across Lucia's face. Should I have lied to her? No, that would've been more for my own benefit than hers, to assuage my guilt at causing her all this pain. In the long run, being honest with her was probably better. At least she wouldn't feel betrayed if she discovered the truth later.

"You've never mentioned her."

"No."

"Why?"

I shrugged. "Nothing to say. She's in the past. Why discuss it?"

"Did you sleep with her?"

"I assume you mean tonight." Nice to know she trusted me.

"Yes."

"No. I didn't."

"Are you sure?"

I snorted and rolled my eyes. "I think I'd remember. How the hell can you even ask me that?"

"You wanted to, though, didn't you?"

I hesitated, and that was apparently all the response Lucia needed. She wrapped her arms around her middle and began rocking back and forth as if in intense pain. She closed her eyes, and one lone tear from each leaked out and made slow tracks down her cheeks. Shit. I should've just lied to her about that part. Unfortunately, lying outside of an undercover op had never been my strong suit.

"Luce."

"What?"

"Come on."

"Come on, what? You wanted to sleep with someone else."

"It wasn't like that."

"What was it like, then?" Her tone was razor sharp and cutting.

"It wasn't a completely formed thought. Not entirely." Well, except for those brief mental pictures I'd had of Allison in the shower. But they'd been fleeting, and I'd pushed past them as quickly as I could.

"So, what? You were just turned on then?"

"Yes." I was relieved she seemed to comprehend my dilemma.

She laughed bitterly. "Perfect."

I frowned. Okay, perhaps she hadn't understood quite as well as I'd hoped. I wracked my brain, desperate for a better way to explain it to her. "Just a little."

"There is no such thing as cheating a little bit, Ryan."

"I didn't cheat on you!" Was it even possible to cheat on her if we'd never talked about the status of our relationship? I wasn't sure. I also didn't want to bring it up.

"You were aroused by another woman!"

"What? You've never been attracted to anyone else since we've been together?"

"So you admit it, then."

Damn. I'd walked right into that one. I wanted to smack myself upside the head. Stupid. "Yes. Fine. I admit it. I was a little turned on tonight. But nothing happened."

"Oh, my God."

"It isn't like that's something I can help, Luce."

"She's your ex, Ryan!"

"So?"

"So, that makes it a little different than you just being attracted to some random woman you've met on the street."

"But it's no different than if you were turned on by Jessie." I thought I'd hit upon the perfect example that she could relate to.

Agony streaked across her features, and I instantly knew I'd said the wrong thing. "I am not attracted to Jessie," she spat, her voice venomous. My heart seized at the heat in her tone, and I clenched my hands into fists on my knees. "No. I wasn't saying that. But, if you were, it'd make sense. I mean, you guys were together before, so you must've been attracted to her at some point. And just because you might feel a spark for her now, it doesn't necessarily threaten what's between you and me. That's all I was trying to say."

Lucia bit her lower lip and shook her head. Her eyes were brimming with anguish and distrust. "Did she make a pass at you?"

That was laughable in a twisted, painful sort of way. "No. She didn't."

A pause. "What if she had? Would you have fucked her then?"

"Of course not!" At least I didn't think I would have. The almost-kiss in the car flickered in my mind, and my shame threatened to overwhelm me. What if Allison had kissed me? Would I have stopped her? Kissed her back? Did it matter if it hadn't happened? I hadn't actually done anything wrong, but I still felt a shade guilty.

"I don't understand." Her voice was a strangled sob.

"What don't you understand?"

"How you can still love someone who broke you?"

"Who said I still love her?"

A bitter smile tugged at the corners of Lucia's mouth, and she tilted her head to favor me with an exasperated-yet-somehow-expectant look. "Are you saying you don't?"

I was being led right into a trap, I was sure, but I was confused because she had nothing to trap me with. I hadn't done anything wrong, so what was she getting at? "Where's all this coming from, Luce?"

Lucia heaved a big sigh and looked away. "Do you love me?"

"Wh—what?"

"You heard me."

This was karma biting me in the ass for something. It had to be. Lucia hadn't mentioned the "l word" once in six months, and now she wanted to know where we stood? If this weren't happening to me, I'd have laughed.

"Are you sure you want to talk about this now?" I asked hesitantly, still hoping to find a way out of this without everything messily imploding.

"What's wrong with now?"

"You're kind of hammered."

"And?"

Damn. I'd been hoping she'd deny it. I wouldn't have believed her, but I could have claimed I'd taken her at her word later. "And I just don't think the best way to have this conversation is when one of us is drunk."

"I'm not saying anything to you now that I wouldn't say sober."

"Oh."

"So? Are you going to answer my question?"

"I just...I don't know what to say. I mean, you've never seemed interested in feelings before."

She scowled at me darkly. "What do you think we've been doing all this time?"

"I...I hadn't ever taken the time to label it. I didn't think you had either."

"Jesus fucking Christ." She sounded miserable. I didn't think she could have sounded any more upset if I'd had an orgy right in front of her. But I still had no idea what I'd done to make her feel that way.

"What is this about, Luce? You're obviously not upset because we haven't talked about our feelings."

"No, I'm upset because I saw you."

I was perplexed and waited for clarification. None came. "You saw me what?"

"I saw you guys together this morning at the diner. After I left. Through the window. I saw you."

Okay, now she just wasn't making any sense. I had no idea what she was referring to, but I knew damn well that neither Allison nor I had done anything to warrant this kind of a reaction. I couldn't wait to hear her explanation. It had to be good.

"Luce, I don't know what you think you saw, but I promise, nothing happened. Not at the diner. Not anywhere." I'd almost slipped and mentioned Allison's hotel room but caught myself at the last second. Thank God. That wouldn't have gone over well. Not when she obviously thought I'd been up to no good to begin with.

Lucia had turned to face me and was studying me with an intensity that made me extremely uncomfortable. Her eyes scoured my face, leaving marks I could practically feel. Her eyebrows rose, and her lips parted in surprise as realization flooded her eyes.

"You really don't know, do you?" Her voice was soft, barely louder than a whisper.

"Know what?"

Lucia's expression produced an ache inside me. "I've waited half a year for you to look at me with a fraction of the adoration I saw in your eyes when you looked at her."

Well, shit. First Stacey, now Lucia. Could everyone in the world see that I still had feelings for Allison? My blood ran cold as a new thought occurred to me. Could Allison see it? Nausea gripped me as it dawned on me that she most likely could. Well, wasn't that just perfect?

I opened my mouth to say something, anything, but nothing came out. How could it? I didn't even know what to say. So many conflicting thoughts and feelings were assailing me, no wonder I couldn't form a coherent sentence.

I wanted to deny it but was afraid any denunciation would come out sounding halfhearted. And Lucia deserved better than lies from me. Hell, she deserved better than the truth, too, but clearly I'd fucked that up royally.

"At least I know it isn't me," Lucia mumbled sullenly.

"Luce—"

She held up a hand. "No. Don't. Do not patronize me by denying what I saw with my own two eyes. You know what? It's fine. Really. At least now I know why I could never get you to love me."

"Were you trying to?" The words were out of my mouth and sounded way more surprised than I'd have liked.

"Did you really not know that?"

Fuck. I didn't want to have this conversation. Not now. Not when she was bombed, and I was exhausted. I paused and prayed for my phone to ring, for any excuse to flee the scene and leave this unfinished until I'd had some time to think. None came.

"I told you when we started this that I wasn't relationship material. You said you were fine with that."

"Yeah, well, things changed." Her brow furrowed, and her eyes were murderous. Her admission seemed to irritate her.

I took a deep breath and mentally squashed all the insects that were buzzing around just beneath the surface of my skin. "Okay. Things have changed. So let's have a calm, rational discussion about that."

She went on as if I'd never spoken. "I'd always wondered why you were emotionally bankrupt. Nice to be able to put a face to the reason."

Ouch. Emotionally bankrupt? Was she serious? Is that how she saw me?

Her words hit bone, and I winced against the sharp gouges of pain they left. I'd always thought we had a good relationship. I'd gone out of my way to dote on her and make her feel beautiful and special. And I'd been under the impression that I'd done a passable job. She'd never indicated that she needed anything I hadn't been giving her.

How, then, did I reconcile the past with the words she'd just flung at me? Part of what'd prompted her to say that was the mix of emotions she was mired in, but what if a nugget of truth were in there somewhere? What if some small piece of her really did see me as emotionally bankrupt?

However, a small part of me railed against Lucia and her accusations. Like I said, I'll take my lumps when and where I deserve them, but I wasn't willing to accept this. She was speaking as if I felt absolutely nothing for her, as if I'd used her. She was acting like I'd deliberately misled her and then cheated on her, and nothing could be further from the truth.

"That isn't fair, Luce."

"Fair? Oh, this'll be good. I'm not being fair."

"No, you're not. How does me looking at Allison in any way diminish how I feel about you?"

"You can't be serious!"

"I'm absolutely serious. Tell me how."

Lucia folded her arms defiantly, and a harsh scowl twisted her features into something unpleasant. I'd never thought I'd ever describe her as anything less than beautiful, but I was close now.

"You never look at me like that," she muttered angrily.

"How do I look at you, then?"

She refused to meet my eyes and didn't answer.

I rubbed the outsides of my index fingers with the pads of my thumbs. If she'd been drinking, she probably wasn't logical enough to rationalize with on this point, but I was determined to try anyway.

"Luce, you and Allison are two different people. I've had different experiences with both of you, and as a result, I have different feelings for you. I don't think you should compare my past with her to my present with you."

Lucia gaped at me. "You don't?"

"No. I don't." I wanted to say a million other things. That I really cared about her. That she was the first woman since Allison who'd made me feel anything. That I wanted to make an honest try at a future with her. But the words stuck in my throat, nearly suffocating me. I swallowed hard, determined to dislodge them and say something—anything—to reassure her, but she spoke first.

"So you do still love her." The statement was forced, and she choked on it a little.

I sighed heavily and sank back into the cushions of the couch, then tilted my head back and briefly passed my hands over my eyes. God, I wished I were better at this lying thing. However, that I wasn't was telling in and of itself. I could lie all day to people I didn't give a damn about. One look from Lucia, and I crumbled, blurting out the truth.

"I honestly don't know. I think maybe I love who she was to me, if that makes any sense. Isn't it always like that with your first love?"

"She was your first?"

I nodded, even though the question had been rhetorical and Lucia wasn't even looking at me.

"She left you, then."

"Yes."

"Why?"

I winced. "It's a long story."

A caustic laugh escaped her lips. "I'm not going anywhere."

The request unsettled me. I wasn't sure whether it bothered me more that she was asking or that it would hurt to tell it. "It doesn't matter now. It's over."

"You don't think I have a right to know?"

Annoyance flashed white hot behind my eyes, and I clenched my teeth. "No one has 'the right' to that story. It was between Allison and me. No one else. And it's finished."

"I just want to know what she did that broke you. What was so bad that I wasn't enough to mend."

I looked away, clenching my jaw and glaring at the far window. My hands trembled. She didn't understand anything at all. Not if that's what she thought. Because she *was* enough to mend me, as much as I was capable of being mended. But she wanted me free of any and all emotional baggage, and that simply wasn't realistic. Not at this stage. We were both way too old for that to be a possibility.

I opened my mouth to tell her so, but before I could get a word out, Lucia rushed on, cutting me off. Again.

"That's what she did, you know. She wrecked you, and then she threw you away just like a child does with a toy that no longer holds her interest. And you know what? I don't know if you can ever be fixed. You're fucked up, Ryan."

The undercurrent of her words was sharp, borderline cruel. I'd never heard her speak with such disdain before. That alone jarred me and set me on edge, but the words themselves would leave permanent scars. I wanted to fight back yet run away.

"That's not true." My voice was a harsh rasp, but she'd expressed my greatest fear. I'd always secretly worried that maybe something was wrong with me. And now she was confirming it.

A cynical laugh bubbled up from inside her, and I winced. "Isn't it? You're detached, Ryan. You talk a good game and act like you feel things, but nothing touches you. At least not the things that should. You won't let them. Instead, you prefer to make people fall in love with you yet continue to feel nothing for them. You get validation without any risk to your own heart. You're cold, and you're heartless, and no one else matters to you but you."

I shook my head. She was hurt because she thought I loved someone else, and that defense mechanism of alchemizing pain into anger was prompting her to say these things. The animalistic response to lash out when injured was causing her to look for my weaknesses and press on them hard. She didn't really want to wound me and would regret her words eventually. I knew these things, but her statements still stung.

I wanted to start swinging back. I was hurt now, too, and infuriated and resentful. I wished I could tear into her, cutting fast and deep, leaving her bleeding. I wanted to injure her for saying those things to me. For deliberately being cruel. For making me question myself. Or maybe for giving me the answers to questions I'd always been afraid to ask.

"I don't know how you can even say that to me after everything we've shared." Normally, I'd have grimaced at the naked emotion in my tone, but at the moment, I didn't care. I wanted her to know she'd upset me. That'd obviously been her goal. I should at least reward her efforts. "And I think if you reflect on our relationship, you'll see you're mistaken."

My voice was deliberately low and even, and it took a considerable effort to keep it that way, as well as to not utter more severe words to her. I didn't feel I deserved her anger or her successful attempts to wound me, but she didn't deserve for me to retaliate. However, my control was slipping, and if this didn't end soon, I might lash out at her, regardless. And I didn't have room in my already overcrowded head or heart for any more guilt or remorse.

Lucia stared at me for a long time with the oddest expression. I couldn't even begin to put a name to the emotion flickering in her eyes, though I tried.

"What do you want from me, Luce? Do you want me to lie? Pretend there was nothing and no one before I met you? That's unrealistic, and I won't do it. I can't feel exactly what you want me to feel, exactly the way you want me to feel it. No one can because everyone is different, and it's unfair of you to hold your yardstick up to my emotions. All I can do is feel what I feel and treat you the best I know how. I was always under the impression that I'd done that, but clearly I was wrong. So tell me what you want from me. Just say the word, and it's yours."

Lucia snatched her cell phone off the table and stood, staring down at me. An eternity lapsed before she finally spoke, and when she did, the jumble of emotions in her tone brought me to tears.

"Nothing, Ryan. Absolutely nothing."

CHAPTER TWELVE

W hoa. What the hell happened to you?" Allison said when I arrived at her hotel room bright and early the next morning to pick her up for breakfast.

"Well, good morning to you, too, sunshine."

"You look like shit, Ryan."

I rolled my eyes. But how could I argue with her? Okay, perhaps she could've been a bit less direct, but I couldn't begrudge her the opinion. Not when she was right.

Needless to say, I'd gotten zero sleep the night before, which, by my calculations, brought my grand sleep total for the past forty-eight hours somewhere close to negative three hours. Of course, I was using the new math. And boy did it show. The sleep thing, not the math. The makeup I'd so painstakingly applied that morning had done little to conceal the dark circles under my eyes, my hair had been less cooperative than usual, and I had a defeated, lackluster air about me that made my reflection virtually unrecognizable.

Allison, naturally, looked stunning. Breathtakingly, mouth-wateringly gorgeous. Not a hair out of place, not a wrinkle or a smudge anywhere to be seen. She was flawless, as usual. I sort of hated her for that.

"Aw, thanks, Allison. You always say the sweetest things."

She eyed me curiously as she motioned for me to follow her inside. "Do me a favor and tell your girl to let you get some shut-eye tonight, okay? I mean, I know how totally sexy you are, and I can't blame the woman for not being able to keep her hands off you, but you can't show up on game day looking like this. You're a mess."

When I was a teenager, I'd taken a soccer ball to the gut once during a pickup game. It'd been kicked hard by one of the older boys and had hit me squarely. I'd saved the point since my body had stopped the goal, but it'd knocked the wind out of me, and I'd spent several long minutes on my hands and knees on the field, trying to force my lungs to inhale and being unable to make my body comply. Allison's words had a similar effect.

A heavy silence hung in the space between us, and I turned my back on her, blinking furiously, trying to keep the tears from my eyes. She'd only been joking. I knew that. But the jest hit a tad closer to home than my already-raw nerves were prepared to handle. I took a deep, shuddering breath and rested my forehead and one palm against the glass of the window, relishing its cool, smooth texture. I closed my eyes, grateful that Allison was otherwise occupied at the moment.

A hand on my shoulder startled me, but I didn't turn around. Instead, I silently cursed my own distraction and tried to scrape together the last vestiges of my game face and slap it on before she was any wiser.

"Hey." Allison's voice was soft in my ear, the tone so tender I wanted to sob. Like I needed another reason at this point. "You okay?"

I nodded, not trusting myself to speak, and swallowed with effort. The lump that'd taken up permanent residence in my throat a few hours earlier felt as though it might actually be growing. It went nicely with the huge weight that'd settled in my chest where my heart used to be and the churning nausea that was making me regret my earlier demand for chocolate-chip pancakes.

Allison's hand pushed lightly in an effort to turn me around, and I resisted, but only for a bit. I may've been stubborn, but in Allison I'd met my match. She just kept nudging until I finally relented. I faced her with my chin to my chest and my eyes downcast, which I'd thought was a great plan. Right up until she cupped my chin in her other hand and tilted it up so she could meet my gaze.

"What's wrong?"

The concern and worry marring her perfect features tore at me, and I nearly collapsed under the onslaught of a completely new stab of guilt. The tears threatened to come again, and I bit my lower lip. Lucia had been wrong. I wasn't heartless. I couldn't possibly be in this much pain if I was. Too bad she wasn't here to see it.

I stroked Allison's cheek with the palm of my hand, and the warmth of her skin dispelled the cold left by the glass. I opened my mouth, but only a weary sigh escaped. I shook my head.

Curiosity flickered in her eyes, but all she said was, "Come here," as she tugged me into a soothing hug.

I wanted to fight it, fight her. I didn't want her to see me when I was weak, and I sure as hell didn't want to need comforting, especially not from the first woman who'd broken my heart. But her scent was too intoxicating, her warmth too inviting, and my need too great. I gratefully gave in.

I sank into her arms and wrapped my own around her, pulling her tight to my body. I soaked up her presence the way a flower soaks up the sun and drew comfort from the embrace. I took as much solace from the gesture as I possibly could and garnered the strength necessary to face the day, despite the new cracks to my battered heart. The hug lasted a lot longer than it probably should've, but I was raw and aching and, frankly, it gave me the consolation I required. It was only when I'd started to become more aware of her body and the old lingering pangs of arousal started clamoring in the back of my head that I let go.

I cleared my throat as I stepped back, thoroughly embarrassed, and swiped at my cheeks hastily to remove any traces of tears. My gaze flitted to her and then skittered away, and I licked my lips, suddenly nervous.

"Thanks," I whispered.

"Not a problem."

"I'm sorry."

"For what?"

I shrugged and chanced a glance at her. I'd been expecting…I don't really know what I'd been expecting. Amusement, maybe? Mischief? I wasn't sure. But I did know it wasn't this sympathetic expression. It might've been easier for me if she'd made fun of me. I would've had a better idea how to respond.

"It was a rough night. You about ready to go?" I made a move toward the door, but she grabbed my arm.

"Hang on there, speed racer. Not until you tell me what the hell that was all about."

"It was nothing. Can we go? We won't have time for pancakes if we don't get a move on." I wouldn't be able to get through telling her what'd happened with Lucia without breaking down again, and we definitely didn't have time for that. Besides, if she thought I looked like a mess now, she really didn't want to see me after that.

The muscles in Allison's jaw tensed, and she folded her arms across her chest as she stared at me. Deliberately and without once breaking eye contact, she slowly lowered herself so she was sitting on the edge of the bed. She crossed one leg over the other and waited, her posture as indicative as her expression that we weren't going anywhere until I bared my soul.

After a flash of misplaced irritation I threw up my hands. "Jesus, will you just drop it? Come on. We've got shit to do. I'm not in the fucking mood for this."

Okay, I'll admit, that was much. Like, completely, totally, over-the-line much. She was merely expressing concern. I had no right to bite her head off. I regretted my outburst immediately but for some reason couldn't bring myself to actually speak the words of apology she deserved. I did, however, place trembling fingers over my lips.

Here's where I'll give Allison credit for her skills at controlling her temper and knowing exactly how to handle me. While other people might've snapped right back and told me to go fuck myself, she merely cocked her head slightly and looked at me for a long moment. Her stern glare was penetrating enough that I flushed and dropped my eyes first.

"Are you finished?"

"I think so."

"Good." She held one hand up and extended her index finger. "First, I'm only trying to help, so I'd appreciate it if you wouldn't yell at me."

"You're right. I'm sorry. I shouldn't have said that."

Allison nodded once, but she clearly wasn't through. She held up another finger. "Second, I will thank you to watch your fucking mouth when you're in my presence. I won't take any more goddamn blasphemy from you."

A small smile threatened to break out across my lips, spurred on by the seriousness of her expression. I dipped my head. "Done."

"And, third, there is always time for chocolate-chip pancakes."

At that, I laughed and held out my hand to her as though to help her up. She took it and accepted my assistance even though we both knew she didn't really need it. It was my way of apologizing and her way of accepting.

"You're right. What the hell was I thinking?"

"I'm leaning toward temporary insanity." Allison flashed me a grin over her shoulder as she made her way back to the bathroom. She clattered around in there for a few minutes, affording me ample time to clean myself up and fix my own makeup in the mirror over the desk. By the time she emerged, we'd both cooled off, and the atmosphere between us had a much more bearable weight.

"Just tell me this much," Allison said as she slid into her suit jacket. "Is Lucia okay?"

The mere mention of her name threatened to catapult me right back into my earlier despondency. I focused instead on Allison's oddly crumpled collar and rolled my eyes, motioning her closer. I adjusted it for her and gave her a friendly pat on the shoulder. I didn't feel even a twinge when I touched her, which spoke volumes about my mental and emotional state at that moment.

"I'm going to go with yes."

She shot me a quizzical look. "What do you mean you're 'going to go with'? Don't you know?"

I shrugged and tried to ignore the misery gnawing away at my insides and making me faintly nauseous. "She was okay when she left my place last night." *Well, physically anyway.*

"Ah. You guys had a fight." It wasn't a question.

I hesitated. A small part of me didn't want to disclose any details to Allison. She'd already seen me break down once. I didn't think I'd be able to look her in the eye if I lost it twice in one day. Besides, despite our past, we really weren't friends. We never had been. Plus, I didn't need pity from anyone at the moment, least of all her.

Also, a miniscule part of me felt stupid admitting that Lucia had dumped me, as if I were afraid Allison would take it as further proof I just wasn't good girlfriend material. Not that she needed any more, apparently, or we'd still be together. But I was humiliated and upset enough about the dissolution of the only relationship I'd been interested in pursuing since her without adding that on top of it. And I deliberately avoided any examination as to why that would even bother me. I could only juggle so many balls at once, and it was best to leave that one on the ground.

"Yeah. Something like that."

"Well, I'm sure you guys will work it out." Allison was making one last visual sweep of the room. "She really loves you."

A bitter bark of laughter bubbled up in my throat, and I couldn't bite it back. The harsh, shrill sound caught Allison's full attention. "And therein lies the problem because apparently I'm heartless." I hadn't meant for that little gem to slip out, either, but there it was. I really needed to get some sleep.

Allison frowned. "What?"

"Yeah, I know. Heartless. That's what she said. Ironic, isn't it? Since you seemed to have the exact opposite problem with me."

I gasped and froze the instant the words were out of my mouth but couldn't call them back, so they hung leaden in the air between us. A multitude of emotions flowed beneath Allison's ebony eyes, and then her expression went cool. She turned to the door.

I grabbed her arm, borderline desperate. She and I had somehow managed to reach a fragile truce over the last couple of days. Hell, we'd even found a way to get along and have some fun, overlooking the specter of the past that would always be between us. And I was threatening to fuck that up with my thoughtlessness. What'd happened with Lucia hadn't been anyone's fault but my own and was a completely separate issue from my history with Allison. I'd do well to remember that and think before I spoke.

"Hey," I said, my voice soft. Past conversations flickered through my mind, and I was grateful she hadn't shaken off my grip, a move she'd been famous for once upon a time. "I'm sorry."

Allison turned back to face me and looked into my eyes. Frustration marred her features for a fraction of a second, and something akin to panic grated harshly against the back of my throat.

"Look, can we forget I said anything? Please?" My clumsy words were ineloquent, as they always were whenever I spoke to her about anything important.

The silence grew as we stared at one another, and a feeling of dread trickled slowly down my esophagus and dripped icily onto the organs below. Finally, much to my relief, she spoke. "You're a jerk." I nodded, and my insides started to slowly warm again. Whenever she said that, I knew she'd pretty much forgiven me. "I know." I flashed her a tentative grin. "But you love me anyway."

Allison didn't return my smile. Her expression was solemn for the instant she continued to regard me before she turned around. With her back to me I almost missed her quiet reply, which I suspect was the point.

"I know."

CHAPTER THIRTEEN

Much like the day before, Allison and I had way too much to do to let something as silly as a few thoughtless words mar the entire day. Before I knew it, it was after nine o'clock, and we were sitting in my office putting together our books for the motorcade, quizzing one another over the details of the visit to make sure we hadn't forgotten anything.

"The motorcade security guys are all settled?" Allison asked. She looked up at me from her place behind my desk.

"Yup. No worries. They're set until we pick up the cars in the morning."

"Cars are going to get gassed and washed?"

"All taken care of."

"Security sweeps start at what time?"

"Oh-six-thirty for the cars. They start earlier than that for the sites themselves." I consulted my notes. "Um…It's looking like oh-four-hundred for the Stock Exchange, oh-five-thirty for the LZ, and I think they said they wanted to start sweeping the airport at oh-four-hundred, as well. I'd have to talk to the site guy to be sure. Drivers are arriving at oh-six-hundred. Wheels down is scheduled for ten-hundred hours."

"So we should leave at maybe five to go out to the airport. I'd like to be there well before the motorcade sweep."

"You're the boss."

Allison made a face at me, shook her head, and handed me a completed book to add to the pile. I took it without a word and immediately went back to compiling the packets of paperwork each site agent needed to have. I was relieved to be almost finished. I was exhausted, both physically and emotionally. The two days of no sleep had caught up to me, and I wanted nothing more than to go home, cry for a bit, and then crash. I quickly did the math in my head. If we left by ten, I could drop Allison off at her hotel and be in bed and hopefully asleep a little after eleven, which would give me a solid four and a half hours of rest. I sighed longingly.

"What?" Allison wanted to know.

"Nothing. Just ready for bed."

"Well, the books are done. Jamie and Robert should be stopping by here to pick up the surveys for their respective sites any minute. Don has his already?"

"Yeah, he picked them up when you went downstairs to grab dinner. He has the earliest report time, so he wanted to try to get some sleep."

"I'm going to run to the bathroom real quick. That way we can get out of here the second they're gone."

I nodded absently. "Sure."

My mind was reeling as I pushed thoughts of Lucia from it for what had to be the hundredth time that day and again ran through the long list of issues I needed to be concerned about for the next fifteen hours. I yawned as I bundled the surveys into piles by their respective sites and read over my notes once more. I always had the lingering feeling I was forgetting something whenever I did an advance. As a result, I had a probably annoying habit of going over my paperwork repeatedly, scouring my notes as I both dreaded and hoped something would jump out at me as a glaring omission.

I was incredibly focused on my task, which was perhaps why I didn't realize Allison had returned until I felt her cold, wet fingers lift the curtain of my hair and stroke the skin just above my shirt collar.

Startled, I whipped my head around and winced as an electric zing shot up the right side of my neck. Allison was standing almost directly behind me wearing a strange half smile. Her hair was free and tumbling down over her shoulders. Her expression stopped me cold.

"Feel better?" I somehow managed to utter after what felt like an eternity of staring at her.

Allison nodded and took a step closer, which forced me to turn a little more in my chair to maintain eye contact with her. Her smile widened, and she placed her hands on my shoulders, gently turning me so I was once again facing my desk. My eyes fell on the notes I'd been rereading, but I didn't actually see them. I was too distracted by Allison's touch, which'd caused my insides to turn somersaults and goose bumps to break out all over my body.

"You just hurt your neck, didn't you?" Allison asked me. Her voice was low and had a surprisingly borderline-intimate tone that made my head spin with a mixture of desire and confusion. When her strong fingers began gently kneading the area in question, I had to force myself not to whimper.

Instead, I settled on a slight shrug. "It's fine." I might've felt a twinge in my neck just now, but the feelings she was currently invoking in me completely overshadowed that discomfort. Completely.

Allison hummed and continued running the pads of her thumbs up and down the column of my neck. She was standing as close to me as she could get, her hips pressed against the back of the chair in which I sat.

I let slip a small sigh of contentment, and my eyes fluttered closed as Allison broadened her explorations to include my shoulders. It was a strange experience, having one form of tension being coaxed from me while becoming slave to another. I wasn't sure what to make of it, so I attempted to think nothing at all. Want to guess how well that worked?

"How's it coming?" Allison leaned closer, and I could feel the barest brush of her breasts against the back of my head.

I held my breath for a moment as her words slowly penetrated the fog enveloping my brain. Coming? Almost. Wait, what? Oh. She was talking about the surveys. Right. Work. I chastised myself for being so easily distracted, but my efforts were halfhearted. "Uh…Good. I'm done. See?" I held a packet of surveys up where she could see it.

"Good," Allison murmured, allowing her hands to slip from my shoulders and trail over my upper chest, not quite far enough to be touching my breasts, but close enough that my nipples had contracted almost painfully, and I was definitely having trouble breathing.

My pulse stuttered, and my mouth went dry. Some small part of me screamed at myself to break the spell. Through my stupor I kept trying to remind myself that just because I clearly—and unfortunately—still had feelings for Allison, she didn't have any for me. Her rubbing my shoulders meant absolutely nothing. I'd hurt my neck. Her offer to help was no cause to get carried away on the fleeting wings of hope. What I'd thought I'd heard in her tone was no doubt wishful thinking, and looking for hidden meaning in any of this was not only counterproductive and bound to end up with me getting hurt, but also just plain stupid.

After an internal struggle, I cleared my throat to speak, but what I'd planned to say would forever remain a mystery because a voice called my name.

"Ryan?"

"Huh?" I snapped my head up and looked at Allison, who was staring at me with a confused, worried expression.

"Are you okay?"

I frowned. She was standing a good two arms' lengths away from me. How the hell had she gotten all the way over there? Holy shit, had I just fallen asleep? Had I just dreamed that entire thing? Oh, my God! Had I said anything? I groaned and dropped my head into my hands, thoroughly mortified.

I could see through my eyelashes that Allison was still watching me carefully, her expression pensive. She took a step closer, and I tensed. If there were ever a time to wish the earth would literally open up and swallow me, now would be it.

"Allison? Where are you?" a familiar voice called. Even through my considerable embarrassment, I couldn't suppress my grin as I recognized those tones. The woman always did have impeccable timing. I'd have to remember to reward her for that.

"I'm in here," Allison called back, shooting me another enigmatic glance.

"Where's here?" The mild annoyance was apparent in the speaker's tenor, and I chuckled, imagining the look on her face.

Allison made a noise in the back of her throat and patted my shoulder absently as she withdrew from me, leaving me to hurtle along the swirling rapids of my confused thoughts alone while she went to find our colleagues.

"This place is a fucking maze," I heard the voice grumble a moment later as Allison returned with two of the detail agents in tow.

The taller one was fairly typical of what one would expect of a Secret Service agent: dark hair, dark eyes, broad shoulders. The shorter one—the one who'd been yelling and cursing—had a wild mane of dirty-blond, shoulder-length curls, arresting gray-blue eyes, and a body that was unmistakably female, despite the suit. They both appeared slightly disheveled and a little tired. I could only imagine how I appeared to them, what with my surely nonexistent makeup and my negative-three hours of sleep. I didn't even want to know how I looked to Allison.

I stood up to greet the new arrivals, my grin growing wider. I didn't know the guy, Robert, so he only warranted the slightest nod and a halfhearted handshake. The girl, on the other hand, I knew well.

Jamie Dorchester answered my grin with a cocky one of her own and flew into my open arms, actually picking me up and spinning me around. I let out an uncharacteristically girlish squeak and laughed into the curve of her neck.

When Jamie finally set me down and pulled back, she took one of my hands in hers and my chin in the other. "You look exhausted."

I rolled my eyes as I squeezed the fingers that held my own. "I look better than you."

"Please. No one looks better than me."

"I bet Joanna looks better than you." I was teasing her, not feeling even remotely guilty about going for the low blow and trotting out the girlfriend. I grinned slyly at her and squeezed her hand again.

Jamie ducked her head, but I still caught the way her smile softened and her eyes danced. Robert, probably wisely, decided he needed to make a phone call and stepped out into the hall.

I'd known Jamie for a long time. We'd met a few years prior to her going to the detail during UNGA, and then we'd gone to rescue swimmer training together. We'd originally bonded over knowing what it was like to date someone on the job and then be unceremoniously dumped by them—although I'd carefully concealed the fact that Allison was the one who'd broken my heart—and since then, we'd become pretty good friends.

The two of us might've fallen into bed a couple of times, but that'd just been friendly, pass-the-time sex, simple and fun because we got along great, and we both knew it didn't mean anything more than that. That had also been before Lucia and before Jamie had fallen in love with a hotshot ER doctor she'd met while at a party she'd attended with me. Now we had an easy, completely platonic friendship, and I was thrilled I'd gotten to see her, even if it was only for a couple of minutes.

"Yeah, well, Joanna looks better than everyone," Jamie mumbled, seeming for all the world like a schoolgirl dreaming of her first crush.

"Careful, Jamie. Folks are going to start thinking you've gone soft. They might actually mistake you for a female! You know, with mushy feelings and stuff."

Jamie ignored my quip and turned to give Allison a dark look. "What the hell are you doing to her, Reynolds? Did I or did I not explicitly tell you to take care of my girl? She's not making any sense, and she looks like a zombie."

"Hey!" I dropped her hand and took a step away from her.

"What? You do. Your skin is all pale—well, paler than normal—and you have huge bags under your eyes. You're a mess."

"I do not look like a zombie!"

"Ryan, you look terrible."

"Thanks a lot."

"No offense."

"You're an asshole." I laughed, thoroughly enjoying the banter. "Hasn't Joanna taught you that you're always supposed to tell a woman she looks beautiful? You don't have to say everything you think, you know. Filter, woman! Jesus!"

"I said, 'No offense.'"

"How the hell am I not supposed to be offended by something like that?"

"I dunno. You're just not. Look, I'm trying to yell at Allison for you. Do you mind? Stop interrupting. You're distracting me. My tirade is losing some of its strength here."

"I'm a big girl. I'm perfectly capable of yelling at Allison myself."

At that declaration, I shifted my attention from our good-natured bickering to the woman in question. I opened my mouth to draw Allison into the fray but stopped.

Allison's expression had shuttered completely, and she was holding herself stiffly. All business, she ignored our mock squabbling and retrieved the packets of paperwork we'd compiled. She handed Jamie one packet and stepped into the doorway to get Robert's attention, so she could give him the other.

"Everything's in there. You should be all set."

Jamie blinked, obviously startled, and glanced at me, seeming puzzled. But when I shrugged, she merely accepted the offered paperwork without comment.

Jamie and Robert flipped through the surveys. They nodded, which I took to mean everything was in order, and relief flooded me.

"Your handwriting hasn't improved," Jamie couldn't resist pointing out.

"Yeah, well, we zombies aren't terribly concerned with mundane trivialities like good penmanship."

"Any changes we need to know about?" Allison's voice was borderline brittle, and I frowned.

Jamie and Robert shook their heads in unison, but it was Jamie who actually spoke. "If I think of something, I'll let you know."

"Sounds good. Have a great night, guys. Get some sleep." Allison turned her back, clearly dismissing them.

Now Jamie frowned, and she glanced from me to Allison and back again. I could see the questions swirling behind her eyes, but I probably wouldn't have been able to answer them even if we'd been alone and able to speak freely. I was just as confused as she was.

"Are you headed back to the hotel?" Robert wanted to know, clearly not picking up on the tension in the room.

Allison shot me a guarded glance. "That was the plan. Why?"

"Think we could hitch a ride?"

Allison looked at me again, and if I didn't know better, I'd have sworn she was annoyed and disappointed. I shoved that thought away. I must've imagined it, projecting those emotions onto her because that's what I'd felt at the question. No way were those her feelings. Damn, I was tired! Why else would I be seeing things that weren't there?

"You mind?" Allison asked me.

I shook my head. "Nope. Let's go."

The ride back to The W was unbelievably uncomfortable, at least for me. Allison and Robert remained absolutely silent the entire time. I suspected Robert was simply too exhausted or distracted to even attempt conversation. Allison opted to stare out the windshield. I returned to mentally reviewing all the moving parts of the upcoming visit, reassuring myself once more that we had everything covered, while trying to chat idly with Jamie so the car wasn't completely quiet.

I pulled up in front of the hotel, and Robert mumbled his thanks as he tumbled out of the car. Jamie leaned forward between the seats to give me a hug and a kiss on the cheek, both punctuated by meaningful looks, before hopping out herself. Allison hesitated. She turned to look at me, the expression in her eyes unreadable.

"Oh-five-hundred?"

I nodded, and a slight flutter of nervousness tickled my diaphragm. I really hoped I hadn't overlooked some vital detail. "Oh-five-hundred."

She studied me for a long moment. "It's going to be fine. We didn't forget anything."

"How the hell do you do that?"

"How do I do what?"

"Read my mind like that? It's spooky."

Allison smiled at me and opened her mouth, but just then Jamie yelled at her from the sidewalk. "Allison, are you coming or what?"

My eyes cut to Jamie for an instant before they locked back onto Allison, and my cheeks burned. I'd completely forgotten about Jamie the second she'd stepped out of the vehicle. No surprise, really. No matter what else might be going on around me, Allison had a way of contracting my world until it encompassed only her. I sighed.

"Good night, Ryan," Allison said as she exited the car. "Sleep well."

"Good night, Allison," I whispered.

CHAPTER FOURTEEN

"Thank God," I breathed as the wheels of Air Force One lifted off the ground. All the tension I'd been carrying around fled at once, and I sagged with relief. Letting out a contented sigh, I watched the plane disappear into the wild blue yonder. It was finally over. The man had been in, done what he'd needed to do, and left in the same condition in which he'd arrived. We'd had no major setbacks or even minor ones. I couldn't have asked for a better visit.

A throaty chuckle sounded over my shoulder, and I turned to see Allison grinning back. "Glad that's behind us?"

"You have no idea." I reached for my phone so I could make the required calls to let everyone know that Harbinger was on his way home.

"Oh, come on." Allison chided me playfully, bumping my shoulder with her own. "It wasn't that bad."

"Nah." I brought my phone to my ear with one hand and released my hair from its confinement with the other, then held up one finger to stall the conversation as someone picked up on the other end. I imparted the necessary information and hung up, replacing the phone in its holster without looking. "Not bad at all, actually. Just a little stressful." I started walking back toward the cars.

Allison and I briefly made some additional notifications and took care of logistics regarding the motorcade cars and the people still on the ground before resuming the conversation back in my vehicle.

"So that was stressful for you, huh?" Allison said.

"Shit, yeah, it was!" I exclaimed, half laughing. "You may be accustomed to shouldering the responsibility for the president's physical safety on a daily basis, supercop, but I'm not." I pointed the car toward the airport exit as I checked the time on the dashboard clock. "At least not to that degree. I'm not built for that type of pressure."

"Well, you'd never know it."

I eyed her suspiciously. Was she messing with me? But something in her expression stopped the sarcastic comment I had locked and loaded before it passed my lips. "Really."

Allison beamed at me with something close to pride. "You did a fantastic job, Ryan."

"Even when your boy mentioned that he wanted to make an unscheduled stop at Hurricane's apartment, and I almost had a heart attack?"

Allison laughed, and the sound washed over me with an almost warming physicality, making a great many parts of my body tingle. "Yeah, you didn't look happy about that. Although I don't know why. We did discuss the possibility of him wanting to see his daughter while he was here."

"I know we did, but I still would've had to get the streets shut down for our trip over. That would've been a nightmare."

"Oh, come on. You could've handled it."

"Could've? Yes. Wanted to? No. I was thrilled to hear Hurricane was out of district."

She laughed again. "I could tell. But you got yourself together. Eventually. In the end. That's all that matters."

I backhanded her lightly on the arm. "Thanks, smart-ass." I grinned at her. "You did okay yourself. I mean, not up to my standards, but who is, really?"

Allison chuckled again and ran her fingers through her thick, black hair, tousling it. "Absolutely no one."

"So, where to now?" Standard operating procedure would've been for her to catch the afternoon shuttle back to D.C.—that's what Jamie was doing, I'd already found out—but Allison hadn't brought her bags with her when I'd picked her up at the hotel that morning. I knew what I wanted that to mean, but, frankly, I was afraid to hope.

"Back to the hotel, if you don't mind." Allison tilted her head to one side and watched me almost speculatively, as if gauging my reaction.

"Will you need a ride back to the airport later?"

One side of Allison's mouth twitched like she wanted to smile. "My flight out isn't until tomorrow."

Damned if my heart didn't soar. "That's unusual, isn't it?" I attempted to tamp down my considerable glee. Part of me was yammering that I really needed to examine the why behind my sudden bout of happiness, but most of me was telling that part to shut the hell up. "Shouldn't you be going back today?"

"Trying to get rid of me?" Allison's tone was teasing, but I caught the barest hint of strain underlying her words.

I laughed. I couldn't help it. But when I glanced at her again and noticed her gorgeous features slipping into that cold mask she wore when she was angry or hurt, something inside me seized. Impulsively, I reached over and took her hand.

"You know I'm not," I said quietly, giving her fingers a squeeze. The jolt that shot through me at the barest brush of her skin against mine was more than I could handle. I let go abruptly, not needing to prolong that sensation. No good could come of it.

"I'm on day off tomorrow," Allison told me. "I figured there was no reason to rush back."

"Oh, that's nice. You'll have time to catch up with some people before you go back."

A sly grin stole over Allison's features then, and her face was alight with barely restrained mischief. "Actually, I'd planned to go to the wheels-up party."

"What wheels-up party?"

Allison laughed and treated me to a playful swat on the arm. "Yeah, peddle that malarkey somewhere else, Irish girl. I used to be a New Yorker, remember? I know exactly what goes on the night after a PPD visit. The entire detail does. We're always pissed because we have to miss it."

"Maybe we're celebrating your departure."

"Maybe you are. Tonight, I plan to confirm it."

"You mean you're going to spy on us and report back to the rest of your PPD buddies."

"Uh, yeah. I thought that was pretty clear."

"Hmm. Guess I'd better warn the guys not to talk shit about the detail then, huh?"

"Damn straight. I don't want to have to throw down, but I'm not afraid to kick a little ass if it comes to that."

"Good to know where your loyalties lie."

"Hey, you know I'll always be a New Yorker first."

"Uh-huh," I murmured sarcastically. "Well, I'll tell you what, oh loyal New Yorker, I have to go back to the office and get some things done because some of us get paid for more than looking stunning in a business suit. So, if you think you can behave yourself and stay out of trouble for the rest of the afternoon, I'll drop you off at your hotel and then pick you up around five. Sound good?"

"Is the staying-out-of-trouble part negotiable?"

"Nope."

She heaved an overly theatrical sigh. "Fine. I'll do my best. But I make no promises for later tonight. Once you pick me up, all bets are off."

Something might have been lurking behind her eyes or beneath the tone of her voice as she said those words, but I was too distracted by the racing of my traitorous heart to be the least bit objective on the subject.

"Deal," I told her, more than a bit giddy at the prospect of what the evening might hold.

Oh, yeah. I was toast.

CHAPTER FIFTEEN

I'd just barely pulled away from the curb in front of The W when my work phone rang. I huffed. Couldn't I have just five freaking minutes to relax and decompress?

"O'Connor."

"Where are you?" Mark's gruff voice demanded.

I gritted my teeth against the urge to snap at him. We'd just had a wheels up, for crying out loud. What did he expect me to do? Beam myself back to NYFO?

"Manhattan."

"Are you planning on coming back to work today?"

"Technically, I've done my eight hours, Mark. I could go home now if I wanted." Okay, arguing about my hours with my boss was probably not my best plan. But clearly I was all about doing the exact opposite of what was good for me these days.

"Not planning on working your LEAP today?"

LEAP stood for Law Enforcement Availability Pay. All gun-carrying federal agents get paid a little extra over and above their base salary to work what amounted to a fifty-hour work week rather than a forty-hour one.

Our HQ tracked LEAP by the quarter rather than the week, so as long as I had enough total hours to cover three months' worth of work, no one looked very closely to see how the hours were distributed. In some agencies, I knew, agents crammed all their LEAP in at the beginning of the month or the quarter, depending on how theirs was accounted for. And I also knew agents who procrastinated and put it off for as long as possible, which usually resulted in them scrambling to pack in an astronomical amount of hours in a few weeks.

I was the kind of girl who preferred to shoot for a weekly target of at least ten LEAP hours, though I'd often have more than that. I liked having that cushion to fall back on. It was almost like putting hours in the bank on the off chance that something would prevent me from working my required hours on a day here or there. I didn't get paid extra if I worked more LEAP, but I also didn't get in trouble.

I clenched my fists on the steering wheel and scowled. Why the hell was Mark giving me shit about this? It said a lot about his feelings toward me that he was concerning himself with an issue like my LEAP. Next, he'd probably be scrutinizing my gas-card receipts and my EZ-Pass records. Or perhaps how many minutes I'd used on my cell phone. Fabulous. I wasn't particularly worried about it. I followed those rules to the letter, so there was nothing he could ding me for. But it was still a hassle, and even a mere suggestion from him of impropriety on my part would grate on my nerves something fierce.

"I've worked more than enough LEAP in the past few days to cover the rest of the week, Mark." I kept my voice deliberately light, but it was one hell of a struggle. "In fact, I probably have next week covered, too."

The silence on Mark's end of the phone lasted so long I started to think we'd been disconnected.

"Mark?"

"You'd better be here for the PT tests," he snapped. A loud clatter told me he'd hung up on me.

Okay, so going to NYFO right now was out. I was definitely not in the mood to get into a knock-down-drag-out with Mark over nothing. Sure, I had work to do, but something told me if I went back there, I'd spend more time arguing with him than I would actually accomplishing anything. I wracked my brain for legitimate ways to kill time until I absolutely had to make my appearance.

A quick glance at my watch confirmed I still had a couple of hours before the PT tests were scheduled to start. Maybe now would be a good time to show my face at the JTTF office. I hadn't been there in a few days, and the impending Iran visit guaranteed I'd be out for several weeks. It couldn't hurt to stop by. I could make my calls to D.C.

regarding the Iran advance as easily from there as I could from NYFO, and I could spend the rest of my time running Akbari's info through the FBI's computer databases. Sure, I had no reason to suspect I'd find anything, but it was something to do, and it kept me away from NYFO that much longer, which was motive enough.

Normally, parking in the area near the JTTF office building was a nightmare, but luck was on my side today. I scored a prime space a few spots down from the front door. In no time at all, I'd stowed my gear in its required place outside the office itself and was sitting at my desk, making my calls to D.C. to ask about intelligence regarding the upcoming visit while I waited for my computer to boot up.

On a blank piece of paper, I jotted down some reminders. I could run basic criminal-history checks on anything I might uncover today from NYFO. It was just easier. The FBI had a special unit of analysts who did that sort of work for them, but it took a few days to get the results, and you needed to submit an active case number for the query. They wouldn't accept the request without one, and since I wasn't necessarily planning on opening an official case on Akbari—and even if I did, it'd be a USSS one and not a JTTF one—I'd need to do that database check myself. I also made a note to ask Amanda to run any new leads through the databases that she had access to for exactly the same reason.

Then I turned my attention to running Akbari's name, address, and social security, passport, and phone numbers through the FBI databases to see whether they popped up in connection to any current or previous FBI investigations. Their system was superior to ours because you could pull up actual report text right on the computer. With just a few keystrokes, I could get an idea of the context of an investigation by reading the actual memorandums submitted in correlation with it. That was extremely helpful.

I fell headlong into my work. As much as I enjoyed being in the field and participating in interviews and arrests, I was much more interested in following trails and uncovering associations between people. I could sit for hours at a computer linking threads and tracking money as it bounced from bank account to bank account all around the world. It was like putting together a really big puzzle.

The name checks didn't do me much good. Apparently the name Amin Akbari was relatively common. The search on the address where he used to reside in Maryland yielded a few more definitive results, and I jotted down the case numbers in which the address was mentioned. I'd read the full text of those reports to see whether it was relevant to my investigation when I had more time.

The FBI's phone-record database was unbelievably impressive and held all the phone numbers that their main target number had made calls to and from. The data was sorted and compiled in such a way that you could see exactly how many calls had been placed between the two numbers during a particular time period as well as the length of those calls. And if you were lucky, the numbers your target was placing calls to and receiving calls from were listed somewhere else in the FBI database.

Entering all of that data into the database was a painstaking process that amounted to hours of work for the analysts, but the information that could be gathered was invaluable. The pictures they revealed and the patterns that often emerged could provide leads that had the potential to make a stellar case, provided you were motivated enough to follow up on them and take the time required to reveal the entire image. I, of course, was.

First, I searched the cell-phone and landline telephone numbers Akbari had provided me the other day. Unsurprisingly, this search yielded negative results. It was about what I'd expected. The man had been in New York for only a few weeks, and the analysts weren't quite that current with their database entries.

Next, I searched for the cell-phone number Akbari had used when he was in Maryland, fully prepared to end up with nothing on that search as well. I was stunned when a long list of numbers that went for several screens was displayed on the monitor in front of me.

I blinked, flabbergasted, as I registered what the case code classifications I'd come up with revealed. I'd gotten multiple hits on Akbari's number in connection with subjects who were targets of terrorism investigations. And at least two of those were main targets, suspected heavy hitters.

That couldn't be right. Could it? I flicked my eyes back and forth between the number from my notes and the number displayed on the computer screen. Huh. They definitely matched, so there was no mistake there. Could I have copied the number down wrong when

I was talking to Sarah? It wasn't outside the realm of possibility, but I always meticulously check and recheck my information when copying something from dictation, so it was unlikely.

I scribbled a note to myself to call Sarah tomorrow to verify the number and then hastily copied the first two dozen hits that had cropped up on the list as the ones my target number had been in contact with the most. I also included any additional information provided, such as the number of calls made and the average length. I wasn't yet positive whether it'd be worth my time to look into every number on the list, but—

The ringing of my desk phone shattered that thought. Without taking my eyes off the screen and while still attempting to make notes with my right hand, I reached for the phone with my left.

"JTTF. O'Connor."

"Where the hell have you been? I've been calling you for hours." My sister's irritated voice floated over the line and conjured up images of what her face and posture surely looked like as she scolded me.

"Hey, Rory. What's up?"

"Well? How'd it go?"

"How'd what go?"

My sister made no attempt to hide her exasperation and allowed me to hear the rude noise she made in the back of her throat. "Tea with the queen. The visit, jackass. Did everything go okay?"

"Huh? Oh. Yeah. Yeah, it went fine. Thanks. Wait, how did you even know about that?" I hadn't spoken to my sister since that assignment had been dropped into my lap.

"That's it? That's all I get? 'Fine'? You'd better come up with a better response than that! I want details, *Ay-vo*, and I want them *nep*."

Rory's use of a couple of our old code words from childhood startled me. She must've felt pretty strongly about this to have slipped back into that habit. I glanced up from my notebook, shocked when I noticed the time. Shit, I had to hurry or I'd be late for the PT tests. Mark would just love that. I made a few more quick notes and then started shutting everything down and storing it, so I could get the hell out of there.

"Ryan? Are you listening to me?"

"Oh, yeah. I'm here. Sorry. What'd you say?"

"Why have you been avoiding me all day? What happened?"

"What? Nothing happened. I haven't been avoiding you."

"Well, I called your cell phone like a hundred times."

"That's a lot of time to invest in one activity. You do still have a job, don't you? How'd they feel about that?"

"I'm working the night shift this week, smart-ass. And I woke up in the middle of the afternoon—hours before I even needed to be awake, might I add—just to call you to see how everything went, and you're giving me shit. Nice."

"Sorry. You still didn't tell me how you even knew about the visit."

"How do you think I knew? Dad told me. I loved finding out something like that from him, by the way. Thanks." Her voice was laden with sarcasm, but I ignored it as the tiny little lightbulb in my head went on. Dad. Of course.

"So why were you ignoring me again?" my sister demanded, not leaving me the space of a breath to sneak in even a word.

My smile widened into a full-fledged grin. "Rory, where did you just call me?"

"Huh?"

"What number did you just dial?"

Her end of the line was quiet for a long moment. "You're in the scow, aren't you?"

I chuckled. "It's a SCIF, Rory."

SCIF stood for Sensitive Compartmentalized Information Facility. Basically, it meant my office had a lot of classified, secret, and top-secret information floating around in it and wireless devices of any and all kinds, whether capable of transmission or not, were strictly forbidden. Cell phones, pagers, PDAs, cameras, iPods. All of them had to be left outside. Rory could call my cell phone a thousand times for all the difference it made. When I was in here, I was more or less on an island, reachable only by the landline telephone at my desk.

"Skiff. Scow. Whatever. It's some sort of boat."

"Yes. You're absolutely right. I'm on a boat. I decided to give up my job and try my hand at piracy. You know how I feel about those eye patches." I had to bite my lower lip to keep from laughing out loud. My sister was a trip.

She was also not amused, if her tone was any indication. "Stop being an idiot. I don't even know why I bother checking up on you sometimes."

"I'm such a bitch."

"Tell me about it."

I laughed again as I attempted to ignore the pangs of loneliness that reverberated within me at hearing my sister's voice. I desperately wanted to talk to her, to pour my heart out regarding everything that'd happened the past few days. Unfortunately, I didn't have time right now. I sighed wistfully.

"Listen, sweetie, I know you're gonna kill me, but I've gotta run." My computer was now dark, and I was shoving all my notes and the envelope containing the pictures Meaghan had taken into my top desk drawer and locking it.

"Oooh, hot-shot federal agent too busy for her big sister now. Fine. I see how it is. Hmph."

I couldn't see her, obviously, but I was willing to bet she was pretending to pout. "Rory, you're only like three-and-a-half minutes older than I am." It was a recurring argument, one we'd had at least a million times and would probably have a million more. "I'm not sure that qualifies you as 'big.'"

"Four. And the difference in our maturity levels is apparent."

"Three minutes and forty-three seconds."

"I rounded up."

"I know."

"So am I going to see you any time soon?"

My mood fell. I had so many things I wanted to talk to her about and get her take on, but I simply didn't have the time. I grimaced, knowing she wouldn't like my answer. "Um, well, I'm pretty tied up the next few days...Two weeks maybe?"

"Seriously?" Now she sounded aghast.

"I'm afraid so."

"Well, who the hell am I supposed to confide in while you're off saving the world or whatever it is you do? By the time you get back, Caleb and I will probably already be out of the honeymoon phase of our relationship, and you'll have missed all the best parts."

That made me pause. "Caleb? What happened to Landan?"

"See what happens when you get all wrapped up in your own world of international espionage?"

I rubbed my forehead against the headache gathering behind my eyes. I definitely didn't like that I was missing important changes in my sister's life. I also didn't like that I couldn't vent to her about the occurrences in mine, but if I began that conversation now, she'd never let me off the phone, and I really needed to leave.

"Tell you what. The second my boy's wheels up, I'm all yours. How's that?"

"I'm going to hold you to that," she warned me.

"I'm good for it," I promised.

"Yeah, well, it doesn't matter if you are or not. I know your boss. I'll get him to make you make time for me."

I rolled my eyes. "Right. Because the SAIC of the New York Field Office has nothing better to do than indulge you and your whims."

Rory laughed. "Somehow, I don't think he'll mind. You know I'm his favorite."

I winced at the thought of her calling in that favor. "Well, let's make sure it doesn't come to that. Seriously, I gotta go. I'll talk to you later."

"All right, honey. Be careful. Call me when you can, okay? In the meantime, I'll dole out little teaser tidbits via text to whet your appetite."

"I can't wait. *La-val.*" Love you.

"*La-val, tow.*"

I hung up quickly and hauled ass out of there, praying the traffic gods would be merciful today.

CHAPTER SIXTEEN

As luck would have it, I made it to the office just in time to administer the PT tests. Mark was milling around in the gym when I arrived—most likely hoping I wouldn't make it, so he could yell at me or try to get me fired or something—but as soon as I breezed in, he left. I guess he didn't want me overseeing his test. Or maybe he'd skulked off to find something else he could be mad at me for. I hardly cared.

I ran the group through the paces at lightning speed and stopped at my desk only long enough to enter the PT scores into the mainframe before dashing off to the locker room to shower and change into more appropriate attire.

Throughout my career, I'd learned to come to work prepared for anything. Running, swimming, shopping, clubbing, walking around Central Park, a last-minute foreign-dignitary visit. I had outfits for every occasion on hand that I could slip into in a New York minute. And on days like this it meant I could get ready at the office without having to stop home first, which meant I'd be able to see Allison sooner. Not that I was looking forward to that or anything. Nope. Not at all.

I stepped out of the office, trying to walk and answer an email on my BlackBerry at the same time. The guys had been at the bar enjoying the wheels-up party for a while, it seemed, and they were demanding my presence ASAP. I was in the middle of sending them a message that I was on my way and to calm down, when my personal cell phone rang, scaring the hell out of me. I'd been working so hard I hadn't even looked at the thing for days. Everyone important who could possibly need to talk to me also had my work cell-phone number, so I hadn't given it any thought.

I glanced at the display. Hmm. Private caller. Rory again? Probably not. She never bothered to block her number. Besides, she should've been napping before her night shift.

"Hello?" I said as I continued to fumble clumsily with my other phone in my left hand. I dropped it and let slip a muffled curse as it skittered across the sidewalk.

"Hey," was the quiet reply.

My heart stopped beating and shriveled to something the size of a walnut as I recognized Lucia's voice. I sucked in a harsh breath, and my throat burned from all the car exhaust and diesel fumes I'd just inhaled. "Hey."

"How was the visit?"

"Fine." I bent to retrieve my erstwhile phone.

"Everything went okay?"

"It did. Thanks for asking."

"No problem."

My mind was working overtime. What could she possibly want? I thought she'd been abundantly clear two nights ago that she never wanted to speak to me again, so the motive behind this encounter escaped me completely. But I didn't appreciate the unpleasant feelings she was stirring up. My insides were wilting, and my chest felt like it was being crushed in a vise.

"So how are you?"

"I'm good. You?" This was insane. I wished she'd just get to the point. I still felt terrible that I'd hurt her, but I certainly hadn't done it on purpose, and my guilt was now taking a backseat to annoyance. She'd called me. She obviously wanted something. But what? I had neither the time nor the inclination to listen to her yell at me some more.

"Good." There was a long pause.

"Are you okay, Luce?"

I heard a heavy sigh. "Yes. I mean, no. I mean, oh, hell, I don't know."

"What's the matter?"

"I think we should talk."

"What's left to say? I think you covered all the bases pretty well."

Maybe that was mean, but she'd effectively wounded me with the insults she'd so callously slung my way. She'd injured me pretty badly, in fact, and, frankly, I wasn't eager to open myself up to any more emotional battery. I wasn't sure my fragile ego could handle it.

"How about 'I made a mistake'?"

"A mistake about what?"

"About you. About us." She took a deep breath. "Okay, so you have a past. Everyone does. I guess I just wasn't prepared for a visual reminder of that fact, and I overreacted." A beat. "Plus, I was pretty drunk when I came to see you, so I wasn't exactly rational."

I gaped at my reflection in the glass of the adjacent building. I looked about as shocked as I felt. She had to be kidding. The words "heartless" and "emotionally bankrupt" still echoed loudly in my head, leaving deep scores. I couldn't even begin to find the words to describe the damage her accusation of me purposely trying to make people fall in love with me for my own amusement had caused. She couldn't seriously expect me to just forget about everything she'd said the other night and go on as if nothing had happened.

"I stopped by your apartment a couple times to have this conversation face-to-face, but you weren't home."

"No. I've been busy. Working. You know, the visit."

"Oh, I know. I wasn't saying anything."

"Okay."

Another long pause. "I'm sorry, Ryan."

"You feel what you feel. I can't change that." I wished she didn't, but I couldn't really argue with her. Feelings were feelings. Right or wrong, they just were. I didn't have to like them, but that wouldn't make them go away.

"I don't though. That's what I'm trying to tell you."

My gut twisted painfully, and my hands shook a little in my nervousness. "I don't understand."

"All that stuff I said. I didn't really mean it."

"Then why'd you say it? It had to have come from somewhere."

"Well…I was drunk, like I said. So I wasn't thinking."

"There must've been something behind it. People don't just say stuff like that for no reason." I desperately wanted to believe her. I longed to accept her excuse and chalk it up to alcohol-induced stupidity, but I couldn't.

Lucia sighed. "I was hurt, and I guess I wanted you to hurt, too. When I thought about it the next day, I felt awful. I accused you of some pretty horrible things."

"It's okay." It wasn't. Not really. But I didn't know what else to say just then. This whole conversation was confusing. I needed time to think.

"It's not even remotely okay. I'm sorry."

I nodded, even though we were on the phone and she couldn't see me. I tried to wrap my mind around the exchange and get a handle on all my conflicting feelings.

"I mean, it's not as if you went out of your way to seek her out, right?" she went on when I didn't reply.

"No. I didn't."

"So she came to you. What, did she want you back or something? Because I wouldn't blame her."

Her halfhearted stabs at teasing or flattery went right through me without making a ripple. "No. She came here for work. We were partnered up for the visit. That's all."

"And you guys didn't fool around or anything?" Her voice was oddly strained.

"No." My answers were flying out of my mouth automatically at this point. My mind was a complete blank, and I was numb.

The silence stretched taut between us, and as I considered what she'd just asked me, something clicked in the back of my mind. Loudly. Unwilling to accept it, I replayed the words against memories of the expressions on her face the night we'd broken up, seeing the situation with new eyes.

Over the past day or so, a little voice had been telling me something hadn't exactly been on the level about the conversation Lucia and I'd had. Now I knew why. I'd assumed the anguish I'd seen on her face had been pure. I'd thought it was because I'd hurt her by failing to live up to her expectations. It hadn't seemed particularly rational, but I'd been unable to come up with a better explanation. I only just now realized that something else had tainted her accusations.

Guilt.

"Ryan?"

"Huh?" My head was spinning, and I was pretty sure I was about to vomit. I sat down hard onto the corner of a cement flower box. It was either that or risk my legs going out from under me.

"Okay, you're right. I totally deserve this. After the way I treated you, I don't blame you for wanting me to grovel a little. And you know what? I'm fine with it. I miss you terribly, and there's nothing I wouldn't do to earn your forgiveness. Just tell me how I can make it up to you, and it's done."

"Oh, Luce," I whispered, unable to draw the necessary breath to speak louder. "Tell me you didn't." I bent over and rested my elbows on my knees, dropping my head as low as I could. Wasn't that what you were supposed to do when you felt like you were going to pass out? Or was it the crash position for a plane during an emergency landing? I couldn't remember.

Lucia hesitated. "Tell you I didn't what?" But the self-reproach lacing her tone confirmed what I already knew.

My heart shattered, spewing painful emotional shrapnel every which way as I finally understood exactly where Lucia's fears about Allison and me had come from. It was the oldest story in the world. Human projection.

"It was Jessie, wasn't it?" My voice was quiet, and for a long moment, I wasn't sure she'd even heard me.

"Ryan, you don't understand—"

"What, Luce? What don't I understand? That you came over to my house the other night to accuse me of cheating on you, when it was *you* who'd been unfaithful? Tell me what I'm not getting. Because it seems pretty clear from where I'm standing."

I clenched my jaw, and tears welled in my eyes as a razor-sharp whip of pain wrapped itself around my middle. I trembled and opened my eyes wide in an attempt to dry the drops before they fell. How the hell could she do this to me? And how could she claim I was the heartless one afterward?

"Listen, Ryan, when I came to see you, I was upset. I'd seen you looking at that woman in the diner, and I was hurt so I—"

"So you spent the afternoon fucking Jessie?!"

"No, that's not it at all." Lucia's voice shook, and she sounded near the edge of desperation. "I was devastated to see the way you looked at her. I mean, seriously just sick over it. You have no idea how painful it was to see your tender expression. So, Jessie took me out after requals to have a drink, you know, to help calm me down, so I could decide what to do."

"And you guys got drunk and had sex. I get it. Thanks for sharing."

I will not throw up; I will not throw up; I will not—

"Ryan, please."

"Please what?"

"Please don't be angry with me. It was an accident. I didn't mean for it to happen, but I was just in so much pain, and when she touched me—"

"Ugh. Spare me the details. I can work out for myself exactly what went down." The words tasted bitter on the back of my tongue, and the irony of the phrase I'd just used definitely wasn't lost on me.

"No, Ryan. I didn't mean that. I just meant that for a few precious minutes, I forgot how bad you'd hurt me, that's all."

"So this is my fault? I pushed you to fuck her with my—what was it?—oh, my emotional bankruptcy. Is that it?"

Lucia let out a huff on the other end of the phone while I focused on gathering all of my wild and raging emotions together and packing them into a neat little ball that I could bury somewhere, never to be seen again, if I could possibly help it.

"No. I just—I just wanted not to hurt. That's all." Her voice was small and sounded far away, but that may have been due to my dizziness. I wasn't sure. I didn't care.

"I gotta go, Luce." My ears were ringing, which made my own voice sound hollow and vacant. It matched my insides perfectly.

"Ryan, please. I'm begging you. Can we at least get together and talk? Grab dinner or something? I hate that I hurt you."

Hurt. Huh. Sure, probably, once the blissful numbness finally wore off, I might hurt. A lot. But right now, my pain had receded, leaving me empty except for a very distant ache in my chest. I didn't even have it in me to cry.

"I'll call you." It was the best I could give her. At the moment, I didn't want to think about her, let alone see her. I needed the perspective that distance and time would give me before I could even conceive of having a conversation with her.

"When?"

Her obvious despondency didn't move me. "Dunno. Later."

I was about to take the phone from my ear and hang up when she rushed on. "I have your phone."

"What?"

"I wasn't paying attention the other night, and I grabbed your phone instead of mine when I left." A beat. "Guess we should've put stickers or something on them the way we always talked about, so we could tell them apart, huh?" The joke fell flat. But it did explain why Rory had such a hard time getting ahold of me earlier.

"Guess so." In the past, our having identical phones and always getting them mixed up had been comical. Not so much anymore.

"Are you busy? I could meet you so we could swap back."

"Right now?"

"Yeah."

"Um, I'm sort of on my way somewhere." Well, that and I had less than no interest in seeing her.

"I understand."

I could tell she assumed I was going out with Allison, and I didn't feel compelled to clarify my evening's plans. Huh. Maybe she was right. Maybe I was heartless. Or maybe I was simply childish. Either way I didn't reply.

"Well, maybe we could meet up tomorrow," she suggested.

"Sure." It actually sounded like the worst idea in the history of ideas, but I really wanted my phone. "I'll be in the office all morning giving PT tests, and then I have interviews for the rest of the day. I'll call you when I'm free. We'll work something out."

Maybe I could get Meaghan to meet her in the lobby and do the switch for me. That was unbelievably cowardly, but I was seriously considering it, strength of character be damned.

"Okay."

Silence again. I was done with this conversation.

"Good night, Luce."

Her voice was small as she replied, barely a whisper. "Night, Ryan."

CHAPTER SEVENTEEN

I hung up and sat motionless on the cement planter in front of my office building for an eternity. The skin on my forehead and cheeks tingled and buzzed. I closed my eyes in an effort to center myself, but the second I did, I saw vivid images of Jessie touching Lucia, kissing her, sliding her hand—

Tears prickled the backs of my eyes, and I snapped them open. Okay. I could do this. No need to fall to pieces. Lucia and I had broken up a few days ago, so I'd had some time to get used to the idea. I wasn't any more thrilled about it today than I'd been when it'd happened, but I wasn't in shock anymore. Getting weepy or emotional now was pointless because nothing had changed. Except everything had.

I took a series of deep breaths, inhaling and exhaling in long, measured movements, willing myself to calm down. It helped. A little. I concentrated on feeling the air as I drew it into my lungs and then expelled it. Nothing and no one else existed for me outside that moment.

This wasn't getting me anywhere. I needed to move. Yes, I was devastated in a way the definition of the word hadn't quite prepared me for, but I also had someplace to be. If I didn't show, the others would question, speculate upon, pick apart, and investigate my absence to the nth degree, and I wasn't in the mood for that. I had to get a grip, push all recent events aside for a few hours, and go pretend to have a good time so I could dissolve into an emotional wreck later at my own leisure. Okay. I could do that. Probably.

I forced myself to step to the curb and raise one hand to hail a cab. I was a wreck and definitely in no state to operate a motor vehicle. I was also inclined to get rip-roaring, balls-to-the-wall, stupidly drunk, so it was better for everyone if I didn't have access to a car. Just in case.

As a taxi pulled up, my work phone rang. I let loose a string of muttered curses as I tried to get into the newly arrived cab, answer the phone, stow Lucia's cell in my purse, and not flash the driver all at the same time.

"O'Connor," I said into the receiver, pressing it briefly to my shoulder to tell the driver the name and address of Allison's hotel.

When I brought the phone back to my ear, I winced as a loud, almost-melodic cacophony of music and many voices raised in good cheer lanced through my eardrum. It sounded like the party was well under way.

"Hello?" a male voice yelled into my ear.

I grimaced and pulled the phone back too late to avoid a near-deafening "Hello?"

"Hello?" the voice said again.

"Who's this?"

"Ryan?" the voice asked.

"Yeah. What's up?" I was pretty sure it was Keith Abelard, but it was sort of hard to tell, what with the music and the screaming and the traffic noises on my end and all.

"Where the fuck are you?" Oh, yes. Definitely Keith.

"I'm just leaving the office now. Keep your shirt on." I immediately became defensive but then reminded myself that he didn't mean anything by his question, and he hadn't contributed to my current mood. *Deep breaths, Ryan. Deep breaths.*

"Is that Ryan?" I heard someone else yell in the background. Several other voices joined in the shouting, and while I couldn't make out exactly what was being said, the basics were pretty apparent. I was late. Very late. They'd started without me.

"Hurry up, Ryan. We're all waiting."

"And you're all half-drunk." I smiled fondly. The guys were nothing if not predictable, and their boisterous spirits were just what I needed to take my mind off the mess my life had imploded into during the past forty-eight hours. "Relax. I'll be there in half an hour. Maybe forty-five minutes."

"Shut up," Keith yelled at someone, not bothering to take the phone away from his ear and almost bursting my eardrum. "I can't hear her. Forty-five minutes?" he repeated, sounding confused.

"An hour, tops." I gauged traffic as my cab driver and I made our way slowly but surely up the FDR.

"It doesn't take that long to get to Piper's from the office."

"I know that. I have to make a stop first."

"For every minute she's late, she owes us all a shot," someone else chimed in. I groaned as everyone else screamed their agreement, and I heard the clinking of glasses in the background. They were probably toasting that suggestion.

"What stop?" Keith demanded in between shushing noises, which apparently had less than no effect on the crowd.

"I have to pick up Allison." And hit an ATM, it sounded like. I barely had the resources to pay for all the shots I was preparing to consume. I sure as hell didn't have the cash on me to cover everyone else's. And I'd learned the hard way never to throw down a credit card to cover a tab. That's how you ended up with a five-hundred-dollar bar bill and no recollection of how you wound up on the floor in your apartment wearing only your bra and a hat. Or so I'd heard.

"Who?"

"Allison. The PPD lead." I hated that I was without my own phone, as I'd wanted to send her a text letting her know I was en route, so she could be outside ready to go. I didn't want to go anywhere near her hotel room. God only knew what sort of an ass I'd make of myself if I were alone with her. I'd probably burst into tears or something. And her seeing me cry once this visit was plenty.

"She's still here?"

"No, I'm going to D.C. to get her."

"Stop being a smart-ass."

"Then stop asking me stupid questions. I'll get there when I get there."

"Okay, but hurry up."

I heaved a bone-weary sigh as I hung up and leaned forward to talk to the driver. "Someone's going to meet us at the curb when we get to the hotel," I told him, raising my voice to make sure it carried over the din of the traffic and through the Plexiglas separating us. "Then I'd like you to take us to Piper's." I rattled the cross streets off the top of my head.

The only acknowledgment that I'd spoken was a sort of curt nod that might or might not have been directed at me. I sat back in the seat with a shrug and sent Allison a quick email from my work phone. Then I allowed my mind to wander as I stared out the window. Thoughts of the work I needed to accomplish over the next few days mingled with images of Lucia that faded into pictures of Allison, all of it going around and around until it made me a touch crazy. I shook my head violently as if to wipe my brain clean like an Etch-A-Sketch. I didn't need to think tonight.

When we pulled up to the curb in front of The W, Allison was just stepping outside. Her well-worn, faded jeans appeared as though they'd been painted on her body; a form-fitting, red cotton tank top displayed a tantalizing amount of olive skin; and broken-in, scuffed black boots completed her casual outfit. Her hair was loose and cascaded to tickle the tops of her bare shoulders. She'd folded a light jacket over one arm, and an eager-looking smile played across her luscious lips.

My mind went blank, and a swarm of dragonflies took flight inside me, their virtual wings tickling the undersides of my rib cage deliciously. I trembled slightly and licked my lips. Well, if anyone could take my mind off the emotional grenade Lucia had just lobbed my way, it was Allison. I wasn't sure whether that was a good thing or a bad thing. I was too fried to think, and it didn't really matter enough for me to try.

Self-consciously, I glanced down at myself. All I'd had available in my bag at the office had been a dark pair of indigo jeans, a black silk halter top that revealed just enough cleavage to get someone's attention without being vulgar, and a pair of black, open-toed sling-backs. I'd piled my hair up into a loose, messy knot on the back of my head and made sure I covered the angry-looking scab on my forehead with some strategically placed wisps of bang.

Getting ready, I'd been grateful that we were still between summer and autumn when warm temperatures weren't unexpected, so I wouldn't need to go home to retrieve a warmer outfit or, worse, don work clothes. Now, however, I felt silly and a little exposed. Normally, I thought nothing of dressing up a little when I went out after work—I was a girl, after all, and occasionally I did like to doll up—but today I was afraid it might seem like I was trying too hard.

I drew in a tumultuous breath and swallowed as I waved to Allison. As I leaned over to open the door for her from the inside of the cab, my heart stopped beating when I glanced up and noticed her eyes flickering to what she could see of the tops of my breasts. A blaze ignited beneath my skin, but that couldn't compare to the heat that rose in my cheeks when she lifted her eyes back up to mine and I recognized the flash of desire in them.

Allison held my stare as she slid into the seat next to me and then allowed her eyes to travel the length of my body. I felt that visual exploration as keenly as I would a physical caress, and it sparked an involuntary hum of arousal in me.

"Wow, Ryan. You look beautiful."

That declaration robbed me of the ability to inhale, and I had to clear my throat. "I was actually just thinking the same thing about you."

It was Allison's turn to flush, as much as she was able with her complexion. "I feel somewhat underdressed."

"You're perfect," I told her honestly. An all-encompassing need to kiss her suddenly seized me, an ache that throbbed dully in every cell of my body. Disregarding that impulse would be like ignoring the desire to breathe. Fortunately, she distracted me by speaking.

"Do you have a curfew tonight?"

"Nope."

"Your better half isn't expecting you?"

I grimaced in response to a searing stab of pain and managed to swallow the bile rising in the back of my throat. "I'm flying solo these days."

Understanding flooded Allison's expression, tinged with a hint of sympathy and something else I couldn't readily identify. "So it was more than just a fight."

"Yup." I really didn't want to get into this right now and hoped my short answer would discourage further discussion.

"Is it something that can be fixed?"

"No."

"You okay?"

"Mmm-hmm." *Aside from the fact that the girl I was seeing slept with someone else and then broke up with me under the pretense that she thought I cheated on her, but I can't stop thinking about you, and I still feel like an asshole because of it, I'm just dandy.*

Allison shook her head, which caused stray locks of her hair to tumble down across her forehead. "Liar."

I reached out before I knew what I was going to do and gently brushed those tresses out of her eyes, reveling in the slide of her silken skin beneath my fingertips. Allison blinked, obviously startled, but she didn't appear upset.

The cab driver slammed on the brakes and screamed loudly, shattering the moment and catapulting me back into my senses. I jerked my hand from Allison's face as though I'd been burned. What the hell was I doing? I really needed to get a freaking grip. Never mind the fact that I shouldn't be touching Allison at all. Now was definitely not the time.

"So, where are you taking me?" Allison's voice was light, her tone nonchalant, and I was instantly jealous. My own emotions were careening wildly out of my control, and I could've used a dash of nonchalance. Hell, even a pinch would have felt like a lot.

"Piper's."

Allison grinned. "You guys still go there for your wheels-up parties?"

"Of course. They take really good care of us. Oh, but I should warn you. I got a call from the thundering horde while I was on my way here. They sounded like they'd been at it for a bit. I can't imagine they can maintain that pace much longer."

"Good."

Surely I imagined that Allison's tone contained an undercurrent of satisfaction mixed with desire. Right? It had to be. It was a classic case of seeing—or in this case hearing—what I so desperately wanted.

I forced myself to focus on paying our accommodating, if slightly suicidal, driver and deliberately avoided Allison's intense gaze. But the fire burning in my cheeks spoke volumes.

A slight tug on my arm forced me to stop my trek to the pub's entrance, and I turned to face my captor with a vague wringing sensation just below my rib cage.

Allison's eyes were bottomless as she stared at me, and I felt myself falling. I glanced down to my feet to make sure the pavement was still solid beneath me. Allison recaptured my attention by resting a hand on my shoulder, making me return to myself and fly apart all at once.

"I'm going to make sure you forget everything tonight."

Promises, promises.

Chapter Eighteen

The place had a good-sized crowd considering it was a Monday night, but Allison and I didn't have much trouble making our way to the bar. I'd predicted correctly that the guys were all well and truly in their cups, so I wasn't surprised that the bartender, Sean, spotted me first.

"What'll it be, Ryan? The usual?" His voice still held a trace of a true Irish brogue, though he'd been in the States for years, and his smile could charm a leprechaun out of his pot of gold. "I hear you've something to celebrate."

Keith must've caught Sean's words because his head snapped around in my direction. Had he been sober, that might not have been a problem, but his inebriated body wasn't quite up to speed with his wildly swiveling head, and he nearly fell off the bar stool and onto Allison. It was a good thing Allison saw it coming and reached out to steady him, or he'd have ended up on the floor. A good thing for all of us, really. Keith was a big boy. It would've been tough to haul him back up again. I knew. I'd done it many times.

"I'm sorry," I mouthed to Allison when she glanced at me. She smiled back at me, and I almost melted.

Keith's face broke into a huge grin as his unfocused eyes finally sent the message to his alcohol-soaked brain that I'd arrived. "Hey, Ryan, you made it. 'S about damn time." His words were a little slurred.

"Yup. Told you I would." I turned to Sean to answer his question. "The usual would be great, thanks. And a Tanqueray and tonic, please, with a lime and two maraschino cherries."

"No, no, no!" Keith shouted, slamming one giant paw down on the bar. Some of the guys snickered and nudged one another, but he was undaunted. He turned his faux wrath to the bartender. "Ryan gets an Irish car bomb. On me." His tone was insistent.

Sean cut his eyes my way, as though checking to see whether the change was okay. I shrugged. "I'll drink it. But just the one. And keep the Tanqueray and tonic."

"Coming right up."

Now that he'd gotten his way, Keith turned his back on me and busied himself making certain everyone else had a drink. Sean set my Guinness and shot on the bar next to the Tanqueray, which I immediately handed to Allison.

"One Irish car bomb."

"Isn't that a little politically incorrect, Sean? I thought we weren't calling them that anymore."

It was Sean's turn to shrug. "I tried to get them to stop, but after a while, the fight just went out of me. You know how hard-headed cops can be."

I grinned and nodded as I tossed some cash on the bar. "Yeah, we're all pains in the ass. Thanks, Sean." I turned so my right side was nestled against the bar and picked up my shot.

Keith stood on the rungs of his bar stool so he towered over everyone and held up his glass. "Way to go, Ryan. The Big Guy went out the same way he came in. You managed not to get him killed. Good job."

I exchanged a quick glance with Allison, who grinned at me and lifted her glass in a mock salute. I rolled my eyes. The rest of the guys chimed in their own raucous comments, and glasses clinked as they toasted.

I protested. "Hey! Why do you all sound so surprised?"

Allison leaned in to whisper in my ear. "I'm not."

The sensation of her lips brushing softly against my skin mingled with the heady scent of her perfume made me shudder. My head swam, and a tendril of molten desire snaked its way toward my gut. "You're not?"

Allison grinned. "Nah. I knew you'd keep him alive. I was taking bets on whether he'd be in one piece though."

"Ha, ha." I wrinkled my nose at her and moved to drop my shot into my beer. "Very funny."

Allison laughed, and the sight of her mirth lifted my spirits.

"Hey, Ryan, wait! Let me get my watch ready."

I paused and turned to find Rico Corazon grinning at me wickedly. The shouts from the guys nearest to us reached a decibel level that made me wish I had earplugs, and I knew I was in serious trouble. I glanced to Allison for assistance, but she was conveniently engaged in conversation with one of the other guys she knew from before she went to D.C. and pretending not to notice my silent pleas for help. Traitor.

"Wait, wait," someone else was shouting. "Let me get one, too. I wanna race."

Several other voices chimed in, echoing the call to Sean to set them up with another round. The rest of the guys started placing bets.

I shot Rico a mock glare. "Thanks, buddy."

Rico laughed, showcasing his dimples and revealing a dazzling smile. He shrugged his broad shoulders and hooked his thumbs into the pockets of his jeans. With his caramel-colored skin, thick black hair, and deep-brown eyes, Rico was stunning. You know, in that brawny, male kind of way. Like drop-dead, mouth-opened, drooling-on-yourself gorgeous. He also happened to be a really nice guy. If I were into men, he'd have totally been my type. Hell, as it was I sometimes found myself studying him a little too closely and giggling like a schoolgirl whenever he teased me.

"That's what I'm here for."

"To be my own personal menace?"

Rico's grin grew. "Exactly."

"Great."

"I put fifty bucks on you," Rico informed me. "You'd better win."

"Bite me."

"Okay, okay," a new voice shouted. "We're all ready. Let's go."

"Sean, call it," someone else chimed in.

Sean made a show of raising his hand in the air the way I was sure only people in bad movies about drag racing did. He grinned at us and counted down. "Three...Two...One..." His hand fell, and the race was on.

We all dropped our shots into our beers and started chugging. Somehow, I managed to avoid spilling mine down the front of myself, but it was a struggle. I slammed my glass triumphantly down on the bar and noted I'd finished well before any of the guys. Pleased with myself, I turned to find Rico beaming at me.

Cheers and groans erupted from the watching throng, followed by some good-natured ribbing of the guys who'd just been beaten in a drinking contest by a girl. I laughed and motioned to Sean to get me my Harp and a glass of water.

Though the number of women in law enforcement was steadily rising, it was still mostly a man's world, and a lot of men, unfortunately, continued to have trouble sharing the field. I'd found two surefire ways to gain their respect and acceptance: kick someone's ass or drink them under the table. It helped a lot if you could do both. I was much better at the drinking part, but I wasn't above fighting dirty in either arena, especially if it meant I was going to win. However, I'd noticed most of the guys handled it better when I outdrank them than when I beat them up. Go figure.

"I knew you could do it." Rico threw one arm around my shoulder and squeezed.

I shoved him playfully. "That wasn't fair, and you know it. Why'd you goad them all into a bet they couldn't possibly win?"

"Hey, it isn't like you're a secret ringer or anything. It's their own damn fault if they overestimate their own drinking abilities and bet against you."

"Yeah, yeah."

"Ryan!" a high, musical female voice squealed.

A petite blonde launched herself into my arms and nearly knocked the wind out of me. Then two deceptively strong hands mashed my face, and someone kissed me rather soundly on the lips.

"I'm so glad you're finally here," the woman exclaimed, snuggling up next to me. "I've been waiting forever."

Out of the corner of my eye, I caught Allison staring at us with an odd expression, but when I turned my head to look at her fully, she'd already glanced away. I hooked one arm around my assailant's shoulder and glanced at Rico.

"How much has she had to drink?"

Rico shrugged, his face split by a sly grin. "I don't keep track of my wife's alcohol consumption. You know that. Makes it easier for me to take advantage of her."

"Clearly."

"Hey, you can take advantage of her, too." Rico grinned lasciviously. "As long as I get to watch."

I backhanded him lightly in the stomach. "Pig."

"Yup." He seemed proud of the label.

"Hey, Paige." I allowed myself to make a lingering examination of the woman. "You look absolutely gorgeous. I might actually make a move on you tonight."

Paige beamed, all pearly white teeth and sparkling blue eyes, and I knew my comment had had the desired effect. Okay, I'll admit it, I was flirting. But that had absolutely nothing to do with threesomes or getting laid. I swear.

Rico and I had been partners back when I was in the Counterfeit Squad. We'd been undercover together on what'd turned out to be the biggest investigation of the year. Not just for New York, but Servicewide. And when I say "together," I mean we'd posed as a couple at a posh Latin nightclub, whose owner had been suspected of printing counterfeit bills in extremely large numbers and giving them back as change, as well as selling them to other people to use however and wherever they wanted.

The assignment had translated to a lot of nights when Rico didn't go home until the wee hours of the morning, and Paige had apparently been jealous of all the time Rico and I were spending together. In what he'd deemed a move of pure brilliance, Rico had decided to diffuse his wife's insecurity by having her meet me.

Working in a male-dominated field for as long as I had, I'd gotten used to women being suspicious of all the time I spent with their men. I found it laughable. I had less than no interest in men in general, let alone their men specifically, but I couldn't blame them for being wary. Not with the rumors circulating in the public about what goes on in this agency.

More often than not, the women calmed down as soon as the guys explained I was irrevocably gay, but in a few cases, it'd taken a bit more than that. Trial and error had taught me that flirting with them would effectively reassure them I had absolutely no designs on their mates. It was a fine line to walk, and I could take it further with some than with others, but the tactic hadn't failed me yet.

While I had to use varying levels of attention to placate all the wives or girlfriends I'd encountered, Paige actually flirted back. Mercilessly and with great enthusiasm.

Now she favored me with a coquettish smile as she slowly looked me up and down. "Dressed like that, I think I might let you."

"Tease."

She blew me a kiss. "You love it."

"So, how've you been? I didn't expect to see you here tonight."

Paige made an impatient motion with her hand. "Ha! Like I was gonna miss your big celebration."

"Paige, it's not that big a deal, really."

Paige's stare indicated she thought I was being an idiot. "Your first PPD visit as counterpart? It's a huge deal. Rico and I are gonna buy you a drink."

"You're just trying to get me drunk."

"Damn right I am. You play hard to get when you're sober."

"How do you know I'm easy when I'm bombed?"

"Wishful thinking." She turned to Rico. "Baby, can you get us some shots?"

"Sure. What would you ladies like?"

"You pick," I told him.

Rico grinned evilly, and Paige let out a low groan. "We're going to end up with Wild Turkey now."

I grimaced. "No way. Pick something else."

Rico ordered Paige and me kamikaze shots instead, in deference to what he called our "girly-ness," and we downed them after a sloppy toast. He signaled Sean to set us up with another round, and I made a mental note to myself to be careful. Despite my earlier vow, I'd concluded nothing good could come of me getting smashed.

I glanced around to see where Allison had gotten to. She met my stare and favored me with her heart-stopping smile. I smiled back and silently motioned to her drink. She nodded.

I placed the order with Sean, adding another glass of water for her, and turned back around to find Paige eyeing me.

"Who's your friend?" She lifted her chin and cut a pointed glance toward Allison, who was now laughing at something one of the guys was saying to her. Of course, she was absolutely stunning, and for a long moment, I forgot how to breathe.

"She's the PPD lead. She was my counterpart for the visit."

"Oh." She continued to size up Allison. "She's pretty."

"Mm-hmm." No way I was going there. Not even with Paige.

"Will she get jealous if you dance with me?"

"I can promise you she won't care."

"Good. I'm going to go pick some songs." Paige abruptly released her hold on me and began weaving unsteadily toward the digital jukebox that hung on the wall.

"You did a good job today, Ryan," Rico told me seriously after his wife had wandered away.

"Thanks. Like I said, it was no big deal. You know how it is. I didn't really do anything other than be Allison's bitch. She did most of the work."

Rico held out a newly filled shot glass to me and clinked his against it when I'd finally taken possession. "Well, here's to your bitchiness, then. Who knew you'd be so good at it?"

I made a face at him and downed my shot. "I seem to recall you complaining about that particular character trait at least once a day when we worked together."

"Shows how much you know. It was more than that. I just did it behind your back most of the time." He grinned at me.

"Coward."

Rico just laughed off the insult and handed me another glass. He lifted his in salute. "We have something else to toast, you know."

"We do?"

"Yup. They moved me back to Counterfeit." His dark eyes sparkled with pride.

I couldn't restrain my grin, and I answered his proposed toast with a lift of my glass. "No way. Really? That's great, Rico."

He nodded and slammed his shot in one quick gulp. "Yeah, I'm the new backup."

I finished off my own drink and gave him a big celebratory hug. "Congratulations. You're going to be a great re-addition to that squad. You were always fantastic at counterfeit. The newer guys will learn a lot from you."

Rico grinned at me. "Thanks. You really think so?"

"Totally. In fact, I may be hitting you up for some assistance soon."

Though we hadn't worked closely together in quite some time, I knew I could trust Rico with any secret. I'd never have to worry about him ratting me out to the bosses for conducting investigations outside my current purview. He could be counted on to do what needed to be done and still protect me—and by extension my friend Sarah—in the process. His transfer back to Counterfeit, as the backup no less, couldn't have come at a better time.

Rico's humorous expression turned immediately serious, and he studied me with concerned eyes. "Everything okay?"

"Yeah. I just got something dropped in my lap the other day that looks like it might be bigger than the one-note pass we originally thought. I don't want to get into it now, but I may be coming to you soon looking to pick that devious brain of yours."

"Well, my devious brain and I are always here for you, whatever you need."

"I know. And I appreciate it."

"Hey, hey, hey!" Paige exclaimed as she stumbled back over to us. Her blue eyes were narrowed, and she shifted her gaze from Rico to me and then back. "What's with all the hugging? You can't hug her without me. You know that."

Rico lifted both his hands. "I just told her about my backup slot, and she started mauling me. You know she can't be controlled."

Paige shot me a conspiratorial little grin, the pride for her hubby's accomplishment shining in her eyes. "Just how out of control are you?"

"Very," I told her, flashing a smile.

In unspoken agreement, Paige and I both pounced on Rico, trapping him rather violently in the middle of an extremely vigorous hug. Rico made a big show of protesting and trying to break loose, but Paige and I held on tight for another long moment before we freed him.

I was laughing—really laughing—for what felt like the first time in days, and I had a lightness in my soul I desperately needed. Automatically, my eyes swept the room, searching out Allison as if to include her in my joy. I caught her watching me from a few feet away. Her eyes were hard and slightly narrowed as she took in the tableau Rico, Paige, and I presented, but when I winked at her, the corners of her mouth turned up in a small smile.

CHAPTER NINETEEN

I glanced at my watch for the third time in less than ten minutes, eager for a plausible excuse to make my escape. The party was still going strong and showing absolutely no signs of flagging. Apparently, the guys had banded together to once again prove me wrong. Thanks, guys!

I sighed and considered my options. True, I was having a blast. Ever since I'd transferred out of Counterfeit to PI and Rico had been shuttled over to Protection, I welcomed any opportunity to spend time with him. That Paige was here as well was just frosting on the cake of my day.

However, the hour was growing late. I'd imbibed all the alcohol I was inclined to for one evening and had switched to a steady stream of water some time ago. And I had to get up early in order to administer the remaining PT tests, which would be the beginning of a very long day for me. It was past time for me to pack it in.

"You keep looking at your watch," Rico said. "You got a hot date or something?"

I smiled ruefully. "Yup. PT tests in the AM."

Rico made a face. "That sucks."

"Tell me about it."

"So you've got to get going, then?"

"'Fraid so."

Rico looked sorry to hear that but didn't argue.

"Wait, you can't go," Paige interjected loudly, her volume just this side of a screech. She'd had a huge lead on me in the drinks department and then had attempted to keep stride once I'd joined the fray, so she no longer had any concept of indoor voice versus outdoor voice.

"Sorry, sweetie. Early day tomorrow. I need to get some sleep." I failed to mention that sleep as a concept had been largely elusive recently and that chances were the trend would continue. It seemed counterproductive.

"But..." Paige's brow wrinkled in an adorable frown, and she was obviously struggling to come up with a reason I should stay.

I continued to watch her in expectation, and Rico and I exchanged amused glances.

"You and Rico have to dance first," Paige proclaimed matter-of-factly, obviously proud that she'd succeeded in her task.

I blinked. "What?"

Paige nodded, and her sage facial expression contrasted with the dazed look in her big blue eyes. "Yup. You guys gotta dance. I picked a song and everything. I've been waiting."

"Paige, honey," Rico said, his voice measured with patience though he was obviously trying not to laugh. "This isn't really a dancing kind of a place."

Paige shrugged, completely unconcerned. "So what?"

Now Rico's brow furrowed. He was clearly trying to think of a compelling argument.

"I wanna see you guys dance," Paige went on. Her eyes fell on someone standing just behind me. "Tell 'em." She put her tiny hands on her slim hips and glared from the newcomer to Rico to me and back again.

I glanced over my shoulder and smirked when I realized Paige was ordering around Allison, who'd just wandered into this conversation and was completely clueless.

She looked to me for help, but I just shrugged. With her reappearance, I was suddenly too busy battling my conflicting feelings concerning her—unlocked and freed from their confines by the copious amounts of alcohol I'd consumed, no doubt—to really take much interest in the discussion.

"You should see these two dance," Paige told Allison, apparently tired of waiting for a response from any of us. "It is so fucking hot!"

Allison raised her eyebrows at me, a small, almost indulgent smile stealing over her oh-so-kissable lips. She appeared intrigued, and a blush rose to my cheeks.

When Rico and I'd first been paired together for that undercover op in the Counterfeit Squad, I'd learned he had four older sisters. They'd enlisted him as a practice dance partner from the time he could walk. Rico told me he hadn't really minded. He got along well with his sisters, and he'd found dancing actually fun. And after he'd grown up a bit, all the little preteen girls in his class at school had practically swooned when he'd revealed he had some serious moves.

I'd taken my fair share of dance lessons as a kid, too, and had gravitated toward styles with a lot of flair, like salsa. While I could perform other steps and had, in fact, tried just about every type of dance around, I preferred the fast ones with a lot of movement and twirling.

Rico and I discovered rather quickly that we moved well together, and the result of our inadvertent pairing for that assignment had been a lot of interesting dance combinations. We became something of a club favorite with the patrons and bartenders and eventually garnered the attention of the club's owner. The relationship we'd built with him and some of his employees had led them to trust us enough to let slip little details concerning the non-club-related activities occurring on the premises. Together with the information we'd gathered during independent investigation as well as tips from another confidential informant, we had all the probable cause we'd needed to get a search warrant for both the club and the owner's residences. After that, it'd been a done deal.

Rico and I hadn't had much of an opportunity to do a lot of dancing since the operation ended. On the rare occasion we did go out together, the music generally didn't lend itself to what I'd classify as actual dancing—bopping, writhing, grinding, flailing, and swaying maybe, but not dancing—and the atmosphere was always less than ideal. I mean, most of our after-work outings were held at some version of an Irish pub, and who really felt comfortable doing a merengue in a place where people habitually did shots and flung darts around? Not me.

"You dance?" Allison murmured out of the corner of her mouth. She definitely sounded amused.

I studied her. Was she was teasing me? It was tough to tell. "A little."

"There's this song," Paige slurred her words. Clearly none of us needed to be present for this conversation. She was evidently hell-bent on driving it whether we actively participated or not. "It's kind of old, but it was on the radio the other day, and the second I heard it, I thought, 'Rico and Ryan would look smokin' if they danced to that.'" She blinked at us expectantly.

"I'm not really dressed for dancing, Paige."

Paige's bleary eyes looked me up and down. She waved one hand dismissively. "You look great."

I held up one foot and hitched up the leg of my jeans a little to show her my shoes. "I'll probably break an ankle in these."

"Ooh, those are cute! Where did you get them?" Paige frowned. "Wait, what did you wear on your sting?"

I tried not to smile. "Lower heels. And it wasn't a sting."

"It wasn't? Are you sure?"

"We don't use the term 'sting.'"

"I thought everyone used 'sting.'"

"You've been watching too many old cop dramas," I told her. Rico put a hand over his mouth to hide his grin.

Paige looked to Allison for confirmation as though she didn't trust me to tell her the truth.

Allison shrugged. "I've never heard any of our guys say it. But I wouldn't be surprised if the FBI did." She met my eyes for an instant and beamed at me before her attention returned to a very serious Paige, leaving a bittersweet ache in my chest.

"I'll tell you what." I was determined to finish this discussion and not above looking for any way to placate her into dropping the subject. "I'll hang out for another half hour, okay? If the song comes on, let us know. Maybe we'll dance to it."

Paige nodded happily and stumbled into Rico. She seductively ran her hands over his chest and then threaded them behind his neck. She tilted her face up to his, wordlessly asking for a kiss. Rico's eyes danced as he complied.

Smiling wistfully at the display, I turned to give them a moment of relative privacy and ended up face-to-face with Allison, which made my heart thud wildly out of control. It was awkward for me to be standing next to her while near such a display of adoration and love as Rico and Paige were putting on, and I didn't know what to say. So I shoved my hands into my pockets and looked toward the bar where Keith was animatedly telling a story.

My scalp tingled, and I heard a definite ringing in my ears as the sensation of déjà vu threatened to overwhelm me. I'd never been particularly suave in this type of situation before. I sure as hell didn't know how to act now.

Once upon a time, Allison and I had been a normal, happy couple. Well, sort of. No, not exactly. We'd gotten along well enough, and we'd never lacked for passion, but for reasons I was never able to get her to confess, she'd wanted to keep our relationship a secret. As a result, I'd spent a lot of nights just like this one, standing next to her while feeling as though we were emotionally miles apart. And that was on good nights. More often than not, we'd spent the evening on opposite sides of a room, each pretending the other didn't exist, though I was always aware of her presence the way you can always tell where the sun is even without looking directly at it.

At first, her attitude hadn't bothered me. I don't want everyone in the entire agency to know my business either. And, let's face it, we're worse than adolescents sometimes. We all spend so much time together it's inevitable that after a while familiarity takes its toll, and conversation degenerates into gossip.

Unfortunately, as time wore on, I'd become less able to hide my feelings for her, to say nothing of actually being inclined to. So what? I was in love. I'd gotten her desire not to express extreme PDA when we were out with the work crowd, but to get pissed because I touched her on the arm? Smiled at her? Tried to have a conversation? That, I hadn't fully understood. And her aversion to almost any amount of interaction with me in a public place had done more than just anger me. It'd fucking hurt.

She'd expected me to walk an extremely fine line, too, because if I didn't pay any attention to her at all—which frankly had eventually just became easier for me than constantly policing my actions—she'd accused me of ignoring her and had become upset. But if I'd looked at her for a fraction of a second too long, well, she'd gotten annoyed then, too. I couldn't win.

Ultimately, the entire situation became too much for both of us. I'd been on edge all the time, worried I'd somehow do something to make her mad. But underneath all that, so much more was tearing me apart. I'd been sad that we couldn't just be happy together and devastated that she seemed ashamed of us—ashamed of me. I'd been angry I couldn't just accept her wishes, because I felt I was pushing her to overreact somehow. And I'd also been pissed off at her for putting me in that situation to begin with. Why the hell couldn't she just freaking relax?

In the end, we'd fallen apart. I think there'd been too much fighting, too much anger, too much resentment, too much pain between us by that point. I hadn't been able to see any way to fix it, and Allison clearly hadn't wanted to. She'd shattered me and never once looked back.

So here we were again, in a setting so familiar that pangs of the old anxiety were tying my nerve endings in knots and making me regret that I'd ever agreed to come. Why had I thought this would be a good idea? I hadn't known what to do years ago. What made me think I'd have a better clue now?

Allison rested one of her hands on my forearm. The sparks her touch inflamed in me lit a path straight to the most sensitive points of my body, and I stifled a gasp. Confused by her action and my own reaction, I looked into her eyes, hoping for answers.

"Relax," she told me softly. She squeezed my arm before letting go.

My thoughts reeled. I hadn't meant for her to see how uneasy I was. "You're doing it again."

"Doing what?"

"That mind-reading thing. I told you before, it's creepy."

Allison chuckled. "Well, you're not that hard to read."

I sighed, mildly irritated. "For everyone?"

Allison shook her head. "I don't think so. Just for the select few fortunate enough to know you well."

Time to deflect. "Oh. And you think you know me well, do you?" I cocked my head to one side playfully.

"Well enough to know what you're thinking about right now."

"Oh, yeah? And what's that?"

"Do I really have to say it?"

I scoffed. "You can't because you don't know."

Allison leaned in so her lips pressed right up against my ear, making me shiver. "You were thinking about kissing me." Her tone radiated confidence.

My jaw dropped. That was the first time she'd acknowledged my attraction to her since before we'd split up. I hadn't expected that. It also hadn't been remotely close to what I'd been thinking.

"I was not!" My protest was a little shrill as I tried to come up with a way to convince her she was wrong. My face was on fire.

Allison's lips quirked in a barely contained grin, and her eyes sparkled. "You are now, though, aren't you?" She blew me a playful kiss and sauntered over to the bar, putting a little extra sway into her hips as she walked.

Game. Set. Match.

Once I'd finally recovered, I let my own lips stretch into a grin. Ooh, she was so bad. She was also right, damn it all. Now that she'd brought it up, I was thinking about kissing her, as well as a host of other things, all of which involved my lips and her body in varying stages of undress.

Okay, I was still incredibly attracted to her. I might not have wanted to be, but facts were facts, and I needed to face them. With one offhanded quip, she could still light a fire in me that threatened to rage unchecked until I was reduced to embers.

I'd been fighting that realization for several days now. Despite the few fleeting looks and brief touches, I'd been convinced she saw me only as a coworker and former lover. And it'd seemed pointless to dwell on something that would never come to pass.

Now, however, I wasn't so sure. Most people didn't say things like that to people they weren't drawn to. Well, not unless they got off on making people want them for mere sport. Which I knew Allison didn't. So, part of her must still desire me. My heart stuttered, and I looked at her with new eyes as she headed back my way with another round.

Granted, the timing could've been better. I was literally just coming out of...well, something, but she knew the score there. I certainly hadn't hidden the situation. Besides, wanting to go to bed and wanting to rekindle a romance were two different desires entirely. One didn't necessarily lead to the other.

How would I feel about that? If she and I were to fall into bed tonight—not that I was expecting us to—could I be content with just sex? Would I be able to handle making love to her, only to have her walk back out of my life? And what if she wanted to stay? Did I even want to go down that road with her again? I wasn't sure. I didn't trust her not to shatter me once more.

"Thinking about kissing me isn't supposed to make you all broody." Allison handed me another water.

I blinked and shook my head, then accepted the offered drink and took a long swallow. I glanced around. It wasn't like her to be so open with these types of discussions when coworkers were lurking nearby. "It's not that."

She took a sip of her own drink, her face serious. "What's got you so tied up in knots, then?"

I studied her for a moment, attempting to decipher the meaning behind her actions and each of the words she'd uttered from her first appearance in my office until now. It didn't work. I was still completely clueless, which drove me crazy.

Maybe it was the alcohol, which was probably a contributing factor. Or perhaps my poor brain had gone into shock and shut down from all the emotional ups and downs I'd endured lately. Maybe my war-torn heart had thrown up its figurative little hands and decided it wanted out of my decision-making process entirely. Or maybe all three. But that was—oh, screw it. For tonight at least, I was through thinking.

"I was contemplating other things besides kissing."

"What other things?" The hint of passion swirling behind Allison's gaze belied her tone of forced innocence.

"You're a smart girl. I think you can figure that out on your own."

When she didn't reply, I fixed her with a long look, not hiding my desire, guessing I had nothing to lose. She stared at me for a long moment, and I tensed in anticipation as I awaited her reaction. The sensation was reminiscent of the moment when the roller coaster's reached the top of that first climb and slowly starts to creep over the precipice of that initial huge drop. I was one giant ball of raw nerves and slithering organs.

Her eyes flared just a little, and she inhaled sharply. She swallowed, and the tip of her tongue darted out to swipe across her bottom lip. The hand not holding her drink came up to brush her hair back off her forehead, and it was trembling. The barbed wire that'd snaked around my esophagus loosened, and my sparking nerves settled to a dull hum.

"Any more silly questions?" I asked so quietly she had to lean in to hear me.

Allison shook her head and gaped at me. "Christ," she muttered.

I smiled and took another sip of my water, forcing myself to concentrate on the cool wash of the liquid as it hit my tongue and slid down my suddenly dry throat. God, I wanted to touch her. Nothing too intimate. Something small. Just a brief meeting of hands or a swift brush of fingers against the bare skin of her shoulder. I ached with desire but wasn't sure whether she was ready for that or what the gesture would even mean to either of us. I didn't want to up the ante too soon.

"You need to stop looking at me like that," she said in a throaty rumble. She'd shifted so she was standing next to me, and I couldn't look at her without turning my head.

"Why?"

The invisible hand around my chest squeezed, and my breathing stalled. Shit. I'd gone too far. She wasn't going to answer, and I'd have only the din of my wildly thudding heart for company.

Allison took another sip of her drink. "Do you remember the day we met?" Her tone was mild, and the seemingly off-topic question threw me.

Did I remember? Which part? The immediate tension between us when we'd first made eye contact? The sparks that'd lit up my entire being when her fingers first brushed mine? Our inability to keep from touching one another, even innocently? Perhaps she meant the way my pulse had raced each time I'd even glimpsed her magnificent smile. Or maybe she was talking about the way everything in my world had suddenly made perfect sense the instant our lips touched. Truthfully, I remembered every single second of my time with her that day.

"Vividly."

Her eyes captured mine and held them for a long moment. The longing in their depths made me totally forget how to think. Now I swallowed hard. I took another gulp of water, trying to dispel the dryness in the back of my throat.

"The stools over by that pool table are about the same height as the benches at the range, don't you think?"

I glanced at the pieces of furniture and remembered our first trip to the shooting range, then imagined treating her to a repeat performance in the middle of this very public bar. My already racing pulse picked up speed, and I closed my eyes as a stab of pure need shot through me.

Allison's lips brushed against my ear, and I felt that touch acutely all over my entire body. "That's why you need to stop looking at me like that. If you don't, I can't be held responsible for what I'll beg you to do to me."

The sensation of her lips gently caressing my sensitive skin suddenly silenced the cacophony of memories rolling around inside my head as I was abruptly propelled headlong back into the moment. The muscles in my lower abdomen clenched, and I struggled for something clever to say, something that would mask my true thoughts. "Okay. Not up for a live sex show. Duly noted."

Allison grinned at me and shook her head. "Not just yet. But I do remember someone promising me a plaid skirt once upon a time."

I laughed. "I'll see what I can do."

"This is it! This is it!" Paige's excited squeals shattered the intimate moment, and she almost knocked me down with an overly enthusiastic lunge in my direction. She tugged insistently on my arm, and I was thankful it wasn't the arm holding the water. That would've been messy. And I was already wet enough in other places.

Paige looked back and forth from me to Allison expectantly, anticipation brimming in her eyes. I tilted my head to one side and listened. I knew this song. Paige had been right. It was kind of old. And it would be fun to dance to. I glanced at Rico, who shrugged.

"I'm game if you are."

I held out my glass to Allison. "Do you mind?"

"Not at all." Her smile made me faintly dizzy.

"Wait 'til you see this," I heard Paige tell her. "My God, I just want to jump them both when they do this."

My jaw dropped, and I glanced back over my shoulder as Rico led me to the dance floor. Allison seemed torn between laughter and intrigue. I shook my head and stepped into Rico's waiting arms. We paused a moment, feeling the beat of the song before we moved. The muscles in his arms tensed, and instantly I realized what part of the song was coming and what he was about to do.

"Dump me on my ass, and I'll pistol-whip you," I told him.

Rico just laughed. And then I was spinning, one revolution for each count the singer made. I'd realized his intentions just in time, too. Whew! If I hadn't been prepared, my legs would've tangled, and I would've gone down. I very likely would've taken him with me. He'd made a gutsy move. I was a tad unsteady in heels this high as it was.

I forced myself to block out everything—the lights, the setting, the guys, the fact that I could practically feel Allison's hot gaze on my skin—and just concentrate on the beat and Rico. It didn't take long to get caught up in our familiar rhythm. The rest of the world faded away as we moved together, and I caught myself grinning.

Rico met my eyes, and he echoed my smile before turning me again. It'd been way too long since I'd been out dancing, and I'd forgotten how much fun it was. I made a mental note to ask Rico and Paige to go out again soon and counted myself lucky that Paige couldn't dance like this and didn't mind lending me her husband once in a while.

The song was over way too soon, and Rico lifted me into his arms and spun me around as the last chords of the music faded away, replaced by an undanceable popular pop song. The five or six work guys still left broke into spontaneous applause, and Rico and I made a big show of bowing to the crowd. I laughed right along with him as we stumbled back over to Allison and Paige, beaming and a little breathless.

Paige's grin was enormous, and her glassy eyes sparkled. "That was great, you guys." She nudged Allison. "Weren't they great?" She didn't wait for an answer as she wrapped her arms around Rico in an exuberant hug.

Allison was staring at me, something not unlike shock painted across her face.

"What?" I wanted to know.

"I didn't know you could do that."

I shrugged and glanced away, embarrassed. Was she complimenting or criticizing me? I kept quiet.

"Have you always been able to do that?"

"For as long as I can remember."

"I've never seen you dance before."

"Well, no, you wouldn't have."

"It was very hot."

A sharp stab of desire cut straight through me, slicing cleanly through the threads of uncertainty that'd gotten tangled inside me. I cleared my throat. "It's even hotter when you do it with someone you're actually attracted to."

She was quiet, something intense and almost primitive flickering in her eyes. "Could you teach me?"

"Definitely." I cocked my head, so I could better hear the song currently playing. No, this wouldn't work.

"Let's go." Allison's voice held more than a hint of a command, and underneath lurked a slim thread of passion.

I shook my head again. "Not now."

Allison looked hurt. She set her jaw. "Okay."

I rested one hand on her bare forearm. "I'm not a very good lead. I haven't had that much practice." I sketched a vague gesture in the air with my hand, indicating the music surrounding us. "I won't be able to teach you how to dance to this. I'm not proficient enough to ignore the beat. Rico might be able to do it, but if you want me, we'll have to wait for another song."

Realization dawned on Allison's face, followed by a tender sort of smile, which confused the hell out of me. What had she thought I'd been talking about?

"No, I meant let's leave."

"Oh. I thought you wanted me to teach you to dance."

Allison shook her head, the sway of her dark hair as it brushed the tops of her bare shoulders mesmerizing me. "I do. But not here."

I colored. How could I have forgotten we had an audience? She wouldn't want them to see us doing something as intimate as dancing. And she was right. We didn't need to fuel their fantasies. Besides, after five seconds of moving with her in my arms while she stared at me with that hungry look, I might ravish her on the spot, audience and probable jail time be damned.

"Oh. Right. Sorry." I hesitated, thinking, and then it hit me what she'd just said. She wanted us to leave. Together.

My eyebrows flew up, and I gaped at her. Her blatant desire left me speechless. Even when we'd been a couple, she'd never wanted anyone to see us depart a party together. We'd always had to duck out separately with at least thirty minutes between our departure times, even though we intended to spend the night in each other's arms. What had changed? Anything? I didn't want to make the wrong assumption.

Allison smiled at me again, probably reading my uncertainty, and extended a hand. Tentatively, I took it. Again, her behavior stymied me. Not that I was complaining. I just didn't understand what was going on, and I didn't like being clueless.

She threaded her fingers through mine and pulled me toward the door. I stopped her with a light tug, and she turned around, looking part bewildered and part irritated. I squeezed her hand.

"Just give me a second to say good-bye to Rico and Paige."

Relief flickered in Allison's eyes, and she nodded.

I made my way back to my friends, who also looked like they were getting ready to call it a night. We quickly exchanged hugs, as well as promises to call and get together again soon. My heart was stomping out a vigorous treble reel as I floated back over to Allison, and a flutter of nervousness tickled my insides.

Allison gazed at me with tenderness and once again offered me her hand. She always could read me better than anyone on the planet, which could be a blessing or a curse. Tonight it was the former. I smiled at her as I took her hand and allowed her to lead me out the door and into the night.

CHAPTER TWENTY

Allison shivered as the cool night air hit her. I took her jacket from where she'd slung it carelessly over her arm and held it up. A secretive smile touched the corners of her lips as she turned her back to me and allowed me to help her into it. I wanted so badly to place a small kiss on the side of her neck just below and behind her ear, but somehow I made myself wait. I sighed softly at the memory the faint scent of her perfume invoked and felt her shiver again. Was it due to my proximity to her? I smiled.

"Do you mind if we walk?" Allison wanted to know.

"No. It's a nice-enough night, and it's not that far."

"Will you be okay in those shoes?"

"If I'm not, will you carry me?"

"Maybe. If you're good."

She started ambling down the street. The expression in her eyes—what I could see of them—seemed distant and vaguely troubled. She had something on her mind, but I'd need to wait it out. Pushing her to talk before she was ready had never gotten me anywhere. So I tried to examine my surroundings and simply enjoy being with her rather than obsess over whatever could possibly be occupying her thoughts to this degree.

After a few minutes, she took my hand with trembling fingertips. The sweetness of the gesture tugged at me, and I brought her hand up to my lips and dropped a gentle kiss on it.

Allison inhaled sharply and studied me out of the corners of her eyes. The longing reflected there made my joints all wobbly, and I was thrilled when she didn't pull her hand away. I hadn't thought about the action before I'd performed it, but once upon a time it would've gotten me into trouble. Though her holding my hand at all signaled she was okay with a little PDA.

Always one to push any envelope presented, I held her gaze and brushed my lips along her knuckles once more. I took my time, drawing out the kiss, teasing her. Her breathing was shallow and quick, and her tongue darted out to moisten her lips as her eyes dropped to focus on mine. My heart might've momentarily ceased beating, but I hardly cared.

Still gazing at her eyes, I deliberately grazed each knuckle lightly with my teeth. Then I turned her hand over and nipped at the inside of her wrist, at the skin over her pulse. I could feel it pounding when I pressed my lips against it and couldn't help smiling. Absently, I traced small circles in the palm of her hand with my thumb.

"You're driving me crazy." Her voice was a low, warning hum, and her eyes flashed dangerously.

"Good."

All of a sudden, on the heels of that declaration, all the reasons why we shouldn't be doing this paraded across my mind and made me pause. But then Allison tugged me to a stop in the middle of the sidewalk and brushed my cheek with the fingertips of her free hand. Any thoughts I might've had about anything else completely dissolved as the raw desire in her unflinching eyes pinned me.

My head started to spin, and a fissure shot up my spine, slamming against each individual vertebrae. I couldn't think about anything else. How could I? Allison was everything, and satisfying her longing was paramount. Nothing else mattered in that moment. Not yesterday, not tomorrow, not next week. Now was everything. And now it was imperative that I kiss her.

I leaned in, determined to capture those luscious lips with my own. She was gravity itself, and I was helpless against her pull. Allison smiled coquettishly and leaned back, shaking her head a bit. I huffed and rolled my eyes but couldn't help smiling.

"Guess I'm not the only one who's going crazy," she said lightly. Her eyes glittered, and she resumed walking, swinging our hands between us.

I pulled her closer to me and threaded my arm around her waist and under her jacket. Before she could protest, I slipped my hand under her tank top, tracing designs on the soft skin of her lower back. She stiffened and gasped. Both the feel of her beneath my fingertips and her little sighs caused my entire body to ache and a flood of moisture to pool between my legs. As far as I was concerned, we couldn't get to the hotel fast enough.

The rest of the walk was a blur of sights, sounds, and sensations, which served only to stoke the embers of my arousal until they burned with the intensity of a four-alarm fire in an oil refinery. I was so hot by the time we walked into the lobby I was ready to come in my pants. The elevator ride was pure torture as Allison snuggled up behind me and rested her chin on my shoulder, scarcely nuzzling my ear. She might've been speaking to me, but I couldn't hear over the roar of blood pounding in my ears on a fast track straight to my throbbing center. The feel of her arms around my waist, her hot breath in my ear, the sensation of her breasts pressing firmly into my back, her hips pushed up against my ass—all of it led me further and further astray from the bounds of propriety, and I craved to take her in the elevator. Too bad she'd already nixed the live sex show.

Finally, finally we reached her room. Her attempts to insert the key card into the lock with trembling hands took way longer than I wanted, and I let out a low moan of impatience. That slip only made her hands shake more and delayed her progress that much longer. When we stumbled into her darkened foyer at long last, I was so happy I wanted to cry.

Allison slammed the door shut behind me the second I was inside and flipped the deadbolt, her movements quick and jerky. She shucked her jacket and tossed it to the floor in a careless gesture, then wasted no more time on foreplay or preparations.

She pinned me forcefully to the door, and I let my purse fall to the floor. Her hands went around my waist and pulled me tight against her. She gazed into my eyes for a heartbeat or two, and all the air in my lungs whooshed out of me as I tried to make sense of the emotions I could see crackling and snapping behind hers. When her lips descended possessively over mine, my attempts to decipher what I'd seen in her eyes scattered along with my thoughts.

Holy fuck, she's an amazing kisser. That was my first coherent notion after who knew how long. Better than I remembered, actually. Time had blunted the memory of how exquisite it felt to have her lips pressed against mine. I was so caught up in the sensation and reeling at how incredible, how right, it felt that it took me a moment to remember I could participate in other ways. Warmth flared in my chest and slowly radiated outward as I tangled one hand in her thick, black hair while I moved the other lower to palm her ass through her jeans. I gave the cheek in my hand a firm squeeze, and Allison let out a low, guttural groan and rocked her hips against mine. I nearly came on the spot.

A warning sounded in the back of my head, faint, but not faint enough for me to ignore. Then it came again. Breathlessly, I wrenched my lips away. It was too hard to think and kiss her at the same time. My head was spinning and not just from the alcohol. No, I was drunk on desire. I wanted her in a way I'd forgotten I could want anyone, and it would've been so easy to get swept away on the torrent of perfectly mind-blowing sensations that her kiss sparked. But I didn't feel right about the situation. We were both more than a little tipsy, and things were wretchedly complicated for me. I was positive I'd never be able to forgive myself if I didn't at least try to talk to her before we gave into our obviously mutual desire.

"Allison, wait," I gasped, turning my head when she leaned back in to kiss me.

A rumble emanated from deep within her chest, and she ignored my protests and immediately started exploring the skin of my now-bared neck with her lips. I shivered and tightened my grip on her, moaning a little as I did. Dear God. Was there anything about this woman that didn't completely short-circuit my brain?

Allison worked one hand beneath the fabric of my shirt and started stroking my skin with her fingernails. Goose bumps broke out over my entire body, and I covered her hand with one of my own. It was an effort, and the part of me drowning in the need for her to touch me howled loudly in protest.

"Allison, please, just wait."

She pulled back a bit and eyed me with a borderline-hostile expression. "What?"

"Are you sure this is a good idea?"

"What do you mean?"

"Well, don't you think maybe we've had a little bit too much to drink?"

She scoffed. "Honey, we've never been too drunk for this."

She leaned in to kiss me again, and I cuffed her on the shoulder, trying not to laugh. "You know that's not what I meant."

She nodded slowly. "On a scale of church sober to that weekend in New Orleans, how drunk are you?"

"Um...I'd say I'm Superbowl Party tipsy. You?"

"Desjardin's retirement, maybe edging toward New Year's Eve."

"Oh."

"Okay?"

I frowned. "Sure." I was glad this wasn't all a booze-fueled hook up, but there was still the matter of...well, everything else.

She regarded me for a long moment, her expression unreadable. And then, inexplicably, she smiled. "Are you married?"

"What?"

"You heard me."

I made a face. "Of course not!"

"Seeing someone?"

I grimaced at the reminder of my recently failed relationship. That was actually a huge part of the reason I'd stopped this. What the hell had I been thinking, coming up here to her room with her? This was—

"Are you really a man?" Allison rushed on before I could fall too far back into my self-loathing or varying degrees of guilt.

I blinked, and it finally hit me what she was doing. She and I'd had an eerily similar conversation the very first time we'd slept together, only then our positions had been reversed. She'd been the one who'd been a touch unsure, and I'd attempted to lighten the mood with inane queries.

Allison brushed some stray wisps of bang off my forehead and tucked them back behind my ear, smiling broadly now that she seemed positive I recalled the exchange. "Whatever it is, it doesn't matter. Okay?"

I bit my lower lip and nodded, not completely reassured but feeling at least a little better.

"Do you want me to stop? Because if you don't want to do this..."

The mere suggestion was like fingernails on the chalkboard of my mind, and I shook my head. "No. Don't stop."

Allison cupped my jaw with her fingertips and scoured my eyes again. She waited a long moment as though to give me time to pull away, if that was what I really wanted, like she doubted my words. And then she leaned in slowly to kiss me again. It seemed to take forever for her lips to finally brush mine, but when they did, I sighed. I could easily have spent the rest of my life just kissing her.

Allison deepened our kiss, easing her tongue into my mouth and stroking mine. It almost tickled in a wonderful way, and I whimpered. Allison's lips curved into a smile, and I pulled back just enough to nip at her bottom lip. She slid her hands around my neck and pulled me tighter against her as she moaned. The sound sparked something primal inside me, and I knew I was seconds away from letting her take me against the hotel room door. As hot as that would've been, it wasn't what I wanted right now.

Using a technique we'd learned in training, I dropped my hands so the heels rested against the front of her pelvis and pushed, tucking my elbows in close to my body and creating a little distance between us. Allison growled and tried to press her body back against mine as she increased the intensity of her kiss. I waited, thoroughly enjoying the pressure of her hips against my hands, and when I thought she was pushing as hard as she could, I released my grip and swiftly wrapped my arms around her to cup her ass. I used her forward momentum to scoop her up into my arms. It was a bold move, tipsy as I was, but she instantly locked her legs around my waist, grinding against my belt buckle. She cried out, but the press of my lips muffled her moans.

Praying she hadn't left anything on the floor for me to trip over and I could pull this off without injuring both of us, I walked us farther into the room and dropped her on the bed. Passion flared even hotter in her dark eyes, and she scooted back, kicking off her boots. I took the opportunity to lose my own shoes as well.

Allison's eyes bored into mine as she wrenched her tank top from her body and quickly went to work on the fly of her jeans. Normally, I loved undressing her, taking my time to discover each part of her as I revealed it. Tonight, however, both of us were too far gone to even pretend to be slow and leisurely. At least this first time. I vowed to savor her later.

Maintaining our charged eye contact, I shimmied out of my clothes. I didn't care where they ended up as I flung them away from me. I wanted nothing between me and the hot press of her skin.

Allison hit me in the face with her panties and then tossed her bra at me. Automatically, I caught both and returned her smile, tossing the bra over my shoulder. The panties gave me pause, and I captured the crotch between my thumb and forefinger. God, they were wet.

"Come here."

The panties slipped from my grasp, and I crawled across the bed and immediately covered her body with my own, dispensing with my usual ritual of feasting on the smorgasbord of her naked flesh with my eyes. Right now, I needed to feel her. The desire was an all-consuming ache, and my head swam.

I groaned deep in the back of my throat as our bodies collided, and a wave of satisfaction-tinged relief washed over me. She felt more amazing than I remembered, more incredible than I could ever have imagined, and my skin hummed everywhere we touched.

Allison cupped the back of my neck with one hand and pulled me to her, crushing my mouth to hers in a bruising, possessive kiss. She wrapped one leg around my hip, and the new position allowed me greater access to her dripping center.

She groaned, tilted her hips, and pulled me tighter to her. Evidently, she wanted me to continue. Smiling into our kiss, I stroked her again, pleased with how easily my fingers slid through her slick folds.

Allison hissed and broke our kiss, throwing back her head and squeezing her eyes shut. The fingers on the back of my neck tensed, and she rocked her hips again. Then she ripped my hair tie out, and I took advantage of my momentary freedom to shift my position, sliding down on the bed so I could lavish my attentions on her breasts with my lips while I used my hand to drive her a whole different kind of crazy.

The sounds wrenched from Allison's throat were the stuff of legends. I could think of no more powerful aphrodisiac than her little moans and gasps of pleasure, except perhaps hearing her say my name as she came. The heat that poured off her was intoxicating and drew me like the proverbial moth to a flame.

"Ryan," Allison pleaded a little breathlessly, tugging on my hair.

"Mmm." I closed my eyes and trailed lingering kisses over the taut planes of her abdomen, tracing the ridges of her muscles with my tongue. I sucked on the skin surrounding her belly button and slid my fingers a little higher, so I was almost brushing the spot where I knew she needed me most. Almost. But not quite.

"Turn around."

"Mmm." I wasn't paying attention to her words, much more interested in the tension I was creating in various parts of her body as I skimmed my lips over her skin. The scent of her arousal enthralled me, and I nuzzled the juncture where her thigh met her hip.

"I want to taste you," Allison whispered softly. She followed her statement with a small sigh and, despite her words, lifted her hips toward my mouth.

Okay, that got my attention. I raised my head just enough to meet her eyes as I dragged my tongue slowly through her wetness, relishing her musky flavor.

Allison moaned and threaded her fingers back through my hair, gripping hard. She tugged my head back, and I glared at her, irritated that she was interrupting me. I had explicit plans for her, and she was the exact opposite of helpful.

"Ryan, please?" Her voice was low and husky, full of desire.

Arousal pierced my gut and tickled that odd spot under my right arm that it did in only the most extreme cases. I closed my eyes against the onslaught, which was almost too intense to bear. Allison loosened her grip in my hair and began to rake gentle trails through it, causing a shiver to run down my spine. I trembled, reveling in the pleasant sensations she was evoking in me.

I opened my eyes to meet hers and saw swimming beneath their depths the very passion that'd shattered me and in the same moment somehow made me whole time and time again. I melted under the weight of that look.

Still unable to form coherent sentences, I simply nodded. I lifted myself, and she sat up to meet me, our lips brushing one another in a long, tender kiss. When we broke apart, she flashed me an impish grin and raised her eyebrows once in an almost playful gesture. I grinned back, recognizing the unspoken order for what it was, and readjusted my position so she could reach me while I lavished attention on her.

Her hot breath tickling the skin of my inner thighs made me completely freeze. The first touch of her tongue gliding over my sensitive folds made me lose my focus altogether.

I lay there for a long moment, my cheek resting against her leg, completely unable to move. My eyes were closed, and sparks were dancing along the insides of my eyelids that seemed eerily timed with the motions of her tongue against my throbbing core.

My muscles all went tight, and my body trembled. Jesus, this wouldn't take long at all, I thought stupidly as I spread my knees a little wider. She let out a sort of growl as she wrapped her lips around me, and the slight vibration made me gasp.

Remembering where I was and what I was supposed to be doing, I bent my head so I could resume my earlier activities. Only I upped the ante and thrust two fingers inside her as well. She made that low, guttural noise again and rolled her hips beneath me. I chuckled as I pulled my fingers out slowly. She whimpered, and I, never able to deny her anything, slid them back home.

Her entire body went rigid, and her thighs quivered. She was moaning more often, and her motions against my swollen sex were becoming almost frantic. She was definitely about to come, and I was thrilled to know she was as close as I was.

It took all my willpower and concentration to remain focused on her pleasure because I was dying to submit completely to her touch. Fighting that instinct was a bitch. But, somehow, I did. And it was absolutely worth it. Feeling her groan of surrender against me as she fell dragged me over the edge with her, and as we clung to one another, riding out the ecstasy of our shared orgasm, I couldn't imagine anything more perfect.

CHAPTER TWENTY-ONE

We lay there for a while, our bodies and limbs tangled, catching our respective breaths. We'd shifted positions so Allison's head rested heavily on my shoulder, and I brushed my lips over her hair as I stroked her back with my fingertips. I was floating in the most incredible post-bliss haze, and I didn't have the energy to even wonder what came next for us. I was spent.

"Wow," Allison whispered.

"Yeah."

"That was…" She shook her head and sighed, snuggling more securely against me and throwing one leg over my hip. "Wow."

"Yeah."

She traced random patterns on my other hip, and I smiled. Then I didn't hear anything but our mingled breathing for a long time. I thought she'd fallen asleep and was drifting off contentedly when she murmured so quietly I almost didn't hear her.

"I've really missed this."

My eyes popped back open, and I tensed. A cannonball suddenly splashed down in my chest, and I didn't know how to respond. Did she mean she missed being held by someone in general? Or was she telling me she missed me specifically? Her words didn't indicate her meaning, and since her face was pillowed against my chest, I couldn't see her expression for any clues. I finally went with the ever-eloquent and appropriate, "Huh?"

"Mmm. So you are awake." Allison's voice sounded a little teasing.

"Yeah. I...yeah." It was lame, and we both knew it, but I couldn't think of anything else to say. Now that we'd slaked our passion somewhat, and I could think, I wasn't sure what I wanted to happen next, what was even feasible. After a long silence, during which Allison inhaled several times as though she wanted to say something, she just exhaled softly.

"You did know I was talking about you, right?" she asked finally.

I shrugged, not wanting to shatter the afterglow by mentioning that she'd slaughtered me once upon a time. Nothing kills the mood faster than bringing up old wounds. Except perhaps giving voice to fears that she might one day do it again.

Allison propped herself up, leaning on one elbow over me and looked intently into my eyes. Her brow furrowed, and she pushed the hair back out of her eyes with an impatient motion. "Please tell me you know that."

I bit my lower lip and thought about how to respond. Apparently, my hesitation was answer enough because her forehead uncreased, and the corners of her lips pulled down slightly.

"I guess I can't blame you. I mean, not after the way we ended things."

You mean the way you ended things? I wanted to say. Thankfully, I managed to keep a lid on that little addendum. Instead, I tucked another stray lock of hair behind her ear and trailed my fingers down her neck to play at her collarbone.

"I'm surprised." I made my voice as gentle as possible. I hadn't planned to discuss this, but since she'd brought it up, we might as well talk about it. "Considering I haven't heard a word from you since you left."

"I didn't know what to say," she said.

"You could've said anything."

"I couldn't have said what you wanted to hear."

"You didn't know what I wanted to hear. And sometimes hearing the opposite of what you think you want to hear is enough. At least it gives you a place to start healing."

"Yeah, no kidding."

I frowned. "What's that supposed to mean?"

Allison scowled, let out a huff, and rolled away from me, yanking the sheet up to cover her exposed breasts. I felt the loss of her warmth immediately.

"Nothing. I'm sorry. Let's just drop it." Allison averted her eyes and crossed her arms over her chest, drawing into herself.

I wanted to touch her, wanted to make her look at me, but wasn't certain how she would react. Instead, I sat up against the headboard, drawing the sheet up to cover my own body. "Oh, I don't think so. Not this time. If you have something to say, let's hear it."

She didn't reply, and a dread crushed me.

She stared at the desk chair in the corner of the room with more interest than was really warranted. I could see the muscles in her throat working as she swallowed. "Do you remember the day we broke up?"

I winced, not expecting the question. "Yeah."

Silence. Where was she going with this? The crushing weight had turned icy.

Allison took a deep breath and clenched and unclenched her fist in the sheet beside her leg. "Do you remember what you said to me that day?"

I frowned slightly. I'd said a lot of things to her that day and spent the past few years trying to forget them. Most I'd sputtered, heartbroken. Why would she want to remember any of that? I didn't.

"You mean what I said about loving you for the rest of my life?" That was the only thing worth recollecting.

Allison nodded but still wouldn't meet my eyes. "Yes."

I waited for another question. She didn't ask one. "What about it?"

"Did you mean that?"

I wasn't sure how to answer. I'd meant it when I said it. I loved deeply and loved forever. But I was reluctant to admit that now. And since our future was uncertain, what would she think of my answer?

"I did," I finally said.

She inhaled and hesitated, tensing. Her arms tightened around her middle. Was she wavering, possibly trying to decide whether to pursue that line of questioning? Not being able to see directly into her eyes, it was tough for me to tell. She took another deep breath. "Do you?"

I blinked. Was she asking me if I still loved her? It sounded like it. It also sounded almost like she was dreading the answer. My pulse raced, and I was so nervous I was physically ill. I definitely hadn't seen this conversation coming.

In a perfect world, I'd declare my love for her, she'd return the sentiment, and we'd live happily ever after. But this wasn't a perfect world. It was real life. I was having a hard time letting go of the past, and I wasn't keen to open myself up to let her hurt me again. Now I clenched my fists in the bedsheet. I wasn't ready for this. Why the hell had I come up here again?

"Where are you going with this?" I asked.

Allison finally looked at me, her eyes narrowed. She studied me, as though trying to determine whether I was being a smart-ass. Her dark look made me uneasy, and I licked my lips, my mouth suddenly bone-dry.

"Just trying to figure out what a declaration of love from you means, that's all."

"What?"

"Well, you fell in love with the girl you started seeing immediately after me pretty damn fast. Do you just say that to anyone or did it really mean something?"

I shook my head. "I didn't even go on a date until almost a year after you left NYFO." I felt like a total loser even admitting that much. I didn't mention that she'd just watched the only real relationship I'd ever actually attempted dissolve. No need to play all my cards at once, right?

Allison looked angry now, and I winced initially, but then my stubborn pride kicked in. What the hell was she so angry about? She'd dumped me. Hard. And then she'd left New York. I hadn't heard from her until a few days ago. How dare she question me about what I'd done or with whom and when?

"Don't lie to me, Ryan. I deserve better."

How had we ended up here? I didn't even know what she was accusing me of.

"Allison, I'd never lie to you about something like this. I have no idea what you're talking about."

Allison's shrewd, calculating stare went on so long I wondered if she was about to toss me out of her hotel room on my ass and in my birthday suit. I struggled to stay calm and remain focused. I would not allow myself to get carried away by becoming all emotional.

She finally spoke. "I heard you." She turned away from me and rubbed tiredly at her forehead.

"You heard me what?"

She slammed her hand back onto the bed and clenched the sheet at her side in a rough fist again. "My last day in New York, before I left for D.C., I came by your office. I...I wanted to say good-bye."

I nodded. The memory was bittersweet. "Okay."

"You were on the phone with someone. Someone named Ashley. You told her you loved her. And you made sure to emphasize her name."

Who was Ashley? Why was Allison so sure she'd heard me declare my love for her? "What the hell are you talking about? Why would you think I'd make sure to emphasize the name? That doesn't even make any sense."

Allison's huff sounded irritated. "You're telling me you didn't know I was standing there? You didn't say that on purpose just to hurt me? To ensure I knew you'd moved on?"

"You thought I was trying to hurt you? Nice. That's great. Thank you."

"It was the only explanation that made any sense."

"Why would you even care? We'd been broken up for months. What difference could it have made to you?"

"Just because we'd broken up, do you think I was okay with you rubbing some woman named Ashley in my face?"

I stopped. I didn't know anyone by that name. I'd never known anyone named Ashley. Allison must've heard wrong because—

The phone rang, and I looked to Allison as though she could tell me who was calling and why. She looked as surprised as I felt, and I glanced at the clock on the nightstand. A call at this time of night was never a good thing.

"Is that your phone or mine?" I asked.

"I don't know." She crawled out of bed and padded over to the desk. We'd just been arguing, so I shouldn't have been distracted by the smorgasbord of delectable flesh on display, but I was.

Allison looked down at her phones and then turned back to me and shook her head. "Not mine."

I groaned and rolled out of bed, then followed the ringing sound. Sure enough, it was coming from my purse, which was still on the floor near the door. I cursed and retrieved it, hoping it was a wrong number or someone had butt-dialed me. The name on the caller ID shattered those dreams.

I looked at Allison. "It's my boss."

Her forehead wrinkled. "Why's he calling you now?"

"No clue." I sighed heavily. I never wanted to talk to Mark on a good day, so I definitely wasn't in the mood for his special brand of shenanigans now. I rubbed my temple as I thumbed the answer button and lifted the phone to my ear. "O'Connor."

"Where are you?" Mark sounded almost angry, which didn't improve my disposition.

I watched Allison as she slid back into bed and pulled the covers over herself. She propped herself up with several pillows and busied herself with her phone. She didn't appear angry, but she didn't look happy either. I didn't blame her. I wouldn't have been particularly pleased if she'd interrupted our fight to take a phone call.

"O'Connor?"

"Yes. Sorry. I'm here. What did you need?"

"I need to know where you are right now."

"Why?"

"Are you at home?"

Alarm bells jangled loudly in the back of my head. He didn't generally concern himself with my whereabouts when I was off duty, and I wasn't willing to set that precedent. "What can I help you with, Mark?"

"I need to know how quickly you can get to NYFO. I know you live in the city."

"Why? What happened?"

Allison glanced up from her phone then and gave me a questioning look. I shrugged and rolled my eyes.

"The two-to-ten guys locked someone up tonight, but obviously they won't be able to get him before a judge for several more hours. I need someone to babysit him until the six-to-two guys come on so they can go home and get some sleep."

Inwardly, I groaned. I closed my eyes and thumped my head lightly against the wall. This was most definitely not the best time for me to come to the aid of my country or my coworkers. For one thing, Allison and I apparently had some issues to resolve. For another, I was still a little tipsy.

"Are the midnight response guys available?" I wanted to know.

"Do you think I'd be calling you if they were?"

I did, actually. But now didn't seem like the best time to point that out. My shoulders sagged, and my heart sank. "I'll be there as soon as I can. Tell the guys to expect me within the hour."

I didn't bother to wait for a reply. I simply hung up and took a deep breath. Would Allison be relieved I was leaving or angry we wouldn't get to finish our argument? With a bellyful of dread, I opened my eyes and met her frank stare.

"I'm sorry," I said softly. "I have to go."

Allison's eyes narrowed, and she folded her arms across her chest, pursing her lips. "Okay."

My intestines tried to climb up into my chest and suffocate my heart. I took a tentative step toward her, unsure how to proceed. I wasn't even sure what I wanted, let alone how to get it. I stared at her as I attempted to divine my own desires as well as hers.

"I really am sorry," I said.

Allison unfolded her arms and ran one hand through her hair. She still seemed annoyed but not necessarily at me. She shook her head and waved her other hand. "Don't worry about it. If anyone understands, it's me. Duty calls. What can you do?"

"Yeah." That about summed it up.

"Are you going to be okay?"

"What do you mean?"

"You had quite a bit to drink tonight."

"I'll be fine. I'm not driving, and I only have to babysit this guy for a couple hours until the day tour comes in. He'll have already been searched by the time I get there. I won't have to actually interact with him. I'll just have to watch him and make sure he doesn't somehow try to kill himself. I won't even need to take my gun out of its lock box."

"Okay." She was studying me intently.

I had no idea what else to say, so I started to collect my clothes. Allison stared at me silently the entire time. I didn't look directly at her, but I could see her out of the corner of my eye, and her attention never wavered. Each second I remained under her scrutiny, I became more tense.

Finally, when I was completely clothed and out of reasons to avoid looking at her, I turned back to the bed. I wanted to rush over to her and fall back into her arms. I wanted to run from the room as fast I could. I wanted to sit down and hash out all the issues we'd never bothered to resolve. I wanted her to never speak to me again because I was terrified of what she'd say. I didn't know what the hell I wanted.

"Allison, I—"

"It's okay." She seemed guarded, almost cold, totally impenetrable. That made me nervous.

"Are…Are you sure?" I hated to leave things with her like this.

She attempted a smile, but the result was pitiful. "I'm sure. Go."

I hesitated. Should I kiss her? I'd never had to leave anyone this abruptly in the middle of an unfinished argument. I'd certainly never had to run out on someone I had a history with, someone I might have a future with. I had no idea what she expected.

Allison pulled the sheet tighter around her and nodded in the direction of the door. "Good night, Ryan."

My heart cracked. "Good night, Allison."

CHAPTER TWENTY-TWO

The cab ride to NYFO was longer than I wanted it to be, not because I wanted to get to the office but because it gave me far too much time to think. Thinking only reminded me how completely at sea I was when it came to the direction of my life.

As the car sped down the nearly deserted FDR, I wondered whether our night of passion was a one-time thing. I sighed heavily and allowed my head to loll back on the seat. Allison and I needed to talk about a lot of issues. When—or if—would we ever do that?

I was still attracted to her, true. Recalling her kiss lit a blazing fire in certain parts of my body. And I obviously still had very deep and powerful feelings for her, but I couldn't just go back to being what we'd once been. Not again. I was older now, if not necessarily wiser. I didn't want to be someone's dirty little secret. Not even hers. Not even for a hundred nights like the one we'd just had. My lungs shriveled and my gut clenched at the thought.

Where did that leave us? Should I reach out to her or give her space and let her determine for herself whether she wanted to speak to me? I definitely didn't want to open myself up for rejection by initiating the discussion, but would the conversation ever happen if I didn't start it? My indecisiveness was irritating the hell out of me.

I'd originally thought the task of watching the prisoner would drive thoughts of Allison from my mind, but he'd had his head down on the table when I'd arrived. After I determined he was merely sleeping and not dead, I didn't have much else to occupy myself. So I stared at him through the one-way mirror from the adjacent interviewing room and tried—and failed—not to let myself get too tied up in knots.

By the time the six-to-two guys finally rolled in, I'd nearly worn a path in the linoleum by pacing and about driven myself insane with all my speculating and worrying. I originally hadn't looked forward to administering the rest of the PT tests that morning, but at least it would distract me from my own overactive imagination, temporarily.

Always prepared, I had a spare suit stashed in my closet at my desk and an extra set of PT clothes in my locker. After the day guys had relieved me, I took the world's fastest shower, dressed, and headed to the gym.

I barreled through the door as I wiped droplets of water from my cheeks, which had dripped down from my still-wet hair. My untied shoelaces flapped about my ankles as I walked.

"Ryan," a deep voice called the second I was in the door.

"What?" I turned toward the sound, and my face blazed as I realized who I was talking to.

Matt Levise, one of the office's three Assistant-Special-Agents-In-Charge—or ASAICs—strode my way, looking all business. He was dressed in his normal attire—dress slacks and a button-down shirt with a tie—so clearly he wasn't there to join the PT test. He had a sheaf of papers in his hands and a slightly amused twinkle in his eye. Not much to go on.

"Oh, good morning, sir," I said quickly. Matt—despite how I might address him or refer to him in conversation, I was still having trouble thinking of him as ASAIC Levise—was two levels above me in the NYFO chain of command, which meant only one other person was between him and the SAIC. It was always a good idea to show a certain amount of deference to a man of his pay grade. Well, unless that man was an ass. Then all bets were off.

Matt gave me a stern look. "Sir? Seriously, Ryan. How many times do we have to go over this?"

I shrugged and smiled up at him. "At least once more, as always. Sir." He made a face at me, which I ignored. Instead, I inclined my head toward the papers in his hand. "Those for me?"

He nodded but didn't hand them over. He cut a quick glance toward where the guys and girls I'd be testing were milling about and chatting idly and then motioned for me to walk with him out into the hall.

"I'll be right back, guys," I called to them. "If you need to hit the head, now's the time. You have two minutes."

Once the door snicked shut behind me, and we were alone in the hallway, Matt fixed me with a steadily appraising look. It was difficult for me to determine what he was looking for or what he found. His demeanor was what people expected of a Secret Service agent, and his countenance gave away nothing. For lack of anything better to do, I held my hand out, wordlessly asking for the stack of PT score sheets. After he'd handed them over, I began to flip through them, counting silently in my head. A lot more folks needed to squeeze this in than just the guys in my squad.

After staring at me, Matt spoke, his tone even and measured. "How are you feeling today?"

I glanced at him from underneath my eyebrows without lifting my head. "I'm fine." Was he asking because I actually looked as exhausted as I felt or because he'd heard I'd been out with the guys the night before. Either was possible, and both were mildly irksome.

"Fine enough to actually take the PT test while you're administering it?"

I frowned. I hadn't been expecting that question. I also wasn't even remotely in the mood. "I already took my test for the quarter."

"I know you did." Matt hesitated and glanced away, but it didn't appear as though his eyes were actually seeing what they were looking at. It did, however, seem as if he was weighing something in his mind. It took a few moments, but eventually he must've made a decision. He tapped the top paper in my hands with the tips of two fingers.

I glanced down and noted the name typed neatly at the top of the standardized Secret Service PT form. Eric Banks. The name didn't ring a bell. I looked back up at Matt and met his steady gaze.

"He's new," Matt informed me as if reading my mind. "He's been out of training for maybe four months. He's in Counterfeit."

"Okay."

"I've been hearing some pretty disturbing things about him. He's cocky. He's arrogant. Apparently he walks around here like he's God's gift to the world."

The muscles in my face twitched as I attempted to rein in a smirk. "Well, all of us are just a shade too cocky for our own good, don't you think? We sort of have to be. I drove you crazy when I first started, remember?"

"You were a smart-ass, true enough. Still are, from what I can see. But I'd never describe you as cocky."

"Thanks. I think."

Matt flashed me a tight-lipped smile. "This kid is different," he insisted. "I've been watching him the past couple weeks. Shows up late. Leaves early. Argues with or questions every single order he's given. Has an opinion on everything. His way is always better. Never mind that he's only been on the job a hot five minutes. He has an answer for everything and won't listen to anybody. In short, he's a real pain in the ass."

And he was about to become Rico's problem. Wonderful. "It's a wonder no one's thrown him a blanket party."

"Believe me, some of the guys are about ready to. He needs the wind taken out of his sails a little bit."

I'd known Matt for several years now. He'd been the AT of the Human Resources and Training Squad when I'd first started, which meant we'd spent a fair amount of time together at the outset. He was the exact opposite of my current boss, Mark. He was kind and fair and patient, so I knew if he was saying all of this about this kid, it was true.

"Did you talk to the scheduling guys? They're excellent at this sort of thing."

"I did. And they've been working on it. Midnight vehicle-security assignments, stairwell post standing, and duty-desk shifts abound for this guy. So far, he isn't getting it."

"I see. So, where do I come in?"

"Turn his paper over."

I did and discovered a small sticky note with some numbers jotted on it. It didn't take a genius to figure out they were the scores recorded from his last PT test, which I presumed had been administered while he was still in Beltsville. "Impressive."

"Yeah," Matt said dryly. "He thinks so, too. Apparently, he was quite the recruit in training. Won both the PT and the shooting award for the class."

"Good for him. Does he know that doesn't mean shit in the field?"

"He appears to be having considerable trouble grasping that concept."

"And you want me to assist him in that arena," I said, finally catching on.

"If you're up for it."

"Is that an order?" I was in an awkward position here. I definitely didn't want to go against Matt's wishes, but I was having a hard time getting excited about competing with a fellow agent, even a cocky new one practically begging to have his bell rung. It simply wasn't my style.

"Think of it as a friendly request."

Damn. I'd been hoping he'd let me off the hook by taking the decision completely out of my hands and making it a directive. No such luck. I glanced back at the kid's scores so I could consider the matter.

"The pull-ups are going to be tough," I said after a moment. "I might be able to swing the push-ups. Maybe. If I can break protocol and have one of the guys count for me."

Matt gave me a quizzical look.

"Bigger hands," I explained. "I won't have to go down quite as far to make contact and have the rep count."

Mentally, I ran through the faces of the guys I'd seen during my extremely brief stop in the gym, trying to decide who'd best be able to aid me. I needed one with big hands, who wouldn't get all immature about the fact that I'd basically be rubbing my breasts against him with every push-up. That was why we generally had the women count for one another and left the men out of the equation. It was easier to avoid sexual-harassment lawsuits—and maintain plausible deniability—that way.

An emotion not unlike triumph flickered in Matt's dark eyes. He knew he had me. "It's the run I really need you to hammer him on. Apparently the guy thinks he's some sort of Olympic-caliber marathoner. If you can even come close to matching him in any of the upper-body strength tests, that's just gravy. And I know you've got the sit-ups locked."

I consulted the score sheet again. That last statement about the sit-ups appeared to be true enough. But I said, "I hate running."

"Really? But you're so good at it."

"Only because I want it to be over as quickly as possible."

Actually, that was only partly true. My sister had run track all through high school and college and insisted on dragging me along when she'd trained. I only ran half as much as I did to this day because she and I tried to meet once a week to run together, if our schedules permitted it, and no way in hell would my pride let me lag behind. I was greatly looking forward to the day when Rory lost interest in running altogether so I could regress to training only as hard as I needed to so I could pass my PT test.

"So, you'll do it?"

I sighed softly. "Yes, sir."

Matt smiled at me and turned to go, but he'd barely gone two steps before he stopped. "Ryan?"

"Yeah?" My free hand was poised on the door to the gym.

"You might want to do the run outside today. Perhaps on the bridge."

"Why? You think he won't be used to the incline at the beginning, and it will give me an edge?"

"No. You can smoke him without that. But it will be useful for you to have an excuse to wear a turtleneck or a scarf or something."

"Why would I need to wear a scarf?"

"To cover that hickey on your neck."

"What?"

Surely he wasn't teasing me. I'd been in such a rush earlier I hadn't even glanced at myself in a mirror, so maybe he was just fishing, hoping I'd give something away.

Matt's smile widened into a full-fledged grin, and that mischievous twinkle was back in his eye again. The tips of my ears burned, and I instinctively sought out the nearest escape.

"I guess that means you and Allison finally worked things out. It's about damn time."

My blood suddenly ran as cold as though someone had injected ice water directly into my heart. I tried hard to cover and keep my face completely neutral, but I wasn't quick enough, if Matt's low chuckle was any indication. Shit! What the hell would make him say that? I knew he and Allison were sort of chummy, but I didn't think she'd actually talk to him about me, no matter how close they were. And what did he mean about us finally working things out? I wasn't sure I wanted to know.

"Allison who?" I said.

Matt made a low noise in the back of his throat. "Really, Ryan? That's what you're going with?"

"I have no idea what you're talking about." I hoped my deliberately bland tone was convincing.

"Oh, I'm fairly certain you do." He was enjoying this way too much.

"What makes you think Allison had anything to do with it?" I demanded, wanting to protect her.

Matt merely gave me a knowing look and pointed at himself with his thumb. "Trained criminal investigator." And with that, he turned and strode away, chuckling.

I scowled and slunk back into the gym.

CHAPTER TWENTY-THREE

I glanced at the clock hanging on the wall in my office as I finished inputting the last of the PT scores. It was still relatively early, and I still hadn't heard from Allison, but I was trying hard not to think about that. I was also trying not to check my email every two seconds. Between the lack of sleep and all my worrying, I was drained. It was going to be an extremely long day—hell, a long two weeks—if I was already this spent. Maybe it wasn't too late for me to call in sick for the next month or so.

I leaned back in my chair and stretched, which caught Meaghan's attention. She looked up from whatever she'd been doing to fix me with a contemplative expression. "Tired?" Meaghan wanted to know.

"I'll live."

"You sure about that? You look terrible. Did something happen?"

I shook my head. "No. I just had to take the PT test this morning. We ran the bridge."

Meaghan blinked. "Didn't you already take your test for last quarter?"

I sighed. Matt had, of course, been one hundred percent correct in his assessment of Eric Banks. Within five minutes of our formal introduction, he'd extolled the virtues of my ass to one of the other guys in a loud whisper; made crude comments in reference to wanting to watch me and one of his female classmates count push-ups for one another in a somewhat louder voice, which I'm positive he meant at least her to hear; and implied that he was in better physical shape than all of us and disappointed no one would present him much of a challenge. Needless to say, I'd thoroughly enjoyed disabusing him of that last notion.

"I did. But I wanted to take it again, and now I'm beat."

"You sure that's it?"

"What else would it be?"

"Don't know." A pause. "Did you go to the wheels-up party last night?" She averted her eyes as she asked that, and I tensed.

"Yeah."

"Good time?"

I narrowed my eyes at her. What was she getting at? "Always."

She cleared her throat, still staring at the papers on her desk in a show of acting casual that was so forced I was positive anyone would be able to see through it. "Was Allison there?" Her voice was strained.

I inhaled sharply and prayed she hadn't heard. "Why?"

She shrugged. "Just curious."

I didn't know what difference that made or how to answer. I also didn't care to share the mental images that immediately popped into my head, although they did make me blush. I adjusted the collar of my dress shirt to make sure the hickey—which was indeed present and extremely noticeable—was covered. Meaghan had most likely already seen it, but that didn't stop me from trying to hide it anyway.

"She was, yes."

"Must've been nice to see her again." I hadn't thought it possible, but Meaghan's voice sounded even tighter.

"It was fine." I didn't know what Meaghan was angling for, but she wasn't getting anything else out of me. Partly because I respected Allison's privacy, but mostly because I wasn't in the mood for all Meaghan's questions or to try to get to the bottom of her sudden attitude problem. Whatever was bothering her was going to have to wait.

But now that she'd brought it up, and I was thinking about Allison again—though admittedly I'd never really stopped—I reached for my personal phone to see whether she'd contacted me. I really hated the dive my spirits took when I confirmed she hadn't, and I hated myself more for even caring. Of course she hadn't reached out to me. She probably—Shit! Lucia still had my personal phone. Maybe that's why I hadn't heard from Allison today. A glimmer of hope blossomed.

I glanced at the clock again before mentally reviewing Allison's schedule. She should be almost to the airport by now. Surely she'd at least text me to let me know she'd made it there safely and on time.

Hmm. Should I email her on her work phone to let her know I didn't have my personal cell? Or would that seem needy and desperate?

"You ready to go?" Meaghan's inquiry startled me out of my reverie.

I yawned and started shutting down my computer. "Yeah. All set. Thanks for waiting."

She was giving me the strangest look. Maybe she didn't even know about Lucia. Had I told her about the breakup? I couldn't remember. When was the last time I'd seen her anyway? Was it before Lucia had broken up with me or after?

"No problem," Meaghan said, her thoughts obviously in a completely different place than mine. "I had some paperwork I needed to finish anyway. Do you have a list of all the addresses we need to hit?"

"Yup. There are four I'd like to get to today. I have two on tap for tomorrow. And I thought we'd squeeze another visit to Akbari in somewhere, if we have the time."

Meaghan's gawk suggested disbelief and exasperation. "That's a lot of interviews, Ryan. And then you still have to actually type the report."

"I know. I'm really sorry to drag you out on all this. I can ask someone else if it's too much or if you have something else to do."

She waved a hand in my direction. "It isn't me I'm worried about. When does Iran come in?"

"Thursday."

"What time?"

"Wheels down is currently scheduled for eleven-hundred."

"How's the advance going?"

"As well as can be expected." I shrugged. No intel was good intel as far as I was concerned, and that's what all my sources on the subject had indicated thus far. I'd keep checking periodically up to and all through the visit to confirm that didn't change.

Meaghan shook her head, looking disgusted. "Ryan, let me write the closing report for the Dougherty case for you."

I scoffed. "No way! I'm not letting you steal cases from me. You get your own."

Meaghan fixed me with a murderous glare. "Stop being a smart-ass. You're going to kill yourself trying to finish all this work before the visit. You're still exhausted from last week. Let me help."

I was touched and prayed she'd understand. "I appreciate that, Meg. I really do. But I need to do this on my own."

"You feel like you have something to prove to him, don't you?"

"If I don't do this, Mark'll think he's been right about me, that I can't handle it."

"And if you do somehow manage to pull it off, he'll keep burying you in work just because he wants to see where your breaking point is."

"Ah. So that's what they mean when they say caught between a rock and a hard place."

Meaghan shook her head but had only sympathy in her eyes. "Please, just promise me you'll let me know if you change your mind."

"I promise. And thanks for the offer."

"What are friends for?"

"Ryan?" a new voice interjected itself into our conversation.

I glanced away from Meaghan's smiling face to see Mark hovering in our doorway. His expression was odd, and I couldn't help wondering how much he'd overheard. While I couldn't put my finger on exactly what was different about him, something was. It wasn't just the manner and tone he used to address me, though that was strange enough. He normally strutted around like he was big man on campus, but now he appeared tense, almost tentative and jumpy. This change made me distinctly uneasy.

"Yes, Mark?"

"I need to talk to you." He hesitated and cut his eyes toward Meaghan. "Do you have a minute?"

"I'll go get the car," Meaghan told me, either unwilling or unable to disguise her worry that'd blossomed when Mark appeared. "I'll meet you out front in five."

I nodded to her but refocused my attention on Mark and waved to the seat in front of my desk. He glanced at it and looked almost lost for a second, as if he wasn't sure what to do with the chair, before settling stiffly in it. He rested his right ankle atop his left knee, and his fingers drummed restless patterns on the tops of his thighs. Wait, was he wearing a skull-and-crossbones tie tack? Was his pirate obsession that out of control? I tried to get a closer look without being obvious about it.

"I know you're busy, so I'll get right to the point," he said, dragging me away from thoughts on his choice of accessories. "We need to discuss that counterfeit call you went out on the other night."

Why was he still dwelling on that? "What about it?"

"I know you used to be some sort of counterfeit superagent back in the day, but you're in PI now. You can't just go out on any kind of cases you want. Regardless of who's asking. You need to drop it."

His tone was almost gentle, which made me wary. Usually he preferred the strong-arm technique, at least when it came to dealing with me. Why the sudden switch in tactics? But I didn't reply.

"You have dropped it, haven't you?" Mark asked, and I thought I detected a faint tremor in his voice. That ratcheted my confusion up another notch.

How should I respond? Now that I had what appeared to be a possible nexus to terrorism in the Akbari case, I was within my rights to investigate it as I saw fit. Mark had absolutely no control over what work I did for the Task Force. And it'd feel rather nice to point that out to him. But why was he even presenting me with that opportunity? It had to be some sort of trap.

Perhaps it was time to try a different approach. For once, he appeared to be attempting to engage me in an adult conversation, sans insults, blustering, and bravado. I didn't understand his sudden change of heart, but maybe I should take full advantage of it. Who knew? Perhaps this would be a turning point for us.

I needed to word my answer just right, give him enough detail to satisfy his curiosity, so he'd feel like he was in the loop, but not divulge too much. Mark may've been my boss, but he was a Secret Service boss, which meant he didn't need to be and shouldn't be privy to the specifics of my terrorism-related cases.

"I'm still looking into it," I told him honestly. "Some new information has come to my attention that, if verified, places the investigation directly in my purview."

"What information?"

"The subject may have ties to known terrorism targets. Like I said, I'm still looking into it."

"And if you confirm he does, he becomes the subject of a JTTF investigation." Mark's eyes held a far-away cast, and he appeared to be thinking rather than having a discussion with me.

I answered him anyway. "That's generally the way it works."

Mark's focus snapped back to me at my admittedly unnecessary quip, and he stared at me for a very long time, saying nothing and moving even less. Only his eyes indicated he'd even heard me, and the emotions swirling around there moved too quickly for me to grasp. But he wasn't exactly happy with what I'd just said.

I held my breath as I waited for the explosion headed my way. The tension in the room was palpable, and if this were a television show, I was certain some Old-West-type music would have underscored the standoff. I was tempted to whistle along with the soundtrack playing in my head, but that probably wouldn't be a good idea. I doubted Mark would see the humor. He never did.

After a while, Mark exhaled noisily. The muscles in his jaw and cheeks tensed as though he were pursing his lips in thought. He slowly pushed himself to a standing position, his dark eyes never once leaving mine. "I see," he finally said, after simply staring down at me.

He turned to go—had actually made it most of the way out of my office—but he stopped abruptly in my doorway as though something had occurred to him. He slowly pivoted back around to face me, his facial expression odd and unreadable. A sort of cold dread seeped over me, but I couldn't pinpoint why.

"Have you told anyone about this?"

"Excuse me?"

"Your superiors over at the JTTF. Have you told them anything about this case?"

"No. Not yet. Why?"

A pause. "I think it would be a good idea for you to brief me, the SAIC, and the AT of the Counterfeit Squad about as much of this as you can before you start talking to the FBI bosses about it. That's all."

Hmm. He wasn't necessarily wrong. The bosses hated it when someone blindsided them with stuff they felt they should've known. It probably wouldn't hurt to fill in all the pertinent parties—as much as I was able, considering the nature of the investigation—before I opened an active case.

"Of course. You're right. And I definitely will. As soon as I get some more concrete info, I'll let you know."

"Thanks."

And with that, he exited the doorway, leaving me to gawk after him.

CHAPTER TWENTY-FOUR

The next few days passed in a hectic blur of driving, talking, and typing, and by the time Thursday rolled around, I was teetering on the edge of exhaustion and ready to drop.

Of course, it didn't help that I still hadn't heard from Allison, and I was cursing that it distracted me so much. Thoughts of her had trickled into the cracks in my day and took up far more time than I'd wanted them to. Sleeping with her had been a terrible idea. I tried to tell myself that her silence was a good thing, that it sent a message on par with the lights on the Las Vegas strip that we wanted different things and would save me a lot of grief and heartache in the end, but the mental pep talk didn't help.

I was also cursing my own stubbornness and wondering what'd possessed me to turn down Meaghan's offer of assistance. If I'd taken her up on it, I might've gotten more than seven hours of sleep in the past two days. Oh, well. At least I didn't have to drive. That would've been disastrous for everyone. No one likes it when you're asleep behind the wheel in a motorcade.

I glanced at the lucky bastard who'd drawn the short straw and had to chauffeur me around for the next eleven-to-infinity days. Michael Prince was the picture of spry and together, damn him, and when he noticed me looking at him, he smiled.

"You okay?"

I sighed. "Yeah." I took a sip of my third cup of coffee and winced at the temperature.

"Mark been beating you up?"

"Nothing I can't handle. You?"

"Nah. I'm good."

"How'd that report work out for you the other day?" Or had it been last week? I wasn't sure. Jesus, I was tired.

"Good. Thanks. You were a big help."

I waved my free hand dismissively. "No problem."

"I gotta tell you, I was really looking forward to this assignment."

"Why's that?"

"I like to take a break from investigations every once in a while, you know? The change of pace is good for me."

"It is that." I didn't even have the energy to converse. The remainder of my day wasn't looking good.

"So, what's the schedule like today, anyway?"

The president of Iran had arrived on time, and we were shuttling him from the airport to New York City, where we had days upon days of meetings and appointments and dinners to look forward to. It wouldn't be very interesting for us, nor would it be much fun. But all our visits couldn't consist of live performances by Jon Bon Jovi or the Edge.

I consulted the mini survey I'd received from the lead advance agent while we'd killed time at the airport waiting for the delegation to land. "Down time at the hotel until seventeen-hundred. Then meetings at the UN for the remainder of the day. Dinner at Nobu at twenty-one hundred. TBD after that."

I groaned as the words left my mouth. TBD was never a good sign. That could mean we were going back to the hotel for the night—and I'd be able to get some much-needed sleep—or it could mean we were going out on the town. We wouldn't know until the president or one of the members of his delegation told us. I frowned at my coffee cup. How much caffeine could the human body effectively consume? I must've conducted that experiment before, but I couldn't remember what I'd come up with.

"You gonna make it?"

"Huh? Oh, yeah. I'm good." I rolled my head from side to side to crack my neck and opened the window a bit, hoping some cool air would enliven me.

"Can I ask you something?"

"Sure. Shoot."

Michael hesitated. "I've never driven in a motorcade before."

I blinked at him and sat up straighter. Holy shit. I must've been really out of it to not have asked him that question. I was a fairly senior agent in the PI Squad and as a result almost always had someone my junior drive. I always reviewed the rules of motorcade driving with my counterpart if I hadn't worked with them before. How could I have dropped the ball on that?

"In a PI capacity or ever?" I asked, just to clarify.

"Ever. Well, except in training. But it's been a while, and I'm a little rusty."

"Oh, Michael, I'm so sorry. I can't believe I forgot to ask."

"It's my fault. I should've said something earlier. I just don't want to do anything wrong, you know?"

"No. I flubbed it. I normally go over that while we're waiting on the tarmac for wheels down. PI driving is easy and actually a lot of fun. While we're here in the city, NYPD will assist us with intersection control. Just follow the pace of the rest of the motorcade. Stick close enough to Follow-Up so no one can get between us, but allow them enough room to maneuver. Help them clear the merges when you can. And if someone who doesn't belong breaks into the motorcade, use your lights and sirens to encourage them to leave. If they don't take the hint, either pit them or ram them, whichever is easier and whichever keeps the rest of the motorcade out of danger."

After a click on the car radio, I heard the lead inform the hotel security room agents that we'd cleared a particular checkpoint, which cued them, and everyone else, that we were about five minutes out. The hotel agent responded and gave a preliminary situation report.

Michael chuckled—presumably at my last statement, as I saw nothing amusing in what'd just come out over the air—and then he glanced at me out of the corner of his eye. He seemed to be waiting for me to laugh with him, and when I didn't, his eyes widened. "You're serious."

"Yup." I shifted my attention from him to the passing scenery, so I could scrutinize folks on the street.

"You want me to ram a car if it gets into our motorcade."

"Yup. Like I said, we'll have intersection control here in the city. If someone gets into our motorcade who isn't us, they already went through a police checkpoint to do it. Which, to me, says ill intent. I have no idea what that could possibly mean, but whatever they're trying to do, we need to make sure it doesn't happen to or near the limo. And if we can take care of it and keep the working shift out of it so they can continue to attend to the protectee, well, then we've done our job."

Silence for a long moment. "You are hard-core, Ryan."

I grinned before resuming my inspection of the people and buildings scattered along the New York City streets. "Thanks."

"And a little crazy."

"I've heard that before."

"This is going to be an interesting week, isn't it?"

"Oh, you can pretty much count on that." My cell phone vibrated on my belt, and my heart leapt. Could it be Allison? My hand was trembling as I retrieved it and checked the caller ID. It was a blocked number, but that didn't mean anything. If she called me from her work cell phone, the number would show up as blocked. Tendrils of hope wound their way around my heart as I answered. "O'Connor."

"Hey, Ryan. It's Sarah."

Those fragile tendrils immediately turned to ash, and disappointment flared inside my chest. I tried to tamp down my violently eddying emotions. "Hey, kiddo. What's up?"

"I got a mysterious email that you had a few requests for me. I'm not sending you pictures of my boobs, so stop asking."

I grinned. "Fine. I'll just do what everyone else does and get them from your website. How about this? When you have a minute, I need you to email me the cell-phone number you have for Akbari, as well as .pdf copies of the source where you got that number from. And I'd like to look at that bill he passed, also."

I broke off to allow the radio chatter between the lead, the Follow-Up, the hotel agent, and the detail leader in the limo to subside. We were less than two minutes out, and apparently the situation over at the hotel was relatively clear.

"Sounds like you're busy," Sarah commented.

"I told you before, we actually earn our paychecks up here."

"Why work harder when you can work smarter? Who've you got?"

"Iran."

"Ugh. Have fun with that."

"You know something I don't?"

"Only that you're not going to be getting much sleep. The guy likes to stay out late."

"Of course he does." I massaged one temple with my fingertips. "Fantastic."

Sarah laughed. "I'll fire that info to you ASAP. Give 'em hell for me."

"Will do." I hung up the phone and slid it back into its holster as I unbuckled my seat belt. As the motorcade rolled to a stop, I hopped out and began my 360-degree perusal of the street and all its occupants. The flurry of activity I could hear behind me gradually tapered off, indicating the delegation had made it safely inside. Only then did I wander back over to Michael in the PI car.

He rolled his window down at my approach. "What's up?"

I glanced past the arrival area toward the front of the motorcade to where I could see the guy in charge of the cars pointing and gesturing as he tried to get everyone lined up for our departure in a few hours. I tapped the doorframe with my palm.

"Hang here until Charlie tells you where he wants you. After that, you can pop inside to hit the head or around the corner to grab something to eat at the deli if you want. Just make sure you leave the keys either with me, if I'm down here, or with the Follow-Up driver."

Michael nodded. "No problem. I probably will hit the deli. You want anything?"

"A bottle of water would be great, thanks." I dipped my hand into my pocket to pull out some cash, but Michael waved me away.

"We have a long trip ahead of us. I'm sure you'll get me back at some point."

"Thanks."

I shifted my attention to the street again. Iran had chosen to stay at the Waldorf Astoria, which took up the entire city block between 49th and 50th Streets and Park and Lexington Avenues. Personally, I loved it when our protectees stayed there. The Waldorf had a covered arrival area that made arrivals and departures relatively drama-free, and they were so used to us being in and out with all of our delegations that working with the staff there was like using a well-oiled machine.

It also happened to be located just across the street from The W Hotel, where Allison and I had recently spent an incredible couple of hours together wrapped up in one another's arms. The thought sparked a myriad of conflicting emotions within me, and a slight flush crept into my cheeks as memories from that night flitted through my mind. I forcibly pushed them away.

"Yo, Ryan?" I felt a tap on my shoulder in time with the greeting and turned to face the speaker. It was Charlie Parker, the agent in charge of transportation security for the visit.

"Hi, Charlie. What's up?"

"I'm gonna back the PI car out onto five-oh, and then I'm gonna park you guys on Lex between four-eight and four-nine, right by the side entrance to the Intercon. Okay?" His stereotypical New York accent and wildly gesticulating hands made me want to smile.

I shrugged and glanced at Michael to make sure he'd heard the instructions before I nodded. "It's your motorcade, Charlie. I'll go wherever you tell me to go."

Charlie nodded once. "Yeah, the well gets crowded, ya know what I mean? Gotta save some space for the guests or the Waldorf gets pissed." I barely managed to dodge a punctuating hand as he said that. "So, we're gonna stage most of the cars out on four-nine goin' counterflow cuz the next movement is to the UN. But I want a presence out on Lex, too. Someone we have coms with. That'll be you." A forceful finger jab in my direction. "And you guys just merge into the motorcade when we make the right on Lex."

I tamped down a smile and fought the urge to point right back at him. "Whatever you need, Charlie."

"Great." He clapped me on the shoulder and strode off.

I turned to Michael and rested my arm on the open windowsill of the driver-side door. "You heard the man. Back this beast out onto five-oh, and then square the block and stage on Lex. I'll have the guys behind you back up so you can get out."

"You want me to block a lane of traffic on Lex?"

I nodded. "That's the only way to do this. Put your hazards on and tell the cops at the checkpoint at the end of the block what you're up to so they know not to give you a hard time."

"The general public won't like that."

"Trust me, I know. And they won't be even a little bit shy about making their displeasure heard."

Michael grinned widely. "It's gonna be one helluva visit, isn't it?"

I rolled my eyes. "Oh, yeah."

CHAPTER TWENTY-FIVE

Most people I've talked to seem to think my job is glamorous. And I guess it sort of is. Sometimes. I've met some really cool people in my line of work, and I've seen a lot of things I never would've had the chance to witness if I worked for someone else.

But those times are the exception rather than the rule. More often than not, especially when I'm on protection, I spend my day in a holding pattern, waiting for someone to move or something to happen. I've often said I get paid not for what I do, but for what I might have to do.

That was true on this visit. We had long days of meeting after meeting and even longer nights of basically waiting for the delegation to finish their endless dinners. Sarah had been right; the guy did like to stay out late, and he started moving way too early. I wasn't getting any closer to catching up on sleep than I'd been several days ago, and I was really beginning to become petulant. As far as I was concerned, the visit couldn't end fast enough. Too bad we were only in the middle of it.

That I still hadn't heard from Allison wasn't helping my disposition. All the sitting around gave me ample time to check and recheck my phone and become more and more agitated because she hadn't reached out to me since I'd left her hotel room. And the more days that passed without word from her, the more unlikely the prospect looked.

Of course, I kept reminding myself that I hadn't reached out to her either, and then I wondered whether I should just put on my big-girl pants and call her. I was obviously still undecided. And the longer I delayed, the harder it became to rationalize that calling would be appropriate. Then I became even more despondent.

I sighed and looked at my watch. Only three minutes had passed since the last time I'd checked it. The day wasn't even half over, and already I wanted to put the protectee in his hotel suite and barricade the door so he couldn't come out. Maybe then I'd be able to get some rest. Or at least I could worry myself into a tizzy over Allison in private. This was going to be a long freaking day.

A tap on my car window startled me out of my fog, and I blinked. God, I was really losing it. I scowled as I rolled down the window. Where the hell was Michael with my coffee? I could use a serious jolt of caffeine. Or maybe an adrenaline shot.

"Agent O'Connor," the auburn-haired woman standing there said, almost shyly.

"Oh. Hey, Anna. It's Ryan, please. I've told you that before."

Anna Strom had been out of the academy and on the job for only a couple of months, and no matter how many times I saw her, she insisted on calling me Agent O'Connor. It was as cute as it was unnecessary. For one thing, I was only a regular hump agent. I may've had a few grades on her, but the gap would close quickly, and it didn't matter enough for her to show me that sort of deference. It wasn't like I was a boss or anything. For another, I'd counted Anna's push-ups for her during the PT test I'd just administered and was convinced that feeling another woman's breasts, regardless of the circumstances, at least put you on a first-name basis.

Anna flushed and nodded. "Right. Sorry. Anyway, I was asked to tell you that the president is going to have a quick meeting at the Intercon before our next move to the UN."

I nodded wearily. I'd really been looking forward to the change of scenery the trip to the UN would provide, which said a whole lot about my mental state, as sitting at the UN kind of sucks. A lot. Now it looked like my reprieve from Lexington Avenue would be delayed.

"What time?" I wanted to claw my own eyes out. If staying in one place for only a couple of hours bored me this much, the rest of this visit would really be rough. I still had at least six days of this fiasco left.

"He's getting ready to move now."

"He'll be walking over, I presume?"

"That's the plan. The cars are going to relocate out here on Lex once he's inside. They'll probably pull right in front of you, actually, so they're stacked for the next movement."

"Okay." I eyed the empty street in front of my car as I attempted to size up the space and mentally calculate whether the necessary part of the motorcade would fit there or whether I should back up my car to make room. I was a little close to the door they'd be using. The pertinent cars probably wouldn't fit if I didn't move. But first, I had a question. "Do they want me to come in and shadow them for the walk? Or do they want me to wait out here?"

Anna's expression turned thoughtful. "Good question. Kyle didn't say. Do you want me to ask him?"

"Nah. That's okay. I'll do it. Thanks, Anna."

"No problem. Have fun. I have to get back up to the security room."

"Okay. Let me know if you need me to bring you anything."

Anna held up a white plastic bag. "I just grabbed some food. I'm all set, thanks."

She turned to go and almost ran into a middle-aged gentleman approaching my car with some sort of purpose. He seemed determined, and his posture radiated focused intent.

Anna stiffened and took a step back, creating distance between her and the man. She shifted her right arm so her forearm brushed the butt of her weapon and put her little bag on the ground, which freed her hands. I presumed this was in case he broke bad on us and started a brawl right here on the street. I'd always found her to be serious and intense, but this was taking it to a whole new level.

"Can I help you?" I asked the man, flashing him a smile.

His gray eyes flicked from Anna to me, and he appeared angry, though I couldn't imagine what could've set him off.

"Who's here?" he demanded, his voice gruff, his words clipped.

Ah. Now I understood the problem. But I played dumb. "I'm sorry?"

I could see the man's demeanor made Anna bristle, but I kept my tone pleasant and light. We were trained to establish rapport with the public, and I took that training to heart. It was an especially good idea when you considered how readily people called the office to tattle on us if they thought we'd treated them with anything less than total professionalism and respect.

He gestured to the police checkpoints and officers scattered all over the nearby corner, as if to emphasize his point. "I want to know who's here."

"You mean besides us?" I asked. I didn't often play the bimbo, but occasionally I found it necessary. It tended to put guys like this off guard.

The man rolled his eyes, clearly exasperated, but his apparent anger seemed to have ebbed. Chalking up his small change to my acting skills, I turned up the wattage on my smile and ran my hands through my hair, brushing it back off my shoulders.

"Yeah, besides us. This whole mess is seriously screwing with my commute. You and your checkpoints and road closures. I work my ass off. My taxes pay your salary! I have a right to know what you're doing here."

I wanted to laugh aloud but was careful not to. It wasn't the first time I'd heard that take on my chosen career. The notion never failed to amuse me. "Well, I pay taxes, too, so does that make me self-employed?"

The man frowned, but before the discussion could go even further south, I made a show of looking around and motioned him closer. He leaned in toward my window, forcing Anna to take another step back in order to maintain a safe distance between them.

"Have you ever heard of the Marshall Islands?" I asked him.

He blinked and eyed me almost suspiciously. I merely continued to smile up at him. Finally, he shook his head. "No, I haven't."

I spread my hands out in front of me and shrugged, allowing my smile to grow.

"Lot of pomp and circumstance for nothing," the man muttered to himself as he abruptly turned his back on me and stalked away.

"Why did you tell him that?" Anna wanted to know.

"Tell him what?"

"That we were working the Marshall Islands."

"I didn't actually tell him anything. I asked him a question. It's not my fault he assumed it was the answer he was looking for."

"Okay, so why'd you ask him that?"

"Why not?"

"It's none of his business who we're protecting. You shouldn't have to answer him at all."

"No, of course it isn't his business. But he was looking for some sort of answer, and I didn't think he'd go away until he got one.

I merely killed two birds with one stone. I preserved OpSec by not actually telling him who was here, and I got him to leave, which was my ultimate goal."

Anna's expression turned thoughtful. "Is the Marshall Islands a real place?"

"Yeah, it's a chain of islands in the Pacific between Hawaii and Australia. They were my first lead when I got out of the academy."

"What if you're actually guarding the Marshall Islands? What will you say then?"

I paused in my reply to pay attention to the radio traffic, which was announcing that the delegation was moving to the elevators. "I'll pick another country I don't think anyone has ever heard of. Mauritius or something."

Anna waved good-bye as she hustled back toward the Waldorf. I hopped out of the car and stretched a little. Slowly, I ambled to the corner of four-nine, gazing around, checking out the foot traffic on the street. I'd made the executive decision to wait for the delegation right there, smack in the middle of the walking route. The president had his entire shift with him. I didn't need to jump into the middle of all that chaos. I'd serve the detail better by remaining where I was and warning them if anything nefarious cropped up.

A minute or two later, Kyle Taggert, the lead advance agent for the visit, popped out of the Waldorf and started heading toward the corner of 49th and Lex where I was lingering. He was scowling darkly and shook his head when he saw me.

"Rough day, Kyle?" I asked softly as he neared. The rest of the delegation was about fifteen steps behind him. I did a quick check up and down the block, looking for trouble. People gawked a little—they always did when we went anywhere with anyone, as we aren't exactly a discreet bunch—but no one seemed particularly interested in approaching the gaggle, which made me happy. One of the many perks of working in New York.

"Dude, this sucks," Kyle muttered as he strode past.

I covered my mouth with my hand to hide my grin and turned slightly so I was facing north looking up Lexington Avenue and had my back to the procession and my eyes on the opposite side of the street. Keeping my eyes off the front door to The W was a Herculean feat, and I'm afraid I didn't manage it as well as I'd have liked. But after a long moment, the din of activity and motion behind me subsided, and a glance over my shoulder confirmed what I suspected; everyone was inside. Now the waiting game began anew until departure.

My BlackBerry vibrated on my belt, and I gritted my teeth. I almost never got good news on that thing. I doubted that now, smack-dab in the middle of the Iran visit, the trend would suddenly change. It was much more likely that whoever was on the other end was about to throw my world into bedlam, and I wasn't in the mood for the complete destruction of my already crumbling world.

"O'Connor."

"Hey," a low voice murmured in my ear, sending shivers up my spine.

My heart raced, and my stomach flailed around like a cartoon character walking across hot pavement. I eyed the motorcade cars as they rolled slowly by, so they could position for the departure. "Hey."

"Are you working right now?" Allison wanted to know.

"Yeah, but the delegation just went into a meeting, so I have a few minutes." I hesitated as I cast around for something to say, my eyes drawn back to The W completely against my will. "How are you?"

"I'm good. You?"

"Good."

"Good."

I was alternating between hot and cold and was light-headed. She'd called. I couldn't believe she'd actually called. I was thrilled. I was terrified. I also had no idea what I wanted to tell her.

"So," Allison said after a long pause. "Are you still mad at me?"

"What? I was never mad at you." I shifted my attention back to the cars. There'd been ample room for the limo in front of my car, but the Follow-Up was double-stacked next to me. I sighed and ambled over slowly.

"Really?" She sounded skeptical. "So you never answered my text because you've been too busy?"

"You texted me?" I rapped forcefully on the driver's side window to the Follow-Up. "Hang on a second, Allison." I rested the phone against my chest to muffle the sounds of my conversation.

Bill Steelman, an agent in our office who I didn't want to deal with on a good day, looked surprised. He cracked the door a little so he'd be able to hear me. "Yeah?"

"Do you need me to back up so you can stack behind the limo?"

He shook his head. "Nah. We're okay here."

"You sure? I don't mind."

"No, you're fine."

"Okay." I turned my back on him and returned the phone to my ear. "I'm sorry, Allison. You were saying something about texting me?"

"Yeah. I did. The day I flew back to D.C."

"I didn't get a text from you. Oh, shit!" My intestines performed a few spectacular backflips as it finally dawned on me what'd happened. "You texted my personal phone, didn't you?"

"Of course. I wasn't going to email you on your work phone."

I closed my eyes and scrubbed the middle of my forehead with the palm of my hand. "I don't have my personal phone."

"Did you lose it?"

"Not exactly. Someone else has it. I'm sorry. I didn't get your text. I would've answered if I had."

"Oh. Okay. Well, now I feel like an idiot."

"Don't. I've been spending the past few days wondering if you were upset with me, too."

"No, Ryan. I'm not upset with you."

"Good."

"But I do think we need to talk."

My heart tried to climb into my lungs. Not that I didn't agree with her. I did. We had a lot to work out. But in my experience, those words never preceded anything good. "Okay. Now?"

"No. Not right now. We need to have this talk face-to-face."

"Ah." That didn't make me feel any better.

"Do you think maybe we could try to set something up for when I get back?"

"Sure. Where are you?"

"I'm doing an advance in Hong Kong."

"Nice. I've never been. How is it?"

"It's okay. Busy." Allison paused. "I'm ready to come home."

"Yeah?"

"Yeah." Another beat. "I—I'm here for two weeks."

"Well, I'm pretty wrapped up with this visit for the next week or so, anyway. So that works out."

"It does."

"So...uh...what time is it there?" I closed my eyes and smacked myself on the thigh with the side of my fist. I couldn't believe I'd just said that. I was such an idiot.

"I think we're—" Allison broke off, and I heard some sort of commotion on her end of the phone. "Hang on a second."

"Sure." I waited as she covered the receiver so she could talk to someone. I could hear muffled bits of conversation but not enough to make out what they were discussing.

A few moments later she was back. "Ryan? I'm really sorry. I have to go."

I was disappointed, of course, but I understood. "That's okay. I'll talk to you soon. Stay safe."

"You, too."

Though we'd left things between us up in the air, my smile lingered long after I hung up. This day wasn't shaping up to be half bad. Speaking to Allison for even two minutes had completely altered my perspective. Wow. Some things never changed. Even our impending talk didn't dampen my mood. It was extremely likely I wouldn't like whatever she had to say, but I refused to let that possibility bring me down. I was floating.

An all-too-familiar voice behind me spoke. "Ryan?"

I tensed. My blood ran cold, and my heart suddenly plummeted from its previous Allison-induced heights to land somewhere in the vicinity of my knees. Clearly, I'd spoken too soon. I turned around very slowly.

"Luce."

Lucia stood a few feet away from me with the strangest expression. I couldn't read it, and, frankly, I was too tired to even try. She didn't look happy, though I had no idea what her current mood was.

"What are you doing here?" I asked, surprised to see her.

Lucia's eyes narrowed, and she studied me with an unnerving intensity. Finally, after a long, uncomfortable moment, she jerked her thumb in the direction of the front of the motorcade where I knew the

NYPD intel car sat idling along the curb several cars ahead of mine. "I was asked to fill in."

"Oh."

Silence fell thick and heavy between us, and I rubbed my palms against the legs of my pants. My insides twitched, and I bit my lower lip nervously, unsure what to say. This was unbelievably awkward. I wanted to ask her whether she was filling in just for today or if she had to work this detail for the remainder of the visit, but I was as afraid of her reaction to the question as I was of her answer. I just kept quiet.

I'd been incredibly busy with the numerous interviews, typing my PI report, and all the prep work for the visit. Not to mention being tied up in knots over Allison. I'd become completely wrapped up in everything, and while I'd meant to meet Lucia to switch our phones, I'd somehow never gotten around to it.

Of course, some people would speculate I'd purposely put off the meeting because I'd been dreading, well, this...the moment where Lucia and I stood face-to-face and our inevitable strained interaction. I'd had no illusions we could fix what'd happened or we'd ever be able to get back together, but the thought of us having one last, stilted conversation brought the situation into sharp focus. It solidified the end of our relationship, made it seem more final somehow, and I hadn't been eager to rush that reality check.

But here we were, tongue-tied and avoiding all but the most fleeting traces of eye contact, as we stood motionless on a New York City street corner. This situation resembled a cheesy Hollywood movie, and the notion made me unbelievably sad.

"You look good, Ryan," Lucia said, eventually. "Happy."

"Uh...Thanks. So do you. Look good, I mean." Her mere presence was like a hot poker being thrust into my chest and twisted around. It threw me off balance. I blinked and then fumbled in the backseat of my car where my bag was stowed. After retrieving her cell phone, I handed it to her. "I'm sorry I didn't return it sooner."

Lucia glanced at the phone I held before taking it. I noticed she made it a point not to touch me as she did. She put her phone in the pocket of her suit jacket and continued to watch me. Then her eyes flicked down to where the wire for my surveillance kit peeked out between the collar of my shirt and my neck and back up again. She pressed her lips together in a thin line, and her eyes hardened, but I couldn't have said exactly why. Perhaps this was as difficult for her as it was for me. The idea only intensified the ache inside me.

The moment stretched out forever. I cleared my throat and held out my hand, dismayed that it was trembling. Pinpricks of pain scraped behind my eyes, and a lump welled up in my chest and lodged firmly in my windpipe, making it tough to breathe. All the best and happiest moments of our relationship played in vivid Technicolor in my mind and made me want to cry.

"Do you have my phone?" I asked finally, my voice barely more than a whisper. I don't think I could've spoken any louder than that. It was taking too much effort not to burst into tears.

"I do." Lucia reached into the cell-phone holster on her belt and withdrew it. She held it aloft but didn't hand it to me.

The pressure in my chest increased exponentially. "Can I have it?"

"Not until you tell me something." Lucia's words were brittle, her tone icy. The coldness in her eyes chilled me and seeped into the marrow of my bones.

"What?"

"Was it good?"

I was stumped. "Was what good?"

"Fucking Allison. Was it good?" Her features twisted into something cruel, and her voice was hard as she glared at me.

"What?" She'd completely blindsided me. No way could I have seen that coming.

Something resembling triumph flickered behind her eyes, and she wiggled my phone for emphasis. A mean smile contorted her lips as she said, "Despite how it ended, I really enjoyed last night. You were incredible. Call me when you can." She was clearly quoting a text message, and I cringed, horrified and embarrassed. "You forgot to tell her not to send any incriminating texts until you got your phone back. Not to mention, you didn't do a very good job hiding the evidence." She gestured toward my throat as she snidely said that.

Okay, so she hadn't been looking at the wire for my surveillance kit. She'd been scouring for telltale traces of my night of passion with Allison. And even though it'd been days, and the mark Allison had left on me had faded considerably, Lucia didn't miss it. I'd never hated the fact that my fair skin bruised so easily as I did now. And I'd never been so disappointed I'd so poorly judged another human being. Why the hell had she been reading my text messages? What happened to honor and respect for someone else's privacy?

Lucia and I stared at one another, the atmosphere between us thick with tension. I wasn't sure what to say. I hadn't meant for her to find out like that and was sorry she was upset. But I also wanted to lash out. She'd broken up with me—after she'd slept with someone else. It was no longer any of her business what I did or with whom. I could run naked down Seventh Avenue during the Macy's Thanksgiving Day Parade, and she should have nothing to say about it.

A click sounded in my left ear, indicating someone was about to transmit radio traffic. "Grayson Follow-Up from lead. Be advised, it looks like we're breaking up. Stand by for imminent departure."

As soon as the mic clicked off, the block buzzed with activity. Agents hurried back and forth to their respective cars or posts. Other agents took up positions surrounding the limo. The uniformed NYPD officers on scene rushed to shut down the street for our next movement. One of the hulking black Suburbans raced off to secure the route with a roar. And I suddenly didn't have to say anything.

"We're getting ready to move, Luce." It was time to work. I couldn't do this with her now.

A bitter laugh escaped her throat, and she sneered. "So that's it? I ask you what it was like fucking your new girlfriend, and you run off to play *In The Line Of Fire*. Nice."

I barely refrained from shooting back a scathing reply. I wanted to—oh, how I wanted to. But I bit my lip so hard I literally tasted blood. Instead, I reached out to retrieve my cell phone from her hand.

She surprised me again by throwing it down onto the pavement with enough force that it shattered, spewing bits all over the place. Spite glittered in her eyes, hard and poisonous, and she smiled that simpering smile again.

"Oops," she deadpanned.

I closed my eyes and pressed the tips of my fingers to my temples. I was dying to let her have it. But we were about to leave, and the last thing I needed was the entire detail seeing me get into a knock-down-drag-out shouting match with my ex on a street corner at the arrival-departure area. Talk about an international incident.

I clenched my hands into fists and dug my fingernails into my palms, seized by the urge to hit something. I even gave in and settled for childishly banging the side of my fist into the passenger-side door of my car once. Or twice.

When I opened my eyes, I saw Michael rushing up the block carrying two paper cups of coffee. Perfect timing, because just then someone came over the air and said, "We're moving to the elevators." I glanced over Lucia's shoulder toward the side door to the Intercon.

"Luce, I'm very sorry you're hurt. But we can't do this now. You have to get back to your car before he comes out."

"You know what, Ryan? You can go fuck yourself. Or fuck Allison. I don't really care." Her voice grew louder with each word, and by the end of that statement, she was practically shouting.

A few people on the street glanced our way—agents and bystanders alike—but no one said anything, which I considered a minor miracle. I looked around to see whether I could identify any threats on the street. The click sounded in my ear again.

"Can someone grab the door?" a breathless voice asked over the air. "I had to take the stairs, and I'm not sure I'm going to make it."

"O'Connor copies direct. I've got it."

I brushed past Lucia and cracked the door to the limo, threading my fingers between it and the frame to make sure it wouldn't latch again. I wouldn't open it all the way until he was out—I wanted to be certain no one would be able to throw anything inside—but I wanted to be able to swing it open quickly once he was.

My head was on a swivel, and my eyes were everywhere at once as I tried to size up everyone I could see with a single glance. I wiped the palms of my hands on my pants one at a time and tightened my grip on the doorframe. I hated arrivals and departures. They edged out my second least favorite place, motorcade choke points, and my third, any scenario involving the protectee in a crowd. I always felt like if something went wrong, those would be the most likely places.

"Coming out," a voice transmitted over the air.

I glanced around one last time and waited a beat for the delegation to start exiting the hotel before I swung the door open completely. I kept my gaze on the surrounding area and held my breath, waiting for the president to get into the car. He was maybe two feet away when he stopped in the middle of the sidewalk to finish a conversation he was having.

My fingers twitched on the door, and I tried not to roll my eyes as I clenched my jaw. I caught movement out of the corner of my eye and turned, but it was just the shift guy who'd had to take the stairs barreling toward the car. He took the door from me with a grateful look. "Thanks. That elevator was packed."

I smiled. "No problem. That's always the way."

I clapped him on the shoulder as I scooted swiftly by to take up position next to my own car, careful not to touch the president as I slid past him. I'd made it maybe four steps before I ran almost bodily into Lucia. My pulse jumped, and an icy stab of fear pierced my heart. What the fuck? Why was she this close to the limo? I mean, I know some NYPD guys can't help themselves around a protectee and tend to spend more time watching them than actually doing their jobs, but this was too much. She knew better than to step into the protective bubble. Especially now.

"Luce, what the hell are you doing? Get to your car. We can finish this when we reach the next stop." I chanced a quick peek over my shoulder toward the president, who was now lingering in the limo's open doorway shaking someone's hand.

I moved to push past Lucia, but she grabbed my arm and spun me to face her. I saw a blur and barely had time to register the rage on her face before I caught her left hook on the right side of my jaw.

Pain, jagged and white-hot, exploded behind my eyes, and I heard a loud crack when her fist connected with my face. It must've been one hell of a hit, too, because I felt a sharp stab near where my right shoulder met my neck as my head snapped to the side. Not being prepared to be sucker punched by a woman I cared about, I was a little off-balance and stumbled at the impact, smacking the area just above the outside edge of my left eye against the open trunk of the limo where a staffer had been loading bags.

I blinked, dazed for a second or two before I dragged myself up off my knees to yell at her. I winced at the agony in my shoulder as I used the bumper of the car to push myself up. The staffer was staring at me like I was a moron, and I was starting to feel like one.

I glanced toward the limo door, pleased that the staffer was the only one who appeared to have seen what'd just happened. Good. The last thing I needed was for my boss or the protectee to watch me get laid out by an officer of the law. Although we were standing so close to them, I had no idea how they could've missed it. Perhaps it was tough for them to see through the press of ever-present hangers-on that always had to surround the president wherever he went.

Embracing the blistering fury roiling beneath the surface of my skin, I sought out Lucia. The angry words died on my lips when I saw her lying on the ground flat on her back. I frowned. How the hell had she ended up there? And where had all that blood come from? A whole lot of it was pouring out of the area near her jugular notch. Holy shit!

"Gun, gun, gun!!" someone screamed frantically. It took me a second to realize it was me.

I dropped to my knees, straddling Lucia's body, and covered the wound in her neck with my hands as I felt two hard hits to my back, like someone had whacked me with a sledgehammer. I glanced over my shoulder but didn't see anyone.

I shifted my weight to my right knee and leaned in that direction to give myself room to turn Lucia to my left and into the car, but as I did, I felt another jolt on the back of my right hip. I rolled back left and tried to shimmy Lucia and myself closer to the limited cover the car provided, but not before I felt a painful slash on the outside of my right thigh.

I looked up again and saw that the working shift was busily attending to their "cover and evacuate" protocol with the protectee. As I watched, the detail leader shoved the president's friend out of the way, elbowed a few staffers, and hurled the president bodily into the car before leaping in after him and pulling the door shut. All around me were shouts and scuffling and car doors slamming. Someone's foot caught the edge of my biceps in their attempt to escape, and I cried out as the impact caused my shoulder to burn.

I gazed down into Lucia's eyes and saw her terror. My heart seized, and bile rose in the back of my throat. I applied more pressure to her wound with my hands, trying to staunch the crimson flow without suffocating her. My own breathing was ragged, just this side of hyperventilation, and the horror on her face scared me.

"Go, go, go!" someone was shouting.

More car doors slammed, and the motorcade started to take off with a squeal of tires. Unfortunately, with such an enormous motorcade, it took what felt like an eternity for it to actually get rolling. It probably wasn't more than ten or fifteen seconds but seemed like forever.

The entire situation was surreal, so close to mirroring a training scenario that I half-expected to hear a booming voice yelling, "Actual stop," halting the action around me so we could huddle up and debrief. I would've given anything for that to have happened, but unfortunately no JJRTC instructor was waiting to save us by calling an end to this nightmare.

I was shaking now, perhaps a result of exertion, shock, or pure terror. Not that it mattered. It was becoming increasingly difficult for me to hold myself up enough to keep steady pressure on Lucia's throat without cutting off her air supply completely. I wanted so badly to just collapse on top of her and close my eyes. I had to force myself not to give in.

"Luce, hang in there, baby," I told her, trying to appear calm.

I tried to use my elbows and my knees to scoot us closer to the front of the PI car, still sitting at the curb next to us. I winced and sucked in a harsh breath at the raging inferno the motion produced in my right shoulder, clenching my teeth. Why was the car even still sitting there? Why hadn't it started rolling with the rest of the motorcade? But I didn't care, as it provided at least a little cover.

Darkness was creeping around the edges of my vision now, and fear shot through me. Every breath I drew was agony, and a woman I cared about was bleeding out on the street corner while I watched, powerless. The red of her blood contrasted sharply with the whiteness of my skin, loudly blaming me for this.

"Somebody call an ambulance!" I screeched, panicking. All sorts of shouting and commotion were echoing up and down the street, but I heard it only dimly and in snatches, as if someone were constantly adjusting the volume on the world at large. I think I was only tuning in long enough to attempt to determine whether help was on the way and then immediately tuning back out again. Apparently, I could no longer multi-task.

Lucia gripped my wrists, jostling my shoulder, and I yelped. Tears welled up in my eyes, and I swiped them away with the back of my hand. Her chest was rising and falling rapidly, and the crimson stain trickling from between her lips told me she was aspirating on her own blood.

"Luce, sweetie, just hang on. I've gotta turn you over, okay?"

I tried to rotate her onto her side, but my body wouldn't cooperate. Moving my right arm at all made me see white flashes in my periphery, and I simply didn't have the necessary strength. I settled for curling up as tight as I could over Lucia's body and pressed my forehead into hers. Squeezing my eyes shut I murmured to her over and over again to hang on, that help was coming, that she'd be okay.

She was gasping now, or trying to, and it was agony to hear the sound of the blood rattling in her airway. Each strangled wheeze was a red-hot ember being dropped down my throat to burn in my chest. I pressed harder against her neck as tears streamed down my face. My sobs sounded like thunder to my ears and mingled discordantly with hers, seeming to drown out everything else.

How unprepared I was for this situation. We'd trained relentlessly in the academy, going through assault scenarios repeatedly until it became second nature to put your protectee's life ahead of your own. And yet, as many times as they'd made me practice, I couldn't help thinking they'd failed me in this. They'd taught me how to take a bullet, how to trade my life for someone else's, how to die so someone who didn't even acknowledge my existence could live. They'd taught me to have pride in that mission and to accept it as easily as a corporate employee would acknowledge the reality of Monday-morning meetings. They'd failed to teach me, however, how to cope with watching someone I cared about shoulder that burden.

And then I stopped thinking altogether.

CHAPTER TWENTY-SIX

An unbelievably annoying beeping sound disturbed me who knows how long later. At first, I fuzzily thought it might be someone's watch or cell phone, but it just kept going, making me want to scream. Each beep felt like someone was stabbing me behind the eyes.

When I tried to snipe at someone to turn it the fuck off, I noticed a tube down my throat and felt like I was suffocating. I heard a low sort of strangled hissing sound, and my lungs burned as they were forcibly filled with oxygen. My heart rate soared, which only increased the tempo of the beeping, and I struggled to open my eyes and sit up. My right shoulder was in agony, and I let slip a muffled grunt. Only one eye would open all the way, and that didn't help me stay calm.

The deluge of air stopped, and I gratefully exhaled before trying to suck in a breath on my own. I tried to grasp the tube with my right hand, but my arm was fastened to my body somehow, and the struggle to free it caused me unnecessary pain. The hiss came again and with it the unsettling feeling of being inflated like a balloon against my will. Panic rose in the back of my throat, and I gave up on my right arm and reached for the tube with my left.

I'd just started to yank, determined to get the damn thing out of me so I could breathe on my own, when cool fingers closed over mine.

"Ryan, calm down," a voice said authoritatively. It sounded eerily familiar, and I opened my good eye, casting around wildly as fear threatened to choke me. A soothing hand stroked my forehead, and I finally managed to focus on my sister's face as she looked down at me.

"Don't fight the machine, *Ay-vo*," Rory advised me. "I know it's uncomfortable. Just give me a second, and we'll get it out of you, okay?"

I nodded and tried to concentrate on lying still and remaining calm, but my body was still fighting to breathe without aid, and I was shivering. The sensation of drowning even though my lungs were being pumped full of air was maddening.

I heard the faint, low sound of switches being flipped, and the hissing stopped. My relief was immediate, and I started to pull.

Rory chuckled. "Hang on a second. You don't want to pull that out just yet." She turned away from me again, and I felt a pressure in the area just below my throat loosen. Rory's face drifted back into view, and she nodded. "Knock yourself out."

With a stifled sort of gasping sob, I tugged. The pull of the tape as I ripped it away from my cheeks stung, but I ignored it and soldiered on. My throat was on fire as something scraped against the length of it for what felt like an eternity. And suddenly, it was out and I could breathe.

I sucked in greedily, gulping the air, ignoring the burning sensation all up and down my windpipe. I was thrilled I could breathe on my own and blinked furiously as a lone tear trickled down my right cheek.

Rory wiped it away tenderly, then brushed the hair back off my forehead as she shone a tiny light in my eye. I scowled and batted my eye against the painful intrusion, trying to pull away from her. My feeble struggle didn't appear to faze her.

After a bit, she flicked her pen light off and tucked it back into the pocket of her white coat. In the same motion, she reached up to retrieve a stethoscope, which'd been slung carelessly around the back of her neck. I must've been really doped up because I didn't notice her attire until then.

"What're you doing here?" I asked, as though the surgical scrubs and white lab coat with her name embroidered on the left breast didn't provide enough of a clue. My voice sounded rough and raw, barely more than a whisper. My throat was a raging inferno. Each syllable that passed through my lips was like swallowing broken glass, and a sharp, stabbing sensation encompassed the entire right side of my back in time with every breath I took.

Rory ignored my inquiry. Instead, she inserted the stethoscope into her ears and placed the pad against my chest, inside the neck of my hospital gown.

"Breathe in for me," my sister directed. Her sea-foam green eyes were unfocused as she concentrated.

I complied, though even that simple act was an effort. The right side of my body from my shoulder down to my knee felt like someone had worked it over with a two-by-four.

Rory relocated the stethoscope slightly farther down my chest. "Again." And when I'd followed that order, she repeated the process. The entire experience couldn't have taken more than thirty seconds, but time felt slippery, the whole thing dreamlike.

Once she'd finished, she replaced the instrument so it dangled off her again like a fashion accessory and took my wrist. She consulted her watch as she held me and then nodded, appearing satisfied.

A heavy-set woman with a cheerful face and a chaotic halo of curly ashen hair entered the room. She, too, wore scrubs and was carrying a folder, but I was too busy trying to keep my eyes open to make much sense of anything. The woman's sparkling eyes landed on me, and she beamed.

The newcomer shifted her attention to my sister and consulted the folder briefly. "Evan O'Connor?" Her tone was questioning, as though she was trying to verify the information. "E-A-V-A-N. Is that how you say that? 'Evan'?"

Rory held out her hand, silently asking for the papers. "It's pronounced 'even,' actually. But we just call her Ryan."

Confusion drifted across the woman's merry countenance much the way clouds float in front of the sun. She glanced back at the papers in her hand before handing them to my sister. "Where did you get 'Ryan' from?"

"Her middle name. Aeryn."

"Oh. Well, that's different." The woman somehow managed to sound happily excited by just about everything, which amused me for some reason. She nodded and smiled at me again. "Nice to finally meet you, Ryan. I'm glad you're awake." She turned back to Rory. "I'll page her doctor now. Unless you need me to take care of something else first."

Rory was flipping through the pages of what I could only presume was my file. "No," she murmured distractedly. "I'm fine. Thank you."

The woman left, and my sister and I were alone. I was exhausted and struggled to keep my eyes open, drifting for a while as Rory read. I wanted to go back to sleep but was afraid of what I'd miss if I did. I had no idea how much time passed before Rory spoke again.

"How are you feeling?"

I shot her a dirty look. Well, as dirty as a look could possibly be with the full use of only one eye, which, if her facial expression was any indication, wasn't very. "Fantastic."

She ignored my sarcasm. "Any headache or nausea?"

A smart-ass response welled up within me, but I didn't let it loose. I considered the question. "Headache. No nausea."

She set my chart down on the nightstand and gently probed the swollen tissue surrounding my left eye. I hissed at the unexpected pain and tensed, which didn't help the aching sensations in the rest of me.

"Your stitches look good. The swelling is definitely going down."

"Hooray," I murmured. I was trying to recall how I'd ended up here, but my thoughts were sluggish.

As if reading my mind, Rory asked, "Can you tell me what happened?"

I frowned, ignoring the dull throb the motion brought to the area of my injured eye. Dim flashes of memory swam around in my head, broken and disjointed. "Maybe."

Something flickered in Rory's eyes as she watched me, and while my brain fog wouldn't let me identify the exact emotion I saw playing there, I did know I didn't like it. My heart-rate monitor picked up speed in time with my racing pulse.

"Well, these definitely aren't injuries I want to read about in my baby sister's chart," Rory informed me, changing the subject abruptly.

I sighed, but my thoughts had strayed back to recent events. I mentally catalogued the battery of aches and pains plaguing me, trying to assign a cause. Something was nagging me, and I was determined to figure out what.

Rory regarded me for a long moment, her countenance serious. Her hair was a little messy—which was unheard of for her—and she looked nearly as exhausted as I felt.

After a bit, she moved to a small rolling table nestled up against the wall and retrieved a gleaming metal bedpan, which she brought over. I eyed it warily, but she didn't relinquish it.

"I don't have to go right now," I informed her.

"I know you don't. You have a catheter in."

I wrinkled my nose. "Ew."

Rory's expression now was vaguely sympathetic. "I can take it out if you want. Or we can wait for your doctor to do it." She shrugged. "Your call."

I looked away from her but didn't reply.

"Or I can tell you about your injuries."

When I refocused on her, I saw she was expectant. This appeared to be a sticking point for her for some reason. I attempted to sit up, the movement pure agony.

Through my haze, I watched Rory roll her eyes and wordlessly push a button on the automatic bed. With a low hum, it slowly folded me into a sitting position, which was still painful, but slightly less so. It was worth it not to be lying down anymore, though. I frowned again as I let my gaze drift around the room.

"Am I on drugs?" It took a while for me to make that connection.

"Oh, yeah. Dilaudid. Why? Are you in pain?"

"Some," I murmured lazily. "But mostly I just feel out of it."

"So, now would not be the best time for me to tell you about your injuries."

"*Asha*, you could tell me when I'm completely sober, and I still wouldn't understand half of what you're saying." My mouth felt sluggish and beyond my immediate control. I wasn't even sure my words were coherent.

She chuckled softly. "When you emerge from your drug-induced haze, I'll explain. I promise to use small words and prop dolls the way I would with the little kids."

"Fine."

A long pause. I'd just closed my eyes and decided it was okay to give in to the sweet siren song of sleep when Rory's whisper broke the relative quiet.

"You scared the shit out of me, Ryan."

I struggled to open my eye again so I could look at her. She was worrying at her lower lip with her teeth, and her brow was creased. The sight nearly broke my heart. "I'm sorry."

Rory appeared faintly annoyed. "Don't apologize. It wasn't your fault that some crazy person decided to—" She bit her lip again.

"Decided to what?" The dim snatches of memory swirling around in my subconscious came into sharper focus, but I still couldn't identify exactly what'd gone down.

Rory swallowed and lowered herself so she sat perched on the edge of my hospital bed, the bedpan lying in her lap. A wobbly smile touched the corners of her lips, and her attempts at bravery tugged at me almost painfully. She took my good hand in one of hers.

"I know this is what you signed up for, but I never in a million years thought it would ever really..." She shifted her focus so it rested on our intertwined fingers.

"I was shot." It wasn't a statement, but it wasn't exactly a question either. Hell, even as drugged as I was, I was able to tell my injuries weren't consistent with something as mundane as a fall or a car accident. My mind worked overtime to put the pieces together, and I winced at the sharp stab of pain the effort produced.

"Five times," Rory confirmed quietly.

"Bummer." I may or may not have actually said that out loud. Bits of the incident were coming back to me slowly. I closed my eyes again, and this time I could almost hear the chaos that'd erupted when everything had broken bad. But the recollection was rather muffled and distant.

"Your right shoulder got the worst of it," Rory was saying from far away. She seemed unable to help herself. Clearly, she needed to get this running diatribe of my injuries off her chest. "The bullet tore through your trapezius, which was actually lucky. The shoulder's a complicated joint. If it'd struck lower, it would've shattered bone, and you might never have recovered full use of the limb. Of course, if it had—"

"Mmm."

I was missing something. Speaking of bones, I could feel it deep in the marrow of mine. In the theater of my mind, I was trying to replay the events as best I could, but they were broken, out of focus, not in the correct order. When I was a kid, I used to dive to the very bottom of the pool and look up at the world above. My memories were wavy like that, and I felt insulated from them as though submerged under ten feet of water.

Sounds were easier. I remembered clearly, for example, the sound of the motorcade taking off, the punching roar of the engines, and the screech of tires attempting to gain traction against pavement. In my head, I could hear distant voices shouting, though I couldn't make out precisely what they said. The slam of doors. The stamp of boots against concrete. I remembered hearing lots of different things. But I couldn't see any of it. Not really. Just useless flashes. The delegation being rushed into the cars. Feet dashing by my head as I lay on the ground. The curve of a tire next to a curb. Nothing useful. Nothing that helped me put together exactly what had happened. Why not? What was I forgetting?

"Your leg's a bit mangled," Rory went on, though whether she thought I was even awake at that point was unclear. Maybe she simply didn't care. On TV, people talked to their unconscious loved ones all the time. Perhaps that's what she was doing now. The sensation of her fingers tracing gentle circles on my hand was soothing. "One of the bullets grazed the outside of your right thigh. You'll have a scar, but there was no major muscle or tissue damage."

I sighed. The urge to just let go for a while and put off remembering until much later was seductive. I wanted so badly to give in to it. I started to drift off, Rory's voice floating to me as though from the other end of a long tube. She was saying something about lungs and kidneys and internal bleeding, but her words weren't hitting home with me. I tried to murmur good night to her but couldn't quite rally the energy to move my lips. I'd tell her later. She'd understand.

"It could've been much, much worse."

At those words, I suddenly remembered everything. The abrupt clarity was almost startling, and I would've sworn I actually heard a click as the missing pieces snapped into place. My eyes flew open, and the nausea Rory had asked me about earlier punched me hard in the gut, but I doubted it had anything to do with my physical injuries. No, this reaction could be attributed to psychic wounds.

"Luce?" My voice was shaky, and I trembled. "Where is she? Can I see her?"

My sister's expression was all the answer I required. My heart shredded, and tears welled up in my eyes, blurring Rory's face. I wanted to beg her, plead with her not to say the words I knew were about to come out of her mouth, but I couldn't make my voice work. The lump in my throat was too big. The sudden, painful pressure inside me was too great.

"I'm so sorry, Ryan. Lucia didn't make it."

A fraction of a second before it happened, I knew exactly what the bedpan was for, and somewhere beneath my anguish, a part of me was grateful Rory knew me so well. She was already lifting the dish with one hand as she helped me turn to the side a little with the other. I expelled the contents of my stomach with such force I was positive I was either reopening old wounds or inflicting new ones. Either way, I welcomed the pain. I deserved it. I hungered for it. Lucia couldn't feel anything anymore because of me.

I have no idea how long I vomited, only that the moment seemed to stretch on into forever. Finally, when my stomach spasms quieted somewhat and I appeared to be through dry-heaving, Rory placed the bedpan on the floor.

I squeezed my eyes shut to block the scalding tears gathered in them. The side of the bed dipped with the weight of another body, and I buried my face in Rory's chest, sobbing. Guilt threatened to drown me, and no words could've offered any comfort.

Rory must've sensed that, too, because she merely held me quietly as I cried.

CHAPTER TWENTY-SEVEN

"A re you still mad at me?" Rory's voice floated through the
open doorway, interrupting my attempts to find anything
even remotely entertaining on TV.

I thumbed the power button on the remote with as much force as I
could and turned to glare at her. "You mean because you refused to let
me attend Lucia's funeral? No. Why would I be mad about that?"

Rory sighed and shuffled into the room. She looked ragged, but I
refused to let that sway me. "You haven't recovered nearly enough to
handle the stress."

"So you said. Just before you fled the room. Coward."

"Yeah, well, you were being unreasonable." She pulled a chair up
next to my bed and flopped into it, tipping her head back and closing
her eyes.

"Is it even legal for you to do what you did?"

She cracked open one eye. "What did I do?"

"Used your position at the hospital to make decisions for me."

She scoffed and closed her eye again. "Please. Like you were even
sober enough to realize you were missing it."

"And whose fault was that?"

"Mine," Rory mumbled, not sounding really interested. "Everything's mine."

"Glad you can admit it."

"Mmm."

We were quiet for a long moment, and I took the opportunity to
really study her as she dozed. The skin beneath her eyes looked bruised,

and I would've sworn the stress lines creasing her brow weren't there before. My heart lurched, and I rubbed my own forehead as though I'd be able to soothe her that way.

"It was best," Rory murmured, startling me.

"What was?"

"You skipping the funeral."

"I should've been there, Rory. I should've at least had the chance to honor the life she'd lived and the sacrifice she'd made."

Rory groaned as she hoisted herself into a more upright position and twisted and turned to work out some kinks in her back. "I know. And I'm sorry. But I didn't want you to have to deal with all the whispers and the staring and the questions."

It was my turn to sigh. "Yeah, I figured it was something like that." A beat. "Thanks."

"Any time. How'd your visit with her family go?"

Even now, I felt like I was being pressed in a vise at the mere memory of that conversation. I forced myself to breathe in despite the tightness in my chest. It wasn't easy. "It went okay."

Rory quirked an eyebrow. She knew I was full of shit. "Really?"

"Well, if you overlook the fact that she hadn't told them anything."

"Anything about...?"

"About anything. Our breakup. Her sleeping with someone else. That she was upset with me because I'd..." I couldn't even bring myself to say that she'd been in the line of fire instead on the far side of the limo by the Intel car because she'd felt compelled to confront me. I didn't want Rory trying to convince me it wasn't my fault. "Nada. Zip. Zero. Zilch."

"Oh, shit. I'm so sorry."

I cleared my throat in an attempt to break apart the heavy ball that'd gathered there and blinked furiously against the tears welling in my eyes. "Yeah, well. I thought they'd come to yell at me. Imagine my surprise when they cried and fussed over me like I was part of the damn family."

Rory was silent for a while. "You didn't tell them, did you?"

I shook my head. "No. But I thought about it." Had teetered on the brink of revealing the truth the entire visit, in fact. I'd even opened my mouth a few times, intent upon confessing everything, but in the end, I couldn't bring myself to do it.

"Why not?"

"If she'd wanted them to know, she'd have told them herself. Besides, that would've been for me, not for them. To make me feel better." She probably had no idea what I was talking about, but that was okay. She didn't need specifics. "I couldn't take advantage of them like that."

Rory favored me with a pitying look that grated on the underside of my skin like a thousand splinters. "Ryan, you know that—" Her pager went off, cutting off whatever she'd been about to say, and I sagged against my pillows, relieved. She checked it and stood, a dark frown washing over her features. "I've gotta go. I'll come back and check on you later."

"I'd rather you get some sleep," I called after her.

She waved over her shoulder and strode purposefully down the hall. I shimmied around in the bed for a bit after she'd gone, trying to get comfortable, but it just didn't seem possible. The best I could do was settle into a position that produced the least amount of pain. But the physical aches were a welcome distraction from the shame and guilt bubbling like a witch's brew inside me. So that was something, I supposed.

My work phone chimed to announce a new email and intruded upon my wallowing. With a sigh, I retrieved it and awkwardly typed in my password with my left hand. God, I wished I knew how much longer it'd be before I could use my right.

The message wasn't from Allison. Speaking of nada, zip, zero, and zilch, I hadn't heard squat from her since the day I'd been shot, and that cut me to the quick. News traveled faster than the speed of light in this agency, so she'd surely heard what'd happened. I'll admit it, I'd sort of been expecting her to call to check up on me. That she hadn't even emailed was devastating.

Whenever I threatened to drown in thoughts like that, my pragmatic side reminded me she was overseas on a protection assignment. She had responsibilities and couldn't just drop everything to confirm what everyone in the agency had surely already told her—that I was going to be fine. Besides, she and I were just finding our way back to one another. I had no right to expect her to magically appear at my bedside.

I sighed. Pragmatism be damned. I was equal parts hurt and saddened that Allison hadn't asked to be released from her assignment to come home. And the frustration and regret that sliced through me at the thought that she hadn't even called or emailed me was painfully acute.

I clenched my hand impossibly tightly around the phone before I slung it onto the nightstand. It clattered before coming to rest against a pitcher full of water. A bitter taste like bile rose in the back of my throat, and I gritted my teeth against all the negative emotions pulling painfully on my insides like they were so much taffy. Unfortunately, all the teeth-gritting caused some pain to my outside, too. I winced at the stab along the right side of my jaw.

"Oh, good, you're awake," a tentative voice said from the doorway.

I glanced up and saw Meaghan hovering there, looking a touch uncertain. I smiled at her and nodded, waving her inside. Agents from the office had been taking turns coming to visit me throughout my stay. Though I didn't always remember much about the visits due to the painkillers my doctors kept pumping through me, in my lucid moments, I appreciated them immensely.

"Hi, Meg. How's it going?"

"Are you, you know...?"

"Sober?"

Meaghan nodded.

"Mmm. Ish," I told her honestly. I'd been moderately successful at getting my doctors to back off on the drugs a bit. But I was still out of sorts.

Meaghan entered the room and took a seat in the chair Rory had recently vacated. Her eyes took in my battered face and my sling, and a strange expression flickered across her features. She reminded me of a little kid, for some reason, and I immediately wanted to put her at ease. "You sure about that?"

I frowned. "Reasonably. Why?"

"Eric Banks is running around telling everyone that when he was here you said you were going to take his badge and smack him hard enough on the forehead with it that it'd leave a permanent indent."

I laughed. "He is, huh? Nice."

"So is it true?"

"Absolutely. Though I'm still not sure why he was even here. I barely know him. I think we've met like once."

"He came over with Anna. She wanted to see you. She seemed pretty shaken up by the whole thing. And for some reason Eric decided to tag along. At least that's what Anna said."

"It was sweet of her to be concerned. She's a nice girl."

"I think she's got a crush on you."

"Come on. She does not."

"If it's not that, then she thinks you're the reincarnation of Wonder Woman. So maybe ease up with threatening the rookies. Don't want to tarnish your image."

"Not rookies. Just the one. I'd never say something like that to Anna. She's squared away. And you're right. It was the drugs talking. I'd never have said that out loud if I hadn't been all doped up."

She grinned. "But you'd have thought it."

"Definitely."

"Do I even want to know why?"

"Probably not. Have you ever interacted with him?"

She rolled her eyes. "Yeah. It was a real treat. I loved having a guy with a couple months on the job telling me how we needed to handle the demonstrators at a site when he isn't even in PI."

"He's a peach."

"It'll be interesting to see how much longer he lasts before Rico kills him."

"That's right. Rico's his backup now. Ha. I love it."

"Yeah, well, Rico told him if he ever even spoke your name again, he'd get worse than a smack on the head with his badge. And then he had Ops assign Eric to midnight desk duty for a week."

I couldn't help smiling at Rico's protectiveness.

Meaghan's expression became serious as she went back to inspecting me. "So how are you doing? Really?"

"I'm okay. Speaking of people I want to smack with their own badge, I only did this in order to show up Bill Steelman because of his huge arrest last week."

Meaghan cracked a weak smile and shook her head before raking one hand through her hair. "Somehow, that doesn't surprise me."

I shrugged, once again forgetting my injured shoulder, and tried to hide my reaction to the resulting pain. "Yeah, well, I couldn't have him hogging all the attention."

Meaghan's brows pulled down, which made me wonder whether she'd caught onto my physical discomfort. "How much pain are you in?"

"Absolutely none."

"Because of the drugs?"

"No. Okay, well, maybe. A little bit."

"Fantastic." She eyed me with a hint of exasperation as she crossed her arms over her chest. I couldn't help it. I laughed at her.

"What were you expecting to hear?" I liked to tease her.

She rolled her eyes. "I don't know. Not that."

"You know me better than that."

"Yeah," she murmured quietly, almost sadly, as her eyes scoured me from head to toe. "I guess I do."

"And yet you still felt as though you had to ask."

"Come on, Ryan. Be serious for once in your life." Meaghan appeared annoyed with my attempts at levity, and the harshness in her voice shocked me. She had a dull fire in her eyes, and she opened her mouth, but she must've changed her mind about what she wanted to say because she closed it again and rubbed her fingertips across her lips.

After a long moment during which she seemed to be gathering her composure, she tried again. "You were shot. Several times. You had to have emergency surgery. You could've died. Someone did—" She clapped her hands over her mouth with a loud slap. Her golden-brown eyes were wide with disbelief and horror.

My heart wrenched, and my gut twisted right along with it. Tears stung my eyes, and I blinked them back furiously. I clenched my jaw and took a deep breath, ignoring the sensation that someone had just sucked all the oxygen out of the room.

I didn't need Meaghan—or anybody else—to remind me of the seriousness of the situation. I wasn't an idiot, and I wasn't capricious when it came to the subject of my life. But I was terrible when it came to dealing with any type of solemn emotion. I also didn't like to dwell on my own mortality. I don't think any of us did. And that, more than anything else, is what prompted me to crack jokes rather than simply answer her pointed question. It was what made me continue to treat the subject lightheartedly, even though I could see that it bothered her. Even though I knew it bothered me.

"I'm sorry," Meaghan said.

"It's okay."

"No, it isn't. I didn't mean to..."

"It's fine." It wasn't, but I really didn't want to get into it. "Your girlfriend just died. And I was being a jerk. It's not my place to tell you how to react to things."

My insides began playing a spirited game of Twister, and I sucked in a harsh breath. The intensity of my anguish startled me, and I had to fight not to cry. I couldn't even bring myself to correct her about the label she'd used, as though I craved the additional agony the word caused.

I almost confessed everything to her then—Lucia and Jessie, the breakup, my night with Allison. But if I did that, she'd realize Lucia's death was my fault. I was having enough trouble accepting that myself. I wasn't even remotely prepared for the look I was sure she'd give me once she was made aware of the facts.

"Don't worry about it."

"So, uh, you ready to get out of here?" Meaghan looked miserable. She cast her gaze toward the floor and started twisting one of the rings on her fingers. Since the move was so uncharacteristic, my eyes were immediately drawn to the motion. I couldn't recall her ever wearing a ring on that finger before. She usually—

"Oh, my God!"

Meaghan's head shot up, her eyes borderline panicked. "What? What's wrong?"

"Did you get engaged?"

Meaghan covered her left hand with her right, appearing uncomfortable. "Oh. Uh...Yeah."

"Congratulations. That's great! When did this happen?"

"Two days ago."

"I'm so happy for you. Let me see the rock." I held out my good hand and motioned her closer with my fingers. She hesitated for a long second before placing her hand in mine. I inspected the ring closely. "It's beautiful. He did a great job picking it out."

"He did." She took her hand back and set it in her lap, keeping her eyes glued to it.

"So, how did he propose?"

"We can talk about that later."

Her reluctance to share the details of something she'd been not-so-secretly hoping for, for the past few months, confused me. It wasn't like her at all. "Did we talk about this already?"

"What?"

"How many times did I ask you that when I was all doped up? I'm sorry. I don't remember."

"You haven't asked me before."

"Then what's wrong?"

"We should just talk about something else. I can tell you all about it when you get out of the hospital. How much longer are they planning to keep you here anyway?"

Her attitude puzzled and slightly hurt me, but I didn't want to push her. If she didn't want to talk about it, that was her business. I pushed my distress aside and tried to go with her chosen topic of conversation. "Uh, I'm not sure. Rory won't tell me."

"It must be killing you to sit still for this long."

I rolled my eyes. "You have no idea."

She didn't know the half of it. The forced inactivity had made it impossible for me to escape the tangled labyrinth of my own thoughts, and I was driving myself crazy with all this thinking. I couldn't wait to get the hell out and go home. I'd likely do my fair share of introspection there, too, but I'd have access to a few more distractions. I'd be more comfortable at any rate. That was something.

"Have you started plotting your great escape yet?"

"Not yet, but it's coming. Although it hasn't been all bad. Half the people in this hospital dote on me because they know my sister, and the other half do it because they seem to think I am my sister." With my free left hand, I plucked at the collar of the snazzy, navy-blue scrubs Rory had given me. "I've got some cool duds, a steady supply of amazing drugs, and all the Jell-O I could ever hope to eat in a lifetime. It's as good as it could possibly be, considering the circumstances."

"So, I don't suppose you need this, then?" a new voice said from the doorway.

Ben Flannigan, the SAIC of the New York Field Office, stood there holding a nice-sized plastic container of what was obviously more Jell-O. "Black cherry."

"Ooh! My favorite. Thanks."

"You sure you want it? I hear they're giving you all the Jell-O you can eat in here. I'd hate for you to get overloaded."

"Of course I want it. They don't have black cherry here. And if I'm forced to eat one more bowl of lime, I can't be held accountable for my actions."

He smiled and set the container on the nearby bed as his eyes shifted to my companion. "Hello, Meaghan. How are you doing?" He unbuttoned his suit jacket, and I took the opportunity his diverted attention afforded me to study him.

His dark hair, which had started gathering gray strands at the temples in recent years, was immaculately coifed, and his suit was meticulously creased and pressed. He looked every bit the part of the always-in-control Secret Service agent. But a tension to his posture and a tightness around his eyes and mouth betrayed his outward calm. I sighed inwardly at the sudden realization of how much this whole mess must be wearing on him. Another pang of guilt roiled inside my already knotted guts.

"I'm fine, sir," Meaghan said. "Thank you. How are you?"

"As well as can be expected, considering. Do you mind if I have a moment alone with Agent O'Connor?"

"Of course not, sir." Meaghan hastily collected all her belongings and gave me a sympathetic look. "I'll see you later, Ryan."

"Thanks for stopping by." I wanted to say more to her before she left, but she was gone before I had a chance.

The SAIC waited a beat after Meaghan's departure and then walked purposefully over to the door. He made sure it was securely closed before turning back to face me. Then he merely remained quiet for a long moment, studying me intently.

"How're you doing, kiddo? I mean, really?" he asked finally, his voice soft.

I smiled at him and struggled to sit up slightly to meet his offered kiss with my cheek. "I'm fine, Dad."

Yes, I'm the boss's daughter. Well, technically, his adopted daughter. But he's known me since before I was born, so we have a long history together. And no, nobody in the office knows. We've taken great pains to keep it a secret because I wanted to make my own name—good or bad—on my own merit.

Dad frowned at me then. "That's not what Rory says. She says you're in pain."

Rory had told me that both Mom and Dad had been in and out of my hospital room with all the regularity you'd expect from dutiful parents, but I'd always been either asleep or too doped up to notice. The one or two times I'd actually been lucid enough to make a stab at conversation, some nurses had been poking and prodding me, so I hadn't had a chance to really talk to either of them. I was grateful to finally have these few moments alone with him.

In answer to his statement, I almost shrugged again but caught myself. A small flare of irritation at Rory ignited for ratting me out, but I attempted to keep the annoyance from my face and downplay the entire situation. Sure, I hurt like hell, but I refused to whine about it.

"Yeah, well, that's to be expected. But it's not too bad. They're keeping me pretty well drugged. It helps dull the pain as long as I don't move around too much. Which reminds me. Where's my gun?"

Dad favored me with an indulgent smile that somehow made me think he'd been mentally timing me, waiting to see how long it'd take me to ask that question. "I have it. It's locked up at home."

I breathed a sigh of relief. I'd been pretty sure someone from my agency had taken possession of it—that was standard operating procedure whenever a law-enforcement officer was injured. I just hadn't been positive where it'd ended up. The knowledge was a small comfort.

"And I wasn't asking about your physical state. I wanted to know how you're holding up emotionally."

"You mean aside from being irritated that of all the people in the world I had to take a bullet for, it had to be that guy?" I rolled my eyes and shook my head.

"Yes, aside from that." When I didn't answer right away, he went on. "I know this must be hard for you, Ryan. You're probably feeling a lot of different—"

"What are they saying?"

"Who?"

"The FBI. The ones investigating this assassination attempt on the president of Iran. Did the guy say why he did it? Did someone pay him, or was it some kind of vendetta?"

Dad regarded me for a long moment, his face carefully blank. I was familiar with that move. He knew something, but he was considering what to tell me or whether to tell me anything at all. If I hadn't known him as well as I did, he might've played it off well enough that I didn't realize what he was doing. Maybe.

"As far as I've been told, they're following up on a few things. I'm supposed to meet with their SAIC later today to get a more thorough update on the situation."

"Wait. What? You mean the gunman isn't already in custody?"

"No."

"How is that even possible? The entire block was crawling with cops. Somebody had to have seen something."

"They're working on it, Ryan."

"You don't know how he got away, do you? You have no idea. Neither do they." My insides began a spectacular free fall as that realization hit home.

"As I said, I'm scheduled to receive a more thorough briefing later today."

I studied him for a time, trying to work out exactly what he was keeping from me. In the end, I gave up. He'd worked for the agency long enough to have perfected his poker face. His expression wouldn't give away anything he didn't want me to know. Not anything specific, anyway.

"This is more than just an assassination attempt, Dad. This is personal."

"Not to them."

"Well, it is to me."

"I know."

I frowned as I reminded myself of what he deliberately wasn't saying. That I needed to take a step back and let the FBI do their jobs. That I needed to let go of any personal stake I might have in this situation. That I needed to try to forget it'd happened at all and get on with my life. Or maybe he wasn't trying to avoid saying any of those things to me. Maybe that was all in my head.

I didn't want to bore him with a long diatribe. I didn't even have the energy or the inclination to sort it all out at the moment. So I went with a summary of the thought that'd been regularly recurring inside my head since the moment I'd opened my eyes in this god-forsaken hospital room.

"I'm going to find out who did this. If it's the last thing I do, I'm going to find out who killed Lucia. And, when I do, I intend to make him suffer for it."

Dad's phone rang then and interrupted whatever commentary he might've had regarding my vow. He winced when he looked at the screen. "I'm sorry. I have to take this." He lifted the phone to his ear and stepped over to the windows. His voice was low, so I couldn't hear any of what he was saying, which I suspected was deliberate.

A knock on the door distracted me from my eavesdropping, and I scowled. "Come in."

The door eased open, and my mouth dropped. I blinked several times, then rubbed my eyes with my left hand, trying to determine whether I was hallucinating.

"Do you see her, too?" I asked Dad, afraid the drugs were starting to affect me more than they were supposed to. But he had his back to me.

Allison let out a throaty chuckle and sauntered over to the bed, all confidence and sex appeal. Christ, she looked amazing. Tired and a tad disheveled, but stunning nonetheless. My heart beat out a rapid, machine-gun-fire rhythm, and I was secretly glad they'd taken that infernal heart-rate monitor off me. The frantic beeping that would've accompanied her sudden appearance would've mortified me.

My immediate grin faded as something finally made it through my painkiller-addled little brain. "What are you doing here?"

"What? Aren't you happy to see me?" Her teasing almost managed to conceal the strain in her voice. Almost.

"Of course. I'm thrilled. But I haven't—" I physically bit my lip to prevent myself from blurting out that I hadn't heard word one from her in days.

"I haven't called," Allison said.

I looked away, hoping my hurt feelings didn't show on my face. "Yeah."

She stepped up to the side of my bed and placed her hands on the railing. "Hey," she said softly.

I glanced up at her, all bated breath and nervous hope.

"I'm sorry." It came out as a whisper, but her face was sadder and more serious than I'd ever seen it.

We continued to stare at one another until the pointed clearing of a throat broke the spell.

"I think that's my cue to leave," Dad said, sounding amused. "Hello, Allison. Nice to see you again."

Allison blinked once, startled, as if just now noticing I had company. "I'm sorry, sir. You don't have to go anywhere. I can come back later."

"Please stay. I have a meeting to prepare for, so I was about to leave anyway." He shifted his focus to me. "Call if you need anything."

"Of course. Thank you, sir."

Dad grinned at me, then walked out and shut the door behind him.

CHAPTER TWENTY-EIGHT

Now that Allison and I were alone, the atmosphere in the room suddenly threatened to choke me. The pressure gathering in my chest was acutely painful. Each one of the scenarios I'd imagined for our reunion rushed in on me at once. I was overwhelmed and couldn't decide what to say.

Allison's eyes raked over me, and she appeared to be assessing my condition. All of her usual swagger had disappeared, and a tension and uncertainty hovering around her now filled me with dread. She gazed at me for an eternity, but finally she reached out to tentatively caress my cheek with her fingertips. My skin sparked where she touched me, and my heart threatened to beat its way out of my body. I closed my eyes and sighed.

"Ryan," Allison whispered.

I opened my eyes, and her bare emotions frightened me. I gently covered her hand with my own.

The in-control, put-together façade she'd strolled in here with had completely cracked, and I doubted she'd recover it. With her other hand, she followed the line of the stitches on my forehead with a feather-light touch. Her eyes reflected back to me such a myriad of ever-changing emotions I scarcely had the energy to keep up.

When she finished exploring my wound, she let her hand ghost across my brow and down the other side of my face and caressed the tender spot on the other side of my jaw.

I opened my mouth to say something, anything, to break the weighty silence between us, but Allison ignored my attempt and leaned down oh-so-slowly to retrace the path her fingers had just blazed across my stitches with her lips. My eyes fluttered closed, and a small moan slipped past my lips.

Allison took her time lavishing my cut with attention before depositing small kisses on each of my eyes and the tip of my nose. My heart pounded, and my lungs seized when she barely brushed my lips as she turned my head in order to pay attention to the aching spot on my chin. I smiled when she finally finished and made her way back to my lips. She rewarded me with a long, lingering kiss that kindled sparks in every single nerve ending in my body.

When we finally broke apart, I was breathing heavily, and my head felt like I'd just jumped off one of those spinning carnival rides. But underneath everything I was so overwhelmed with love for her that it actually hurt. That love silenced the voices clamoring in the back of my head reminding me that things between us were still unsettled. And it almost carried me through my guilt and despair over the death of Lucia that violently sucker punched me at the oddest times. Like now.

Allison rested her forehead against mine. Her breath tickled my lips, making me want to kiss her again. Her fingers wound their way around the back of my neck to tangle in my hair. I used my free left hand to cup her cheek, surprised to discover it was wet. I tried to pull back so I could look into her eyes, but she tightened her grip on me, forcing me to remain where I was.

"Don't cry," I murmured.

She let out a strangled half-laugh, half-sob. "Easy for you to say."

I wiped all traces of moisture from her cheeks, then kissed the tracks her tears had made. And when fresh tears took their place, I repeated the process.

"Hey," I said. "You're undoing all my hard work."

That did get a laugh. Well, sort of. A halfhearted chuckle, at any rate. "Stop trying to make me feel better. That's my job."

"You already have, just by showing up here." I paused. Did I want to add the next part? Was I ready to make myself vulnerable with the admission? "I'm happy to see you."

"Did you really think I wouldn't come?" She drew back from me just enough to look into my eyes. Her hands were still threaded through the hair tumbling down across my neck. Her expression was dark, almost morose, and a nervous flutter tickled up and down my spinal column before landing directly on top of my diaphragm.

I shrugged and hissed at the pain in my shoulder. Damn it! Would I ever remember not to do that? "When you didn't call..."

"You're right. I should've called. I'm sorry. But you should know I have never, ever, in my entire life been as terrified as I was when I heard what happened to you." She held my gaze as she said that, her voice low and teeming with raw emotion. She slid her hands around my face and cradled it tenderly between them, skating her thumbs across my cheeks. "I couldn't book a flight home fast enough."

I winced against the remorse that pummeled me at learning she'd been so upset, but then her words struck me. "*You* booked your flight home."

Allison nodded. She'd caught her lower lip between her teeth, and her eyes told me she knew exactly what I'd just realized.

"Operations didn't book it for you?"

"No."

"You weren't finished with your assignment."

"No."

"How did you convince them to let you leave?"

"I just said I had to go."

"You told your boss you had to leave in the middle of an assignment?"

"Yes."

"And did he ask for an explanation?"

"He didn't have to. Considering I told him I needed to go home about three seconds after he finished briefing us about what'd happened to you, I think it was evident."

Holy shit. I gaped at her as my mind spun helplessly. Her rushing here the way she had was a definite, concrete declaration about our relationship. Surely she had to realize that. How would she react when she finally comprehended what she'd done?

"Huh," I finally came up with. Should I be pleased or concerned? Allison might be okay now, but after some time passed, she might freak the hell out. And that would land us right back where we'd started. I couldn't go through that again.

"You know what's funny?" she said, her dark eyes starting to twinkle and a dimple appearing on one cheek.

I shook my head, not even wanting to guess.

"Not one of the guys on that trip seemed surprised when I announced I wanted to beam myself back here to New York to be with you. Guess I wasn't as good at hiding my feelings for you as I'd always hoped."

I studied her, trying to determine whether she was as fine with that as she pretended to be. Again, I briefly suspected she might one day decide having the guys know we were—well, whatever we were—was a catastrophe. But before I could voice my concern, she went on.

"Maybe now's a good time for us to have that talk."

My insides combusted, then turned immediately to ash, and the sudden departure of heat made the cold that followed that much more pronounced. I tried to swallow and give a halfhearted nod. "Sure. I'm not going anywhere. Do you want to sit down?"

Allison shook her head. "No, thanks. I sat enough on the flight home to last a lifetime. I'll stand."

"Okay."

"Do you know why I broke up with you, Ryan?"

I winced. Wow. Way to ease into this. Her words were like barbed wire. They caught on my heart and twisted, mangling tender flesh. God, the woman knew how to deliver a timely hit. I swallowed, successfully this time, and tried not to allow my pain to show on my face.

"Honestly? No. I have no idea." And I hadn't, because all she'd said to me had been, "Ryan, I'm really sorry. But this just isn't working." I'd questioned, pled, and attempted to appeal to her sense of fairness, but she'd refused to give me more than that.

If someone or something had pressed me—by, say, threatening to have a crocodile named Glocamorra maul me—I'd have guessed she'd wanted to stop seeing me because we'd been fighting so much about people finding out about us. I'd have speculated that I'd loved her more than she'd loved me and that she hadn't wanted to deal with the depth of my emotions for her. But no one had pressed me, with crocodiles or otherwise, so I hadn't been forced to articulate what I assumed her reasoning had been. Thank goodness. That wasn't a conversation I'd been prepared to have—ever.

When she didn't reply, I shrugged. "You weren't exactly forthcoming."

"I probably should've brought this up before now. I mean, I suppose it would've been best if I'd discussed it with you at any point during the past few years, but now I really feel like we should have talked before we..." Allison's eyes flitted to the vicinity of my breasts. My breath caught, and I shivered as my nipples immediately hardened. "But I couldn't stop myself from touching you long enough to think." She smiled at me wistfully.

My heart soared, and I started tingling. I wanted to say something but decided she needed to get through this, so I remained silent.

"It was always that way with you, you know." Allison's voice was barely more than a whisper, and another nameless emotion glided beneath the surface of her eyes the way a shark slinks smoothly underneath the ocean.

"What way?"

"I always felt completely powerless around you. And confused and out of control. And wonderful." And now the barest hint of a frown flowed across her face. "Did you know I used to spend most of my day sitting at my desk thinking about you?"

I shook my head. "No. I didn't."

"I don't think I could quantify the amount of time I spent wondering what you were doing, who you were talking to, whether you were dazzling everyone with that gorgeous smile. I vacillated between dreading to see you, terrified anyone with eyes would take one look at me and know instantly how I felt about you, and hoping you'd storm into my office and kiss me breathless."

Her words made me weak, and I hated to dispel the feeling, but I had to insert a very important truth. "You hated it when I came to your office." True, I'd never kissed her in there, but toward the end of our relationship, the majority of my visits had earned me mostly dark scowls and clipped answers.

Allison shook her head. "No, I didn't."

"You acted like you did. You always seemed pretty annoyed to see me." So much so, in fact, I'd stopped bothering. The look of irritation on her face when I turned up, even if I was there for a justifiable, work-related reason, had become too painful for me to handle.

Allison sighed, her expression becoming pensive. "No, I wasn't. Well, not at you anyway."

"Why, then?"

"I was annoyed at myself. Well, maybe a little bit at you for making me feel the things I felt, but mostly at me."

"I don't understand."

"Do you know what I love most about you, Ryan?"

I opened my mouth to make a smart-assed remark or comment on the present-tense classification of that statement but reined in the temptation. Instead, I simply shook my head. Her lightning changes in topic were giving me whiplash.

"You're fearless."

I snorted indelicately. "Yeah, right."

"I'm serious. You are. It was the first thing I noticed about you." And then she smiled. "Well, one of the first. The very first was your eyes and how when you looked at me, no matter how innocently, my heart stopped and I couldn't think."

That was a surprise. Allison had never waxed poetic about feelings, so all of this was news. I didn't know what to say, so I said nothing.

"But right after that, I noticed how easily you could just be you. You were completely comfortable in your own skin. You didn't care what anyone thought. If someone said or did something you didn't agree with, you told them. If you wanted something, you just went for it. You never let anyone else stand in your way."

Guilt blossomed in me, and I struggled to keep it from showing. Her assessment of my character flattered me, but I thought she was founding her judgment on false pretenses. She also had no idea Ben was my father, and I was terrified her opinion of me would instantly change when she discovered the truth. The secret itself wouldn't impact our relationship as much as the fact that I'd hidden it for this long.

"I was always a little envious of that," Allison broke into my thoughts.

"I don't know why," I told her, still fighting with my inner remorse and trying to decide whether to come clean. "You seem pretty in tune with what you want. I mean, you're on PPD. They're tapping you to handle last-minute leads. You're a shoo-in for a promotion when the time comes. I thought that was the plan. Isn't that what you told me the first day we met?"

Allison sighed and looked away. "It was. Until it wasn't."

"I don't understand."

Allison's eyes shifted back to capture mine, pain etched on her face. "I've always had one dream, Ryan. Ever since I was a kid and the news of the assassination attempt on President Reagan riveted everyone, I wanted to be a Secret Service agent. And then, when I got a little older, I set my sights on being the first female director. It was my all-consuming focus, and I put all my energy into working toward that goal. It defined me as a person."

"No, that's not what defines you."

Allison smiled. "It is, though. Because I let it be. And I'd become so comfortable with just that image of myself that when I realized I might want something else, I was afraid. I didn't know how to handle it or whether I even wanted to. And so I ran."

"I don't understand." I felt like a broken record repeating that phrase, but I just didn't see what she was getting at.

Allison took a deep breath, and I could see varying emotions at war in her eyes. "The day I broke up with you was the day I got the call that I was going to PPD."

"Okay. So, you didn't want to have a long-distance relationship, was that it? Because you could have just told me that."

"That was only part of it, actually. And, be honest. With yourself if not with me. Tell me if I'd mentioned that you wouldn't have come up with a hundred ways for us to work that out."

I rolled my eyes, tamping down a grin. She had me there. "So what if I had?"

"Ryan, you drove me to distraction more often than not, and that was when I got to see you all the time. I was afraid that with you in New York and me in D.C., us having different days off and not knowing when we'd get to see one another again, we would've fallen apart."

I gaped at her. "So, basically, you're telling me you dumped me because you'd already decided how our relationship would play out, and you couldn't be bothered to wait to see whether you were even right." Bitterness stuck to my tongue even after I'd gotten the words out.

Guilt flickered in Allison's eyes. "I never thought about it that way. It just seemed like the best thing for everyone at the time."

"The best thing for you, you mean." I'd thought those words would have an edge to them once I uttered them, but they came out sounding almost weary.

"No, I honestly thought that—"

"Don't." I impatiently waved my good hand. "Please. Don't insult either of us by claiming you knew what was best for me and therefore had the right to make my decisions for me. It's asinine and demeans us both."

"Ryan." Allison frowned.

"What? It is what it is, Allison. I'm not mad at you. I don't agree with your reasoning at all. In fact, I strongly suspect you're lying to yourself about your true motivations, and I really wish you'd consulted me before you started making changes that affected my life. But I can't do anything about it. What's done is done."

That was a pretty pragmatic attitude, considering. And I really meant it. Well, mostly. I was hurt, and furious, but I had to accept the situation for what it was. No emotion would change anything, so I saw no sense in letting my feelings run wild. That's what I was telling myself anyway. It helped me retain my forced calm. Sort of.

Allison sighed and focused on the ceiling, but she didn't seem to be really seeing it. She was obviously occupied with something in her mind. Now I needed to be patient and not push her to speak before she was ready.

The silence lingered, making me even more uneasy, and it was my turn to sigh. I could barely keep my eyes, which had the consistency of sandpaper, open. The past several days had been the psychological equivalent of unsuccessfully navigating a minefield. Things had been exploding around me at every turn. At this point, I just needed to get some real, non-drug-induced sleep and postpone any further emotionally draining discussions until I could think coherently. Too bad life didn't have a pause button.

"You're right," Allison said finally.

"You can't possibly—Wait…What?"

"I said you were right."

"I was?"

Allison smirked. "Yeah, smart-ass. You were."

"Oh."

"Not used to hearing that, huh?"

"Not from you, no."

Allison scoffed.

"Okay. So, uh…What was I right about exactly?"

"I did think breaking up with you was the best thing for everyone at the time. But it was definitely more right for me."

I cleared my throat. "Thank you for telling me."

"There's something else I haven't told you."

"What?"

"I almost told them no."

"What?!"

I was stunned. That was definitely news. People waited for years to be called to The Show. As far as I knew, no one had ever turned down PPD when they'd gotten the nod. It was just too risky. You couldn't be sure you'd ever be offered the opportunity again. Entire careers had been broken over less.

Allison nodded, her expression once again deadly serious. "I told them I needed to get back to them, and I spent most of the day thinking about it."

"But…Why?" That made no sense. The very first day I'd met her, within the space of our first conversation, she'd told me she wanted to go to PPD. She'd wanted to use that as a stepping stone on the way to a promotion. I couldn't imagine anything that would make her hesitate when she was offered the one thing she'd always wanted.

"Because I had you."

I gaped at her. My thoughts were twisted and snarled, and while my lips were moving, nothing resembling words was coming out of my mouth.

A small, understanding sort of smile stole over Allison's face as she watched me react to that bombshell. "I was actually considering changing the entire course of my career—my life—because I didn't want to leave you. But then, when I realized what I was doing…" She bit her bottom lip again. "It terrified me. Wanting…Needing someone so much I was willing to throw away everything I'd ever dreamed of… It—I couldn't."

Comprehension clicked inside of me. Finally. For the first time since Allison had left, I actually understood why. She hadn't left because she didn't love me. She'd left because she'd been afraid.

Allison recognized the instant I realized what she couldn't bring herself to say and looked away, appearing slightly embarrassed. Wanting to give her the illusion of a moment of privacy as well as garner a second for myself, I closed my eyes.

"So, now you know." Her voice was quiet and a little rough with choked emotion.

I tried to shift so I could settle more on my left side and rest my left cheek in the heel of my hand. I was slightly bitter that we'd wasted so many years apart because of her fear. But I didn't have time to dwell on that. Not when so many important questions about the future remained unasked and unanswered.

"And now?" I managed to say.

"And now what? Are you asking if I still love you? Because I think I made that pretty clear."

My heart boomed like thunder and threatened to drown out the sounds of regular life around me. My nerves were shot. I was terrified to continue down this path, but I needed to know something before I got in any deeper.

"No, I'm asking if you can now. You said you couldn't back then, but I need to know if that's changed. Because I have to be honest here, Allison. I've never loved anyone as much as I love you, and I'd kill for another shot at us, but I can't go back to the way things were. I won't."

That'd been the hardest thing I'd ever had to say to anyone, and I'd been on the verge of throwing up as I'd forced those words out of my mouth. My hands were shaking, and my entire body was buzzing as I waited to see how she'd react.

Allison looked at me with regret, tenderness, affection, and her expression broke my heart. She cupped my cheeks in her hands and ran the pads of her thumbs across my skin. Her dark eyes looked intently into mine, and I trembled. She seemed to see straight to my soul.

"I'd never ask you to do that, Ryan. I was wrong to treat you that way. I was selfish, and I didn't consider how much my attitude was hurting you. I'm so sorry."

Relief flooded me, and I was glad I was already stretched out because I think my knees would've failed me otherwise. My heart swelled like the Grinch's in that Christmas movie, and my smile was so wide my cheeks ached.

Allison grinned back. "So, we're okay?"

"We're more than okay." I tried to lean up so I could kiss her, but her hand on my shoulder stopped me. "What?"

"Since we're clearing the air, are you ready to tell me who Ashley was?"

I smirked at her, surprised she was still dwelling on that. "You really care that much about some woman you heard me talking to once several years ago?"

"Humor me."

"It wasn't Ashley. It was Ashlyn."

Allison's face crumpled into a puzzled frown. "What?"

"Ashlyn. That was the name you heard me say."

Allison appeared surprised, but then her expression became guarded. "Yeah. That's it. Ashlyn." A pause. "So you remember."

"I do."

"And you admit you told her you loved her?"

I nodded. "Oh, yes. I told her I loved her. I told her again earlier today when I saw her. And I'll probably tell her again tomorrow. I'll always love her. And she'll always love me. I can't imagine any situation on earth that could change that."

Okay, I was teasing her now, being immature and probably a little spiteful. Sadly, I'm not always the bigger person I strive to be.

Allison looked as if she couldn't decide whether she wanted to murder me or burst into tears, whether she was triumphant because she'd been right or devastated for the same reason.

"I was talking to my sister."

Allison's expression now was puzzled. "Your sister?"

"Yup."

"Your sister's name is Rory."

"Rory's what I call her. It isn't her name any more than Ryan's mine."

Allison continued to gape at me, obviously mystified.

"Her given name is Ashlyn Aurora. We've always called her Rory for short. But when she was going through med school and starting her career, it was easier to use her given name than explain the nickname. The day you overheard me, she'd called me from the OR because she needed to cancel our dinner plans for the evening. She'd had one of the nurses dial for her and put me on speakerphone, and when I picked up, the nurse told me who she was and said she'd called on behalf of my sister Ashlyn."

It wasn't until I'd seen Rory a few days before in her white lab coat with her name embroidered on the breast that it'd clicked with me what Allison had overheard that day. And when I'd finally realized who she'd been talking about, I was amazed I hadn't reached that conclusion sooner. "What you heard was me teasing my sister. I'd never called her Ashlyn before, and I haven't since." I called her *Asha* occasionally—a holdover from when we were kids and more or less had our own special twin language—but only rarely and when we were alone.

"You were really talking to your sister?" A fragile hope had begun to bloom in Allison's eyes.

"Yup."

The optimism flickered. She clearly wasn't ready to relinquish the belief she'd held so steadfastly for years. "But what about Meaghan's reaction? I heard her say she thought you two were adorable together."

I shrugged and smiled. "We are."

Allison shot me a dirty look.

I laughed. "Well, look at me! Hell, I'm adorable all on my own. How could we not be together? We are identical, after all."

That comment earned me an even darker look and an eye roll. I did some damage control with a serious answer. "Meaghan isn't close to her older brothers, and I think sometimes she envies my relationship with Rory." I paused, reflecting on my bond with my twin. "She's my best friend." I may or may not have said that last part out loud, but I didn't suppose it mattered.

Allison looked thoughtful yet a little bitter. "You were talking to your sister." Her voice was quiet.

I didn't reply as it didn't really seem like a question.

"I feel like an idiot," Allison admitted after a time.

"Why?"

As she brushed her hair back off her shoulders, her hand shook slightly. She hesitated again, as though she wasn't sure she wanted to continue the conversation. "I've spent years thinking that...that you just got over me. Like what we'd had was easy for you to leave behind. Like it hadn't mattered."

I took her hand and threaded our fingers together. "Allison, whether I wanted it to or not, it always mattered."

Allison's body sagged, all her tension leaving her, and she brought my hand up to rest over her heart and cradled it in both of hers. "I love you, Ryan." Allison's voice was low, barely a whisper, but her words hit me as hard as if she'd shouted them. "And I plan to spend as long as you'll let me showing you exactly how much."

My heart began to pound out of control, and my head spun. And as she leaned in to brush her lips against mine, I couldn't help but smile. I'd deal with Lucia's death and finding her killer later. Right now I just wanted to enjoy this moment with the woman I loved.

THE END

About the Author

Kara A. McLeod is a badass by day and a smartass by night. Or maybe it's the other way around. Or quite possibly neither. A Jersey girl at heart, "Mac" is an intrepid wanderer who goes wherever the wind takes her. A former Secret Service agent who decided she wanted more out of life than standing in a stairwell and losing an entire month every year to the United Nations General Assembly, she currently resides in Colorado and is still searching hither and yon for the meaning of life, the nearest comic con, and the world's best margarita.

If anyone has any leads on any of the above, she can be contacted at kara.a.mcleod@gmail.com.

Books Available from Bold Strokes Books

A Reluctant Enterprise by Gun Brooke. When two women grow up learning nothing but distrust, unworthiness, and abandonment, it's no wonder they are apprehensive and fearful when an overwhelming love just won't be denied. (978-1-62639-500-8)

Above the Law by Carsen Taite. Love is the last thing on Agent Dale Nelson's mind, but reporter Lindsey Ryan's investigation could change the way she sees everything—her career, her past, and her future. (978-1-62639-558-9)

Actual Stop by Kara A. McLeod. When Special Agent Ryan O'Connor's present collides abruptly with her past, shots are fired, and the course of her life is irrevocably altered. (978-1-62639-675-3)

Embracing the Dawn by Jeannie Levig. When ex-con Jinx Tanner and business executive E. J. Bastien awaken after a one-night stand to find their lives inextricably entangled, love has its work cut out for it. (978-1-62639-576-3)

Jane's World: The Case of the Mail Order Bride by Paige Braddock. Jane's PayBuddy account gets hacked and she inadvertently purchases a mail order bride from the Eastern Block. (978-1-62639-494-0)

Love's Redemption by Donna K. Ford. For ex-convict Rhea Daniels and ex-priest Morgan Scott, redemption lies in the thin line between right and wrong. (978-1-62639-673-9)

The Shewstone by Jane Fletcher. The prophetic Shewstone is in Eawynn's care, but unfortunately for her, Matt is coming to steal it. (978-1-62639-554-1)

A Touch of Temptation by Julie Blair. Recent law school graduate Kate Dawson's ordained path to the perfect life gets thrown off course when handsome butch top Chris Brent initiates her to sexual pleasure. (978-1-62639-488-9)

Beneath the Waves by Ali Vali. Kai Merlin and Vivien Palmer love the water and the secrets trapped in the depths, but if Kai gives in to her feelings, it might come at a cost to her entire realm. (978-1-62639-609-8)

Girls on Campus edited by Sandy Lowe and Stacia Seaman. College: four years when rules are made to be broken. This collection is required reading for anyone looking to earn an A in sex ed. (978-1-62639-733-0)

Heart of the Pack by Jenny Frame. Human Selena Miller falls for the domineering Caden Wolfgang, but will their love survive Selena learning the Wolfgangs are werewolves? (978-1-62639-566-4)

Miss Match by Fiona Riley. Matchmaker Samantha Monteiro makes the impossible possible for everyone but herself. Is mysterious dancer Lucinda Moss her own perfect match? (978-1-62639-574-9)

Paladins of the Storm Lord by Barbara Ann Wright. Lieutenant Cordelia Ross must choose between duty and honor when a man with godlike powers forces her soldiers to provoke an alien threat. (978-1-62639-604-3)

Taking a Gamble by P.J. Trebelhorn. Storage auction buyer Cassidy Holmes and postal worker Erica Jacobs want different things out of life, but taking a gamble on love might prove lucky for them both. (978-1-62639-542-8)

The Copper Egg by Catherine Friend. Archeologist Claire Adams wants to find the buried treasure in Peru. Her ex, Sochi Castillo, wants to steal it. The last thing either of them wants is to still be in love. (978-1-62639-613-5)

The Iron Phoenix by Rebecca Harwell. Seventeen-year-old Nadya must master her unusual powers to stop a killer, prevent civil war, and rescue the girl she loves, while storms ravage her island city. (978-1-62639-744-6)

A Reunion to Remember by TJ Thomas. Reunited after a decade, Jo Adams and Rhonda Black must navigate a significant age difference, family dynamics, and their own desires and fears to explore an opportunity for love. (978-1-62639-534-3)

Built to Last by Aurora Rey. When Professor Olivia Bennett hires contractor Joss Bauer to restore her dilapidated farmhouse, she learns her heart, as much as her house, is in need of a renovation. (978-1-62639-552-7)

Capsized by Julie Cannon. What happens when a woman turns your life completely upside down? (978-1-62639-479-7)

Girls With Guns by Ali Vali, Carsen Taite, and Michelle Grubb. Three stories by three talented crime writers—Carsen Taite, Ali Vali, and Michelle Grubb—each packing her own special brand of heat. (978-1-62639-585-5)

Heartscapes by MJ Williamz. Will Odette ever recover her memory or is Jesse condemned to remember their love alone? (978-1-62639-532-9)

Murder on the Rocks by Clara Nipper. Detective Jill Rogers lives with two things on her mind: sex and murder. While an ice storm cripples Tulsa, two things stand in Jill's way: her lover and the DA. (978-1-62639-600-5)

Necromantia by Sheri Lewis Wohl. When seeing dead people is more than a movie tagline. (978-1-62639-611-1)

Salvation by I. Beacham. Claire's long-term partner now hates her, for all the wrong reasons, and she sees no future until she meets Regan, who challenges her to face the truth and find love. (978-1-62639-548-0)

Trigger by Jessica Webb. Dr. Kate Morrison races to discover how to defuse human bombs while learning to trust her increasingly strong feelings for the lead investigator, Sergeant Andy Wyles. (978-1-62639-669-2)

24/7 by Yolanda Wallace. When the trip of a lifetime becomes a pitched battle between life and death, will anyone survive? (978-1-62639-619-7)

A Return to Arms by Sheree Greer. When a police shooting makes national headlines, activists Folami and Toya struggle to balance their relationship and political allegiances, a struggle intensified after a fiery young artist enters their lives. (978-1-62639-681-4)

After the Fire by Emily Smith. Paramedic Connor Haus is convinced her time for love has come and gone, but when firefighter Logan Curtis comes into town, she learns it may not be too late after all. (978-1-62639-652-4)

Dian's Ghost by Justine Saracen. The road to genocide is paved with good intentions. (978-1-62639-594-7)

Fortunate Sum by M. Ullrich. Financial advisor Catherine Carter lives a calculated life, but after a collision with spunky Imogene Harris (her latest client) and unsolicited predictions, Catherine finds herself facing an unexpected variable: Love. (978-1-62639-530-5)

Soul to Keep by Rebekah Weatherspoon. What *won't* a vampire do for love… (978-1-62639-616-6)

boldstrokesbooks.com

Bold Strokes Books

Quality and Diversity in LGBTQ Literature

victory
EDITIONS

Drama

MATINEE BOOKS

SCI-FI

E-BOOKS

MYSTERY

erotica

SOLILOQUY

EROTICA

BOLD
STROKES
BOOKS

LIBERTY
EDITIONS

YOUNG
ADULT

Romance

W·E·B·S·T·O·R·E

PRINT AND EBOOKS